# Taken

## by

# Vampires

I0742481

# Joy Mosby

Taken by Vampires
Joy Mosby

Copyright © 2018 by Joy Mosby
All rights reserved.
ISBN: 978-1-7325793-1-6

Editor: A Fading Street

Cover By: Anelia Savova AKA Ann RS

Ruby Gulch Enterprises LLC
P.O. Box 64
Craig, CO 81626

*For Amy,*
*My partner in crime*

# Chapter 1

## *Katie*

I squeezed Vince's hand as the taxi driver wove through the streets of Heraklion taking us to the house Theron was renting. I missed my dog, Vinny, and I wanted to know who 'my friend' was. According to Theron someone found my suitcase and dog on the ferry, after Alex abducted me, and took them to Theron. I didn't talk to anyone or see anyone I knew on the ferry which made me wonder who this stranger was.

*It will be fine love, find your breath,* Vince thought to me and I looked up into his eyes. It had been three days of bliss, getting to know the vampire I loved with no distractions on Milos. There hadn't been a lot of talk, and what talk there was came out in the form of moans or screams of ecstasy. He wanted to stay in our own little bubble for the rest of the week, but I needed to know what was going on with Theron and my 'friend.' Plus, I missed my dog.

I closed my eyes and took a breath, concentrating on it and nothing else. *Good, everything will be fine.* Vince let go of my hand and rested his high on my thigh making me lose my breath again.

*If you keep that up I'll make the driver blush,* I thought back to him and moved so his hand would rest a little higher on my thigh.

*You want more?* he asked, inching his hand to the inside.

*I always want more when it comes to you,* I thought as the taxi slowed down and stopped behind a gate. He rolled the window down and pressed the call button.

"Yes?" a strange voice asked.

"I have two people who say they are staying here," the cabbie said, and I saw him roll his eyes in the rearview mirror.

"It is Vince and Katie," Vince added, talking over the cab driver's shoulder.

"Come on up," the voice said, and the gate opened. The driver pulled through the gate and stopped at the front. It was big, with three stories of white stucco, but nothing like the mansion Alex had destroyed. This was closer to a McMansion. I bet if I looked through the windows on the second floor I could see the neighbors having sex. There were no cars in the driveway, but that didn't surprise me, Theron loved his cars and would never leave them outside unless he had to.

I got out of the cab, leaving Vince to pay the driver and waited for him to pop the trunk. When the trunk opened, I pulled Vince's suitcase out and rolled it to the front door then waited for him to catch up. Once he reached my side, I rang the bell.

"You are going to stay calm, right?" Vince asked, grabbing my hand.

"That completely depends on who it is and what they have to say." The door opened, and Vinny, my German Shepherd mix, came bounding out almost knocking me over. "Vinny, I missed you so much." I bent and wrapped my arms around him and breathed in the smell of dog as he tried to lick my face. I let go of him and straightened, finding Theron standing in the doorway. He was a little paler and thinner than I remembered but his brown hair was still buzz-cut, and his goatee was short and perfectly trimmed.

"Katie," he said, staring over my shoulder, refusing to meet my eyes. Guilt was pouring off him in waves so tall I felt like I had to

2

hold my breath, or I would drown in them.

"Theron." I stepped in to him and wrapped my arms around him. "I thought you were dead. When I saw the news, I couldn't get here fast enough." His arms came around me and the guilt he had been drowning in melted away.

"I missed you too, please come in. We have much to discuss." He stepped away from the door allowing us to enter. "I'll show you to your room first. I'm sure you want to freshen up after your journey."

We followed Theron through the house. It was almost as nice as his mansion, but it was missing something. The floors were marble, and white hand-textured walls were decorated with paintings from mythology. The hallway was wide, and the doorways arched with beautiful cedar stained-wood doors. "This place is nice. Are you planning on buying it?" I asked as we stopped outside a closed door at the end of the hall. It was nowhere near as grand as the mansion, but it could've been much worse.

"No, merely renting it from a friend. It will feel like I bought it once my mansion is rebuilt though." His good mood dissolved.

"Theron, I'm sorry you lost everything, it's my fault. We shouldn't have stayed with you." I could not help the guilt saturating my mind.

"Stop, right now," Vince said, pushing past me, and walking into the room. "Drop it, we all feel responsible for what happened in August, but there is nothing we can do to change it now."

"OK." I was shocked at his tight tone, I didn't expect him to be so bitchy about it. I followed Vince into a huge master bedroom. There was a canopied king-size bed against one wall and a fireplace on the wall opposite with a sofa and two wingback chairs in front of it. Floor to ceiling windows, that must have been UV protected made up one wall, while the other had three doors, I was guessing they led to closets and the bathroom. "Wow, are all the bedrooms this nice?" I asked, changing the subject as I peered out the window into the night.

"No, I gave you two the master because no one wants to hear what you get up to in here." Theron sat down on one of the wingback chairs and crossed his legs.

I couldn't help the blush flushing my cheeks. "Thanks, I guess." I kept my face to the window until my color went back to normal. "Which door leads to the bathroom? I have to pee."

Theron pointed to the door closest to the bed. "That one."

I ran to the door, closed it behind me then looked around. It was just as opulent as the rest of the house. There were two sinks with a marble counter. A walk-in shower with four shower heads, a soaking tub overlooking a window, a vanity with a stool, and a separate room for the toilet.

After I peed, I washed my hands and looked in the mirror. My hair was almost halfway down my back now, but it looked horrible. From the top of my head to my shoulders it was almost black while from my shoulders down, it was almost white blond, I looked like a black and white cookie. I was wearing a pair of leggings and an oversized T-shirt Vince bought in one of the few stores open on Milos, and my katana, as always, was on my back.

I went back into the bedroom when I was done and joined Vince and Theron who were sitting in the wingback chairs. I took a seat on the sofa while Vinny sat at my feet. Vince stared at him in disbelief. "I still can't believe you named your dog after me."

"Hey, I thought you were dead. I was keeping your memory alive." I pointed a finger at him before scratching Vinny behind the ears.

"You should have named your firstborn after me then, not your dog." Vince ran a hand through his hair.

"I wasn't planning on living long enough to have kids," I said, thinking back to my plan to kill Lolita then Alex. This was spiraling into a fight, I needed to change the subject. "Tell me about my *friend* who brought you Vinny and my stuff."

"She says her name is Jean," Theron said, looking at the dog. "The only reason I allowed her to stay was because she had your things and the dog. When I heard the dog's name I knew he belonged to you."

"Where is this *friend* of mine, and why didn't you run a background check on her?" I pulled my eyebrows together in confusion, I had no idea who Jean was.

"She's in her room." Theron uncrossed his legs and leaned forward to rest his elbows on his knees. "And I did run her through the facial recognition software. Nothing came up. I ran her name through my background check site and came up with nothing as well. It's like she doesn't exist."

"Well, let's go talk to her and see what we can find out." I stood and adjusted my katana. Whoever it was, had some explaining to do. No one could get away without a background unless they were lying about who they were and had excellent connections.

"Wait, we need a plan. She's smart and hardheaded." Theron stood but put his hands up to stop us from leaving.

"We have a plan, see if I know her, then force her to tell us what she's doing." I walked around Theron to the door and turned to see Vince and Theron having a nonverbal conversation. I rolled my eyes. "Come on, Vinny, show me who saved you." I opened the door and followed Vinny to the other side of the house.

We came around a corner and found a man sitting in a straight-backed wood chair next to a door. When he saw me, he stood. I ignored him and went to open the door, but he put a hand out to stop me. "Sorry, Miss, no one is allowed in without Theron's permission," he said in English.

"Really?" I asked in Greek, feeling my temper boil. "I couldn't care less about his orders. She saved my dog, now open the door."

"Oh, you're Katie?" he asked, looking me up and down.

"Yes, now move aside." He still didn't look like he planned on moving, but it didn't matter. The door opened and a tall, thin girl who looked younger than her nineteen years stood in front of me. She was wearing black leggings, an oversized pink sweater, and Chucks. She had ivory skin, four piercings in each ear, long pink hair, and a smile on her face.

"Katie, you're alive." She squealed and pulled me into a hug.

"Uni, wait." I pulled away from her and went into her room. She followed, closing the door behind her. The room was small, there was a full-size bed against one wall with a dark red quilt rumpled on top, and a desk in the corner a few feet from the end of the bed. There was a teak dresser, and along the other wall there were two doors.

"I was so worried about you. I tried to get Alex, but I slipped and fell on the icy deck. Did you get your stuff?" she asked, jumping onto her bed and sitting cross-legged without a care in the world.

"Yes, and thank you for trying to save me and taking care of Vinny, but what the hell were you doing on the boat?" I pulled the chair out from under the desk and sat on it backwards facing her.

"I was going to see my mom, I wasn't lying about that." She trailed off as her phone chirped. She picked it up and read the message.

"Uni, give me the phone." I held my hand out, I needed her undivided attention.

She huffed and handed it over. I turned the ringer off and set it on the desk without looking at the screen. I rested my arms on the back of the chair then rested my chin on them. "Start talking."

"I can't." She ducked her head and played with a thread hanging off her sweater.

"Uni, do you know whose house you are in? Do you know what he will do to you if you don't tell me?" I had no idea what Theron would do, but it wouldn't be good.

"You don't understand how much trouble I'll be in if I tell you." She sniffled, and a tear raced down her cheek.

"You can trust us, Uni, we are good at keeping secrets. Why don't you tell me why Theron can't find any information about you? Is it because of Kevo?"

She looked up with tears brimming. "If I tell you, promise

not to tell anyone else."

"I can't do that. Theron and Vince need to know. Theron needs to protect his island, and Vince is my partner; I won't keep anything from him."

"OK, well you can't tell anyone in Kevȯ." She wiped her hand across her face and I waited for her to start talking. "Theron can't find anything about me because I work for Interpol. My real name is Jeanette Vang. I hacked Interpol's system when I was fourteen and they recruited me. They sent me to Kevȯ, undercover, since my dad worked there. When I first arrived, I couldn't wait to bring them down, but then I learned about all the good they did for the world, and I couldn't turn them in."

"It was you," I said as all the pieces of the puzzle lined up. "You were the mole."

Her head jerked. "I tipped off the commandos, yes, but I did nothing else. When I went to work there I thought they would be doing horrible things to people. When I found out what they were doing, I couldn't bust them on it."

"Then, why did you arrange the raid?" I was confused. If she loved Kevȯ so much, why would she try to end it?

"You are going to hate me for this." She hung her head again.

"Just tell me."

"I wanted to scare you away, so I could follow you," she said so softly I had to strain to hear.

"Why?"

"I wanted to arrest Alex and prove to my handler I should be doing more than hacking and spying on a group who does more good in the world than bad." She stood and went into the bathroom, closing the door behind her.

I was glad she left the room; my anger was simmering just below the surface and it was about to explode. Jean put the safety of everyone in Kevȯ at risk and was probably the reason Alex found me. She pulled the hat off my head at the restaurant. She said there weren't any cameras, but I remembered her messing with her phone. She used me as bait. She was the reason Alex kidnapped me, she failed to arrest him, and I almost died.

I closed my eyes and found my breath, I needed to not explode and scare her away. She'd been my friend, at least I thought she was. I needed to give her a chance to explain, but I didn't know if it would make a difference, I was ready to kill her.

When she came out of the bathroom a few minutes later, with bloodshot eyes and a tissue in one hand, I felt no sympathy for her. "You put the photo of me online, you used me as bait. You knew Alex would see it and know I was on my way to Crete. Why would you do this? I almost died, Uni, or should I call you Jean?"

She looked at the floor. "You can call me whatever you want. I'm sorry, KK. You don't understand what arresting him would mean for me. I'll never forgive myself for almost getting you killed. If I hadn't slipped on the damn deck, I would've had him, and you would've had one less person trying to kill you." She blotted the tissue under her eyes.

"Next time you have a grand scheme, let me know what it is, and I might help you." I felt my anger disappear. She'd been my only friend for too long, and friends didn't come easily.

"You don't want to kill me?" she asked, looking at me with her mouth gaping open.

"Only a little, and I'll get over it. I can't make any promises about Theron and Vince though, they can be... overprotective." I stood and went to her.

"Can we not tell them?" she pleaded.

"No, we have to tell them. They won't relax until they know who you are, and why you're following me."

"Do you think they will let me leave?" She went back to the bed and sat on the edge.

"I don't know. It depends on how much you know." I went to the door and opened it, letting Vince and Theron in. I felt them

8

standing outside the door since shortly after we went in.

"How much of that did you guys hear?" I asked, staying between them and Uni, I mean *Jean*.

"Enough," Vince said, flexing his hands. He was ready to kill her. "She put your life in danger to get ahead in her career."

"She works for Interpol?" Theron ignored Vince. "Do you know what will happen if anyone finds out I have an Interpol agent staying at my house?"

"Boys, calm down. No one will find out she's here unless someone tells them." I looked at them both. "Jean was trying to help me Vince, not get me killed. She knows she should've told me about her plan now, right Jean?"

She opened her mouth then closed it as new tears appeared. "I'm so sorry Katie, I should've told you." She brought the damp tissue to her face and turned away. "If you want me to leave, I will. I won't tell anyone I was here."

Theron walked over to the desk and picked up her phone. "What's your passcode?" he asked, hitting a button on the phone.

Jean turned, ran to Theron, and tried to take the phone out of his hand. "Give me my phone," she yelled as he held it above his head. She jumped but didn't have enough vertical height to reach it.

I rolled my eyes. "Uni, I mean, Jean. If you want Theron to trust you, you need to let him look at your phone and computer." I walked over to Vince and leaned into him. I needed to touch him, feel him, I still couldn't believe he was alive and with me.

"It's an invasion of privacy," she panted, still thinking she could jump high enough to reach the phone.

"And you invaded my house." Theron narrowed his eyes at her.

"You forced me to come to your house."

"You're the reason Katie almost died."

"Aren't you the one who let Alex stay at your compound in the first place?"

Theron blew out a breath and handed her the phone. She took it, entered her code, and gave it back to him. "None of us are perfect."

Theron tapped on the phone, reviewing the messages and emails she sent. He gave the phone back to her after a few minutes with a blank look on his face.

"What did she send?" Vince asked.

"She asked for a holiday. She pointed out she hadn't had one in over two years and she was going to take some time off."

"Jean, why? What are you going to do?" I asked.

"I want to help you get Alex, and Lolita." She turned to me with a solemn face.

"No, out of the question." I moved away from Vince to stand in front of her and put my hands on my hips. "I don't want you to get hurt."

"If you don't let me help you, I'll go after Alex on my own. Don't treat me like a child, KK." She put her hands on her hips, mirroring me.

"You don't understand how dangerous he is," I said in a small voice.

"No, what you don't understand is that I've been tracking the bastard for years. I almost had him in May, but he disappeared. He didn't pop back up until you did. I know him better than his own mother." She crossed her arms over her chest and narrowed her eyes at me. "Besides, I'm the best hacker you will get your hands on."

I looked at Theron and Vince questioningly. *She can't stay, she's Interpol,* Theron thought.

*Do you think you can trust her?* Vince thought.

"We need to talk about it." I wouldn't make any promises without talking to the guys and thinking to each of them would take too long. Plus, Uni might think it was weird if we stood around staring at each other without saying anything.

"Fine, but while you're talking, Alex is getting away." Jean went over to her computer and opened a program with a dot moving across a blue field.

"What are you talking about?" Theron was at her side in an instant.

"He's been rescued." She pointed to the dot.

"How do you know it's him? He could be dead for all you know. It was a bad storm, and Katie said he wasn't wearing a lifejacket." Theron leaned over to watch.

"He has a search and rescue company on retainer. All he has to do is push a button on his watch and they come to him." She tapped a few buttons and Alex's photo popped onto the screen.

"How do you know?" I asked, looking over Theron's shoulder.

"Like I said, I've been tracking and studying Alex for years. I know most of his tricks. My mentor at Interpol was kidnapped, and tortured by him five years ago. Alex is going to pay for what he did." Jean turned in her seat and looked at us. "Are you going to let me help you or not?"

"We'll talk about it." Theron stormed out of the room.

"Please stay here until we figure out what we are going to do." Vince turned and followed Theron.

"He's getting away, don't you see? We could go after him right now and have him. He's going to Athens." Jean's face was turning red in anger. "Why are they going to talk about it?"

"They won't do anything until they have a plan. Alex thought he killed them all after the attack. Heck, I thought they were all dead too. It's a lot to take in. You come here saying you're my friend and you work for Interpol. Then you show them exactly where one of our enemies are." I sat on the bed, I knew she wouldn't like what I said next. "Jean, when they find him they are going to torture him and kill him."

"But he should be arrested and tried for his crimes."

"Maybe you're right, but that isn't what they're going to do."

"I don't understand. I didn't think you would be one to side with criminals."

"Normally, you'd be right, but not this time. I don't think he will ever stop. If he's arrested, he'll just break out and pick up where he left off." I

11

crossed my arms, not knowing what she would do, but I didn't care. I was done trying to make everyone happy. It was time for hard truths.

She said nothing for a long time, just sat at the desk thinking. "I'll go along with whatever you and the guys want to do."

"You will?"

"Yes, but you have to let me help." She pulled her legs up onto the chair and wrapped her arms around them. "You have my word."

"You're willing to keep this a secret from Interpol?"

"Yes, I want to avenge my mentor more than I want a raise."

"I'll go talk to the guys, see if I can convince them to let you work with us." I stood, and she jumped to her feet.

"I'm sorry I didn't save you from Alex. I thought I could do it."

"Like I said, next time clue me in on your plan and I'll help. I'm not helpless you know." I tapped the katana on my back.

"I will. Are we OK?" She looked at the carpet and danced on the balls of her feet.

"I think we will be." I went to the door and called to Vinny. "Don't let her go anywhere alone," I said to the guards after I closed the door and looked for Vince and Theron with my mind.

## Chapter 2

### *Katie*

I found them in a room near the living room. I went in without knocking and looked around. It was a good-sized office. The walls matched the rest of the house and there was a large rug in shades of gray on the floor; I wasn't sure if it was meant to look like sand or ripples on the shore. There was a wood desk set back near narrow windows and two club chairs before it. Vince was sitting in one while Theron was sitting behind the desk. On the left side of the room there was a couch and two armchairs arranged before an unlit fireplace.

"Why don't you tell us where you've been and what you know about this woman?" Theron asked.

"Where's Helen then?" I took the chair next to Vince.

"I'll text her." Theron picked up his phone and typed a message quickly. "Did you enjoy your time on Milos?" he asked, putting his phone back on the desk.

"It wasn't long enough," Vince said, as a blush tinted my cheeks. "But we have things to do." He reached across the distance between the chairs and I met him halfway with my hand. He gave it a squeeze then let go.

"You two make me sick. Please keep the foreplay in the bedroom." Theron shook his head and turned away.

I was about to tell him to get over himself when Helen joined us. She too had changed little, she was a few inches shorter than me, and her dark brown hair was in a tight bun, as always. From her appearance, she looked about the same age as me, but when you watched her walk and listened to her talk, it was obvious she was decades older. Her face looked a little thinner than last time I saw her and some of the shine I remembered in her eyes was missing. I got up and ran to her. "Helen, I'm so glad you're alive." I wrapped my arms around her in a hug. She patted my back awkwardly before pulling away.

"I'm glad you are well, too." She looked me over and cringed. "We have to get something done about your hair."

I frowned, no one had said anything about it, but I knew what she meant after looking in the mirror earlier. "I know, I didn't have a way to cut it." I ran my hands through it.

"I have a lady who will come and fix it." She smiled, but it didn't reach her eyes.

"If you two are done with the girl talk. Katie, tell us what you've been doing since we last saw you," Theron said, moving to one of the arm chairs by the fire place. We sat, and I told them what I had been doing while I thought they were dead. When I was done, They started with the questions.

"I have never heard of Tad, how old do you think he is?" Vince asked.

"He's really old, older than you." I trusted my vampires, but if my mother ever found out about Tad, he would kill me. I hated keeping a secret from Vince, but I didn't know if Mom could force them to talk. I wasn't going to risk pissing Tad off by telling his secret.

"Interesting, do you know how long he has been living there?" Theron asked, stroking his goatee in thought.

"I don't know, but he made it sound like hundreds of years."

"I would like to meet him someday," Helen said. "I love to hear the stories the old ones tell."

"Do you think he will help?" Vince asked curtly, I had a

14

feeling he knew I wasn't telling the whole truth.

"No, he won't leave Kevò. I think he likes to stay out of vampire politics." I was fumbling for excuses, but I didn't want them to know he was the first vampire.

"That is too bad, we could have used an old one on our side."

"What happened here? I know about Miguel saving you but that was weeks ago." I looked around, trying to ease the tension.

"When I woke, another vampire, one of Lolita's, was trying to take over the Syndicate. We took care of it." Theron didn't look like he wanted to go into the details, but I pressed him. He told me about The Turk, what he had done to the humans in the bar and how he had turned a member of The Syndicate into a slave. Then he told me how they executed the vampire; it sounded like a horrible way to die.

"What happens to slaves if their vampire dies?" I asked, the thought had never crossed my mind. The only slave I had run into was Antonio, but I hadn't realized he was a slave until he tried to take me back to Miguel and Lolita when I was trying to leave San Sebastian.

"It depends on the amount of blood exchanged," Vince said, standing and pacing around the room. "If they have not completed the bond, nothing happens. If the bond is completed but new, the slave loses all sense of himself, similar to Bram's Renfield. They usually end up in a mental hospital. If they were enslaved for a long time, they die when their master dies."

I thought of Mordor, Tad turned him into a slave for trying to kill me. He would pay for what he did by being Tad's slave and blood donor for the rest of his life. I shook my head to clear it. "What are we going to do now?"

"We're throwing a party," Helen said, returning to her seat with a smile.

"Why?" I could think of a million other things we should be doing.

"Because Theron has returned from the dead and we need to garner allies if we are going to destroy Lolita's army." Helen crossed one leg over the other. "And it's time for the rest of the vampire world to meet you."

"So, you believed my dream? That she's creating an army?" I told Vince about the army I dreamt about before the attack on Theron's compound.

"Yes, I believed you," Vince said, but hesitated before he continued. "Miguel has been sending us information, and he confirmed your prophecy." Vince stood and started to pace. "He counted over five hundred vampires all trained for combat."

"I bet that's why she moved to Venice, it was getting hard to control them in Paris," I said, more to myself than the vampires.

"You know where she is?" Theron asked, his eyes wide. "How? We didn't find her until Miguel reached out to her."

"It's a long story. Actually, Uni, sorry, Jean, figured out she was in Venice. I was getting ready to go after her when I saw the news that you were alive." I looked down at my folded hands.

"What were you going to do?" Vince knelt in front of me.

"I was going to sneak into her club and cut her head off or die trying." Vince pulled my chin up forcing me to meet his eyes.

"Did you think you would survive?"

"I didn't care. I didn't want to live in a world without you." I blinked back the tears that wanted to fall every time I thought of him dead.

"Katie." He pulled me into a hug. "Never do something that stupid again."

"I wasn't going to die on purpose, I just didn't know if I would win. Then I was going to go after Alex." I took his face in my hands and ran my thumb over his cheek bone. "I'm so glad I won't have to face them alone."

He pressed his forehead to mine. "Me too, love, me too." He kissed me then got to his feet.

"Back to the matter at hand," Theron said, pulling us out of our moment. "Even if we kill Lolita, we will still need to deal with her army. We can't simply kill her and let the vampires she created go with a, *here are the rules, have a nice day.*"

"That's why we're having a party. We are going to need help destroying Lolita's army," Helen said, looking at me.

"How are we going to convince them to help us?" I asked, not really seeing the point of a party.

Helen looked at me like I was crazy. "We will tell them about Lolita's plan to start a war with the humans and show them your power."

"Why don't we just call them and have them meet us in Venice?" My katana was thirsty for Lolita's blood.

"Because the vampires we want to help us are big on pomp and circumstance. If we don't have a party, they'll think the threat isn't as world-altering as it is," Theron said.

"So, we're having a party." I rolled my eyes, thinking this wasn't going to end well.

"I will call my hairdresser right now. We have to do something about your hair. I can't look at it anymore, and your wardrobe. It's time you dressed like a ruler and not a twenty-something backpacking through Europe," Helen said changing the subject.

"You mean like ball gowns?"

"No, like modern day royalty, think Kate Middleton."

"OK..." I wasn't sure I liked the sound of that.

"Who are you planning on inviting?" Vince asked, getting back to the party.

"Anyone who will take our side in this war. Do you have anyone you want me to invite?"

"Yes, I have a few ideas. When is the party going to happen?"

"In two weeks if everything goes to plan. I would like to wait but my position will remain in jeopardy until I announce that I'm still in charge."

"Very well, we have plenty of time. I'll give you the names later."

"What's next?" I asked, yawning, I needed sleep, but I missed these

17

vampires and I would rather spend time with them than with my pillow.

"Let me introduce you to two of my children who were not here when the attack took place," Theron said, getting to his feet as the door to the office opened and two vampires came inside. From the feel of them they were younger than Helen but not much. The man was on the shorter side, with a lean build and shoulder-length black hair. He wore thick, brown pants and a clean, but thin, button-up shirt. The woman was tall with long, straight, black hair hanging loose around her shoulders. She was wearing a black sheath dress with matching kitten heels. The two could not be more different.

"Katie, I would like you to meet Argyris and Natalia," Theron gestured to each as I got to my feet. "Argyris lives in Mongolia and Natalia lives in the mountains of Romania. This is Katie Hunter, the daughter of our goddess."

"Nice to meet you," I said, offering my hand to Argyris. "Will you be staying with us long?" He took my hand loosely in his and bowed over it.

"As long as Theron needs me, I will be here." He let go of my hand and stood at attention in front of me. "And as long as you need me."

"Wonderful, we appreciate the help." I nodded my head to him and moved to Natalia. "Nice to meet you as well."

Natalia looked at my hand a second before taking it in hers and shook it gingerly. She let go of my hand and bowed her head. "Theron has told us all about you. I look forward to serving you."

I wasn't sure how to react. I was supposed to be queen of the vampires, but this was the first time anyone said anything about serving me. "Great, I'm sure we'll need your help."

Natalia stepped back and looked to Theron, who was looking at his watch. "Now, since we are all together, we are going to the compound, or what's left of it, and sending our fallen friends to the afterlife." Theron opened his drawer and pulled out a small velvet bag.

"I guess I should go change," I said, looking down at my leggings and T-shirt.

"We are paying our respects to those we have lost in this war, I think it's only right." Theron rose from his chair. "We will meet in the garage in twenty minutes."

"What about Uni, I mean Jean?" I asked, as Helen open the door.

"Everyone will come," Theron said, and I felt his distrust for Uni.

"I'll go tell her to get ready," Helen said, smoothing out the nonexistent wrinkles in her navy skirt suit.

"I'll call The Syndicate, they knew almost everyone we lost, it would hurt them if I didn't include them," Theron said, pulling out his phone as Vince and I left to change.

I wished for nothing the past three months but to go back to the compound and live happily ever after with Vince, Theron, and Helen, but now that we were going back I didn't know if I could handle it.

"What's wrong?" Vince asked, as we entered our room.

"I haven't been to the compound since the attack," I said, going to my suitcase still sitting on the bed. "I don't know if I want to. I would rather think of it as it was before." I pulled the zipper open and flipped the lid back. I had nothing suitable for a funeral, so I settled on a pair of black skinny jeans, a black V-neck sweater, and the black boots Uni bought for me.

"I know it will be hard, but Theron has already started clearing the rubble. It is not as bad as it was." Vince came out of the closet dressed in a suit. I couldn't remember ever seeing him in one before. His large frame seemed bigger somehow encased in the single-breasted black shiny jacket that fit snugly over his wide shoulders and tapered down to his narrow hips. He wore a white button-up shirt with a thin black tie. He pulled his shoulder-length hair back into a low ponytail, and with his hair away from his face it seemed to accentuate his large forehead and brown eyes. His coco skin seemed to glow in the light from above and his lips were so full I wanted to run to him and feel them against mine.

"You're right, we will get this done, say goodbye, then we can move on to revenge." I changed my clothes quickly and we headed for the garage but stopped when we saw Helen in the living room.

"What are we going to do with Vinny?" she asked, scratching him behind the ear.

"If there's room, I'd like to bring him with us. He's part of the family now." I didn't want to leave him after I just returned.

Helen smiled, "We'll make room for him. Theron acts like he doesn't like him, but he does."

We went down the hall to the garage, finding Uni and Theron glaring at each other.

"What's going on?" I asked, looking at them.

"He won't let me drive my car."

"She could take off and tell her boss everything about us."

"I've been here for almost a week and haven't told anyone where I am. Why would I leave now?" she asked, putting her hands on her hips.

"Because now that you know Katie's safe, your work here's complete. Why should I believe you?" Theron asked, crossing his arms over his chest.

"Fine, I'll drive Jean's car," I said, holding my hand out for the keys. Jean dropped them into my hand and the four of us went to the cherry-red Mini Cooper.

"Let me drive and you can ride in the back with Vinny," Vince said as we approached the car.

I looked over at him, Vinny and Vince would never fit in the back of the two-door car. I laughed, thinking about Vince contorting himself to get in. I held the keys out to him. "You're right and it's Uni's car, she shouldn't have to sit in the back.

Twenty minutes later we arrived at the compound and my

heart squeezed as tears pricked my eyes. The gate was gone, and even though the sun had set hours before, I could see the ruins of the place I called home the summer before.

We were silent as we drove down the road toward the beach and I wiped a stray tear from my eye as we passed what was left of the house Vince and I shared. I thought about the dojo and the hours of training at Vince's side, it was hell, but it was the kind of hell I looked back at and smiled about, knowing that making it through the training made me the person I was now.

We drove past where the mansion once stood and I didn't understand what I was seeing. Instead of a massive Greek mansion there was nothing but skeletal remains. Half the walls and beams were crumbling like they had been slowly wasting away for thousands of years not months.

Vince took the road around the mansion and came to a stop at the edge of the beach. After we unloaded we silently followed the path to the water's edge. Vince held my hand and Vinny stuck to my side as I lightly ran my free hand through his fur.

"Friends, we will begin as soon as the rest of the group arrives," Theron said with his back to us. He was somber. Grief and pain for those he lost plagued his thoughts.

Vince pulled me down the beach toward what was once our home. "Are you all right?" he whispered.

"No, I'm not. I'm miserable," I stopped walking and turned to face him. "This was my home. A place where I felt safe, where I thought I could always return and be welcomed with open arms." I rubbed my arms with my hands and turned away from the beach to look at the debris covering the landscape. "I'm pissed Alex thought he could get away with this. I'm pissed that we had no warning and there was nothing else we could have done to save more vampires." I lost it then and let the tears of anger and loss stream down my face. Vince pulled me into a tight hug and kissed the top of my head.

"We will make him pay," he whispered before stiffening.

"What?" I asked, pulling away from him and following his gaze.

21

Several sets of headlights were coming down the road.

"That will be The Syndicate, Theron will start soon." Vince took my hand and led me back to the group on the beach. We rejoined them at the same time as the rest of the humans arrived. We fell into a loose circle and waited for Theron to begin. He was looking out at the inky black waters with his hands behind his back. After a few seconds he turned.

"Friends, we gather here tonight to send those whom we have lost across the River Styx to join the afterlife they have waited so long to reach. Their deaths were an act of war that will not go unavenged. The men and women we lost in the attack were friends, lovers, and comrades in arms. They will always be close to my heart and I will not rest until the one responsible for their demise is brought to justice." Theron bowed his head and took a step back in prayer.

Vince let go of my hand and stepped forward. "We lost many and we will mourn their absence for years to come but we must move forward and look to the future while keeping them close to our hearts."

Helen stepped forward then. "We will restore this place to the glory it was before, while remembering those who died defending it."

Vince looked at me and I froze. I had no idea they expected me to speak. I didn't even know most of the ones who died, Vince kept me away from them in case they got any ideas. *Find your breath, Helen and Theron need you to say something,* he thought. I matched my breath to his and took a step forward, my mind blank until I spoke.

"The treachery that occurred here has not gone unnoticed. We will find the ones responsible and make them pay for what they have done. We are at war. We must fight to protect all we hold dear. It will take more than we have, but we will not give up and we will conquer our enemies and restore balance to the world." I stepped back and took Vince's hand. I didn't know where the words came from, but they were everything I had been feeling since the attack.

"If everyone will please take two coins from the bag," Theron said, pulling the velvet bag from his pocket and passing it to Helen. She opened it, pulled out the coins, then passed it to the next person. Once we all had coins, Theron put the bag away. "As our brothers and sisters did not survive the fire and all we have are their ashes, please throw the coins into the sea and pray to Poseidon that these coins make their way to our lost, so they may gain passage across the river and into Hades.

Vince pulled me out of the circle to the edge of the water while everyone followed. Vince shook the coins in his hand, looked at the sky, closed his eyes, and threw the coins into the night. After watching him, I did the same, praying that the souls who lost their lives would find peace in the afterlife.

When everyone finished, we went our separate ways driving home in silence, each of us lost in our own thoughts.

# Chapter 3

## *Alex*

Alex had never been happier to take a hot shower as the cascading, scalding water rained down on him until it turned cold. He got out and dried himself off before wrapping the towel around his hips and tucking it in. Grabbing another towel off the shelf he wiped the steam from the mirror. He looked a little rougher after his ordeal on the deserted island and lost a few pounds based on the way his face looked. The skin was pulled tight against his high, almost feminine cheekbones. He lifted his arm over his head and turned to inspect the stitches in his side. They were angry red with the beginnings of infection.

The stupid bitch cut him just above where Vince cut him a few months ago. He brought his arm down and inspected the bite in his forearm where the dog attacked him. They weren't the worst wounds he ever had but they still hurt like a bitch.

He left the bathroom and changed into the first clean clothes he had worn in a week. Once dressed, he headed down to the kitchen and opened the fridge. There was nothing but week-old takeout and condiments inside. He ate on the way home from the island, but it had been hours ago, and he was starving again.

He put on his coat and shoes, then walked down the street to the restaurant he ate at almost daily. He took his normal seat at the counter and pulled the menu from the holder. He tried not to think about the dream he had while floating in the sea. He had been trying not to think about it since he woke up on the deserted island. He told himself over and over it was only a dream. No way was Zeus his father. His subconscious was trying to give him a reason to kill all the people who annoyed him.

The waiter came over and filled his coffee cup and Alex ordered eggs, sausage, and toast. Then went back to thinking about the stupid dream. He laughed out loud when the thought hit him and looked around to see if anyone noticed the half-starved crazy man laughing at himself. No one seemed to. Why hadn't it occurred to him before? If he killed Lolita, he would have one less enemy on his back. Katie didn't survive the storm. She was a strong swimmer, but she was a girl, and probably died of hypothermia thirty minutes after she jumped overboard. He wished there was a way to prove it to Lolita, but Katie being dead meant one less person on his list of people to kill.

The problem with killing Lolita was he had no idea where she was. He didn't even know what she looked like. He only communicated with her by phone or email. He had no way to track her.

He wished Jared was around, he might be able to track the IP address where her emails came from or her phone number. It was an option; he decided. After he finished eating, he would see if Jared would help. If not, he would have to come up with a different plan. Which brought him to the next person on his list.

Theron was alive, and he would not leave his island when he was weak. He would stay and reinforce his power base. Still, Alex needed to figure out how to get to Crete without Theron finding out about it. When he got there, he would have to take Theron out from a distance. Alex couldn't beat him in a close fight, he was too fast. *Fucking vampires.*

Alex's food came, and he scarfed it down like he hadn't eaten in a week. When he was done, he paid his bill and went back to his rented house. He sat down at the computer and pulled his phone out. He sent a message to Jared about locating Lolita then opened the search program on his computer. There were alerts all over the world for Katie, but it had been almost a week since he had been home to check it and he always pulled a dozen false positives a day. Seeing them wasn't a huge surprise. He was clearing the alerts when one of the locations caught his eye. *Milos, that wasn't that far from where the lifeboat capsized*, he thought to himself, opening the link to the photo. Katie was walking hand in hand with Vince on a sidewalk smiling at each other.

"Fuck me," Alex yelled into the empty room. Not only was Katie alive, but so was Vince. Could his luck get any worse? He went back to the program and reviewed each alert. Katie and Vince had taken a boat from Milos to Crete two days before. He clicked on the most recent picture of Katie. She was running with the dog who attacked him on the boat. How did she get her dog back? She had to be the luckiest woman on earth.

Alex got up and stomped around the room running his hands through his hair. Why wouldn't she die? Why wouldn't Vince die? Alex watched Vince buried alive when the tunnel collapsed. Now, not only was Theron alive, but Vince was too? How many others could there be?

He needed to get ahold of himself. Raging wouldn't get him anywhere, he needed to be calm and think of a plan. He would kill all the vampires on Crete if it was the last thing he did. A buzz came from his phone, he ran to it hoping it was Jared.

**Let me see what I can do, but I'm crazy busy right now. What kind of payday?**

Alex thought about the balance of his bank accounts, there was enough to get by on, but not if he had to pay for Jared's hacking skills.

**Nothing, I'm all but broke.**

27

**I'm not a charity, Alex.**

**I know, but come on we've worked together for years, this is personal.**

Alex stared at the phone willing Jared to text him back with a positive answer. How was he going to find Lolita's location without Jared's help? He was about to give up and go back to figuring out how he was going to take care of Katie when his phone buzzed.

**Fine, but it's going on the back burner and you will owe me one.**

Alex let out a breath. It was the best he could hope for, he was lucky Jared would speak to him after they walked away with nothing following the attack on Crete.

**Deal, I'll email you everything I have on the mark. All I need is a location.**

Alex forwarded all the emails from Lolita and her phone number to Jared. With some luck, by the time he caught Katie, he would also have Lolita's location, and he could kill two birds with one stone.

"In other news, the Coast Guard released the name and photo of a man wanted in connection with stealing a lifeboat last week. Alex Jorgenson is wanted for questioning for the theft and also in connection to the mob-style attack that took place on Crete last August."

Alex's head snapped up, he looked at the television screen and a photo of himself taken from a security camera at the ferry port.

"Fuck," he yelled, and ran his hands through his hair. How was he going to get back to Crete now? His picture was everywhere. He paced around the room trying to think. How was he going to get there without taking public transportation? The sound of a motor on the television brought his head up. He shook his head, sometimes he took way too long to see what was right in front of him. He went back to his computer and began shopping for a boat.

Chapter 4

*Katie*

We didn't get to bed until early in the morning, and then Vince kept me up for another few hours bringing me pleasure in ways I didn't think were possible. When sleep finally took me I found myself in my mother's temple.

"Daughter, you are well?" she asked, almost running from her place on the dais to take me in her arms.

"Yes, I am well, so are Vince, Theron, and Helen." I clung to her for a moment before taking a step back.

"Tell me where you have been and why you were gone for so long." She took my hand and led me to a table set with tea and two chairs.

I took a seat, feeling awkward. We were having tea in my dream? Normally we met for brief conversations concerning the horrible things about to happen to me. She sat down across from me, picked up the teapot, and poured us both a steaming cup.

"Would you care for cream or sugar?" she asked, as I took my seat.

"No, thank you." I picked up my cup but waited for her to take a sip before bringing it to my lips. It was a herbal tea I had never had before, it was delicious. "Why are we having tea?"

She grinned and put her cup back on its saucer. "I wanted to spend some time with you since you are safe."

"How am I safe? Lolita is still out there trying to kill me, she plans to unleash an army on Europe. Alex won't give up, and who knows who else is going to try to kill me." I put my cup back on the table and folded my fingers together resting them in my lap.

"Lolita will not stop looking for you, this is true, and I do not know what became of Alex, but we have time." She smiled sweetly at me and picked up her cup to take a sip. "Now, tell me where you have been the last three months."

I looked at the tea and then back at her. Was she trying to drug me into telling her where I was? "I'm not sure," I went with as much of the truth as I could. "They blindfolded me to take me there."

"Why couldn't I feel you? I thought you were dead." She nodded at my cup.

I picked it up and brought it to my lips. I let the tea touch them but didn't drink more before placing it back on the table. "I needed time to mourn. I thought everyone I loved was dead. Alex was tracking me using cameras and my credit cards. I had nothing, no money, no friends, and nowhere to go. I had to hide, I didn't know it would be in a place where you couldn't find me."

"Were there any vampires there?" she asked, and I tried to keep my body relaxed and my heart rate even. I didn't know if I could lie to my mother, but I made a promise to Tad, and I would not break it.

"Yes, there was one. He kept his distance. I think he was afraid of me."

"I am glad you were not completely on your own then. Now, tell me your plan to kill Lolita and destroy her army." She brought her tea back to her lips and sipped it.

"We're working on it. Before I learned Vince, Theron, and Helen were alive I was going to get Lolita alone and kill her."

"Why can't you still? I am sure you are strong enough to win a battle with her."

"What would happen to the hundreds of vampires she created if she died?" I picked up my tea and pretended to drink from it again.

"True, you need an army of your own to defeat hers." She looked past me. "Twenty-five hundred years ago I could have given you the army you needed, but I do not have enough followers now." She looked down at her lap then back. "Are you planning on staying in Crete for a time?"

"Yes, Theron needs to shore up his authority and can't leave until he does. It's well-protected and we need to plan our attack."

"Good, how are you planning to recruit your army?" She pushed her chair away from the table and stood. I got to my feet, and we walked around the room.

"Theron is planning a party to celebrate his return from the dead. We plan to recruit vampires then. There aren't very many who like Lolita. When they find out what she plans to do, they will join us."

"Good idea," she said as we walked around the temple. "You will gain much of the support you need, but how will you stop Lolita from crashing the party?"

*Crap,* I thought to myself, *why hadn't we thought of that?* "I don't know, but if she does I'll kill her, and we'll worry about the army later."

"You are truly becoming the leader I need you to be." She stopped and turned to me. "Your future is not as clear to me as it once was but be true to yourself and your friends and all will be well, daughter." She kissed me on the cheek and my dream flashed to Lolita and Miguel.

They were both bent over a woman lying on the floor. Miguel was holding the woman's wrist to his mouth while Lolita was at the junction of her neck and throat. The woman was naked, and I couldn't see her face, and something told me I needed to know. I walked around Miguel and Lolita as quietly as I could to get a better look. Lolita's hair was blocking my view, and I almost reached out to move the hair away from her face, but I didn't want her to know I was there.

"That was better than I ever imagined," Lolita said, pulling her head up and looking to Miguel. I pulled my gaze away from Lolita and stared at the lifeless face of the woman they had just killed. It was me.

Chapter 5

*Lolita*

Lolita tore down the hall to her office. She glanced at the text message from the priest again.

**Theron is alive as is the false savior**

"Miguel," she bellowed at the top of her lungs. She needed to speak with her brother, he would calm her. He was good at keeping her on an even keel. Had it not been for him, she would be finding a boat big enough to take her whole army to Crete and destroy the entire island if it meant getting rid of Katie and her followers.

She slammed the door to her office open and took her seat behind the desk. She dialed Ilhami's number. It had been a while since she heard from him. He was trying to make a name for himself and wanted to take over Crete on his own to prove to her he was a worthy ally, but it had been weeks, and with news of Theron being alive, she had a feeling Ilhami was not.

"Yes, sister?" Miguel asked, closing the door behind him and taking the seat across from her.

Ilhami's phone went straight to voice mail, she ended the call and threw the phone on the desk. "I believe Ilhami is dead and Theron is alive."

"How did he survive the attack? I went to look myself, all I found were collapsed tunnels, and ashes of the vampires who burned in the sun after their shelter was destroyed." Lolita watched his face while he talked; he looked genuinely surprised Theron was alive. She was having a hard time trusting him since he arrived, but he had done nothing to warrant it.

"I don't know but with Theron alive, who knows who else survived. Katie is still out there, I would bet she's already on Crete or will be there soon." Lolita didn't know what to do. This weak human was proving harder to kill than most vampires. It was dangerous to bring Miguel into any dealings with Katie but maybe he could succeed where Alex failed. "Can you locate her?"

"Me? I could, but she wouldn't come willingly." He looked down at his hands. Lolita didn't understand the infatuation her brother had with the girl. She believed Miguel didn't want to worship the girl, but he couldn't help himself. It must be part of her magic. Any vampire who spends time with Katie would do whatever she wanted just to stay in her good grace.

"I don't care if it is willingly or not. Do you think you could find her and bring her here?" Lolita rolled her eyes, if he found Katie, he probably wouldn't come back. "Never mind, you are more useful here." She picked up her phone and clicked on Alex's number. It rang through to his voice mail. "Alex, where are you? You told me Theron was dead, and he is not. You have some explaining to do. Call me back." She hit the end button on the phone.

"I'm sorry your hitman didn't work out, but there is nothing we can do about it tonight. Let's go get something to eat. It will help you relax." Miguel got to his feet and dusted off the imaginary dust on the shoulder of his suit jacket.

"Very well, I need to change. Meet me at the front door." Lolita went to her bedroom and straight to her closet. She pulled out a black, long-sleeve dress accented with sequins winding their way through it in a swirling pattern. After unzipping the blue sheath dress she was wearing, she let it drop to the floor and stepped out of it. Greta would pick it up and arrange for it to go to the cleaners after she left. She slid the heavy dress over her body and pulled the side zipper up, then went back to her closet, took off the navy heels and put on the black, patent leather, spiked heels that matched the dress.

She checked her face in the mirror. She wore makeup on occasion, but the black of the dress left her face paler than ever and she loved the look. Pulling her favorite red lipstick out of her clutch she applied it to her lips. After one final look in the mirror she went to the other closet and peeked inside at her pet.

"I'm going out for a little while," she looked down at the creature who sniffled as tears welled in his eyes. "If you're a good boy, I will take you out to play when I get back." The creature, who had once been a man, beamed at her giving her a toothless grin and nodding his head, silently promising he would be a good boy. She nodded once, closed and locked the door then swept out of the room and down the stairs to the awaiting boat.

The boat ride to the club was quiet as usual, her bodyguards and Miguel kept a silent watch for any danger that may cross their path. There was none, but Lolita could never be too careful. Over her long life she had created a few powerful enemies, if they found her, she would have to fight for her life to escape them in her weakened state. She had created too many vampires lately, her body felt slow and almost weak from the loss of its spirit. It wasn't a problem now though. She had Miguel, and he had never created a vampire, he was strong, and she was confident he would protect her with his life as she had saved him all those centuries ago.

When Lolita stepped off the boat fifteen minutes later she looked over the line of people waiting to get in and smiled. She bought the club as soon as she moved to Venice and completely revamped it, making it the hippest club in town. It was not a place for Americans to come and drink beer and rub against each other. It was an intimate club where people came to enjoy the ambiance she created. The music pumped in the background but not so loud that one could not have a conversation. The booths were intimate while the tables allowed the patrons to see and be seen.

The sunken dance floor allowed the people in the booths and tables to watch the dancers and the VIP area had a view of the entire club. There was no bar, or tables in the VIP section, only booths with high backs and privacy curtains that could be raised or lowered depending on what the VIP wanted. It was designed for intimate conversations or more private interactions.

Lolita and her entourage bypassed the line, being waved through by the bouncer. They went straight to the VIP section and claimed her booth. Miguel took the seat across from her and perused the crowd. "Madame, would you like a glass of wine this evening?" her usual server asked, bending slightly.

"Please. Miguel, what would you like?" She looked over as he turned to look at her.

"The same will be fine." He pulled on the cuffs of his shirt, then looked over the crowd with a wistful look. Lolita thought he must have been thinking of San Sebastian and his favorite club.

Lolita joined him in perusing the crowd below looking for something to tide her over for the evening. She did not need to drink blood every night, but she enjoyed it too much not to indulge.

She was still waiting for Miguel to find a candidate to change. It had been part of the agreement for him to join forces with her. He had to help her build her army, and he had been putting it off. Every time they came to the club she would point out good candidates, but he would find a flaw with each one. That would change tonight, it was time for him to pull his own weight.

"Miguelito, tonight you must find a suitable candidate and change them," Lolita said after the waiter put their wine on the table.

"I want to find the perfect person, Lolo, it takes time." Miguel pulled his flask from the inside pocket of his jacket and added a few drops of blood to each of their glasses. "I have yet to create a prodigy, and I want to choose well."

"I don't care if they are perfect or not, we need bodies."

38

Lolita picked up her glass and took a sip while looking over the crowd. "There he is," she whispered, seeing a familiar face.

"Who?" Miguel asked, trying to see who she was looking at.

"The man who was traveling with Katie in San Sebastian." Lolita smiled to herself. If Miguel would not change him, then she would throw him out and change the human herself. Anything to hurt Katie.

Lolita watched as Miguel studied Mark, his face was stoic and unreadable. She hadn't seen him with his mask in place in a long time. He didn't want to change the man. It was a good thing she wasn't giving him a choice. "Mark? Very well, I will get him." Miguel took a sip of his wine then moved to stand.

"No, Tony, come." Lolita beckoned one of her bodyguards to come closer. After he approached, she turned his head toward the crowd below. "Do you see that man?"

"Yes, Madame," he said, looking at Mark and memorizing his location.

"Please bring him up here. Tell him he has earned VIP status."

"Yes, Madame." Miguel and Lolita watched as Tony approached Mark and spoke quietly in his ear. Mark's face lit up as he followed Tony off the dance floor and up to the VIP section.

Lolita watched Miguel gulp the rest of his wine and she wondered if it was because he knew changing Mark would hurt Katie or because the man was slime. "Good evening, Mark," Lolita said with sex rolling off her lips. "Please have a seat next to Miguel. Can I offer you something to drink?"

Mark's eyes dilated, and he licked his lips as he stared at Lolita. He quickly glanced at Miguel as he moved over to make room in the booth. Mark's eyes widened. "Where is Katie?"

"She left me for another," Miguel said, his voice tight. Lolita smiled, it wasn't often she could make her brother uncomfortable.

"Where is she? Her parents think she's dead. This is all your fault." Mark moved to strangle Miguel a second before he caught Mark's eye and took a hold of his mind.

"You will sit quietly," Miguel said to Mark as his posture relaxed. "I don't know if changing him is a good idea."

"Why? We just need to make sure Katie finds out he was changed. It will make her furious and weaken her. I want to show her how ruthless we can be," Lolita said, standing in front of the booth while the waiter waited to lower the privacy curtain.

"What if he doesn't make a good soldier?"

"It doesn't matter if he will be a good soldier or not." Her voice carried a sharp edge telling Miguel if he did not do this, his punishment might be the last thing he experienced on this earth.

"As you wish, sister," he said in a quiet voice.

"Of course, it is. You already have so much in common. You no doubt have lots to talk about, so I will leave you to it." Lolita turned and nodded to the waiter standing at the end of the booth. "Please close the curtain."

## Chapter 6
### *Miguel*

As the curtain closed, Miguel let out a breath and stared at the worthless human next to him. "Why did I let you live? I've wanted to kill you since the first time I laid eyes on you in San Sebastian. Now you will make my life hell." There was no reply from the rapist since Miguel had taken hold of his mind, Mark would not speak unless Miguel allowed it. "Maybe it's fitting that Lolita is forcing me to change you. We both are worthless with women. We are both rapists, we both treated Katie horribly, I guess it's fitting for us to end up together."

When Miguel volunteered to spy on Lolita for Katie and Vince, he was aware he would be forced to do things he would never normally do, but he didn't think it would come down to this; turning Katie's piece of shit ex-boyfriend into a vampire for Lolita. At least they found Katie, and she was safe, he didn't know what he would have done to his sister if Katie had drowned. Lolita still hadn't heard from Alex, maybe he drowned in the sea. He still wished he had killed the men on the island the night before they attacked Theron's compound, but he couldn't change the past. He looked at the man across from him, Mark was nothing more than a walking blood bag, but he could not defy his sister. It was too important for him to stay on her good side.

Miguel leaned in and pulled Mark's neck to his mouth, then slid his teeth in. If he thought about it too long he wouldn't go through with it. He wanted to bring Lolita down just as much as Katie did, but to do that he had to keep Lolita happy until the time came.

Miguel drank from Mark until the gush of blood slowed to a trickle and he was holding the man in his arms to keep him from slipping to the floor. He pulled away and propped Mark against the booth with his head tilted back against the cushion. Miguel pulled a pen knife from his pocket and sliced long ways up his wrist. He forced Mark's mouth open with his uninjured hand and let the blood fall into Mark's mouth.

Miguel had never changed anyone, but he knew how to do it. He'd watched Lolita turn many people over the years. He silently chanted the prayer that was always said when changing a human into a vampire. Once he was done, Mark regained some of his strength and latched onto the cut on Miguel's wrist, sucking the blood from his vein as quickly as he could. Miguel kept track of every ounce of blood he fed Mark. No matter what his sister said, Miguel refused to make him as strong as he was. After a few minutes had passed, Miguel pulled his arm away and pushed Mark back into the booth.

"More," Mark said, licking his lips looking for any spare drops.

"You will have more after your change is complete. Now, sit there like a good boy for a minute." Miguel looked at his watch. When a vampire was born, the first stage was to take all but the smallest amount of blood from their body. The person would lose consciousness until the vampire let the human drink from them, then they would come alive again to drink as much blood as possible. When they finished, they would stay awake and be very strong for a few minutes until the change took them. Then, they would lose consciousness and wake up as a vampire a few days later.

"More," Mark said, slurring his words.

Miguel ignored him, it wouldn't be long before Mark lost consciousness as the change took him. *Forgive me, Asteria, for changing one who is not worthy of your gift. I do this to protect your daughter.* Miguel silently prayed, looking at the ceiling. When he looked back down, Mark was slumped in the booth, dead to the world.

# Chapter 7
## *Katie*

I woke up to someone gently kissing my spine between my shoulder blades and continuing down. I let a small moan escape my lips.

"Good morning," Vince said, grabbing my hips and pulling them against his. His cock was hard against my ass and I relaxed into him.

"Morning," I turned my head and kissed him. "I love waking up in your bed."

"I love waking you up in my bed. Did you sleep well?" he asked, pulling me on top of him so his cock rested below the junction of my thighs.

"I had tea with my mom." I tried to scoot down, I needed him inside me, but he stopped my squirming.

"Tea? Is that normally what you do when you dream of her?" He moved his hands to my ass to keep me from moving.

"No, it was strange. Usually, she warns me about something or other. This time we talked about the party and gaining allies."

"What does she think of the plan?" One of his hands found its way to my moist center and began to caress the outside.

"She likes it, thinks it will work, but," I moaned as he dipped a finger into my opening.

"But what?" He pushed his finger in a little further, and I tried to move down, forcing him to go deeper, but he held me in place.

"We need a plan in case Lolita crashes the party."

"Why, do you think she will show up?" He stiffened and moved his

45

hand away from my junction.

"Theron isn't making it a secret that he's alive. Lolita knows through Miguel I'm friends with him, she would probably love to kill us all." I rested my hand on his chest, then rested my chin on my hands so I could look him in the eye.

"You are right, we need to be ready."

"I kind of hope she shows up." I laughed and rested my cheek on my hands and looked around the room.

"Why do you say that?" Vince ran his hands up and down my sides making me shiver.

"Because I'm tired of hiding and looking over my shoulder."

"We would still have her army to deal with." Vince moved a piece of hair out of my face and pushed it behind my ear.

"I know, but they won't be that hard to kill, they are mostly young vampires, right?"

"You say that now, wait till you are fighting them." He ran his hands down my back.

"We'll have help though, isn't that half the point of the party? I'll kill Lolita, then we will go after her army."

"What do you mean, you will kill Lolita?" Vince asked, meeting my eyes as the corners of his mouth pulled down.

"Exactly what I said, I am going to kill Lolita. She is the reason I've been running and hiding for the past nine months Vince. What? Did you think I was going to let you or Theron do it for me?"

"Not necessarily, it's just that she is old and strong."

"I thought the entire reason you trained me to fight last summer was so I would be strong enough to beat her."

"It was, but I hoped it wouldn't come to that. I just got you back, I don't want to lose you again." Vince buried his face in my shoulder and squeezed me.

"And you want me to stand by while you do my dirty work for me? I need to do this Vince."

46

"Why?" he asked, his voice muffled.

"It's not only because I want my life back. My life will never be the same as before. I need to do this to prove to myself I belong in your world, that I'm not just a wimpy human playing with vampires. I need to prove to you, Theron, Helen, and all the vampires who will be at the party, that I'm part of you. I may not be a vampire, but I am part of the goddess who created you. Plus, I want to be free, I want to stop wondering who's going to make a grab for me next."

"Do you think Lolita will be your only opposition? You will always have enemies Katie; a ruler always does." He caressed my ass again, and I arched into his hands.

"But with Lolita off my back, I could have a few days of freedom. A few days where I won't have to worry about someone wanting to kill me. I know it won't last forever. All I'm asking for is a day, or a few hours, of not having to worry."

"Running and hiding is all you have known for the better part of a year." He moved his hand back to my core. "I will do everything I can to help you find the freedom you seek." I gasped as two fingers found their way inside me and began stretching me. "In the meantime, I am going to take your mind off everything."

I yelped as he flipped me onto my back and made good on his word.

A few hours later, dressed in my running tights, a tank top, and katana, I went to the kitchen to grab a pre-run snack. It was going to be a nice day, the sun was out, but it wasn't warm enough for shorts. Vinny was already outside ready to go, but he could wait for me. When I reached the kitchen, I found Uni / Jean sitting at the bar eating a piece of toast. I pulled a bottle of orange juice out of the fridge. "Morning."

"Morning, how did you sleep?" she asked, around a mouthful of bread.

"Pretty good, had a weird dream. What about you?" I asked, getting a glass from the cabinet and filling it with juice.

"Good, I had weird dreams too."

Jean told me she dreamed her dad told her to become friends with the new person who came to Kevó months before I had arrived. It was something I hadn't figured out yet, but with the way my life was going I was going to take it seriously. "What did you dream?" I sat down at the bar and stared at her.

"That you still needed me. I was thinking about leaving and hunting Alex on my own, but my dream said I should stick with you for a while."

"Are you going to?" I still wasn't sure I could trust her, but she wouldn't be a bad person to have on my side.

"I'm going to see this through, but then I'm gone. Everyone here is weird." Her eyes darted around like someone was watching her.

"Yeah, they're an odd bunch. Look I'm going for a run. I haven't done anything but lie around for a week and I'm dying to get out of here for a while. Do you want to come?" She had been stuck under guard since she got off the boat.

"I would, but there is no way I'd keep up with you." She looked down at her feet.

"It's OK, come on, we'll go easy," I said, taking my now empty glass to the sink and running water into it.

"Really? I would love to get out of here for a while." Her eyes brightened.

"Yes, hurry up and change. I'll clear it with Theron. We don't want him to freak out."

"OK, give me five minutes." Jean ran down the hall to her room and I went to Theron's office.

I knocked lightly on the door. "Come in Katie," he called through the door.

"That will be all, Argyris," Theron said as Argyris turned and bowed to me. I gave him a smile and a wave as he passed me, leaving

48

us alone.

"Did you hear me talking to Jean?" I asked, sitting down in the chair across from his desk.

"Yes, although I tried not to. The woman is infuriating." He looked at the ceiling before lacing his hands behind his head. "She doesn't know when to shut up and she is always bouncing around. I swear she has more energy to burn than the sun."

"Well I'm going to help her burn some of it. She is coming running with me."

"Does Vince know you are going out on your own?" Concern filled his eyes. "We can't lose you again. It would kill him."

"I agree, but this is your island and I have to move. I haven't done anything for a week. I'm about to go insane." I blew out a breath and looked at Theron. He looked tired. "Is there anything I can do to help you?"

"Only what we already talked about. I want Lolita and Alex out of the way. I lost almost all my vampires. I feel like I am starting over and there's more work to do than ever before. Having Argyris and Natalia here helps, and when Marios arrives it will be better. I used to delegate almost everything to my vampires. Now I have to do most of the work myself. I haven't worked this hard since before Vince turned me."

"I'm glad you didn't lose everyone, Theron. I'll never forgive myself for bringing danger to your doorstep."

"We went over this already. It was no one but Alex's fault and we'll make him pay." Theron leaned forward.

"What was with the way Argyris and Natalia greeted me yesterday?" I asked, remembering how they treated me.

"They were told who you are as soon as they arrived. They believe in the prophecy and think you deserve to be treated as a queen." Theron gave me a quizzical look. "Maybe we all need to treat you as a queen now."

"Please don't." I backed up a step and put my hand up in surrender. "At least while it's only us here. I'm not ready for that."

Theron smiled. "Good, I don't think we are either."

"Are you going to turn more people?" I wanted to change the subject and wondered how he was going to run the island and help us at the same time.

"Yes, but with everyone I make, I lose a bit of myself and it takes time to recover. Beyond that, I need to make sure they will be good candidates and will benefit my goals before I decide they are worthy of the gift." He leaned back in his chair again.

"You believe it's a gift?" I never thought of being turned into a creature of the night as a gift.

"Of course, it's not a gift without sacrifice though. Some people might think of it as a curse, giving up food and wine, and living as a human, but think about what you get in return. Near immortal life, never growing old, strength that no human can match, the ability to bend others to your will if you wish." He brought his chair level and stared at me. "I could see how you don't understand since you already have so many gifts without sacrificing the things you love."

"You don't think I've had to make sacrifices?" I asked, feeling my anger rise.

"That's not what I meant Katie, you had to make many sacrifices in the past year and it's been hard on you." He laced his fingers behind his head. "I guess I'm jealous. If I had your gifts before Vince changed me, I don't know that I would have accepted his offer."

I relaxed in my seat. "But you would be long dead now." Being faced with a choice of becoming a vampire or living a human life hadn't crossed my mind before. No one had talked about changing me since we learned what the prophecy really said. Most of the time I wondered if I would make it to my next birthday. With my vampires back, I felt like I might. What would happen to me when I turned old and gray? Would Vince still be at my side?

"Death isn't always a bad thing. I don't want it now, but as a human I never thought of it as an ending, only a new beginning." Theron shook himself out of his thoughts and looked at me. "I must get back to work. Take Jean with you on your run but keep an eye on her."

"I will, and I can help if you need me to. Jean might be willing too."

"An Interpol agent helping me? That is the last thing I need. She'll turn me in, then where would we be? Our existence would be out, and I would likely burn in the sun."

"I wonder how loyal she is to Interpol. You might be surprised," I said before leaving Theron in his office and going to find Jean.

Chapter 8

*Katie*

I searched the house for Jean, but couldn't find her anywhere, and was wondering if she left without me when I looked out the back door and found her playing with Vinny.

"Are you guys ready?" I asked, sticking my head out the patio door. It was cool outside but not cold like it was in Kevò. Vinny came bounding over, jumping and spinning in circles as Jean took the leash off the table.

"Yeah, I can't wait to get out of here for a while." She handed me the leash, and I attached it to Vinny's collar.

We took off around the backyard and into the street, heading toward the beach. "Am I going too fast for you?" I asked as we hit the pavement.

"No, I'm good. I'll let you know if I need to slow down," she panted, keeping up with me and Vinny who was almost walking.

We jogged through the neighborhood of white stucco two- and three-story houses surrounded by olive trees, until we reached the beach. I stopped to let Jean catch her breath before the real work began. We were on the opposite side of the island from where the compound was but the sand was the same, almost white, soft and deep. If she wanted to get into shape, running in the ankle-deep sand would do it.

"Why did we stop?" she asked, putting her hands above her head, and huffing.

"That was the warm up. The real work will start after we stretch." I dropped Vinny's leash, and he laid down in the sand to watch us.

"What's the real work?" She copied me as I bent to touch my toes, I held it for a second then stood and reached my arms over my head.

"We are going to do sprints in the sand." I grabbed my foot behind my back and stretched my quad. "It will suck."

"Then why are we doing it?" Jean asked, grabbing her foot as I had.

"Because it will make us stronger and faster. At least the sand won't be hot today." I grabbed my other foot.

"You never did sprints in Kevò. Why are you starting now?"

"Because when you get tired you can stop and I can keep going, and because I need to work on my speed. Are you ready?"

"I guess."

I picked up Vinny's leash. "Don't go at a hundred percent, go at about eighty," I said before taking off down the beach pushing myself to run faster through the sand.

When I reached the end of the beach, I grabbed my knees and breathed deeply. I heard Jean come up behind me a few seconds later. "OK, you get two minutes to catch your breath then we go again." I stood and watched her chest heave in and out as I adjusted the timer on my watch.

"Only two minutes?" she wheezed. "It took me longer than that to run over here."

"Two minutes." I repeated, stretching my legs as my breath came back.

We sprinted back and forth on the two hundred yards of beach for forty-five minutes until Jean fell backwards in the sand. "I'm done. I can do no more, just bury me here."

"One more time down and back, and we're done."

"Are you punishing me?" she asked, struggling to get to her feet.

"What would I be punishing you for?" I asked, pulling my

54

eyebrows together in confusion.

"For not telling you about my plan to arrest Alex." She stood straight and put her hands on her hips.

"No, you're the one who said you wanted to get in shape." I looked at my watch, we still had sixty seconds.

"That isn't what this feels like. I wanted to go for a nice run around the block not run back and forth through the deepest sand I have ever seen."

"Then quit. I don't care if you want to run with me or not. I have fifteen seconds before the next sprint." I got ready, watching the time count down to zero. My watch beeped, and I took off, giving it everything I had. *Only one more*, I thought to myself. When I reached the end, I turned to watch Jean jogging down the beach toward me.

"I'm not a quitter," she said with her hands on her knees.

"Good, one more and we're done." I gave Vinny a pat on the head. He was getting tired too. "Thirty seconds," I said, moving to an invisible line in the sand. Jean stood next to me waiting for my watch to beep. When it did we ran down the beach until we reached the end. I sank to my knees and thought about throwing up. It had been a lot harder than I was used to. I thought the elevation change would be more help than it was.

"You really aren't mad at me for what I did?" she asked, laying on the ground in front of me. Vinny lay down next to her and licked her face.

"Mad you didn't tell me you were using me as bait to catch the one man on this earth I want to kill? That you took my hat off in the restaurant, solely so he would find me? Yes, I'm mad. If you told me, we could have taken him down together, but I won't punish you over it." Jean had made a stupid mistake that had nearly cost me my life, and as much as I wanted to walk away from her, she helped me more than anyone else in Kevȯ when I needed it the most.

"Thank you and I'm sorry. I really thought I could do it on my own and make Ed proud."

"I still can't believe you lied to everyone in Kevȯ." I rolled onto my side ignoring the sand sticking to my arms and legs and looked at her.

"I didn't, Tad knew who I worked for, he okayed all the intelligence I sent to Interpol."

"But he didn't know you were the one who arranged the raid?"

"No, he would have never gone along with it, and I didn't know the sensor was down. As I told you last night, all I wanted to do was scare you into leaving so I could follow you." She rolled on her back and stared at the clouds floating above us.

I was still pissed at her and she was lucky I was too exhausted to move.

"I wanted to scare you into leaving, then I planned to follow you. It would've been a matter of time before Alex found you." She picked up a handful of sand and let it slide through her fingers. "I'm sorry, I had no right to do what I did to you."

"Jean, it's not just me you put at risk, but everyone in Kevȯ." When I thought about all the people there who had become my friends, I wanted to wring Jean's neck.

"I know it was stupid. I'm glad you warned us, you really saved us Katie. Are you going to tell Tad it was me?"

"You know he asked me to find out who the mole was," I said, rethinking everything that happened while I was in Kevȯ. The answer had been right in front of me, but I missed it. I should've known it was Uni.

"He did? Are you going to tell him?" She sat and looked over her shoulder at me.

"I think I should, after everything the town did for me, I owe them that much." I jumped to my feet. "Come on let's go back, the guys are probably starting to worry about us." I held out my hand, offering her a hand up. She took it and I pulled her to her feet.

"Do we have to run?" she asked, giving me puppy dog eyes.

"No, we don't." I gave her a smile, and we started back to the house. "Do you think Tad will be mad that you ratted the location?"

"Yes, he'll probably ban me for life." She pouted.

"I know you don't want me to tell him, but what if he thinks it was someone else and they get in trouble for what you did?" I wasn't sure what to do. Part of me felt like I owed it to Tad for all the help he gave me when I needed it the most, the other part of me thought about all the help Jean gave me.

Jean was quiet, thinking over what I said for a minute. "That is the last thing I would want to happen. Tell him, please."

I looked at her out the corner of my eye. She looked like she didn't care. I was about to tell her I would tell him, but then I thought about what he did to Mordor. He enslaved him. I didn't know what to do with Jean, but I knew she didn't deserve to be turned into a slave. "You know, if I tell him you can never go back right?"

"I know, but I don't want to go back," Jean said.

"What about Theron, are you going to try to arrest him?"

"Depends on what I find out, is the short answer. I do work for Interpol." She looked down at her feet as we walked toward the house, thinking. "If I don't find something on Theron, my handler will be pissed." She looked at me with fear in her eyes. "Katie, I don't know what to do. I don't know how far Interpol will go to force me into finding a way to put Theron behind bars."

"Wait, you said you were on holiday and Theron checked your phone and your computer, he didn't find anything," I said, stopping in the middle of the street.

Jean stopped and turned to face me. "My handler said no to my holiday request, and I wouldn't be good at my job if I couldn't cover up my own communications."

I crossed my arms over my chest. "Do you know what Theron will do if you try to arrest him?"

"He'll probably kill me, but if I don't do my job, I'll probably be marked a rogue, so there isn't much difference." A tear ran down her cheek and she quickly wiped it away.

"I won't let you turn in Theron, he's a good man, but I don't want you to end up as a rogue either. You have a tough decision to make." I left her and kept walking toward the house with Vinny at my side.

"Katie, wait. What will I do with my life if I'm tagged a rogue?" She jogged up to where I had stopped to wait for her.

"I doubt you'll have any problems finding a job Jean. You're smart and funny, I wouldn't be surprised if you found other ways to do good in the world." I put my hand on her shoulder.

"You really think so?" she folded her arms over her chest and stared at her feet again.

"Yes, I do, but if you cross me, Theron, Vince, or Helen you have no idea what you will be in for." My voice was flat and stern as the words left my lips.

"Let me think about it." She walked down the street.

"OK, but I have to tell Theron what you told me." I matched my stride to hers.

"God, I wish you wouldn't, but I know you have to. Katie, I'm sorry for everything I've done."

"I know, and I'm trying to forgive you, but it's hard when you tell me about all the ways you manipulated me." I put my arm on her shoulder and brought her in for a one arm hug. "It will be OK."

I let Jean go just as Vinny jerked on his leash so hard I lost my balance and hit the ground. "Vinny," I cried as my knees scraped the pavement ripping my running tights. He lunged again as a pop sounded and the car window behind me exploded.

## Chapter 9

### *Theron*

Theron leaned back in his chair and blew out a breath, relieved to have a break from Jean for at least an hour. He laughed out loud, even the dog would be gone. He wasn't sure what he wanted to do first, run screaming through the house, only because he could, or have a bag of blood and savor it instead of sucking it down in the bathroom as quickly as he could in fear of Jean catching him. Decision made, he went to the mini fridge and pulled out a bag of blood. He opened it and went back to his desk. He opened his laptop and clicked on his tracking program. Before it had time to load, his phone vibrated, and he looked at the screen to see who was calling. *Tolis the harbormaster? Why would he be calling?* Theron wondered before answering the call.

"Tolis?" he asked, leaning back in his chair.

"Theron, sorry to bother you but I believe the man you're looking for just rented a slip from me," Tolis said with a shaky voice.

"What name did he give you?" Theron asked, jerking his chair to level, jumping to his feet, and heading for the door. He had to find Vince.

"Robert Hope was the name on his passport," his voice shook as he spoke. "I'm sorry I didn't stop him, but there was no way I could've beaten him."

"You did fine, Tolis. Is he still on his boat?" Theron asked, finding Vince in the gym practicing a kata.

"Yes, do you want me to follow him?" The old man had been useful

59

in the past and Theron considered changing him for a time, but his love of liquor made him less than an ideal candidate.

"No, old friend, but will you tell me when he leaves?" Theron asked, making eye contact with Vince who stopped what he was doing to listen.

"Of course, anything to help an old friend."

Theron ended the call and stuck his phone in his pocket. He wasn't sure if he wanted to jump for joy that Alex had come to him or run into the sun to find Katie.

"Alex is on the island?" Vince asked, pulling his phone out and hitting a button. He brought his phone to his ear.

"Yes, he hasn't left the boat yet. Are you calling Katie?" Theron asked, as Vince walked toward the door.

"Yes, but she is not picking up. Where are Vasilis and Yannis? We need them to find the girls and bring them home." Vince pushed through the door and ran up the stairs, taking three steps at a time.

"Fuck, I sent them on a grocery run." Theron pulled his phone out and dialed Yannis. As soon as he answered, Theron barked, "Katie and Jean went for a run. Drop whatever you're doing, find them and bring them home."

"Yes, sir," Yannis said, before ending the call.

"It will be fine Vince. Tolis will call me when Alex leaves," Theron said as he entered his office and pulled up the security cameras positioned around the property.

There were too many places for people to hide on the grounds. The trees were beautiful and gave a much-needed respite from the sun in the summer, but currently, they were providing cover for people who wanted to kill Katie. Theron ran his hands through his hair and laughed. If someone told him a year ago, he would be willing to lose everything for a human he would have laughed them out of his home, yet, here he was, helping his sire keep

60

the woman he loved safe.

Theron got to his feet and paced around. The allergy to the sun was the worst part of being a vampire, he wanted nothing more than to race into the sun and find the girls, but there was nothing he could do. Theron trusted that Tolis would let him know when Alex left the marina, then again, if the old man fell asleep they would have no idea. All Theron could do was pray Yannis would find Katie and Jean before Alex did.

# Chapter 10
## *Katie*

I flattened myself on the pavement and looked around. Jean was next to me, her eyes pinched closed in fear. Vinny was barking and pulling at his leash. I let go, thinking he would have a better chance surviving if he wasn't with us. "Vinny, go home and get help." I almost laughed at how corny it sounded, but he tore off down the street towards the house. "Are you OK?" I asked Jean.

"Yeah, for the moment. Do you think they're after you or me?"

"I don't know, but we need to split up and get back to the house." They were after me I had no doubt and I didn't want to get Jean killed when it was me they were after. I put my hands flat on the ground ready to run.

"You go toward the house and I'll double back." Jean got ready to run.

"I wish I had a gun," I said more to myself than Jean. "On three. One, two." Another gun shot rang out, the bullet hit the street a foot from my head. "Three." We jumped to our feet and took off in opposite directions. I was right, the sniper was after me based on the barrage of bullets following me down the street. I ran behind a parked car and fell hard on my knees, ripping another hole in my tights. My hands shook as I reached behind me to grab the handle of my katana then let it go. My sword wouldn't help me against a gun. I closed my eyes and reached out with my vampire sense to see if I could reach Vince, but I was too far away from the house, besides it was the middle of the day, what could he do?

I closed my eyes and found my breath, I was on my own, with no idea what to do. I had to get back to the house, then everything would be OK. How was I going to get there with someone shooting at me? Was it Alex? Was he playing with me? Making me freak out before he put a bullet in my head? How was I going to outrun a bullet? Would I be OK if I waited until the cops showed up? I reached into my bra looking for my phone to call the police, but it wasn't there. *Fuck*, I thought, remembering that my phone was sitting on the nightstand in my room. How could I be so stupid?

I took a breath, I needed to calm down, I wouldn't survive without a clear head. I closed my eyes and concentrated on my breathing. Bullets were hitting the car I was crouched behind, but I ignored them and let my mind empty of everything except for my breathing. When I was calm, I looked up the street. The next car was about twenty feet away, but if I ran in a straight line, I would be dead in a second. The surrounding houses all had privacy fences, and it would take me too long to jump over one. I would have to make a run for it.

I let out a battle cry and prayed my super-speed would get me home before a bullet found me. I sprinted out from behind the car and ran in a random zigzag pattern up the street, forcing my arms to propel my legs to go as fast as they could carry me. Bullets hit the ground all around me sending chunks of asphalt flying up and hitting my legs. When the gate came into view, I saw Vinny standing outside of it barking his head off.

I felt six vampire minds and broke into them thinking, *someone open the fucking gate, I'm under attack*. If they didn't get the gate open, I would have to keep running and find somewhere else to hide.

The gate opened when I was ten feet away, I slowed down for half a second for it to open wide enough for me to fit through. Vinny ran ahead of me, stopping at the front door and barking to be

64

let in. The door opened as I approached, and we ran inside. The door slammed shut as soon as we were through.

*Katie,* Vince thought from where he was standing against the wall. I dropped to the floor a second before the glass in the door exploded inward, raining glass shards down on me and Vinny then covering the floor. I crawled deeper into the house as glass dug into my knees and Vinny whimpered as he tried to make his way to me.

"Vince, there's a sniper outside shooting at me," I said, turning my head to see him glued to the wall almost paralyzed with fear. "What's wrong?" I asked, looking around. I knew I was bleeding, but it wasn't anything serious, I hadn't been shot.

*Sunlight,* he thought.

I looked around and realized I was bathed in sunlight streaming in through the now windowless pane. "Right, I got this," I said, moving to the shadows and gasping when a piece of glass lodged itself in my knee.

"Stop," Vince said a second before he ran through the sunlight, scooped me up in his arms, and ran down the hall with Vinny at his heels. It took me a moment to realize a cloud of smoke was following us, Vince must have stayed in the sun for too long.

He yanked on the door to the basement when we reached it and carried me down, taking two steps at a time. When we reached the bottom of the stairs, he set me on the couch. "Theron, we are under attack," he yelled up the stairs.

"I called the police, they are on their way. Is anyone hurt?" Theron asked, coming down the stairs. "Why are there bloody dog prints running through the house?"

I pushed Vince away. "I need hot water, a washcloth, peroxide, and a pair of tweezers, now."

"Katie, wait you are bleeding too. Let me get you fixed up then we can deal with the dog." Vince put a hand on my shoulder and tried to move me back to the couch.

"I'm fine Vince. The glass in Vinny's feet will work its way in further every time he takes a step. I need to get it out now." My voice was cold. Who cared if I was bleeding? My dog needed help first. I felt Vince leave the room as I rubbed Vinny's belly and made him stay where he was.

"Katie, where's Jean?" Theron asked, hitting the end button on his phone.

"We split up, she was going to double back." I looked up and saw fear in his eyes.

"Do you trust her?"

"Only as far as I can throw her, but she knows I can make her life hell if she hurts us." I thought for a moment. "All her stuff is here and her car. She won't leave without her computer."

"Are you truly unhurt?" he asked, looking at my blood-covered legs.

"Yes, just some road rash from when Vinny saved me and cuts from the glass." My legs stung but getting the glass out of Vinny's feet was more important than my legs.

"I'll wait for her to come back then." Theron turned and raced back up the stairs.

Vince came back a moment later with the supplies I asked for. "Here." He thrust the first aid kit and a bowl of water to me. "How can I help?"

"Sit by his head and pet him. Try to keep him calm." I took the washcloth, dunked it into the hot water, then wrung it out before blotting the blood off the worst looking paw. There were tiny shards of glass sticking out everywhere. "Oh, Vinny, I'm sorry, bud, this will hurt." I took the tweezers and pulled the glass out, sliver by sliver. He whined once, and Vince held him still, speaking to him in a language I didn't understand. When I got one paw done, I opened the bottle of disinfectant and looked at Vince. "Hold him, this is going to hurt." I poured it on his foot then rubbed his belly telling him he was a good boy. "I think that one was the worst." I moved to the other paws, and twenty minutes later I had all the glass out. I wanted to bandage them, but I figured he would lick off the bandages. "OK, you can let him up. I think I got it all."

Vince let go and Vinny stood then sat and began licking his paws. "Should we stop him from licking?" Vince asked, getting to his feet.

"No, they say it is the best thing he can do." I looked at Vinny wishing I could've saved him from being hurt.

"Your turn," Vince said, picking me up in his arms and taking me back upstairs.

"Is it safe?" I asked, feeling awkward being carried around. "I can walk you know."

"Yes, but I love to carry you. I will carry you every chance I can get." Vince gave me a smile. "It is safe, the police are looking for the culprit."

"Was it Alex?" I asked, mentally crossing my fingers.

"No, but it sounds like it was someone trying to collect on your bounty."

"Damn, I thought Alex would be the only one I would have to worry about." I shook my head. "I shouldn't have gone running."

"I agree. I am sorry, but you are grounded until we resolve the issues with Lolita and Alex." Vince kicked the door to our room open and went straight to the bathroom. He sat me on the counter, went to the soaking tub, and turned on the water. He came back and pulled my shoes off one by one before looking at the bottoms and throwing them in the trash.

"Hey, those are my shoes. I kind of need them," I said, folding my arms over my chest.

"The soles are full of glass. I will get you a new pair, I do not want you running in those anymore." He pulled my socks off and threw them in the trash too. "You can't be too careful." He opened a drawer on the vanity and pulled out a pair of scissors. He bent down and took the hem of my tights then positioned the scissors in between my skin and the fabric.

"Wait, don't you want to knock me out first?" I asked, half laughing that he was, yet again, cutting my clothes off.

"It might be easier. Hold still." He cut the fabric to my knee on one leg, then did the same to the other. "You are no better off than the dog."

I looked at my legs. Tiny pieces of glass stuck out from my knees to my ankle. "It doesn't hurt much. It just stings."

"Let's get your tights the rest of the way off." He pushed my shoulder back, so I was leaning against the mirror. "Please hold still." He cut up the outside of one leg before doing the same on the other side. "Lift up." He pulled the tattered material away leaving me naked from the waist down. "No underwear?" he asked, cocking an eyebrow.

"They chafe, it's more comfortable to run without them."

He turned back to the tub, turned the water off, and came back. "This is going to hurt, try to stay still." He knelt with a clean pair of tweezers and a towel. He picked the glass out of my legs while I tried to hold still and hissed in pain. I told myself I would not scream, Theron and Helen could probably hear my racing heart as it was, they didn't need to hear how much it hurt. "Why are you covered in sand?" Vince asked, pulling out a long piece of glass.

"We ran sprints at the beach," I said, closing my eyes, trying to think beyond the pain.

"That is a hard workout for someone who is not in shape."

"I know but I needed a hard workout and Jean did it, she was slower than me, but she didn't give up." I flexed my foot and reveled in the tightness of my calf.

"I am glad you have not stopped training." Vince moved to my other leg and started digging the glass out.

"I have to stay in shape to have any chance of beating Lolita." I leaned forward to watch him work.

"Good, it is probably what saved your life in the water last week."

"It helped, but I think Mom had more to do with it than my

68

stamina."

"You said something about her making a deal with Poseidon for your life?"

"Yeah, I think she owes him a favor now." I hissed as he pulled out a long shard.

"I am glad you did not make a deal with him. You never want to owe a God a favor." He got to his feet and took the disinfectant off the counter. "Can you swing your legs over the sink? This is going to hurt."

I moved, putting my feet in the sink, and he poured the germ-killing liquid over my legs. I screamed, clenching, and unclenching my hands until the pain subsided. So much for not letting everyone in the house know how much pain I was in.

"Are you done screaming like a little girl?" he asked, giving me a small smile.

"You like watching me in pain, don't you?" I swung my feet around and slid off the counter.

"No, I hate to see you hurting. Never forget it. When you hurt, I hurt." His voice took on a dark note as he put his hands on my shoulders and stared into my eyes. *I am nothing without you. I was terrified when we found out Alex was on the island and you were out there on your own. Then you thought to us and...*

I cupped his face with my hand and rubbed my thumb across his jaw. "I was scared too. I need a gun. If I had one, I would've ended it before I got cut up and you were burned." I took a step back and pulled my tank top over my head followed by my sports bra. "Wait, Alex is here? When did you find out?"

"Are you trying to drive me insane?" he asked, staring unabashedly at my breasts.

"Earth to Vince," I said as he shook his head and looked at me blankly. "Alex?"

"Shortly after you left. I called you, but you did not answer."

"I left my phone here. Believe me, it's not a mistake I will make

69

again." I turned and stepped into the still hot water. It made all the cuts on my legs sting like I was getting the Chinese paper cut torture, but I kept the pain inside and sank into the water, letting my body relax for the first time since I got out of bed. "Where is he now?" I asked when I could speak without screaming.

"We think he is still on the boat he arrived on, but we cannot be sure."

"What are we going to do?" I opened my eyes finding Vince kneeling near my legs with a washcloth in his hand. "Are you going to bathe me as well?" I gave him a smirk.

"Yes, I want to make sure I got all the glass out. Then we will meet with Theron and talk about how to capture Alex." He soaked the washcloth in the water, then ran it up and down my legs, watching my face for any sign of discomfort.

"I think you got them all, I don't feel any other pieces in there."

"Then lay back and enjoy." He smirked as the clear water turned a shade of red from the blood on my legs. He shook his head at me.

"What?"

"You care more about the dog than you do about your own wellbeing."

"In this situation, yes, he was worse-off than me."

"With the amount of adrenaline running through your body you could have been shot and not noticed it. Next time, let me check you out before you take care of the dog."

He was right, I cared more about the dog than I did about myself. "Vince, you have to understand when I thought you were dead, he gave me companionship when I had no one else. He really is my best friend. I would do almost anything to save him."

"I hated that I could not come after you as soon as I woke up, but I could barely walk. Then Theron had a mess with The Turk.

70

I wanted to find you first, but the longer The Turk was on the island, the harder it would be to get rid of him. I am sorry you thought I was dead." Vince lowered his head and kissed my knee cap.

"You would've had a tough time finding me. Kevò is well hidden." I leaned back and closed my eyes. "I'm just happy we found each other again."

"If I had my way, you would never leave my sight, but as it is Theron still needs help and we need help vanquishing our enemies."

I sighed, what I wouldn't give to have all my enemies dead, so Vince and I could just be normal for a while. Well, as normal as human and vampire could be. "Yeah, when it was just me it didn't sound like such a daunting task, but with Lolita's army, do you think enough of the vampires Theron invited will help us?" I brought my knees up and wrapped my arms around them as Vince washed my back.

"They have to, or we will all be doomed." Vince stood and wrung out the washcloth. "You probably want to get in the shower and rinse off. The water is pretty dirty."

"Only if you shower with me." We had danger all around us, and part of me thought sex should be the last thing on my mind, but the other part didn't want to waste an opportunity to have the man I loved. Who knew when it would be our last?

"I want to, but I want you to heal first." He bent and kissed my forehead. "When you are dressed, come and find me."

## Chapter 11

*Jean*

Jean ran the opposite way Katie had, but she wasn't running away. She was a trained Interpol agent after all. She found cover behind a car and, while catching her breath, she watched bullets pepper the ground around KK. Her legs were killing her, and her lungs were on fire after the workout Katie made her do, but she wasn't giving up.

She listened to the gunfire with her eyes closed, praying Katie would make it to safety. Jean had to find the sniper and stop him. She owed it to Katie, in fact she would probably never stop owing her. Jean felt horrible for how she treated her friend. Katie had no reason to call Jean her friend, she had done nothing but hurt Katie or almost get her killed since they met.

She had to make better decisions, or someone was going to kill her. She didn't think it would be Katie, but she would not put it past Vince or Theron. Part of her wanted to give up on Interpol all together, heck, she had only been feeding them the information that Tad allowed her to send. She really wasn't doing a very good job for them, and now she had to decide if she was going to be true to her job, one of the few things she really cared about, or her friend who needed her help. She didn't have time to decide at the moment though; she needed to do everything in her power to keep Katie alive.

The sniper couldn't be too far away since he was still shooting. The area was covered in trees and while there were houses all along the street most of them were hidden. Jean watched for movement in the trees, it was the only realistic location the sniper could be. A flash of metal halfway up a tree on the other side of the street caught her eye, there he was. There was a six-foot, cedar privacy fence between her and the sniper. She didn't know if her legs would hold up if she tried to scale the fence, but she didn't have much choice; she had to catch whoever it was. *What if it was Alex?* The thought had her adrenaline kicking into overdrive. This could be her chance to avenge her mentor. She ran across the street; her legs screaming with every step. Damn Katie for making her run sprints. She scaled the fence, ignoring the pain in her muscles, and landed almost silently on the other side. She looked around the yard, getting the lay of the land. There were half a dozen, ten- to twenty-foot-tall, well-pruned trees in the yard surrounded by short, brown grass. She found the tree the sniper was in and approached it from behind. Walking slowly and calming her mind she pulled a knife out of the waistband of her shorts.

How was she going to get to the man? He was over halfway up the tree. None of the branches were low enough to use as footholds, he must have shimmied up it. There was no way she was going to be able to sneak up on him. She looked around, trying to find something she could throw to disable him. She could throw her knife, but it wasn't a throwing knife, and she wasn't good at throwing knives. She would probably hit him with the handle, cause no damage, and he would start shooting at her. He wasn't a good shot, but if she was right under him, he wouldn't have to be a good shot.

There was nothing around she could use, not even a rock. The shots continued, but she never heard Katie cry out in pain. Sirens wailed in the distance and she figured the sniper would have to come down from the tree if he wanted to escape. She moved to the far side of the tree she was hiding behind and waited. When she heard the thump of feet hitting the ground, she took a deep breath, held the knife behind her back and came out from behind the tree to find a short man dressed in all black with his rifle slung across his back. *Damn,* she thought, *it's not Alex,* but when she thought about it, the Alex she knew wouldn't have missed. This guy was an amateur at best. She could take him on a good day but after running forty-five minutes of sprints in the sand? She wasn't as confident.

"Hi, what were you doing in the tree?" she asked, acting naïve and younger than she was.

"I was looking for my cat." He stumbled over the words and looked around.

"Wow, with a rifle?"

He ran at her, and Jean wasn't sure if he was trying to kill her or just knock her down. She lowered her center of gravity, held her arms out to the side, and gripped the knife tighter as she prepared for impact. When he was within arm's reach he made a grab for her and Jean turned her back to his front allowing him to get his arms around her, then sank the knife into his thigh. He yelled, let her go, and she spun around to punch him in the throat, but she missed, and he backhanded her, sending her into the fence where she bounced off it with a curse, and landed on her hands and knees. She watched as he wrapped his hand around the base of the knife.

"I wouldn't pull that out if I were you," she wheezed.

"Why not?" He stopped to look at her.

"It's in your femoral artery. If you pull it out, you'll bleed out in less than five minutes." She had no idea if it was anywhere near the femoral artery, but she needed to stall him until the police arrived. She got to her feet and ran at the man while he tried to pull his rifle off his back. She tackled him, forcing him to the ground on his front and dug her knee into his back. She pulled his hands behind his back and waited for the police to arrive.

"If you help me kill her, I'll split the money with you," the sniper offered, turning his head so she could hear him.

"Shut up, you greedy bastard," Jean replied, shoving his head into the ground with her free hand. She heard car doors slam and the sound of running feet on the other side of the fence. "Over here. He's over here," she called, wanting to stand up but afraid he would get away.

She listened as someone climbed over the fence. Once the officer dropped to the ground, he pulled his gun and took aim at Jean and the sniper, "Don't move."

"I won't, but hurry, my arms are getting tired of holding him." The sniper tried to buck her off, and she dug her elbow into the small of his back. "I stabbed him too."

"Shut up and don't move," the officer said, looking confused that such a small girl had taken down an armed man with only a knife.

"I'm trying not to."

Another officer came in through a gate, leveled his gun on Jean and the sniper. "Get off the man slowly, keep your hands up."

Jean rose to her feet, keeping her hands where the officers could see them, and backed away from the sniper who rolled onto his back and put his hands up. "Step to the fence young lady, and put your hands on it."

Jean did as they asked. She knew the routine; do as they say and nothing bad would happen. "Take his gun, I have you covered," the officer who came over the fence said.

"Stand up slowly and keep your hands where I can see them," the officer handling the sniper said.

Jean watched as they arrested the man, staying where she was. If she moved, she might give the sniper the distraction he needed to get away. Then the other officer pulled Jean's hands behind her back and cuffed them.

"Why are you arresting me? I stopped him from killing anyone."

"Because you stabbed him." The officer led her out the gate

to the squad car when another car pulled up and an older man jumped out with a phone to his ear. "Yes, she's right here and looks unharmed." He motioned for the officer to un-cuff Jean. The officer quickly unlocked the cuffs, and she rubbed her wrists. "Yes, sir, I will send her home now." The man hit the end button on the phone then stepped closer to Jean.

"What happened?" he asked, putting his hands on his hips.

Jean quickly told him about the sniper in the tree, and that her friend made it to safety, but she stayed behind to catch him.

"Don't ever do anything like that again," the detective shook a finger at her. "He could've hurt you."

"Sorry, I couldn't let him get away." Jean looked at her feet and clasped her hands together behind her back.

"Thank you, for what you did. You can go home now, if we need anything else we'll call Theron."

"Thanks," Jean said in a weak voice and began to half walk, half limp back to Theron's house. Jean was never working out with Katie again.

## Chapter 12

### *Vince*

"How's Katie?" Theron asked as Vince entered his office. "And the dog."

"They will be fine. She is a pain in the ass sometimes though." Vince sat down heavily in the chair across the desk from Theron and nodded his head at Natalia in greeting.

"Thank you Natalia, that will be all," Theron said as the woman stood and left.

"I know, she was bleeding out, and all she cared about was the stupid dog." Theron laced his hands behind his head and looked at the ceiling. "Jean is earning her keep though."

"What do you mean?" Vince leaned forward in his chair.

"She caught the sniper, then waited until the police came and turned him over."

"Who was it?" Vince asked, leaning forward in his chair, and resting his forearms on his knees.

"Don't know, he gave them a fake name, an amateur I think." Theron leaned forward in his chair. "We're lucky it wasn't Alex. He wouldn't have missed his target."

Vince understood Theron's anger at the sniper not being Alex, but he was right, Alex would not have missed. Vince had not missed being able to go outside during the day in centuries but, today, he would have given almost anything to be out with Katie. "What happens now?" Vince asked, sitting back in his chair.

"We go to the police station, the guy won't talk. He's sitting in the interrogation room quiet as a mouse. The chief asked if I would come down and see if I could get some answers out of him."

"When do we leave?" Vince asked, ready to spring to his feet and leave right then. Someone had tried to kill his Katie, again, and he was going to make the bastard pay.

"At sundown. Are you comfortable leaving Helen and the others here to keep Katie safe?"

"Yes, I am sure they can take care of any threats." Vince smiled, he loved knowing Katie could take care of herself. "She asked me if you could get her a gun though."

"When did she learn to use a gun?"

"In Kevö, I guess someone there showed her how to shoot."

"She is getting better and better prepared to take care of herself, isn't she?"

"Yes, I do not think she will ever cease to amaze." Vince could not stop the prideful smile from crossing his lips.

"What kind of gun does she want?"

"A Smith & Wesson 9mm semiautomatic, with a grip safety, night sights, and a holster." Vince almost had to write down what she wanted, so he would not forget anything. He had used guns in the past but did not have much use for them.

"She really learned how to shoot if she wants that gun. I'll call Serafeim and arrange it."

"Thank you. What are you going to do with Jean?"

"I don't know yet. I have a feeling she's spying on me, so she can hand me over to Interpol. I want her out of the house, but she knows too much, and she could be an asset if we trusted each other."

"Katie talked to her. It sounds like Jean does not know what to do, but I think she will choose her life over being killed by you if she tries to arrest you."

80

"I can't trust this woman, but I think we need her."

"You want her in your bed?"

"No! She has connections I've only dreamed of having, and she can go places I can't." Theron drummed his fingers on the desk. "My bed? As if I would take her, she is nowhere near what I look for in a lover."

"Only you know who you want. Anyway, she does not seem entirely dedicated to Interpol." Vince looked at his watch, they only had a few more minutes until the sun went down.

"Shall we make our way to the garage?" Theron got up, changing the subject, making Vince wonder what he really thought of the girl.

"Where are you going?" Katie asked, as they exited Theron's office and came toward her. Dressed in a pair of tight black yoga pants and a thin black camisole, Vince almost wanted to stay and take her to bed.

"To interrogate the shooter," Vince said, trying to figure out a reason why she should not go with them.

"Can I go?" she asked, turning and walking at Vince's side when they reached her.

"It isn't a good idea," Theron said, and Vince let out a breath. It would sound better coming from Theron than it would him.

"Are you going to kill him?" Katie asked, not sounding surprised they did not want her to come.

"If we can get away with it, but he is in police custody." Vince took her hand and gave it a squeeze.

"Good, he tried to kill me." She squeezed his hand back.

"Are you all right staying here while we deal with him?" Vince stopped when they reached the kitchen and turned to face her.

"I guess, if he wasn't at the station I would demand to go, but I don't want to go to the police station. It makes me nervous."

"We will not be long. How are your legs?" He looked down at them, glad he no longer smelled blood.

"They are scabbing up and pulling on the skin. They hurt, but I'll live."

"Good, I think Helen's hair stylist is coming over soon. Enjoy a girl's night, and I will find you when we return." Vince took her in his arms and kissed her for longer than necessary before joining Theron in the garage. He would never get enough of her.

When they were in the car on the way to the station, Vince looked out the window at the possible locations a sniper could be hiding. "Do you want to move?" Theron asked, watching Vince.

"Yes, but I do not know where. This house is very nice, but it is in such a residential neighborhood. I worry about what the neighbors may see and all the places for assassins to hide."

"I've been thinking about it too. This house worked for the time being, but with the party, we are going to have vampires from all over Europe on the island, we need a more secure location." Theron turned down the street leading to the station.

"You must have an idea if you are talking about it."

"I do, my old house, but there's another compound that will work. I called the owner before you came into my office tonight."

"What did he say?"

"I can rent it, but only because it's winter, and they aren't planning on visiting until July."

"When do we move?" Vince asked, as Theron pulled into a parking spot.

"Tomorrow night. It's a massive house with twenty bedrooms, and twenty-five bathrooms. Everything is state-of-the art including their security system. It's in the middle of an olive orchard. It will give us the privacy and security we need. Are you going to call Maria?"

"Yes, I am sure she will help us, to get even with Lolita for sending a spy into her house, if for no other reason."

Theron turned off the car and opened the door. "The invitations for the party are going out tomorrow. Are you sure you want to send one to your maker?"

"No, but he has sway with the old ones and is good in a fight. If we are going against an army, we are going to need all the help we can get.

"Agreed."

They walked into the police station and found the Chief of Police waiting for them. "Theron, it's good to see you, especially after we thought you died in the bombing."

"It's good to see you too; can you take us to the sniper?" Theron shook his hand. Vince was impressed that Theron had a good relationship with the police. It was the only way Theron could run his business.

"Yes, follow me." The Chief turned and walked down the hall, leaving Theron and Vince to follow.

"What have you found out about him?" Vince asked, walking next to Theron.

"He's an amateur. We are still trying to track down his real name and nationality." They stopped outside an interrogation room.

"Listen, Theron, I know this guy shot up your house and tried to kill your friend, but I can't let you kill him. He needs to stand trial for what he did. We need the Cretans to know we are still in charge, especially since we weren't able to catch the man who killed all those people in the bar last month."

Vince was planning on killing the bastard and now he couldn't. He looked down at his hands and fisted them to stop them from shaking in fury.

"You turned off all the monitoring devices?" Theron asked.

"Yes, as per usual." The Chief opened the door for them.

"Thank you, we won't kill him this time, but if he escapes, I can't make any promises," Theron said, walking into the room after Vince, and closing the door behind him.

The sniper was sitting at a table with the chain of his cuffs strung through a bar in the middle. Vince wanted to bash his head into the table until there was nothing but slivers of bone and brain matter left, but instead he stood in front of him with his hands behind his back.

"You guys aren't cops," the man said, looking from Vince to Theron. "Are you my lawyers?"

"No," Theron leaned in so close their noses almost touched. "The woman you tried to kill is his wife. He's trying to keep himself from killing you right now."

The man tensed. "How did you get in here? I want my lawyer. You can't be in here." The man began yelling for help.

"Shut your mouth, scum." Vince took hold of the man's mind and the screaming stopped. "Thank you, now tell me why you were trying to kill my wife." Vince had to admit he liked the way the word sounded when he associated it with Katie.

"There is a bounty on her head." The man answered with no emotion. "I think there's a bunch of people coming after her. The payout was too good to pass up."

"How did you find her?" Theron asked.

"Someone leaked her location on the web."

"Tell me the name of the website you found it on." Vince was trying to remain calm but knowing there were still people trying to collect the bounty on the woman he loved was making him insane.

The man gave them the website and Theron entered it into his phone. "You will not escape, you will take the punishment you are given. Now tell me your name, your real name."

They extracted the information the police needed then banged on the door. "Everything you need is written on the paper on the table along with a signed confession," Theron told the chief when he let them out of the interrogation room.

"I'm sorry you couldn't kill him. I know it would've made you feel better," Theron started as he drove back to the house.

"I am too, but we got some useful information from him. I think we need to put Jean to work on this. She can delete every mention of Katie on the internet, about the bounty at least. It will stop anyone else from getting into the game."

"But it won't stop the ones who are already looking for her," Theron pointed out. "Do you want to get something to eat before we head back?"

"What are we going to do about that? I need Katie safe and no, I will have bagged blood tonight." There had to be something he could do to keep Katie safe, even though it was becoming harder and harder to do so.

"We are doing everything we can right now. I feel like an idiot for not trying to find out more about the contract before now."

"Thank you, Theron, you have been more of a friend to me this year than anyone ever has been." Vince sighed, he wished he knew more about computers. He could run one, but he had no idea how to remove Katie's contract from the dark web.

"You would do the same for me. Don't worry Vince, we'll find a way to get the contract off the web and take care of Alex and Lolita, then you and Katie can live your life the way you want to."

"I hope you are right," Vince said, staring out at the night and wondering what he and Katie would do when they were truly free.

## Chapter 13

### *Alex*

After Alex docked his boat in the slip he rented, he looked around the small cabin; it had a galley, a head, and a berth big enough for two people. He debated staying on the boat, but there was a problem, there was only one way off it. Bailing into the sea would only work if he could swim faster than whoever was chasing him. He shook his head and went up the stairs leading to the cockpit. He needed a place where he could sleep without worrying about waking up with a gun to his head and he knew where to go.

He grabbed his pack, made sure his hat covered most of his face, got off the boat and walked down the dock toward shore. Waving at the harbormaster as he passed the office as the man took a long swig from his bottle. Alex shook his head, there was no way the drunk would remember what he looked like, let alone that he rented the slip for a month.

Once he was away from the marina he pulled out his phone and opened a ride sharing application. It would be a long walk to the safe house and, after the long boat ride, the last thing he wanted to do was walk five miles to town. When his ride showed up, he got in the back and threw his backpack on the seat next to him. He gave the driver an address a few blocks from Sanctuary. There was no way he would let him drop him off at the front door.

Alex walked down the narrow cobblestone street almost feeling claustrophobic from the three-story stucco buildings encroaching on him. The tourist shops were open, but their doors were closed to keep the heat inside on the chilly day. He came to an alley and turned down it. The street was narrow, and he wondered if a compact car would be able to transverse it. The buildings felt like they were sagging toward him with large chunks of concrete missing from the walls. They kept the front clean and in good repair for the tourists, but no one would want to venture down the alley unless they knew where they were going and wouldn't care about the façade.

He stopped when he reached a large rusted iron door with Σαράντα δύο carved into it and knocked. He waited until a small rectangular slide opened and filled with brown watery eyes. "What do you want?" a gruff voice asked.

"I seek sanctuary under the holy law of mercenaries." Alex forced himself to stand up straight and look the man in the eye.

The man eyed him up and down before shutting the slide, unbolting the door, and allowing Alex to enter a small reception area that reminded him of a budget motel that rented rooms by the hour instead of per night. The walls were probably once white but were now an ever changing shade of yellow. There was a tall reception desk made of dark wood paneling that was all the rage in the 1970s and two plastic chairs sitting against one wall. There were two hallways leading off in different directions. Alex felt like they left the place like this because they didn't want anyone to get too comfortable. They were right, he almost turned around and went back to the boat, but he thought of all the people looking for him. This would be the safest place for him.

After confirming Alex was a member using fingerprint and retinal scanners, the man gave him the rundown of the place. "There are showers and beds upstairs. The bar is through that door." The man pointed behind him to a hallway.

"Thank you, how long am I permitted to stay?" Alex asked, ready to go to his room and sleep.

"A month is the limit," the man said in broken English. "If

you do harm to anyone here, you will be banned from here and all other safe houses."

Alex nodded as if he had heard the spiel before, but he hadn't, he never had to resort to staying in a mercenary's safe house before, from what he heard they were worse than a hostel but better than sleeping on the street. For what he needed it would be perfect. He doubted Theron even knew there was a safe house on the island. "Understood," Alex said before taking the stairs three at a time until he reached the second floor. He walked down the narrow hallway looking for an empty room. There was a surprising number of people staying there based on the number of occupied rooms. When he reached the end of the hall, he found a room with its door open and a sign with the words *vacant* hanging from the door handle.

Alex took the sign off the door as he entered and closed it behind him. He sat the sign down on a dinged, darkly stained dresser that looked like it had been around since World War II. He threw his backpack on the single bed with nothing more than an off-white sheet covering it. The walls were painted white at some point but were now a nicotine yellow. At least the place smelled clean. He went to the blackout curtains and pulled them back to get a look at the view. He could see the street where his ride dropped him off. There were a few people strolling up and down it, but it was nothing compared to high season when the streets would be teeming with people from around the world at all hours. Alex let the curtain fall back in place and took his backpack off the bed. Setting it on the small desk that matched the dresser in appearance and age he pulled out his laptop and plugged it into the wall. While it was charging, he put away two of his three changes of clothes. He took the last set and went down the hall to the communal bathroom. After showering and putting on clean clothes he laid back in the bed and fell asleep almost instantly.

Alex woke from his nap feeling better than he had in weeks. He was doing something instead of sitting behind a computer waiting for a miracle to happen. He listened to the voice mail Lolita left the night before. She was pissed, and he needed to check in with her, but not yet. He wanted to call her with positive news for a change. His stomach growled, it had been hours since he ate. He put his phone in his pocket and went down to the bar.

The dimly lit room had a long bar along the wall near the entrance. The walls were stucco, but he couldn't tell what color they were since there were no windows and the light was dim. There were tables scattered around with little red candle holders sitting on top, toward the back he saw pool tables and a dart board. It was cozy and clean from what he could see, not the grimy hole in the wall he was expecting. It was crowded, but most of the people were hovering around a television screen in the back. When the bartender saw him sit on a stool away from the crowd he reluctantly stepped away from the television and made his way over to Alex.

"What's going on?" Alex asked, glancing at the screen but unable to see anything with all the heads in the way.

"An amateur tried to take out the target they're all going after." He pulled the towel off his shoulder and made a show of cleaning off the bar in front of Alex. "What can I get you?"

"Can I get a cheeseburger, fries, and a beer?" Alex asked, wondering who all these people were after. "Who's the mark?"

"Some girl, the payoff is huge, but no one has gotten close to her. I'll put your order in." The man went to a computer next to the liquor bottles and tapped in the order. "The police haven't said if he hit his target or not, but it doesn't matter, he'll spend the rest of his life in jail."

"Yeah, right," Alex said, only half paying attention. *Were all these people after Katie? How did they find out where she was?* It wasn't like her picture was all over the internet or anything, plus, she had been off the radar for months. Now suddenly, people were swarming Crete to complete the contract. Alex slammed his hand against his forehead. Lolita must have amped up the publicity after he failed on the ferry. The bitch, Katie was his mark, and Lolita knew it. His subconscious was right, all the fucking vampires needed to die.

"Attaboy," a huge man with a deep voice said, taking a seat next to him. He was tall, had to be almost seven feet and almost just as wide, but not with fat. The man had brown, shoulder-length, curly hair, and a neatly trimmed beard, with brown eyes that swirled from milk chocolate to dark.

"Excuse me?" Alex asked. He had to look down and confirm the stool had not folded in on itself due to the weight of the man sitting on it.

"You heard me, kill them all." He winked at Alex before looking for the bartender who was back at the television watching the news with the rest of the assassins. He slammed his fist on the bar and Alex jerked when a jolt of electricity shocked him. The bartender froze and robotically turned and staggered over to the man.

"What can I get you?" he asked, looking everywhere but at the man.

"A beer and hurry." The man turned back to Alex as the bartender jumped at the demand and poured the man a beer.

"Do I know you?" Alex asked, after studying the smile lines on the tanned skin of the man. He reminded him of someone, but he couldn't put his finger on who.

"I would hope so. I'm your father, the one who saved you from Poseidon's wrath last week." He crossed his arms over his bulging chest and gave Alex a sideways grin.

"I thought it was a dream." Alex jumped up from his stool and took a few steps away from the would-be god.

"It was a dream, but everything I said, and the deal we struck, remains. If you do not kill all the vampires I will kill you," Zeus said in a low voice, trying to keep other people from hearing him.

"You've got to be kidding me." Alex didn't want to believe him, but how else could he know about vampires and the weird dream he had while swimming for his life? "There are no such things as vampires, it was just a dream." He tried to leave, he didn't like the feeling he was getting from this guy, but the man's hand shot out and held him where he was.

"You can't leave now, here comes your food." Zeus nodded his head toward the bartender coming from the door of the kitchen with a plate of food in his hand.

Alex needed food, and he wasn't ready to go out and look for Katie yet, hell he might have been too late if the assassin on the news got her. He was so fucked if Katie was dead. His stomach clenched, but he needed the fuel. He picked up his burger and took a bite. "So, what are you doing here?" he asked around a mouthful of food.

Zeus gulped half his beer then turned on his stool to look at Alex. "Checking on you, of course, you didn't think I would come here for a beer when I could be in a brewery in Germany, did you?"

"OK, I'm fine. You can go now." Alex took another bite of his burger. He didn't like to be watched while he ate, and he didn't trust Zeus.

"You are anything but fine. You come to this island with no plan, trying to take out one of the Titans' offspring." He laughed then gulped the rest of his beer.

"For all I know, the guy on the news already killed her, then all I would have to do is kill the vampires, easy." Even Alex didn't believe his own bravado. He had no clue how to kill them, he wasn't even sure shooting them would work.

"Bullets will not work, take their head or remove their heart unless you can secure them and let the sun's rays burn them." Zeus answered Alex's thought, and he jumped to his feet dumping the rest of his food and the beer onto the floor.

"What the fuck? How did you do that?" he asked, ignoring his dinner laying on the floor and taking a few steps away.

"God, remember?" Zeus turned back to the bar and slammed his glass down on the bar to get the bartender's attention.

"This is so fucked-up," Alex said more to himself than to Zeus. "So, can you help me? I don't know how I'm going to do it." He went back to his stool, there was no reason for him to run away even though it was what his body wanted him to do.

"Help you? No, but I can give you information, the girl is not dead." Another beer appeared in front of Zeus even though the bartender was ignoring them.

"How can you be sure?" Alex asked, wishing he had another beer. He was still having trouble believing he was sitting in a bar talking to his dad, who was a god, and not just any god, but *Zeus*.

"Because I watched the whole thing unfold. She escaped, as did her guardian and her friend. The man had no chance, he didn't understand who he was dealing with." Zeus picked up his beer and drained half of it as a full pint appeared in front of Alex.

"Where is she?" Alex picked up the beer and took a long sip. What did he have to lose? He didn't know where to start looking.

"I am not so good with directions, but I know where she will be."

"Waiting with bated breath here." Alex pulled his phone out ready to enter the address into his map application.

"OK," Zeus said, then spat out directions Alex could never follow. They were along the lines of; find the old olive tree that no longer produces fruit and turn toward where the sun sets.

"That's it? How in the hell am I supposed to find her with directions like that? This is the twenty-first century old man." Alex blew out a frustrated breath after saving the directions. When he looked up to see if he could get something better, the stool next to him was empty.

"I'm losing my mind," he said to himself, finishing his beer and going back to his room.

## Chapter 14
### *Katie*

After Vince and Theron left, I went to Jean's room and knocked on the door.

"Come in." I heard her call and opened the door to her room.

"Hey, Jean? Are you all right?" She was sitting on her bed, her pink, long, wet hair was hanging over her shoulders getting the white T-shirt she was wearing wet.

"Yeah, kind of a crazy day." She looked back down at her laptop for a second before pointing and flexing her toes. "I don't know if I will be able to walk tomorrow."

"Why? What did he do to you?" I asked, running to the bed and looking at her legs.

"Not from the sniper. All he did was backhand me." She giggled. "From the torture you put me through at the beach."

"Oh, well, I wish I could say I was sorry, but we both needed it." I sat down on the bed and waited for her to look up from her computer.

"Katie, what's wrong?" she asked when I had been silent for too long.

"Thank you for catching the bastard," I said, looking down at my hands.

"Don't worry about it. The only reason I got him was because he was after you. You should've seen the look on his face when he realized I was waiting for him." She laughed and closed her laptop.

"Katie?" Helen called. "Are you in here?" She pushed the door open the rest of the way.

"Hey Helen, what's up?" I asked, getting up from Jean's bed.

"My hairdresser is here. Are you ready to get rid of that two-tone mess?"

I pulled my hands through my hair. "Yes, do you want to come hang out while I get my hair cut?"

"Yeah, sure," Jean said, and we went to the living room.


An hour later I looked at my hair in the mirror. I finally looked like myself again. The blond was gone, leaving my dark brown, almost black, hair just above my shoulders like a curtain to hide behind.

"It looks so good. Vince won't be able to keep his hands off you now," Jean said, sitting back on the couch and taking a sip of her wine.

"Man, I needed a haircut so bad. Thank you," I said to the stylist as she packed her equipment into a box.

"You're welcome, if I can help you with anything else please let me know." She picked up her bag and went to the door. "I'll see myself out."

"I'll walk with you," Helen said, getting to her feet. "I'm going that way anyway."

Helen left the room with the stylist and I got up from my chair, put my sword back on and moved to sit on the couch across from Jean. "It's been a long day," I said, picking up my glass and taking a sip.

"You were almost shot and all you have to say is that it was a long day?" Jean's eyes almost bugged out of her head.

"It wasn't the first time, and I doubt it'll be the last." I stretched, wincing when the scabs on my legs pulled at the skin.

"You live a dangerous life." Jean took another sip of her wine.

96

"Not by choice, believe me." Vinny came and sat down in front of me raising his paw. "Do you need to go outside, buddy?" He jumped to his feet and ran in a circle. "OK, I guess I'm taking him outside."

"Please be careful," Jean said from her spot on the couch. "I already saved you once today, I don't want to have to do it again."

"Deal, you only have to save me once a day." I laughed

"I'm sorry all this is happening to you. I know you didn't ask for it or want it. I've been thinking about what we talked about before the sniper." She paused and looked at the floor.

"You've decided?" I asked.

"I'm with you. I won't turn Theron in, and I want to help you kill Lolita and Alex. I'm not big on murder, but I don't think there's another way to stop them." She looked up at me with a hopeful look on her face.

I wished I could tell if she was lying like I could with vampires. I went with my gut and trusted her. "I'm glad you're with us, but you need to build some trust with us before we will believe you."

"I know, it starts now. I won't hide anything from you anymore." Jean sat a little straighter.

"Good, I've got to take Vinny outside before he makes a mess and Theron freaks out."

I took Vinny into the backyard but stayed in the light of the house. I pulled my katana out, thinking I could go through one form before Vinny would be ready to go back inside. I closed my eyes for a moment then moved, blocking and slicing my way through invisible opponents the form was designed to prepare me for when I heard it. The sound of someone trying to be quiet while walking on the dormant grass.

I continued with my form, wondering where Vinny was and why he hadn't alerted me to an intruder. When the footsteps came within striking range, I spun around, breaking my form and leveling my katana a hair's breadth from the neck of the intruder. I let the katana fall away from Theron as a smile blossomed on his face.

"Vinny? Where are you?" I called into the darkness. "You're lucky you didn't lose your head, Theron." Vinny came bounding out of the dark and sat in front of Theron waiting to be petted. "Thanks for being such a good guard dog, Vinny." I shook my head at him.

"You've been practicing, or you wouldn't have been able to stop yourself from injuring me." He took a step back. "I don't remember showing you that form."

"No, I found it on the internet while I was in Kevo." I lowered my sword and cursed myself. I could have killed Theron. If I had been paying attention to my vamp sense, I would've known it was him sneaking up on me. I was out of practice. I needed to start using it before I hurt someone I cared about.

"Will you show it to me some time?" he asked, finally giving in and scratching Vinny behind the ears.

"Sure. What was the deal with the sniper?" I asked, sheathing my katana, and walking to the back door.

"He found your hit on the dark web, and someone spotted you on the island." Theron looked at the ground to avoid meeting my eyes. "I wish it would've been Alex."

"Me too. What happens now?" I asked, looking around like Alex would pop his head over the fence any second.

"Now, we need to find Alex and kill him. I am tired of playing defense, it's time we were on offense for a change."

I looked over at Theron, I didn't want to admit it, but he was right. "Defense sucks. What did you do to the sniper?"

"We wanted to kill him, but the chief wouldn't let us. We managed to get some valuable information out of him though." Theron held the back door open for me and we went inside.

"Really?"

"Yes, let's find Jean and Helen and we'll tell you about it."

"So, my name and picture are on the dark web?" I asked, floored, I would never be able to show my face in public again. We were in the living room scattered around sitting on various chairs in front of the fire.

"Yes, but we're hoping with the help of our hacker, it won't be there much longer, and she can make sure it never shows up again," Theron said, taking a sip of his wine.

"Who, me?" Jean looked up, shocked, then thought about it. "Yeah, I can do that if you have the right security on your network." Jean got to her feet and walked toward her room.

"Where are you going?" Theron asked, cocking his head to the side.

"To get started. I have nothing else to do."

"We are moving to a new location tomorrow night. Would it be better to wait until we are there?" Vince asked.

"Well that depends on your security, if I have to change it then it would be a waste of time if we're moving tomorrow. If it's ready to go, then I can start now and finish when we get to the new house."

"Of course my security is good enough," Theron barked, obviously insulted that Jean thought it might be subpar. "You're not the only one with hacking skills."

"Then why don't you do it yourself?" Jean shouted back at him. I didn't understand why they were making such a big deal about this.

"Because I have an island to run, a qu... Katie to protect and a party to plan." I nearly gasped when he started to say queen and squeezed Vince's hand.

"Fine then, I'll go do your hacking for you." Jean stormed out of the room and down the hall.

"Are we moving because of Alex?" I asked, wanting to get Theron's mind off Jean.

"That, and because we need to make a show of strength," Vince said, squeezing my thigh again.

"This location isn't secure, and it's too small. We are moving to a compound in the heart of the island with an orchard. It's a large property, not as big as mine but big enough." Theron moved back to the couch and sat.

"What are we going to do about Alex?" I asked, wishing Jean hadn't left.

"What we have been planning on doing from the start; find him and kill him." Theron paced around the room.

"But how are we going to find him? Where would he go?"

"This is my island, I already have everyone I trust on the lookout for him."

"You won't find him that way," Jean said, coming back into the room with her computer in her hand.

"Why not?" Theron stopped, put his hands on his hips, and glowered at her.

"Because he knows you're looking for him, hell he's probably aware you know he's here. He'll be at Sanctuary." Jean sat down on the couch next to Helen and opened the computer.

"What *Sanctuary*?" Theron asked, stepping in front of Jean and forcing her to look up at him.

"Σαράντα δύο, haven't you heard of it? The mercenary's safe house?" Jean looked up at him and rolled her eyes. "It's in Herculean, I thought you knew everything about this island."

"This is news to me, tell me about it." I could feel envy rolling off Theron, *why wasn't I told about it?* he thought, but it wasn't directed at me so I kept quiet.

"There are safe houses all over the world for mercenaries, hit men, and other criminals. I thought you would have okayed its creation on Crete since you are the head of the crime syndicate." Jean rolled her eyes again, and I held in a laugh. She was right, how had Theron let this place go up knowing nothing about it?

"Go on, how does it work?"

"It's a member's only club, there's an initiation fee, then a monthly fee if you want to use their services. Members can stay at any of the locations worldwide without having to worry about someone stabbing them in the back. They're crazy with the rules though. No weapons are allowed on site, and if you are being chased you have to prove that you lost whoever is chasing you before you enter. It's totally worth the money to be a member."

"How do you know all this?" Theron asked, tapping his lips with a finger as if he was thinking.

"I joined it when I joined Kevȯ, Tad is the one who started it." Jean shrugged her shoulders. "Most of the people in Kevȯ are members. You never know when you'll need to lie low for a few days."

*How do you feel about Jean going in undercover?* Theron asked me.

I blinked. My first reaction was hell no, I didn't want Alex anywhere near my friend, but the more I thought about it the more the idea made sense. *It could work, can you trust her?*

*No, but what other choice do we have?* Theron turned and began pacing again. "Jean, would you be willing to go undercover to spy on Alex for us?"

"What? No, that's not allowed, I could get kicked out if anyone found out." Jean put the computer on the seat next to her and exploded to her feet.

"Jean, you're good, just don't get caught," I said, folding my arms over my chest. "We aren't asking you to kill him, we just want to know what he's planning, where he will be, so we'll be ready for him.

"If you do it right, they will never know," Helen said with a sly smile.

"It would be just like you were out in the field with Interpol," I added, and Jean's face brightened, we had her right where we wanted her.

"You could be the reason Alex goes down," Vince said, relaxing, he liked the idea.

"But what if they find out what I'm doing?" Jean asked, her voice going an octave higher than normal. "What if Alex recognizes me?"

"Where would he have seen you?" I asked.

She pulled her eyebrows together in thought. "You're right, he didn't see me on the ferry. He had no way of knowing I set the whole thing up. It could work." Her face went bright with excitement. "I'll do it, but first, let me make it look like the hit on Katie was filled, then I'll pack and go to Σαράντα δύο. To do this right, I'm going to need some supplies." She bent and picked up her computer.

"What kind of supplies?" Theron asked, cocking an eyebrow at her.

"Surveillance equipment, very small, very expensive equipment. Sanctuary is full of people who know what to look for. I need the best there is if this is going to work."

"Give me a list and I'll get it for you." Theron nodded. Jean nodded her head, picked up her computer and went back to her room.

Vince stood. "I hope you know what you are doing."

"I don't, but it's the best chance we have. It doesn't sound like we can just walk in there and take him. Plus, it gets her out of my hair for a few days."

"But, she hasn't proved herself trustworthy yet," Vince said, starting to pace. "What if she tells him where we are moving?"

"Jean won't rat out Katie. Haven't you seen the guilt in her eyes when she looks at her?" Theron smiled and looked at the floor.

"What? I know she feels bad about what happened, but..." I trailed off and thought about how Jean acted since Vince and I arrived. She was feeling guilty and, based on our conversation this morning, she wanted to get Alex just as much as we did. "Can we move back to this party? I still don't understand why we have to have one to stop the war. Why are vampires so difficult?"

"Because we, or the ones whose help we need, are old and bored," Helen said, picking up her wine. She looked tired, Vince told me she wasn't back to her full strength after what happened at the compound, but this was the first time I had seen it. "They are old world and expect to be wined and dined before there's talk of war."

"Helen's right," Vince said, draining his glass and setting it on the nearby table. "We need to not only tell them what Lolita is planning but prove to them who you are."

"What are we going to do if they don't believe or care?" I had some pretty kick-ass powers, but would they be enough to convince a roomful of vampires I was destined to rule them?

"I don't think it will be an issue," Theron said as he tapped his free hand on his thigh. "But if it is, we will find another way. You need to practice though, if you aren't confident with your gifts no one will believe you."

"You're right, and I am out of practice, I'll start tomorrow but right now I'm going to bed, it's been a long day." I finished my wine and snapped my fingers at Vinny to get his attention.

"I will be there in a little while," Vince took my hand and squeezed it. "I need to speak to Theron and Helen." He brought my hand to his mouth and kissed it.

"Goodnight, everyone."

Once Vinny and I were back in our room, I took my clothes off and laid in bed stared at the ceiling. I should have been freaking out, knowing my name and my picture were all over the dark web, but I expected it to be. Lolita was offering a lot of money for someone to kill me, and Alex wasn't the only mercenary out there. I felt stupid for thinking he would be the only one to come after me.

I don't know why I thought that once I was reunited with my friends the threats would go away. Maybe I thought I was safer with them around. I needed to be careful, and unfortunately that meant I still wouldn't be able to go out on my own. At least I had Vince and Vinny to keep me company.

"You know Vince will be mad that you're on his side," I said when the dog jumped onto the bed. He rolled so his back pushed up against my side. "I missed you too, sweetie, but you are going to have to sleep on the floor." He didn't move, and I didn't care as I closed my eyes and drifted to sleep.

"Vinny, get out of bed," I heard a little while later, followed by a growl. I cracked my eyelids open and saw Vince standing next to the bed with his hands on his hips, frowning at the dog.

"Vinny, get on the floor," I said, snapping my fingers and pointing to the ground. He whined, then jumped off the bed and lay down on the floor next to me.

"Sorry, I knew he wouldn't want to move when you came to bed." I rolled on my side and closed my eyes. I felt the bed dip then strong arms pulled me into Vince's chest and I let out a contented sigh.

"He loves you and does not know me yet. He will come around." Vince kissed my shoulder and rested his arm over my side. "I love you, Katie, sleep well. Tomorrow will be another trying day."

"Love you too, Vince."

## Chapter 15
### *Jean*

Jean got out of the taxi a few blocks away from Σαράντα δύο, she smoothed down the front of her jacket before pulling up the handle on her rolling suitcase and walking toward Sanctuary. Butterflies were swarming her stomach. She'd been a member for years, but she had yet to visit one. Add to that, going in undercover for the head of The Syndicate and whoever Katie really was.

She didn't know what was going on with Katie, Vince, Theron, and Helen, but whatever it was, they were keeping it close to their chests. Jean would find out, then maybe she would understand why so many people wanted Katie dead, in the meantime she had a job to do. Find Alex, befriend him, and figure out a way for her to arrest him. She never promised she wouldn't go after him herself, she promised Katie she wouldn't pass on anything she knew about Theron. Alex was different, he was more than a thorn in her side; he was the fricking stigmata. She blinked back tears when she thought of her mentor and Alex torturing Ed to death.

Ed and Jean were on assignment, the last one before Interpol sent her into the field. Their mission was to hack into a computer system of a crime organization in Prague and set up a monitoring system. The hack had gone without a glitch. Ed went out to get a bottle of champagne, to celebrate when Alex found him in the hotel lobby. The organization learned what they had done and hired Alex to make an example of Ed. The bastard set Ed's phone up to record what Alex did to him.

While Ed was having his fingernails slowly removed, Jean was taking a bubble bath thinking about her future. She didn't worry about Ed until an hour later, and by then it was too late. When her handler showed her the video, she cried, vomited, and begged her handler to stop it, she couldn't take anymore, but her handler ignored her pleas and forced her to watch all of it. When it was over Jean felt dead inside. She still woke up in the middle of the night sometimes in a cold sweat after dreaming of what Alex did to Ed. She made it her life's mission to track Alex down and make him pay for what he did to the one person at Interpol Jean looked up to.

She pushed the memories of Ed to the back of her mind as she approached the door. She took a deep breath then knocked and waited until the slide pulled back. "What do you want?" a man asked in Greek.

"I seek sanctuary." She pulled her shoulders back and rallied her courage, this would be the biggest undercover assignment she had so far, and she wasn't going to mess it up. The slide shut then she heard the unmistakable sound of a bolt sliding back before the door opened. She stepped inside as soon as it was open and looked behind her.

"Were you followed?" the burly man with a scraggly beard asked.

"No, this is the first time I've required the services of Sanctuary." Jean let go of the handle on her suitcase and crossed her arms over her chest.

"First time, huh?" The man went behind the desk and pulled a fingerprint machine out and extended it to Jean. "Place your thumb here, I need to verify you're a member before you go any further." Jean placed her thumb on the screen until it beeped, took a step back, then held her face still while he completed a retinal scan. The man stared at the computer screen until it beeped. "Good, since this is your first time, let me go over the rules while I show you around." He came around the desk and walked down the hall, gesturing for her to follow him.

"There are no weapons allowed and don't bring whatever brought you here with you," he said as they reached the end of the corridor and went through double doors at the end of it. "This is the bar, you can order a drink or food here. This is the only social area we have, most of the guests spend at least a little time here."

Jean looked around the dimly lit room and frowned, she expected more for the money she spent to be a part of this, but it was better than nothing.

"Rooms are first come, first serve." The man turned, leading her out of the bar area and through a door leading to a stairwell. He started up the stairs, and she followed. *They have quite the setup*, she thought, making a mental note of the cameras they passed. She was glad she kept paying her dues, she never knew when she would need a place to hide.

"What about The Syndicate? Do they know you're here? What if I am running from them?" Jean asked, just to get the lay of the land. If she ever made Theron mad, she needed to know if she could still come to this place.

"The Syndicate? You have nothing to worry about there, Evangelos knows we are here and follows our rules, but the moment you step foot outside the door, you'll be on your own." They reached the landing on the second floor and he opened the door for her. She expected him to ask why she asked about The Syndicate, but when he didn't she blew out a breath. These guys knew how to mind their own business. "There are six rooms on this floor, I think a few might still be open. There's a bathroom with a shower at either end of the hall." He continued down the hall as they passed closed doors every fifteen feet. "If a room is vacant, the door will be open and there will be a sign that says so." He stopped outside an open door and gestured for Jean to go inside.

Jean took a few steps into the room and looked around. It was basic, there was a small desk in one corner, a single bed with a thin mattress, and

107

a dresser. The one window was too small for her to climb out of if she needed to make a run for it, but it was clean. "Do you have Wi-Fi?"

"Yes, but you have to pay for it. After you get settled come back down to the desk and we'll get you set up." He turned to leave.

"Thank you. I'll be down shortly." Jean put her suitcase on the bed and unzipped it. She heard the door quietly shut as she opened it and pulled out her computer. She looked at the door noticing the sign was now hanging on the inside. She went to the door and flipped the lock before she moved her suitcase to the dresser but didn't unpack. She didn't know how long she would be there, and she wanted to be able to make a quick escape if she needed to.

As settled in as she planned to get, she took the key off the hook hanging inside the door and went back downstairs to the front desk. After she had her password, she went into the bar and took a seat at a table against the far wall. Sitting with her back against the wall she opened her computer and logged into the Wi-Fi.

"Can I get you anything?" a tall blond woman asked, stopping at Jean's table with a pad of paper in her hand.

Jean looked at her watch, it had been a long time since breakfast. "Do you have chicken fingers?"

"Yes, would you like fries with that?"

"Please, and a Coke." Jean gave the waitress a smile then waited for her to leave before going back to her computer and putting her security protocols into effect. Once she had everything set up, she watched the few people in the bar, none of them were Alex, but who knew what horrible things they had done. It was too bad she wasn't allowed to carry her gun, she could've made Interpol proud.

She went through her email as she ate, keeping one eye on the door. She'd just finished the last of her food when a group of men came in laughing and pushing each other around in a male bonding exercise. They went to the bar and ordered drinks while Jean kept her head down and her eyes on the computer. She didn't know them, but she had a bad feeling, being the only woman in the room besides the waitress. One man turned around and leaned his back against the bar. Jean didn't make eye contact with him hoping her evasiveness would make her invisible to him.

It was time to go, she could come back later to look for Alex. She closed her laptop and put it in her bag, she was about to stand when someone set a beer on her table.

"Well, hello. What do we have here?" The man pulled the chair out on the other side of Jean and sat down. He was tall with blond hair and blue eyes, probably in his late twenties. By the cut of his biceps protruding through his T-shirt, Jean thought he must have been in the military at some point and his accent sounded German.

"I was just leaving." Jean tried to stand but was stopped when the man pushed the table toward her, trapping her between it and the wall.

"Why would you want to do that? My friends and I just got back from a mission and we almost didn't make it. We would love some company right now." He wiggled his eyebrows at her.

Panic was trying its best to take hold of her, but she refused to let it win. "Congratulations on your survival, but I'm not in the mood to celebrate. If you'll excuse me." Jean pushed the table back at the man and shot to her feet with her computer bag in her hand. Without stopping to pay her bill, she started for the door.

"Wait, cutie-pie, where do you think you are going?" Another man from the group blocked the door and Jean stopped in the middle of the room.

She looked around for a weapon but the only thing she could throw were the candle votives. "Look, you seem like nice guys, but I really have to go."

"If we seem like nice guys, then stay and have a drink with us," the one who trapped her said.

"Normally, I would," she said, surprising herself with how steady her voice sounded. "But I have a job tonight and I need a clear head."

"A job, really? You don't look like a mercenary, you look like a whore," the one by the door said, coming closer and licking his lips.

Jean looked down at her loose-fitting jeans and black crewneck T-shirt. Who knew whores dressed so casually when they were out on the prowl? "I am not a whore." Jean looked around the bar, wasn't there anyone who would help her? The bartender was nowhere to be seen, and the waitress was sitting on the lap of one of the other men. Jean was on her own, but she wouldn't give in to these scumbags. She put her computer bag on a nearby table and thought of how Katie would wipe the floor with them. Jean could fight, she had been through all Interpol's hand-to-hand combat training, now she hoped she remembered it.

"Look, brother, we have a fighter," the one blocking the door said, taking a step closer.

"I love a good fight," the one behind her said, only he sounded much closer than he had been before. Jean spun ready to kick him in the balls, but she was too slow, he grabbed her arms and forced them behind her back. The other man stalked forward. "You go first, brother, we will have her eating out of our hands in no time."

Jean's heart was thundering in her chest and she couldn't seem to take a deep breath. She knew how to get out of the hold the man had her in, but her body didn't want to do what she told it. The man in front of her ran a rough hand down her cheek. She shuddered as her body finally decided to obey her commands.

She picked her foot up then slammed it down on the foot of the man who was holding her, forcing him to loosen his grip. As soon as her foot touched the ground, she brought it forward in a kick that landed in the groin of the man in front of her. He doubled over, as she broke free of the man behind her, grabbed her computer and ran for the door. She was almost through when one of them grabbed her by her ponytail and dragged her back.

"You stupid bitch, you're going to pay for that," the one whose foot she stomped on said.

Jean lost her hold on her computer and it spun across the floor. She reached up and grabbed the man's arm where he was grabbing her hair and dug her nails into his skin. He yelled but didn't let go.

"What is going on in here?" a man asked, and Jean looked up as Alex strolled into the room.

"Help me, please," she pleaded, and let the tears she had been fighting streak down her face.

"This bitch kicked my friend in the balls," the man holding Jean by the hair said, while jerking her onto her tip toes.

"They were trying to rape me." Jean looked down at the floor and wondered if she should keep fighting the thugs or if playing the damsel in distress would be a better way to garner help from Alex.

"Do you guys want to get kicked out?" Alex put his hands on his hips and took in the four men scattered around him. "Do you think you'll make it off the island without being caught when they kick you out for harming another guest?"

The man holding Jean by the hair let go and took a step back putting his hands in the air. "Look we don't want any problems. We're just looking for a good time."

"She obviously wasn't, I suggest you get out of here before the bouncer comes in and kicks you out." Alex moved to the side of the door, allowing them to leave without having to walk near him.

Jean ran to her computer case and picked it up. She wanted to run and hide in her room, but she didn't want these men to know what room she was staying in.

"Screw this, come on guys, let's go," the one she kicked in the balls said, before storming out with the rest of the men following.

Jean found the nearest chair and slumped into it gingerly touching her head to gage how much hair he ripped out. She didn't have a bald spot, but her head hurt. She put her elbows on the table and buried her face in her hands. Part of her meltdown was a show for Alex, from what Katie told her about him, he was a chauvinist and thought women were the weaker sex, the other part was scared, if Alex hadn't come in she didn't know what those men would have done to her.

She heard a chair across from her scrape across the floor, then someone sat next to her. "Hey, you OK?" Alex asked, in a quiet voice.

"What?" She looked up from her hands, sure her mascara was making her look like a clown. "Yeah, I'll be all right. Thanks for saving me from them. I thought this was supposed to be a safe place."

"Normally, it is, I don't know what those guys thought they were doing, but you better watch your back. They may not allow weapons, but they still have fists." He looked like he wanted to reach across the table and comfort her, but he stayed where he was.

"Thanks for the warning. All I was doing was working on my computer. They thought I was a whore or something." Jean shook her head, she wasn't sure how much of the *damsel* she should play, she wanted Alex's attention, but she didn't want to lay it on too thick.

"Assholes," Alex leaned back, crossed his arms over his chest, and looked around the room. "Yesterday, this place was packed I wonder where everyone went."

"The mark everyone was going after was filled," the waitress said, setting a beer down in front of Alex and grimaced at Jean before handing a napkin to her. "You might want to clean your face up, sweetie."

"Thanks," Jean said, taking it from her and blotting it under her eyes. She wanted to punch the waitress for not helping her, but it was four on one, and the woman didn't look like she could make a proper fist, let alone take on those ruffians.

"Wait, what do you mean the mark was filled?" Alex asked, as his face turned red. "You mean that joke of a sniper hit her?"

Jean carefully controlled her face. The work she did the night before paid off, they thought Katie was dead. Now, maybe, the poor girl could rest for a while.

"That's what I heard, whatever website everyone was looking at said it was no longer available. Can I get you something, sweetheart?" she asked Jean.

"No, I think I'll go up to my room for a while." Jean stood up and looked down to Alex. "I owe you one for helping me."

"Yeah, see you around," Alex said, pulling his phone up and pretending Jean wasn't there.

Jean forced herself to walk out of the bar even though she wanted to run. Her plan was working, it wasn't going exactly as she planned, but at least she piqued Alex's interest. She went back to her room and sent Theron an email to update him on what she learned.

After an hour of staring at the wall of her room and afraid of going back to the bar Jean couldn't take it anymore. Theron was going to call her later to arrange to bring her the equipment she wanted, but no one said she couldn't go out before he called. She went to her suitcase and pulled out the short, flirty dress she packed. She needed to dance, but not at the Sanctuary.

## Chapter 16
### *Lolita*

"That was a wonderful meal, Lolo, where did you find her?" Miguel asked, wiping his mouth with a handkerchief even though he hadn't spilled a drop of blood.

"Orphanages are one of the best places to find rare vintages," Lolita said as two vampires entered the room, picked up the lifeless body, and left. "Tell me how your protégé is coming along."

"Slowly, he has an addictive mind, and he doesn't seem to want to let go of the bloodlust." Miguel leaned back in the sofa and stared at the ceiling.

"What are you doing about it?" Lolita asked, pulling a nail file from her pocket and shaping her already perfect nails.

"I'm rationing him and talking with him about what he will be able to do once he overcomes his lust."

"Is it working?" Lolita kept herself from rolling her eyes, *Miguel didn't know what he was doing,* she thought to herself.

"No, do you have any ideas?"

"Give him all the blood he wants for a day, if he isn't over it after that then starve him. If he doesn't learn control, he will be of no use to us. You really must choose your children better." Lolita was tiring of the games she was playing, she was ready to act. Spending all her time on the island or in the club was becoming monotonous.

"I didn't," Miguel started but then stopped. "I will go now and see how your idea works." He stood abruptly and stomped out of the room.

Once the door was closed Lolita let out a belly laugh, she had Miguel right where she wanted him. He was her partner, but she was in charge. She didn't care if Mark was a poor choice to become a vampire, she only did it to hurt Katie. If he learned to control his bloodlust, he would be an asset, if he didn't, he would be a sacrificial lamb to make Katie even angrier.

Lolita looked at her phone on the coffee table as it vibrated. She picked it up and looked at the incoming call. It was Alex, he almost never called any more. Something important must be happening.

"Alex, what can I do for you?" Lolita asked.

"Did someone else collect the bounty on Katie?" His voice cracked like he could barely control his anger.

"No, what are you talking about?" Lolita leaned back in her seat giddy with excitement. If someone else had killed the girl, Lolita would still get Alex.

"The page with her contract shows it was filled."

"What?" Lolita yelled, before standing and running to her computer. She pulled up the website and waited for the photo of Katie to pop up, but now, instead of a picture of the girl, it was nothing but a pixilated screen with the word 'filled' across it. She screamed and logged in as admin, determined to fix the picture. She clicked on the photo to remove it, only, instead of removing it, a file downloaded onto her computer. Forgetting Alex was on the phone she tried to stop the download, but it was too late. Whoever had hacked her page set a trap for her and she fell for it. She blew out a breath and threw the computer across the room.

"So, Katie is still out there?" Alex's voice became tentative.

"Are you calling to confirm this or are you actually going to do what I hired you for?" Lolita couldn't believe it, someone hacked her.

"Both, no point in going after her if she's already dead. I'm close, I just need time."

"Haven't you already had enough time?" Lolita rolled her eyes. Why did she hire a human in the first place? "I'm getting impatient."

"I'm on it."

"You better…" Lolita started then stopped when her phone showed the call had ended. The little shit thought he could hang up on her? Well he had another thing coming. She hit a button on the phone then brought it to her ear. "Thomas, could you come up here, please? I have a job for you."

Chapter 17

*Katie*

I was standing in our 'suite' in the mansion we moved to. It was probably the easiest move ever since all we took with us were our suitcases. The new house was enormous, the outside was a cross between a traditional Greek stucco and rock. It sprawled on an olive orchard in the middle of the island. This house made Theron's mansion at the compound look like a McMansion.

Theron, again, gave us the master suite, saying something about not wanting to hear us go at it like rabbits. The master suite had a bedroom with a king-size bed, down comforter, and more pillows than anyone would need. There were French doors leading out to a lawn along one wall, and a fireplace that could be enjoyed from the bedroom or the adjoining sitting room. The furniture was modern and sleek almost at odds with the rustic design of the house. There was a huge bathroom with a walk-in shower and bathtub made for two with jets. There were two walk-in closets both now full thanks to Helen.

I had always been a jeans and T-shirt girl, but the dresses, slacks, and blouses she bought for me made me look smarter, more professional and I had to say sexy. She said I needed to look the part of a half god, and I think she was right. I was wearing a pair of black slim-fitting pants and a long-sleeve red silk shirt tucked in at the waist. The matching red heels I wore to move were laying on the floor by the door.

"This is too much, I'm feeling spoiled." I turned to Vince after putting my things in the bathroom. He was lounging on the bed with his stuff already put away.

"You deserve to be spoiled after everything you have been through."

"No, I don't, I've caused you guys more drama than you've had in hundreds of years I'm guessing."

"You have definitely livened things up, but it will be worth it. You will be a queen and I hope to be your consort."

I turned to look at him. "Why would you hope? You already are my consort. I don't see that changing."

He smiled. "Good. I am planning to call one of my old friends today. I think she will help us."

"Who?" I went to the foot of the bed and sat down on the corner.

"Maria, she lives in Madrid and I sent an invitation to my maker too, since he doesn't have a phone, at least he didn't the last time I saw him. Come, lay with me." Vince patted the empty spot next to him.

I went over to the bed and lay down with my head resting on his chest. After everything we had been through, I was still amazed that we were lying in bed together. "What's he like?" I asked, remembering that Livius had owned Vince as a gladiator before he changed him into a vampire.

"As I said before, he has not adapted to the age of technology well, and he still has his ideas of slavery and a woman's place in the world. He will be an ally though, he still believes in the old gods, the Roman Parthenon, not the Greek, but he will not have a hard time believing who you are."

I had a bad feeling about this vampire. "Does he think he still owns you?"

"The short answer is I do not know. Last time I saw him he treated me as a favored son, but it has been a few decades and I have

120

not spoken to him in sometime." Vince paused before he continued. "He can be very moody."

"OK, so why aren't you just sending Maria an invitation? Why are you calling her?"

"Because Maria is a friend. She deserves more than a card in the mail." Vince was holding something back. I could have broken into his mind and found out what it was, but I wouldn't stoop that low.

"What aren't you telling me?" I asked, sitting up and turning to face him.

His eyes flicked from me to the ceiling as he let out a sigh. "I was not trying to keep it from you, but I was trying to find the right way to tell you," he hesitated as if he was trying to find the right words. "Maria and I were lovers for a few decades."

I rolled my eyes at him wondering why he thought it would bother me. "Vince, neither of us were virgins when we met, why would you think it would bother me that you had a lover?" He probably had ten times the number of lovers I had taken to bed.

"Because when I stayed with her on my way to meet you in Athens she came on to me."

I wanted to be mad, but it felt like it was a lifetime ago and we were nothing close to lovers then. He was saving me, nothing more. If he slept with her, there was nothing for me to be mad at. "That was before my training at Theron's, right? It's OK if you slept with her."

"I did not sleep with her, I turned her down." I felt bad, but those words made me relax a fraction. "I am telling you this because I will almost guarantee she will try again. I will not take her up on it, but I would not put it past her to try to start something with you."

"I'll put her in her place if she tries." I gave him a squeeze. "Who else is coming?"

"I'm not sure, Theron is inviting every leader in Europe. I doubt they will all make it, but many will. We have not had a gathering of this magnitude in a long time."

"How many will help us?"

"I don't know but enough take care of Lolita and her army. They are the strongest vampires we know and Lolita is not a well-liked vampire."

"I hope so, then we can go after Alex, and my enemies will be gone."

"What do you want to do then?" Vince moved quickly, grabbing me around the waist and pulling me on top of him.

"I've been running and training for so long, I haven't thought about what I want to do when we win." I rested my head on his chest.

"You should think about it because we will win. There is no other option."

"I would like to see my parents again. They're probably worried sick." I hadn't thought of them in so long. The guilt brought tears to my eyes.

"Go to America then? I have never been there." Vince squeezed me tighter.

"You would come with me?" I asked, I didn't know why I was surprised.

"Of course. I want to meet the people who raised such an incredible woman." He kissed the top of my head. "Your mother, the Goddess, I mean, might have other plans for you though."

"She can wait. I've given up everything for her. She can let me visit my parents if she wants my help."

"Good, now we have something to look forward to. I need to find Theron, see what he needs help with."

"I'll go with you, maybe there's something I can help him with," I said, pulling away from Vince and sliding off the bed.

"I do not know, but I am sure he would appreciate the offer." Vince got off the bed and took my hand.

"What are in these rooms?" I asked, as we walked down the

hall.

"More bedrooms I think. Theron said there are twenty, five in this wing and fifteen in the other."

"It feels lonely being the only ones in this wing." The old wood floor creaked under our feet as we walked.

"Would you rather hear what everyone is doing and have them listen to us?" He squeezed my hand and I blushed.

"I'll take the privacy," I mumbled as the hall ended and we found ourselves in the sunken living room. The floors changed to a gleaming marble and the high ceilings and huge paintings on the walls made me think we were in the lobby of a luxury hotel, not someone's home.

I looked around the room, everyone was sitting looking at their phones. "What is going on?" Vince asked, as Theron glanced up.

"Jean did it. She not only took down all traces of the contract on Katie, but she made it look like it was filled." Theron passed his phone to Vince, and I looked over his shoulder to see the word 'filled' across my pixilated picture.

"Thank the Goddess, I will have to buy her a shot of ouzo for that. Has there been any news of Alex?" I sat down on an empty couch and crossed my legs.

"He's at Sanctuary according to Jean. He actually saved her from an attack," Theron rolled his eyes. "Does that girl know how to stay out of trouble?"

"No, I don't think she does. What about Alex? What are we going to do?"

"You can't enter Sanctuary," Helen said to Theron before he could speak. She uncrossed her legs then crossed them the opposite way. "You need to draw him out, go out on the town and be seen. People need to see you to believe you're alive. If you go into Sanctuary; you are asking for every merc in Europe to descend on us. We already have enough enemies."

Theron's eyebrows climbed his forehead. "You're right, I've been so busy getting settled I neglected my island. Should we go out on the town then?" He looked at his watch.

Going out in public sounded like just what I needed, but I wasn't dressed to go out. "Sounds like fun. I just need a minute to change." I got to my feet ready to make the long walk back to our suite.

"Katie, I am sorry, but you are still grounded. We need to let the news of your canceled contract circulate for a while before you are seen in public." Vince took my hand as I slumped. "I'll stay here with you," Vince said. "I need to call Maria, anyway."

"No, go, you can call her on the way," I said, shrugging off his arms. "Besides, you need to eat something besides bagged blood. I'll be fine with Vinny, Argyris, and Natalia. No one knows we're here, right?"

Theron looked down at his phone as it vibrated then hit a button to answer it. "Serafeim, what can I do for you?"

Vince tensed next to me and I looked from him to Theron. Of course, he could hear everything Serafeim was saying while I had no clue.

"We are heading to the club shortly; can you meet us there? Then we can talk about it in more detail." Theron looked at Helen then Vince before he walked away. "Good, see you then."

"I know you all know what is going on, but could you let me in on it?" I asked, following behind Vince.

"Katie, I'm sorry, I forgot you don't have the hearing we do. Serafeim is the only arms dealer on the island and is part of The Syndicate. It sounds like a new player is trying to weasel his way into the arms trade and Serafeim is concerned..."

"After everything we have been through this year, the last thing we need is for someone to think we are ripe for the taking. If this man overthrows Serafeim, it may open us up to others who want to find a foothold on the island."

"Wow, yeah, good thing you guys already planned on going

out." The last thing we needed was another hostile takeover attempt while we were trying to stop Lolita's war.

"Be safe," Vince said, pulling me into his arms.

"You too, I'll see you when you get back." He touched his lips to mine then followed Helen out the door.


After everyone left, I wasn't sure what to do with myself. Theron had Argyris and Natalia working on the day-to-day operations of the business and I barely saw them. The last thing I wanted to do was bug them while they were trying to work. I went back to my suite and started a fire. It wasn't cold in the house, but the humidity gave the air a chill. After the fire was roaring, I pulled out my computer, deciding I needed to see what Lolita was up to. I hadn't tracked her in over a week. While I waited for my program to load, I pulled up the email account I created while I was in Kevó. There were a ton of emails and none of them were junk. I had taken off, promising to keep in touch, and ignored my computer since I found my way back to Crete. I started at the bottom and opened an email from Hound.

**KK, are you OK? We saw on the news that someone was kidnapped on the ferry. Please let us know if you are alive.**

*Crap*, I thought to myself, *way to leave your friends hanging*. I clicked on the reply button.

**Hound, I'm so sorry I haven't opened my computer since I left Kevó, things have been a little crazy. I'm fine, survived the kidnapping and found out the love of my life is still alive. We're staying in Crete for a while. I hope everything is going well with you. Please spread the word. I have a ton of emails and I will try to reply to them all but let everyone know**

125

**I'm fine.**

I hit the send button and moved on to the next one from Copperhead. She wanted to know the same as Hound. I quickly sent her a similar reply. I skipped the next few emails knowing they were from people wondering if I had survived. I clicked one from Tad, sent the day before.

**Katie, I hope this letter finds you well. I was wondering if you had seen Uni. We have not heard from her since she took you to Athens and I fear the worst. If you know how to get ahold of her, please have her contact me. I would like to know if she is coming back to us.**

I hesitated over the reply button. I wanted to set Tad's mind at ease, but knowing Jean was the one who jeopardized the safety of the town I didn't know what to tell him.

**Tad, I'm sorry I haven't checked in. I'm well and found my friends alive. As for Uni, she's with me. I don't think she will be back to Kevó for quite some time. She is staying to help us, and it may take some time. In other news, I don't think you need to worry about a mole any more.**
**Tell everyone I said hi,**
**KK**

I sent the email then clicked on one from Vangel.

**Hi, I hope you are all right. Everyone is worried about you and wants to know if you are alive. If you**

126

**need help, I can come.**

I clicked the reply button. Vangel had become important to me somewhere along the way and he didn't deserve to hear from anyone else that I was alive.

**Vangel, hi. I'm fine. Sorry I forgot to tell you all that I made it to Crete. I'm a little the worse for wear, but I'll survive. I'm staying with Theron and we're recruiting people to help us neutralize our enemies. Before the year is over, I will be enemy free. Alex survived the lifeboat ordeal and followed me to Crete. We have a plan in the works to capture him, then go after Lolita. I hope everything is well with you.**

After going through the rest of my email, I went to the program I used to track Lolita and pulled up the oldest. After it loaded, I fast-forwarded to the time she typically arrived at the club. Her boat pulled up, the bouncers got out first, then offered her a hand. She stepped out of the boat and I almost clicked off the screen before I saw Miguel step out the boat behind her. I paused the feed and zoomed in. Two people I hated most in the world were together again. Chills ran down my spine as I looked at Miguel's perfect smiling face. Vince said Miguel was the reason they survived the attack on the compound, but it didn't change the hate I had for him. The bastard raped me. I would never get over what he did to me.

According to Vince, Miguel was on our side but how could I believe that when he looked so happy with Lolita on his arm. I shook my head and pushed the play button. They went into the club, as they always did, and I fast-forwarded to closing time. Lolita normally left around three, but when I looked at the time stamp it was closer to four. I wondered what had kept her. She got into the boat, then Miguel and one of her bodyguards came out holding a man in between them.

I paused the video when they stepped into the light and zoomed in. My mouth went slack as I recognized the face of the unconscious man between them. Mark? My creepy ex-boyfriend was still in Europe? He should have gone home months ago. More importantly, what was he doing with Miguel and Lolita? I pulled my phone out ready to call Vince when my computer beeped at me. I had a Skype call coming through.

I clicked on the answer button and Vangel's face filled the screen, now that I knew Vince was alive, I didn't see the resemblance as much as I did when I first met Vangel. They looked similar, and from a distance I couldn't tell them apart, but up close nothing could keep my eyes from Vince. "Hi, you're alive." His smile went from ear to ear. I should've emailed them sooner.

"Sorry, I didn't mean to make everyone worry. I've been super busy since I got here." I cringed, how could I have been so selfish? I was so used to being on my own with no one caring if I lived or died I let them slip my mind.

"It's all good. We are all just happy you survived. What are you doing now?"

"Still coming up with a plan to take down Lolita and Alex. It's more complicated than I thought."

"Do you need help?" he asked, bringing his eyebrows together in concern.

We needed more help than he could imagine. "It's really dangerous. I don't want you to get hurt."

"KK, I've been sitting on my ass since you left. What can I do to help? Tad will let me go."

*What good could he do against vampires?* I wondered, not a lot, but with humans like Alex still looking for me he could help during the day when the vampires couldn't. "I need a bodyguard. Someone to watch my back during the day. We took down the post with my contract, but there are people who don't know it's been taken down yet."

"OK, I can protect your body. Let me check with Tad, and I'll let you know."

"Thanks, Vangel, please don't feel like you have to do this. Trouble seems to find me no matter where I go."

"It's fine, I need to stay sharp. I have to go, but I'll be in touch with you soon." He ended the call, and I leaned back in my chair. Why was I allowing another human to get involved with my mess? I thought about Mark and wondered if he was dead, alive or were they changing him? I saved the video and stood. Too much was happening for me to think straight. I went to my closet and changed into my workout clothes. The house didn't have a dojo, but it had a ballroom with hardwood floors and a high ceiling.

Vinny and I padded down the stairs to the first level of the house and made our way to the enormous room. I flipped on the lights and kicked off my shoes. The wood floor was cold since the room was rarely used, and I wiggled my toes to get used to it. I walked to the middle of the room while Vinny laid down to watch. I bowed, pulled my katana off my back and worked through my forms. With every cut and block I made against my invisible opponents my mind cleared. I thought of nothing but fighting Lolita. Of winning the fight. There was nothing before or after just the moment when our swords met and who would have the upper hand. As I moved, I deviated from the set movements of the form. Coming up with my own combinations. In my mind they would lead to the death of my enemies. In a final move I swept my katana across the invisible neck of Lolita and imagined her head falling from her body. I stood and bowed to the imaginary woman before applause startled me.

I spun around with my sword ready to take on whoever was behind me. Vince stood there with Vinny at his side. I lowered my sword and mentally gave myself a slap. I needed to use my vampire senses more. If I'd been paying more attention, I would've noticed Vince watching and never thought of raising my sword toward him. I lowered it and looked at the floor ashamed.

"What's wrong, you did brilliantly." He put a finger under my chin and pulled it up, forcing me to look at him.

"I'm out of practice with my vampire sensor. I should have known you were behind me. I never would've raised my sword to you if I had been using it."

"Hey, you have not been spending time with vampires, right? Even Tad, you only saw a few times. It is hard to stay in tune when you have nothing to practice with." He took a step back and looked into my eyes. "You will be back where you were on the compound before you know it."

I sheathed my katana and leaned my forehead against his chest. "I know, it just makes me mad. How was town?"

"I realized tonight that the club scene is not as fun without you at my side." He put his hands on my shoulders and kissed the top of my head. He pushed me back and looked down at me. "Are you done?"

"Yeah."

"Good, let's go to bed." He put his arm around me and walked us toward the door. "What else did you do tonight?"

"I talked to one of my friends in Kevò. He's a mercenary, and he offered to help." I didn't know how Vince would handle me bringing in another human to help.

"We have had bad luck with mercenaries," Vince said in a wistful voice. "Are you sure you can trust him?"

"Yes, he had a chance to cash in on the bounty but instead he helped me take down Mordor." I hit the light switches for the ballroom as we exited and walked toward the stairs. "He kind of looks like you, maybe you are from the same place."

"What do you mean he looks like me?" Vince stopped before we started up the stairs and turned me to look at him.

"I mean," I closed my eyes trying to find a tactful way to tell him. "The first time I saw him I thought he was you."

Vince closed his eyes for a second saying nothing. When he opened them, I could see the turmoil he was in. "Did you date him? You thought I was dead, I would understand if you did."

"No, we hung out, he taught me how to use guns, he was a friend, nothing more. I was thinking he could be my bodyguard. Then I wouldn't be stuck in the house all the time." I took Vince's hand and squeezed it. "You ruined me for other men."

His eyebrows shot up almost to his hair line. "Really? When you thought I was dead you were never going to be with another man?"

"No, you were the only one I ever wanted and when you were gone, I felt nothing for anyone else. Vince, you are it for me." Tears pricked my eyes when I thought of how it felt to be without him. "I love you and no other."

He smiled, looking truly happy for the first time in a long time. "I love you too. There will never be another woman for me Katie." He swept me over his shoulder in a fireman's carry and sprinted up the stairs.

"Vince, put me down, I need to tell you about what I found while I was stalking Lolita tonight," I said, playfully pounding on his back.

"What did you find?" he asked, moving faster up the stairs.

"Put me down and I'll tell you," I said, as blood rushed to my head. When he reached the second floor, he put me down and put his hands on his hips.

"Tell me."

"I only want to tell it once, where are the others?" I asked, closing my eyes and looking for Theron and Helen with my mind.

"They are not back yet. Tell me, and I will tell them later."

"I watched Lolita and Miguel go into her club. When they came out, Miguel had Mark slumped in his arms."

"Mark? Your ex-boyfriend?" Vince froze. He was looking at me but not seeing me, like he was a million miles away and he was mad, so mad I could feel the anger bubbling inside him.

"Yes, I don't know what he's still doing in Europe. He should have flown home in August." I looked down at my feet. What ever happened to Mark was my fault. The vampires thought Miguel was on their side, but if he was turning people, people who had been close to me, then whose side was he really on?

"I will talk to Theron when he gets back, and we will see what he thinks, then I will call Miguel and see what he has to say. I am sorry." Vince put his hands on my shoulders, forcing me to look up at him.

"It's not your fault, I just don't understand what they were doing with him. He is a useless piece of shit, but he was an important part of my life for a long time." I held back the threatening tears. I needed to stop being so emotional about people who didn't care about me, but the damn vampires were doing everything they could to make my life hell.

"We will figure this out. Come." He took my hand and led me to our rooms.

When we got there, he told me to strip, and he went into the bathroom to start a bath. I numbly pulled my clothes off, put them in the hamper then went into the bathroom where Vince was pulling his clothes off as the room filled with steam from the water running in the tub. I stepped into it and hissed as the hot water almost scalded my feet. I eased in and Vince came in behind me.

"We all make our choices in the world Katie, Mark did not leave when he was supposed to. There was nothing you could have done to change it. Whatever happens to him, he will have to learn to deal with his life, and you cannot blame yourself for it." Vince picked up a luffa, squirted some soap on it and washed my back.

There was nothing I could say or do to change the situation, and Vince was right. If Mark had left when he was supposed to, he would have never been caught by Miguel and Lolita. There was no way for me to change what happened. I needed to move on, but no matter what, we needed to find out which team Miguel was playing for. He saved my friends from the attack, but after what he did to me, I would never trust him.

"I need to toughen up. I can't keep everyone safe," I said, more to myself than to Vince.

"Good. Now, let me help you relax."

Chapter 18

*Theron*

As soon as they arrived at the club, Theron spoke with Agapios about setting up catering and entertainment for the party. Theron was pleased with the change in Agapios, he no longer sat in the corner daydreaming of simpler times. He was now surrounded by people and was taking his job seriously.

Theron relaxed once the details for the party were finalized. All the vampires would bring their entourages and The Syndicate would bring their wives. He would need to not only have human food, since there would be humans there, but donors as well, and Agapios could handle it all.

Agapios had just rejoined his party and Theron was taking time to enjoy a moment alone when Serafeim took the seat Agapios vacated. "Theron, is now a good time?" he asked, looking around the room like he was being followed.

"As good as any, what is going on?" Theron asked, leaning forward.

"Last week I called one of my buyers to arrange a transaction." The normally cool and collected man wiped at the sweat beading on his brow. "He said he found someone else who could deliver the goods at half my price and believe me, I gave the man a good price."

"Did he give you the man's name? Where did he pick up the weapons?" Theron asked, resting his elbows on the table and pushing his palms together.

"He didn't get his name, but he picked up the weapons at the port authority a few warehouses down from mine." Serafeim ran his hands through his hair. "We checked out the warehouse, hoping to get rid of the man and his supply, but it was empty. I want to put a warrant out for his arrest, but no one knows what he looks like. The only helpful thing I have is that he has a contact staying at Sanctuary, but I can't set foot in there, and neither can any of my men."

Theron wondered how he had never heard of the place before now, he had been on the island for over a hundred years and yet it snuck passed him. It didn't matter now. The only thing that mattered was helping his friend. "I can help you there. Actually, the more I think about it, I think I can help us both."

"What do you mean? What trouble do you have?" Serafeim leaned forward and pulled his eyebrows together.

"The man who attacked my compound is staying at Sanctuary and, as you said, there's no way to reach him while he is there. However, I have a spy in place. Maybe we can play the two off each other and solve both problems at once." Theron smiled as a plan formed in his mind. All he needed was for Jean to play her part and they would have both the interloper and Alex without spilling any blood.

"You do? That is a tricky thing to accomplish. Are you sure he will help us?"

"It is a she, and yes I think she will, but I need some equipment." Theron bent his head and spoke in a low voice explaining his plan.

Thirty minutes later Theron returned from his car where he stowed the supplies Serafeim gave him and went in search of Vince and Helen. He found Vince first, leaning against the bar with a martini glass filled with a pale red liquid in his hand. There were women all round him trying to get his attention. "You look bored," Theron said, taking the spot next to him at the bar.

"Yes, well the club scene isn't as fun when the woman of my

dreams is at home." He took a sip of his drink and stared past the women into the nothingness beyond them.

"Go home then. I'm sure Katie misses you." Theron took a sip of his martini and looked over the women. He could take his pick of them just as Vince, but none of them looked appealing.

"Don't you need me? How were your meetings?"

"Good, Agapios is back to his old self. He's doing better than ever which is good. Before the attack I was thinking about replacing him. Serafeim and I came up with a plan to not only solve his problem but the Alex problem. As long as Jean does her job we'll solve two problems with one plan."

"What is the plan?" Vince asked, turning to face Theron.

"I'm still working on it, but it will be easier than what we've been doing. Where's Helen?" Theron turned to looked over the crowd.

"On the dance floor. I think I saw Jean out there too."

"Jean? What's she doing here? She's supposed to be hiding out," anger coursed through Theron.

"She is, in a way. Let her be, letting off some steam will help her concentrate later. I'm going back to the house, if you are sure you will be all right on your own." Vince put his empty glass on the bar.

"Go, be with your lover. You two have wasted too much time as it is. We won't be out late."

Vince gave Theron a nod and went to the exit ignoring the woman who stepped into his path. Theron laughed to himself. His maker had changed so much in such a small amount of time. The year before, Vince would have taken two or three of the women home to fuck and snack on, now he only had eyes for Katie. It had to be because she was 'The One,' Theron couldn't think of another reason why a vampire would stop drinking blood from the source and reduce himself to only fucking one woman for the foreseeable future. He shook off the thought. It was time to find something to eat.

Theron found his way to the dance floor moving with the thumping beat of the music looking for someone who would satisfy the hunger growing inside him. He was recovered from being buried alive, but he still needed to eat more often than before.

He saw the pink hair whipping around from side to side a second before Jean's hips grinding into the crotch of a thirty-something man came into view. She was wearing a short, figure-hugging, bright pink dress that accentuated what curves she had. Jean looked five years older with her three-inch heels that matched the dress. Her small breasts were perky and bounced with every grind into the man.

Theron made eye contact with the man, he looked sleazy with slicked back hair and five o'clock shadow. He nodded his head at Theron as if he was saying. 'Yeah, look at the piece of ass I found.' Rage Theron hadn't experienced in decades had his body moving up behind Jean and pulling her back into him before he could stop himself. He didn't know why he was grinding his pelvis into hers, but he wouldn't let the blood bag have her. Jean ran her hands over Theron's before turning to see who she was dancing with. When her eyes met his, she pushed him away with a look of disgust that almost made him fall to his knees.

"What do you think you're doing?" she yelled from a few feet away.

"Dancing of course, you didn't seem to mind a few seconds ago." Theron had to be the tough guy with her.

"That was before I knew it was you." She put her hands on her hips as her pale skin turned a shade of red.

"You would rather dance with a stranger who could do who knows what to you?" Theron countered, based on the shade of red she turned, she hadn't minded dancing with him.

"Why don't you mind your own business?" she yelled and moved off the dance floor.

Theron could not be seen with a woman walking away from

him, he had to stop this. He followed her to the bar, took her hand and forced her to turn and look at him. "We have a plan, you shouldn't even be here."

"I made contact with Alex, he will be putty in my hands before you know it, but tonight I needed to dance, and I wasn't hanging out in the bar at Sanctuary." Jean raised her hand to get the bartenders attention then ordered a beer.

"Why not?" Theron asked, sandwiching her between himself and the bar.

"Hey, man," a voice said from behind him and put a hand on his shoulder. "Can't you see the lady doesn't want you? Why don't you leave her alone?"

Theron closed his eyes for a second and let out a breath. *Goddess save me from Good Samaritans.* Theron turned and looked up at the man. He was well over six feet and beefy.

"Mind your own business." Theron turned back to Jean and watched as she took a sip of beer.

"Finish your beer then I'll take you back to your hotel. I have the supplies you asked for," Theron said, looking around for Helen. He found her leaning against the wall with a man kissing her neck as she drank from him. *Well, at least someone was having a good meal tonight.*

"No, I'm not done dancing." Jean chugged the rest of her beer and tried to walk around Theron to get back to the dance floor.

"You're going to ruin the plan." Theron grabbed her arm trying not to squeeze too hard when something crashed against his head from behind and he was covered in beer, glass, and his own blood. He let go of Jean and turned to the Good Samaritan. Theron put his hand to his head and brought it down to look at it. Blood covered his fingers. His arm shot out and he wrapped his hand around the man's throat before lifting him until his feet left the ground. Theron grabbed ahold of his mind. "You will do exactly what I say," he said in a low voice and walked the man toward the back room.

"Theron, are you all right? Let him go," Jean said from behind him as she followed them. "Helen," she yelled, and Theron took the man into the back room, closed, then locked the door.

"You just fucked with the wrong guy." Theron let the man go and he doubled over trying to catch his breath. Theron paced back and forth in front of the door deciding what to do with the man. He wanted to kill him, anyone who didn't know who he was and what he was to Crete didn't deserve to live, but the pounding on the other side of the door brought him to his senses. Jean would know if he killed the man, and that would cause more trouble than it was worth.

Theron stopped pacing, lunged at the man, took him into an embrace and buried his fangs in his throat. He did not make it feel good for the man, like he normally did when he drank directly from the source, he didn't deserve it. When he had his fill, he ran his tongue over the puncture marks to coagulate the blood and let the man lean against the wall. "Now then, you will forget everything that happened since you met me except for the girl, you will think she is the most revolting human you've ever seen. Do you understand?"

"Yes," the man said in a groggy voice like he was talking in his sleep.

"Good, now go." Theron unlocked the door and held it open. After the man left, Theron went to the utility sink and cleaned the blood from his head and face, the cuts were already closed, but the blood was still there. When he was presentable again, although his shirt was still covered in beer and blood, he left the back room ready to collect Jean and Helen and go home.

When he emerged Helen and Jean were waiting outside the door. Jean had her head on Helen's shoulder as Helen patted her back. Theron snapped his head to the side indicating that they were leaving and walked to the exit. He heard Helen whisper something to Jean as they followed behind.

Once they were in the car, and driving to Sanctuary, Theron's hell began. "What right do you have telling me I can't dance with whoever I want?" Jean yelled from the back seat.

"I'm not only trying to protect you, but Katie as well, what if he was a hit man and planned to kidnap you hoping Katie would try to rescue you?" He wasn't lying to the girl, but he wasn't telling her everything either, he wasn't ready to think about why he didn't want her dancing with another man. "Besides, the man was almost old enough to be your father."

"He wasn't a hit man and you know it," she fumed as a tear leaked down her cheek.

Goddess he hated it when a woman cried. "Was he the love of your life? You knew by the way he sweat all over you?" Theron was being childish, but the girl was trouble.

"Helen was making out with a guy against the wall and you didn't even bat an eye. Why is what I do more important than what she does?"

"Because she was..."

"He was an old boyfriend, I wanted to see if he was as good as I remembered," Helen cut Theron off before he could tell Jean that Helen was drinking his blood.

Theron shot her a look of thanks. "I knew him and knew Helen could take care of herself. She isn't as young as she looks."

"Whatever, I don't need a protector." Jean fumed but said nothing else.

Theron rolled his eyes. This girl was going to be the death of him. They pulled over a few blocks from Sanctuary and turned off the car. He turned and looked at Jean. She was staring out the window with her arms crossed over her chest. He blew out a breath. If he didn't fix the situation, he risked losing her help, and he needed it more than anything at the moment.

"Jean, I'm sorry," he said in a soft voice. "I don't want anything bad to happen to you."

"Yeah, then your plan wouldn't work," she said without looking away from the window.

"True, but you want to get Alex too, right?"

Jean looked at him from the corner of her eye for a second before her gaze returned to the window. "Yes."

"Then we need to keep up appearances. Look, the surveillance equipment you wanted is in the trunk, do you want me to get it for you?"

Jean's eyes brightened. "No, I'll get it. Thanks for the ride." She got out of the car and walked behind it, then waited for Theron to pop the trunk.

"That went well," Helen said from the passenger seat as Theron hit the trunk release button.

"Shut it, I'm in no mood to talk," Theron said, watching as the trunk closed and Jean walked down the street. He shook his head before putting the car in gear and heading home. The girl would be the death of him. She was a pain in his ass, but she was beautiful, even with her pink hair. Her high cheekbones, big blue eyes, and her soft lips called to him. Driving back to the mansion was the first time he had allowed himself to think of her as the beauty she was. He shook his head, he couldn't let anyone know how attractive he found her, or he would never live it down.

142

## Chapter 19
### *Jean*

Jean woke up the next morning with a pounding headache, the night before had not gone to plan. All she wanted to do was go out and forget about everything for a few hours. The last thing she expected to happen was Theron freaking out because she was dancing with a guy. What did it matter to him, anyway? She didn't belong to him.

She rolled over and looked at the clock; it was just past nine in the morning and she was starving. She wanted to go down to the bar to eat, but she didn't want to run into the guys who attacked her the day before. She got out of bed, went to her computer, booted it up and started a hack; she didn't know why she didn't do it as soon as she arrived at Sanctuary, but she would do it now. Ten minutes later she was looking at the security feed for the entire place. Now she could keep an eye on the guys who attacked her and watch Alex without following him around like a puppy.

The bar was almost empty, which was a relief. She could go down to get something to eat, then figure out how she would get the tracker, on Alex. It would have to be on his skin since who knew how often he changed his clothes. The instructions said if she placed it on a part of the body he didn't touch very often, it would last for a week and it was so small that no one would notice it unless they walked through a metal detector. She picked up the case and wondered how she could get it on Alex's bare back. She wouldn't sleep with him to put it on, but she needed a plan. Her stomach growled again, food, then she would figure it out. She ran to the bathroom, brushed her teeth, peed, and ran a brush through her hair. When she got back to her room, she pulled on a pair of jeans and a black, V-neck T-shirt. She checked the cameras one more time, then put her computer and the other goodies Theron gave her the night before, in her bag and went down to eat. She sat at the bar this time; she wanted to be near the exit and closer to the bartender.

"What can I get you?" the man asked.

"Red beer, and some scrambled eggs please." Jean pulled her computer out of her bag and set it up on the bar.

"Hair of the Dog who bit you?" the bartender asked while making her drink.

"Something like that. Hey, what's your name?" she asked, looking over the top of her computer.

"Most people around here call me Shaker."

"Nice to meet you, Shaker, you can call me Uni." Jean wouldn't go by her real name in a place like this, plus she was known in the hacking world by her codename. It might end up helping her in the long run.

"Yeah, you too," Shaker said, putting the red beer down in front of her. "I'll go get your food order in."

"Thanks." Uni turned back to her computer. She checked the cameras again to make sure none of the a-holes from the day before were on their way to the bar. When she saw nothing out of the ordinary, she pulled up her email program and caught up on her correspondence. She had dozens of emails from her friends back in Kevó, but she ignored them. She wasn't ready to tell them what she was doing. If they found out what she'd done to capture Alex, they would never forgive her. She had a few from her handler at Interpol and she hovered over the email with the subject line, *I need an update. You need to check in*. She looked up and realized she'd been alone in the room for a few minutes.

She pulled the bugs out of her bag and looked around the

room. If she were Alex, where would she sit when devising a plan to kidnap Katie? There were a few tables that light did not touch. That would be where she would want to talk to someone about nefarious plans, but this was Sanctuary, no one would pay any mind to what was said, hell it would be safer if you only listened to your own conversations.

The bugs had a twenty-five-foot radius. If she placed them around the room, she could catch a conversation wherever Alex sat. She went back to her computer, put the video coming from the cameras in the bar on a loop and quickly placed the bugs under tables and under the lip of the bar. She'd just sat back down and taken the video off the loop when Shaker came back with a plate of food for her.

"Here you go." He put the food down in front of her and pulled out silverware rolled in a napkin.

"Thanks, I'm starving." Jean unrolled the silverware, put the napkin in her lap and ate while watching the feed on the security cameras. Alex left the room right next to hers wearing only a pair of gym shorts. He had a small bag in one hand and a towel over his shoulder. He was going to the communal bathroom. If she hurried she might *run into him* in the hall. It might be her only chance to place the tracker.

She shoveled the rest of her food down, packed up her computer and was about to leave when Shaker stopped her. "You're not running out on your bill again, are you?" he asked, folding his arms over his chest.

"What? I thought you just billed my room and my credit card is on file." Jean shrugged her shoulders then dug her wallet out of her back pocket. "How much do I owe you?" she needed to be on her way back to her room not paying her bill.

"I'm just kidding, I'll bill your room." Shaker laughed and turned to finish watering down a bottle of ouzo.

Jean shoved her wallet back into her pants and tried to walk casually out of the bar and to the stairwell. When she reached the stairs, she took them two at a time until she reached the second floor, then she pulled her computer out and brought up the hallway on the security camera. It had been less than five minutes and she doubted she missed Alex.

Jean looked at the layout, the bathroom was at the other end of the hallway and her door was just past Alex's when she walked from the stairwell. Her timing would have to be perfect. She pulled the tracker out of its case and put it on the tip of her finger, then she pulled out the book she was reading. As soon as the bathroom door opened, she shoved her computer into its bag and walked down the hall pretending to be engrossed in her book. She looked up when she entered the hall and judged the distance she would have to cover to meet Alex in between the two doors. It would be tight, but if his door was locked, she would make it.

Ready as she would ever be, she walked a little faster until there was three feet between them and she veered into his path. His arms shot out to stop her. "Hey, you need to watch where you're going," Alex said as she pulled her eyes up from the book.

"I'm so sorry, I wasn't paying attention," Jean said, floundering. This was not going to plan. She wanted to run into him and force them both to the floor, then she could stick the tracker on while they untangled themselves. He wouldn't notice the slight pressure on his back. "Hey, you're the guy who saved me from those thugs yesterday, aren't you?"

"Oh, yeah, I guess I was." He tried to move past her, but she sidestepped just as he did.

"I wanted to thank you again. I don't know what would've happened if you didn't show up." Jean looked at the floor. She wanted to ask him for a hug, but it wouldn't work, everyone there was very particular about their personal space.

"No problem, they need to learn not to force a girl, they'll have a much better time." Alex looked past her then back, tapping his foot on the floor.

"Yeah, no kidding. Hey, I would love to buy you a drink or something to thank you." Jean was barely paying attention to what she was saying, there had to be a way to touch his back, she probably wouldn't get another chance.

"Yeah, maybe, but look I'm going to be late for an appointment. Maybe I'll see you around." Alex quickly stepped around her until he was at his door and pulling his key out of a pocket.

"Sorry, I'm just new here and scared. Thanks anyway." Her face fell, and she slouched, she failed. *What am I going to do now?*

"Look, it's not that I don't want to have a drink with you, it's just that I have a meeting." Alex put a hand on her shoulder, startling her. She whirled around with her leg outstretched. It got caught in Alex's and they both hit the ground with Alex half on top of her. Before he could move she reached around and pressed the tracker into his back.

"What the hell?" Alex yelled and scrambled to his feet.

"Oh my gosh, you scared me. After what happened yesterday, I've been a nervous wreck. Are you OK?" Jean did her best to sound concerned and tearful, but inside she was giddy with excitement, part one of the plan was now in motion.

"Leave me alone. You're crazy," Alex said, hurrying to unlock his door and get away from her.

Jean smiled to herself once Alex was in his room, she did it. Who said she wouldn't be a good spy? She went into her room, pulled her computer out of her bag, and set it up at the small desk. She opened the tracking program and watched the tiny blip as it moved around on the screen.

She pulled her phone out of her pocket and sent a group text to Katie and Theron.

**The tracker and bugs are in place.**

She hit the send button then kept her eyes glued to the screen. *If there was only a way to bug his room*, she thought before her phone vibrated.

147

**Way to go, be careful.** Katie replied.

**Took you long enough,** Theron replied.

Jean put her phone away and spent the next twenty minutes playing solitaire on half her screen and watching the blip on the other half. It hadn't moved in a while. *What if it fell off?* Jean thought, getting worried. She brought up the security cameras and checked them all to make sure Alex was still in his room. She didn't find him, but that didn't mean much. She was about to knock on his door to apologize again, and make sure he hadn't left, when the blip started to move toward the door. She let out a relieved breath as she switched cameras and followed him to the bar.

*At least he is staying on the property*, Jean thought. If he left to meet someone she could follow him but would have no idea what he said.

## Chapter 20

### *Alex*

Alex looked over his shoulder as he entered the bar. The girl staying in the room next to his was stalker-crazy. He still didn't understand how he ended up on the floor when he was just trying to be nice. *Fucking women*, he thought, sitting down at the bar. He was hungry, and he wanted to eat before his contact arrived. He wouldn't get anywhere chasing Katie down without weapons. His new plan was to shoot her, wound her just enough to slow her down, then take her to Lolita. After she was out of the way, he would bomb the crap out of Theron and whoever else was with him. Then he would do the same to Lolita.

He ate his food without looking at anything; he was lost in thought about what he wanted to do to Katie when he finally had her. Lolita said she wanted her alive, but she didn't say in what condition. Alex smiled to himself then straightened as a short, skinny man entered the bar. He had short, curly, brown hair and an olive complexion. He took a table in the corner and blew out the candle in the votive. That was Alex's cue. Alex threw some money on the table, picked up his glass of water, and joined the man.

"You're Alex?" the man asked with a heavy Greek accent.

"Yes, you're Fenix?" Alex asked, taking a seat and relaxing back into it like they were old friends.

"Yes, what can I help you with?" Fenix asked as his eyes shot from one corner of the room to another like a cop would appear at any moment to arrest him.

"I need guns and C-4." Alex didn't like this guy, he was shifty, but if he got him what he needed, it would be worth spending a little time with him.

"What are you going to do with it?" Fenix asked, leveling his stare on Alex.

"I have some unfinished business on the island."

"Then you'll have to buy your weapons somewhere else and smuggle them onto the island. Serafeim won't sell anyone weapons they plan on using on the island. If you think he won't find out, you're kidding yourself and you don't want to be on his bad side. I saw what The Syndicate did to the last guy who crossed them." He moved to get up from his chair, but Alex put his hand out.

"What did they do to him?" Alex asked as he thought of all the ways he had tortured people in the past. Pulling fingernails out was one of his favorites.

"Do you know what a brazen bull is?" Fenix asked, almost whispering.

"No." Alex pulled his eyebrows together.

"They put this guy in a huge statue of a bronze bull and locked him in." Fenix's eyes roamed round the room, making sure no one overheard him.

"And they left him there to die?" Alex asked, thinking The Syndicate would be more creative than that.

"No, they started a fire under the bull, cooking the man alive, every time the man screamed it came out as a bull's bellow. Believe me you do not want to be captured by them." Fenix got to his feet.

"Wait, there has to be someone else who will sell to me. I'll pay." Alex slid a five hundred euro note across the table.

Fenix looked down at it a split second before sitting, placing his hand over the money and pulling it under the table. "There is someone new trying to make a name for himself. I don't know him

150

well, but he might help you, he doesn't have the morals Serafeim has."

"Good, can you arrange a meeting?" Alex asked, as he heard someone enter the bar. If it was the girl, he was going to bash her head against the bar.

"Yes, let me step outside to use the phone." Fenix stood and walked casually out of the bar.

*He had better come back,* Alex thought to himself, otherwise he was out a lot of money with nothing to show for it. Alone, sitting with his back toward the door Alex turned and looked around the room. There was an old man sitting at the bar, nursing a beer. It must have been who he'd heard since the rest of the place was empty.

Alex looked at his watch, he would give Fenix five more minutes before he started looking for him. He signaled the bartender he was ready for a beer and relaxed back into his seat. He looked like nothing in the world was bothering him but in reality, if he couldn't get weapons, he would never catch Katie and kill the bastards who made his life hell for the past six months.

The bartender brought him his beer and Alex heard the light footsteps of Fenix cross the floor. He resumed his seat and gave Alex a smile. "What did your man say?"

"He would love to do business with you, but he is not a member of Sanctuary, so he wishes to meet you here." Fenix slid a folded piece of paper across the table to Alex.

"When?" Alex said, glancing at the address then slipping it into the pocket of his jeans.

"Tonight, at nine."

"Are you going to be there?"

"No, I'm only the middle man. It was a pleasure doing business with you." Fenix offered his hand, but Alex ignored it.

"The pleasure was all yours, I'm sure." Alex picked up his beer and drained it. He was going to have a long night and needed to rest before the sun went down.

Fenix left without another word and Alex leaned back to think about his plan for the night ahead. The man wanted to meet at night, idiot, it would be safer to meet during the day.

## Chapter 21

*Jean*

"Seriously," Jean cursed before backing up the video and zooming in on the paper Alex looked at for a split second before folding it back up. She spent an hour finding the right moment to pause the feed and manipulating the video before she could make out the address. When she was finally done, she sat back and let out a breath. They were going to get Alex.

She grabbed her phone, changed into a robe, and grabbed her makeup bag. There was only one place she could talk to Theron and Katie without anyone overhearing, the bathroom. This was it, it was going to be too easy. She knew exactly where Alex would be. Theron would be excited too, maybe he would stop hating her after they captured Alex. She opened the door and took a step back as she recognized the thug from the day before in the bar, standing on the other side of the door. She backed away from the door.

"Hey, little girl, we never got that dance," he said, giving her a smile that made her take another step back. He was missing three or four front teeth and with the evil grin he was giving her, he looked like he had been spat out of hell for bad behavior.

"And you never will." Jean ducked and weaved under his outstretched arm while slamming the door to her room. She sprinted down

153

the hallway and into the bathroom where she slammed and locked the door behind her.

"We will just see about that, sweet one," he yelled through the door before Jean heard his heavy footsteps move down the hall.

She needed to leave Sanctuary, and soon, the locks on the room were enough to keep the honest thieves out, but that guy could kick the door in barefoot with an ingrown toenail. Jean shook herself and got on with her plan. She turned the water on in the shower and the faucet then dialed Katie.

"Jean? Is it you? Are you OK?" Katie sounded worried, which didn't surprise Jean. Katie wanted to protect everyone, not send them out on dangerous missions.

"I'm fine, look, I don't have a lot of time. Can you find Theron and put this on speaker phone? He'll want to hear this." Jean put the lid of the toilet down and sat.

"I'm already on my way. I'm glad you're OK."

"Of course I am. I'm not the child everyone thinks I am," Jean said, looking at the chipped, blue nail polish on her hand not holding the phone. She needed to reapply soon.

"I know you're not a child, I just worry," Katie said before stopping. "OK, we are all here and you're on speaker phone."

"OK, Alex is meeting with an arms dealer tonight at nine," Jean said before relaying the address.

"Did you get the name of the dealer?" Theron sounded agitated, and Jean wondered if it was because she completed her mission, or because of Alex.

"No, but it's not Serafeim. He's a new guy trying to get a foothold. The contact didn't give him up until Alex bribed him. What do we do now?" Jean asked, wanting to be there when they caught him.

"We will come up with a plan to capture him. In the meantime, I want you to lie low until tomorrow morning, then you can join us at the mansion," Theron said, and she imagined him leaning back in his chair.

"But..." Jean started but Helen cut her off.

"Jean we could have never gotten this far without you, but we don't want you to get hurt. Stay there one more night. Come home tomorrow." Helen was using her motherly voice even though she looked too young to have kids.

"Fine, but if you need backup, call me." Jean huffed out a frustrated breath. When would everyone stop treating her like a child?

"Jean," Vince said from further away in the room. "You did good. Thank you."

"Sure, see you guys tomorrow." Jean hit the end button on her phone, turned the faucet off and stripped off her robe. She needed to, at least, make it look like she was in there for the shower.

After she went back to her room, she finally opened the email from her handler.

> **Uni, you were supposed to check in three days ago. I need a status update ASAP. If I do not hear from you in the next forty-eight hours, I will have no choice but to mark you rogue and you know what happens after that.**

Jean took a large gulp of air, if she was branded rogue, she would be on her own and they would put her on the most wanted list. She couldn't let that happen. She'd been thinking about quitting her job and going out on her own, which she thought they would let her do, but leaving, quitting without telling them was a big no-no.

She hit the reply button on her email and posed her hands to type, but she had no idea what to say. She stared at the blinking curser for a long time before she started typing.

> **Dear Mam, I'm sorry I've been out of touch. I'm still trying to win Theron's trust. It isn't something that can be earned overnight. If you wish me to continue I'll be out of contact for the foreseeable future so I can gather the evidence required to arrest him. Alex Jorgenson is also on the island, if everything goes to plan I will arrest them both.**

She crossed her fingers and hit the send button. That done she went through the rest of her emails and told her friends in Kevó that she needed a break and was spending time with Katie. When she finished, her handler at Interpol had replied to her message.

> **Uni, you didn't have authorization to go undercover, but I allowed this because you said it wouldn't take more than a few days. I can't cover for you any longer. If you do not show up in London within the next forty-eight hours you will be tagged rogue, unless you can produce the evidence we need to arrest Theron or capture Alex.**

Jean stared at the email until her eyes burned and she had to blink to keep her eyes from watering. She couldn't be labeled a rogue, the last three agents they tagged didn't make it a year before someone killed them, and they actually knew how to hide. She couldn't go back to Kevó, Interpol knew where it was thanks to her and she wasn't going to London, they would have her in a cubical working nine to five like a normal person, but she wasn't ready to go off the grid either. She had never needed to stash cash, or identities around the world like they do in movies. She wouldn't last a week as rogue, and maybe it was selfish, but she wasn't ready to die yet.

She only saw one answer to the problem, and no one was going to like her for it. She packed up her stuff and was about to leave when someone pounded on her door. She let go of the handle on the suitcase and tiptoed to the eyehole on the door. She peered through it and wanted to scream. Whoever was on the other side had covered the hole, keeping her from seeing who it was. She looked around the room for a weapon but found nothing she could use.

She looked at the window, it was too small to fit through even if dropping two stories was something she knew how to do without hurting herself. She would have to face whoever it was. She unlocked the door and opened it before falling back into a fighting stance.

The man with the missing teeth was standing there with a long piece of rope in his hand. "See, now you and me are going to have fun tonight," he said, taking a step into the room.

Jean looked for a weakness on the hulk of a man but only found one, she faked a kick to his shin, and he moved to block it with a laugh. "I do love me a fighter," he said before her boot-clad foot shot out and connected with his balls. Dropping the rope, he bent over to cup himself, she grabbed him by the hair and rammed his nose into her knee. He screamed and fell to the side leaning against the wall.

Jean grabbed her suitcase and ran past him before he could recover. She ran down the stairs and out the door before anyone could stop her. She didn't care if she was running away from a fight, the man would do terrible things to her. She ran down the quiet street until she hit the main drag and slowed to a walk. She flagged a cab down with shaking hands and got in, not waiting for the driver to put her suitcase in the trunk. When he asked where she wanted to go she blanked for a second before remembering what she planned before she was attacked. Her voice cracked as she asked him to take her to a shopping center near the mansion Katie was staying in.

"Are you all right?" the driver asked as he started down the street.

"What? Yes, just leaving my abusive boyfriend," Jean said, clenching her hands together to stop them from shaking.

"Good for you," the man said, picking up some more speed.

Jean leaned back and looked out the window. She was going to write a very strongly worded email to Sanctuary, it wasn't safe at all.

## Chapter 22

### *Katie*

I hit the end button on the phone then looked around the room. Everyone was looking into the distance, probably visualizing catching Alex. I took a moment and thought of cutting him to pieces digit by digit. "What do we do now?" I asked, grossing myself out at the thought.

"Now, we call Serafeim, he has a stake in this too." Theron picked up his phone, hit a few buttons, and we waited as the sound of ringing filled the room.

"Theron, what is it?" Serafeim asked, breathing heavily.

"We know where your usurper will be tonight."

"Your spy found this out?" Serafeim's voice almost sang with delight.

"Yes, and she wants Alex just as much as I do." Theron leaned back in his chair and laced his hands behind his head.

I didn't know how he could be so relaxed, I was sitting on the edge of my chair drumming my fingers on my leg. It had been incredibly boring since Jean left and I was ready for some action.

"This could be fun," Serafeim said after a long pause.

"It will be fun, let's meet as soon as the sun goes down," Vince said, looking around the room at us.

I looked down at my workout clothes and sneakers, I would need my combat boots and leather jacket for this fight.

"Very well, see you at the bar." Serafeim ended the call and Theron gave me the biggest smile I had ever seen.

"Jean.might be a royal pain in the ass, but if she's right about this, I will forever be in her debt. Tonight, we go to war and we will be victorious."

"Are you sure this is smart? We don't want to risk civilians," Helen said, stopping behind Theron.

"We will make sure no one is hurt except for Alex, and the one trying to cut in on Serafeim," Vince said, leaning forward in his chair.

"What are we going to do with him?" I asked, thinking about all the ways I wanted to hurt the man who had once been my friend.

"We'll make an example of him, of course. We need to let the world know what happens when you mess with the head of The Syndicate and Katie Hunter." Theron smiled. "I was thinking of crucifying him and leaving him on the beach at the compound. He wouldn't be found for days and there would be no evidence pointing to us."

"I like it. When do we leave?" I was ready to change into some ass-kicking clothes and join the fun.

"Katie," Vince started, then stopped, looking at Theron. I knew where he was going before he finished, he didn't want me to go.

"Vince is right. It's safer for you to stay here. You're too important to our cause to be hurt," Theron said, looking to Helen for support. She turned up her nose at him.

"He hurt us all, Theron, we almost died because of him. You can't leave her out of this." Helen's voice was cold and calm. It surprised me she was on my side.

"How about we pick you up after we have him?" Vince offered.

I wanted to pout, but they would have a better chance of catching him if I wasn't there. "I'll wait here, but only because this is Alex." I made eye contact with each of them, giving them my best don't fuck with me look. "If you try to pull this with Lolita, I will fight you tooth and nail. She's mine."

"Agreed," Theron and Helen said, looking a little too pleased.

"But, Katie," Vince started until he caught my look. "We will talk about it when the time comes."

"No, Vince, we won't. When the time comes, Lolita is mine." I drummed my fingers on my leg and raised my eyebrows.

"I just don't want you to get hurt." Vince turned and took my hand in his.

"I don't want to get hurt either, I want to kill Lolita. If I'm not the one to kill her, it will ruin what little reputation I have with the vampires. It's bad enough I'm human. I love you and I want to spend the rest of my life showing you how much, but I will not stand by while someone else kills the woman who made my life hell." I wanted to cry but I wouldn't let the tears come. I had to show everyone I was tough, that I could handle it.

"As you wish." Vince got up and went to the door. "What time are we leaving?" he asked before opening it.

"As soon as the sun goes down. I want to make sure Alex is alone. He will not get away this time." Theron looked at Vince with hatred in his eyes.

"I will be ready." He walked through the door and closed it loudly, not quite slamming it but not shutting it gently either.

I looked at Helen and Theron who were staring at me with frowns. "What? I'm tired of being treated like a helpless human." I stood up and went to the door. "What do I have to do to prove to you people that I can beat Lolita?"

"When you believe it, I'll believe it," Theron said, spinning his chair around in dismissal.

"Do you think you can beat her?" Helen asked, her voice soft and thoughtful.

I thought about it. I thought about sparring with Vince, I thought about how hard I had been pushing myself with the katana. I thought about my original plan to kill Lolita. "I'm ready, I can beat her." *As long as it's one on one, and I didn't have to fight anyone else to get to her,* is what I didn't say.

"Then you will, and we'll support you, but Alex is mine," Theron said, from behind his chair.

"Very well." At least Theron and Helen thought I could beat Lolita, and I did too, most of the time.

# Chapter 23

## *Jean*

Jean had to pee, but there was nothing she could do about it, she was hiding in the trunk of the BMW waiting for Theron, Vince, and Helen to get out. Terrified of moving; she didn't know what kind of training Theron and his friends had, but they seemed to notice the tiniest movement or sound. If she moved in the slightest they would catch her and who knew what they would do to her.

After her escape from Sanctuary she went to the mansion, used her computer to bypass security, and broke into the garage. She planned to trade her suitcase for the gun in her car and leave, but before she could, she heard people on the other side of the door. She looked at the trunk of the BMW and made her decision; she popped the trunk and jumped in moments before Theron, Helen, and Vince entered the garage. At least they would take her where she wanted to go.

A bumpy car ride later, her whole body had a cramp. If they ever got out of the car; she wasn't sure she would be able to move. She would find a way, Alex killed her mentor and tried to kill her friend not once but twice. Plus, she had to arrest him if she didn't want to be a rogue. She wouldn't arrest Theron to keep her from being tagged. He was an ass, but a good guy for the most part.

She closed her eyes and forced herself to stay calm; she didn't want to think about what would happen if they found her in the trunk. She wondered where Alex was. What if she hadn't read the address correctly?

What if it was a code for another place? She could track him on her phone but, if she moved, and they found her it would jeopardize catching Alex.

The car doors finally opened, and they got out. As they walked away she let out a breath and stretched her legs. The beep of the car alarm made her freeze. *Crap,* she hadn't thought this through. *Will the car alarm go off when I pull the emergency release cable to open the trunk?* It was too late now; her mission and her bladder couldn't wait any longer. After waiting a few minutes to make sure Theron and the rest of them were in the bar, she scooted over and pulled the emergency release. The trunk opened, and she tensed, waiting for the car alarm to go off, but it remained silent. She let out an audible breath, *thank God,* she looked around the dark parking lot, made sure no one was watching, then rolled out and hit the ground, hard. She probably looked like a freak but the cramps in her legs were too painful, she couldn't stand yet.

Lying on the ground she slowly worked the cramps out of her muscles. When she could stand she closed the trunk as quietly as she could and took off around the back of the bar. Damn, she needed to pee. There was a dumpster on the far side of the building and it gave her the cover she needed to take care of business. With that accomplished, she snuck to the back door and put her ear to it. She couldn't hear anything; the fire door was too thick.

She pulled the gun from the waistband of her jeans and clicked the safety off. She put her hand on the door knob and twisted. To her relief it was unlocked. She cracked it first and looked inside the dimly lit store room. It was empty; she went inside then closed the door quietly behind her. She walked the room, trying to keep her boots from making too much noise on the concrete floor. Jean had no idea what Theron's plan was, but she had to arrest Alex. She walked over to the only other door in the room and pushed her ear against it.

"Grigoris, what are you doing here with him?" a voice dripping with disappointment asked. Jean didn't know who was talking.

"Father, I am twenty-three years old, it's time for me to go out on my own," another voice said with a slight tremble.

"Why didn't you talk to me? Instead, you go behind my back, steal my supplies, and try to sell them on your own?" *It must be Serafeim*, Jean thought, wondering where Alex was.

"This family reunion is touching, but can we get on with this? Are you going to sell me what I need?" Alex asked, sounding bored.

"So you can attack one of my best friends, and the man who has kept Crete safe for decades? Never," Serafeim said, and Jean heard a gun chambering a round.

"There is no one on the island who will help you, Alex," Theron's voice boomed through the room making Jean wonder where he had been hiding.

"You won't take me alive," Alex yelled as gun fire exploded. There were muffled sounds of flesh hitting flesh for a moment then moaning.

Jean couldn't tell if it was from Alex, Serafeim, or one of the others but it was now or never. She turned the door handle and burst into the room. "Interpol, put your weapons down and your hands up," she yelled, sweeping her gun around covering everyone in the room.

Jean looked around in a split second and cataloged everything. Theron looked up from where he was propped up against the wall with blood trickling down his right shoulder. His eyes told her everything she needed to know. He was going to kill her. Alex had his face pinned against the wall with a gun pointed at his head by Vince. He looked over to Jean with a grin. Vince shook his head at her and Helen ignored her completely. Serafeim had a gun trained on the only other person in the room, Grigoris she guessed. There was blood trickling from his nose and the look of betrayal in his eyes.

Alex took the moment of distraction and twisted out of Vince's arms, took the gun, and started shooting. Jean dropped to the ground, rolled across the floor and took a shot at Alex, she missed, and he shot back at her

165

hitting her gun arm, forcing her to drop the gun. Theron sprang to his feet and rushed Alex, going for a tackle. Alex spun out of Theron's way and went for the door, Jean searched franticly for her gun, and finally found it under the table. She grabbed it, and took off chasing after Alex, when she reached the bar floor the patrons were running for the door. She pushed her way through and as she finally reached the parking lot, she watched a scooter tear off down the road in one direction and a Mercedes in the other. She ran to the BMW and searched her pockets, *fuck* she forgot she rode in the trunk and didn't have the keys.

Theron, and the others were going to kill her. Did she even want to ask them for a ride back to the house? Would they let her go back to the house? She could call her handler and beg her not to tag her, but it would be worse than dealing with Theron. Her arm stung, and she slumped, sat on the ground, leaning against the car holding her stinging arm close to her chest.

A few minutes later, Theron, Vince, and Helen exited the bar moving toward her. They wore the same expressions, lips pulled into a tight line, their eyebrows pulled together and murder in their eyes. She looked back down at the concrete under her.

"Where did they go?" Theron asked, stepping up to her, she didn't bother to look up.

"One took off on a scooter heading that way and the other was in a Mercedes going that way." She pointed bringing her injured arm up and wincing.

"Are you all right?" Helen asked, bending down to look at her bleeding arm.

"Just grazed." She looked up and met Helen's eyes. Helen shook her head still looking pissed.

"We need to stop the bleeding." She took ahold of Jean's shirt sleeve and pulled, ripping it off at the seam.

"She better not bleed in my car," Theron growled, getting

into the driver's seat.

Helen ignored him and tied the sleeve around Jean's arm. "Come on let's get you home."

Theron spent the drive home on the phone asking the other members of The Syndicate to stake out Sanctuary and the marina where Alex's boat was moored. Jean looked out the window, ignoring the others. She could not take the hate and disappointment in their eyes. All Jean wanted to do was get back to the mansion, get her stuff and leave. She would hide, she could ask Barkley to make a new identity for her. Then she could ask Copperhead to help her move her money. At least she would have something to start with. Maybe she would go to a small town in the American West where she could blend in and start over. She messed up before, but never this badly. Now she would be on her own and tagged rogue.

As soon as the car stopped in the garage, she opened her door and ran into the house blowing past Katie who was waiting for them. "What are you doing here? I thought you weren't coming back until tomorrow?"

"They'll tell you," Jean said, looking behind her before running to her room.

# Chapter 24
## *Alex*

How had Serafeim and Vince found him? Fenix must have ratted him out. No one else knew what Alex was planning. He shook his head and sped down the road as fast as the little scooter would go. He needed to ditch it, and damn it hadn't been cheap. He brought the scooter to a halt in the parking lot of a shopping center and walked away leaving the keys in it. He didn't know where he was going or what he was going to do, with his luck they would have people waiting for him outside Sanctuary.

He said a prayer, thanking his father for the stupid girl who allowed him to get away. He stopped mid-stride. How did a girl working for Interpol become a member of Sanctuary? It was unheard of, but it might explain how they found him. If she bugged the bar she could have found out what he was planning, but still, how did she know where he was going? What if she bugged him? She had the chance when she all but tackled him in the hallway. *Fuck*, he thought, he needed a shower and soon. What he really wanted to do was leave Crete, but with all the vampires he thought were dead after him he stood no chance of leaving the island alive and leaving wouldn't solve his problem with Lolita or Zeus. He could call her, tell her where Katie was and maybe she would let him walk away, but his father wouldn't be happy. Alex was supposed to kill all the vampires for him. He didn't know why or how and hell, maybe it was just his subconscious telling him the only way he would ever be free of vampires was to kill them all.

*Screw Zeus*, he thought and pulled out his phone. He dialed a number with no name attached to it.

"Are you calling to tell me you have her?" Lolita's voice purred on the other side of the line.

"No, but I know where she is." Alex stopped under an olive tree on the side of the road and rubbed his free hand over his skin. If that bitch put a tracker on him he needed to get it off as soon as possible.

"If you know where she is you should be able to take her and bring her to me." The purr in her voice was still there, but it was becoming sharper, no longer like silk, closer to rough linen.

"It's not that easy. I thought if I told you where she was you could come and get her. I won't even ask for a finder fee. I want out." His hands shook as he spoke. He hadn't realized how much he wanted this over until now. He still wanted Katie to suffer, but he wasn't willing to risk his life anymore. He took his free hand and ran it down his back starting at the base of his neck and felt something smooth. Using his fingernail, he pried it off and brought it around to look at.

Lolita laughed high and sensual. "You know it's too late to back out. We had a deal and if you don't come through, I get to keep you for myself. I'm so fond of making men beg."

"Please, Lolita, I don't think there's a way for me to get her. Believe me, I want her dead just as much as you do, but I have no help and no way of getting to her. Theron and Vince guard her like she is the queen of fucking England." He squinted at the tiny almost translucent chip before dropping it on the ground and stomping on it.

"Then find some help," she snapped.

He took the phone from his ear and ended the call. How was he going to get out of this? It was time to go, leave Greece and go somewhere far away then put the past year of his life behind him. He thought about returning to Sanctuary for his stuff, but it was too dangerous, Theron probably had all the roads leading there watched. Instead, he started toward the marina where his boat was and his way off the island. It was his best chance to escape.

It was late, near three a.m., when he arrived at the marina. It should have been dark and empty, but all the lights were on, and men with assault rifles were standing around talking and smoking in the cold winter air. He'd been made, they were waiting for him to come after his boat. The morons, standing around like he would walk right up to them and ask what they were doing there.

He wanted to run in the opposite direction but, instead, he backed into a shadow cast by the moon and waited to see if any of them would come investigate. After a few minutes he turned and walked along the coast. It wasn't the first time he'd been stuck somewhere, but it changed nothing. He needed off the island. He would steal a boat. It was his only option with Theron tearing the island apart looking for him. He walked the coastline looking for a deserted marina, but each one he came to was guarded. Even the private villas with docks had guards on them. He was stuck, and the sun was about to come up. He needed sleep, but couldn't get a hotel room, they would recognize him in a second.

He finally found a cave where he could rest and not worry about anyone finding him. He used his bag as a pillow and settled in to get a few hours of sleep.

He jerked awake hours later forgetting for a moment what happened the night before and wondering where he was. It all came back in a flash and he got to his feet confirming he was still alone. No one was in the cave with him, but it was far from empty. The night before may not have gone as planned but looking around the cave he realized it wasn't time to leave Crete yet.

He risked going back to Sanctuary after he hid what he found in the cave, he couldn't think of anywhere safer and he needed help. He watched the road from the shadows for hours before he risked knocking on the door, sure the coast was clear. Once he was inside, he checked the room where the Interpol agent had been staying but there was no sign of her. He tried to tell the manager about her, but he had no name and no proof. Giving up, he went to his room then showered. After his shower, he looked at the bed, his body wanted more sleep, but his mind wouldn't allow it. He had too much planning to do.

He went down the stairs and found a seat at the bar. When the bartender came over, he ordered a beer and a burger. He needed fuel, he hadn't eaten in over twenty-four hours and his body wouldn't do him any favors if he didn't eat. After he had his first sip of beer, he looked around the sparsely populated room. There were a few pairs sitting at tables talking in low voices and a man sitting a few stools down from him sipping a cup of coffee.

When Alex finished eating, he waved the bartender over. "What else can I get you?" the man asked, throwing a towel over his shoulder.

"Do you know anyone looking for work?" Alex asked the man.

"What kind of work?"

"Delicate work, setting explosives in a populated building."

"Why don't you do it yourself?"

"Because everyone on the island is looking for me. I can't go anywhere without being seen."

"I might be able to help," the man at the end of the bar said, looking at him from the corner of his eye.

"Do I know you?" Alex asked, trying to make out the features, but the bar was too dark to see much from where he was sitting.

"We did a few jobs together about five years ago." The man moved to the stool next to Alex.

"Vangel? What are you doing here? This is Sanctuary, you

172

can't touch me in here." Alex jumped to his feet and felt for the gun that wasn't on his hip.

Vangel held up his hands in surrender. "I'm not here to hurt you."

"What brings you to Crete? I thought you joined that pussy Kevò group."

"I did but then I found out about a hit on this winey American that would set me up for life."

"You mean Katie? I heard it was filled."

"Yeah, but I know she's still alive."

"How?"

"She called me, wants me to be her bodyguard."

"You know her?"

"Yeah, she was real cozy with me until she found out her boyfriend was still alive."

"Fucking cocktease," Alex said, sitting back down at the bar.

"No kidding, when she thought Vince was dead, she was all poor me, everyone I love is dead. She flirted with me and led me to believe we would have a future together, but then she finds out Vince is alive and drops me like a dead cat. Goes on about how she only wants to be friends. I want to hurt her."

Alex blew out a breath, it was almost the same thing Katie had done to him over the summer. He didn't want to trust this guy, he could be working with Katie but what other choice did he have? "What do you have in mind?"

# Chapter 25
## *Katie*

I watched Jean walk down the hall; she looked like she had been in a fight: one of her shirt sleeves was missing and there was blood on her face. She walked with a limp and looked like she was about to cry. Theron, Vince, and Helen walked through the door a second later and I took a step back with a barrage of feelings coming off them. Disappointment, anger, pain. "What happened? Where's Alex, and who's hurt?" I asked, running my eyes over Vince as he took me in his arms and held me. "Vince, talk to me, are you OK?"

"Yes, just wounded pride. Theron was shot, Jean was grazed, and Alex got away." He pulled back but took my hand. "Come on, let's go to Theron's office and we will tell you everything."

Vince and I followed Theron and Helen down the hall to the office. Vince shut the door behind us and Theron peeled his shirt off. "Will someone tell me what the hell happened? How did he get away?"

"Jean, that's how." Theron turned around and groaned.

"Are you all right? Should I get the first aid supplies?" I asked, looking at the grizzly wound on his shoulder.

"I'll be fine as soon as we get the bullet out." Theron sat down in one of the visitor chairs as Helen went around the desk, opened a drawer, pulled out a knife and a long pair of tweezers.

"You are going to cut it out of him?" I asked, taking a step back. I wasn't sure I wanted to watch this.

"It's the only way, otherwise his body will heal around the bullet and the pain won't stop until it comes out," Helen said, standing between Theron's legs as he leaned back in his chair.

"Shouldn't you sterilize the knife?" I asked, remembering the first aid class I took in college.

"Vampire, remember?" Vince whispered in my ear, startling me. He put his hands on my hips. "Watch, you never know when we will need you to do this for us." He led me closer for a better angle.

Theron gripped the arms of the chair as Helen stuck the knife in Theron's shoulder, she wiggled it around for a second. "There it is," she whispered. She left the knife buried in Theron's shoulder and picked up the tweezers. She stuck them in the incision and moved them around until she smiled and pulled them out. There was a mushroomed bullet, covered in blood, in between the tongs and she put it on the table. She pulled the knife out of Theron and moved out of the way.

Theron grunted then stood and went to the mini-fridge. He opened it, took out a bag of blood, ripped the top off it and drank it. I stood frozen in place not sure how to react. As long as I had been around vampires I'd never seen them drink blood other than the drops they put in their wine. Watching Theron chug a bag was not as disturbing as I thought it would be and I decided it wasn't a big deal, everyone had to eat. When he finished, he dropped the empty bag in the trash and smiled at me.

I took a step back running into Vince's back. Theron's teeth were covered with blood and his fangs were dripping with saliva. I cringed, thinking back to Lolita and the chunk she took out of my shoulder, maybe it was a bigger deal than I thought. Theron saw my face and turned his back on me. *You have to get over this*, Vince thought, wrapping his arms around my middle and pulling me close.

"I will, I know Theron won't hurt me." I found my breath, matched it to Vince's, and closed my eyes. "Can you tell me what

176

happened? What about Jean, she was covered in blood, do I need to go check on her?"

"Who cares?" Theron moved to his chair and slumped. "She's the reason we don't have Alex right now."

"What happened? What was she doing there?" I asked, looking from one vampire to another.

"She showed up as soon as we had Alex and tried to arrest him. The bastard got the better of me," Vince said, letting me go and pacing around the room. "How was he able to do that anyway?" he asked no one in particular and ran his hands through his hair.

"He was stronger than I remember," Helen agreed. "Do you think someone turned him into a slave?"

"No, it's something else." Theron leaned back in his chair and groaned as he laced his fingers behind his head. "I don't know how, but he is stronger."

"Wait, can we back up?" I asked, still not understanding what happened. "Tell me what happened?"

"Very well," Theron said, sitting up and looking at me. "We waited for Alex and his arms dealer to enter the bar. Once they were inside we went in, one of us from each exit. Alex was surprised and tried to run when he saw us, but we had the upper hand. We had him pinned to the wall and were about to sedate him when your friend exploded into the room telling everyone to freeze because she works for Interpol. We let our guard down for an instant and the place was filled with bullet holes and Alex got away."

"We better check on Jean, knowing her she will try to leave." I got up and went to the door.

"Why not let her?" Helen asked, crossing her arms over her chest.

"Because she knows a lot about the head of the Cretan Syndicate and she works for Interpol." Vince got to his feet meeting me at the door.

"Christ Katie, you have the best friends," Theron said, leaning back in his chair again.

"Don't start, you're the one who let Alex stay at your place." I opened the door and flew down the hall to Jean's room with Vince at my side.

"That was a little harsh," Vince said, as we came to a stop outside her room.

"He started it." I knocked on Jean's door and when she didn't answer I went in. The room was a mess. Clothes and shoes littered the floor and Jean was sitting on the bed staring at her computer. "Are you OK?"

"I don't know, right now I need to find Alex," she said, sounding panicked.

"How?" I asked, moving her suitcase to the floor and sitting on the edge of the bed.

"I put a tracker on him earlier today." She turned the laptop around showing me a map with a blinking dot.

"That's Alex?" I asked as the dot slowly moved across the screen.

"Yeah, as long as he doesn't know he has it, we can find him." As soon as the words left her mouth, her face fell. "Damn it."

"What happened?" I tried to move around to see the screen.

"I lost him." Jean put the computer on the bed and went into the bathroom. "Everyone must hate me right now."

"They'll get over it," I said, following her. It was about half the size of ours, but it was still opulent with marble floors and counter, a soaker tub and walk-in shower. "I want to make sure your arm is OK. Do you need stitches?"

"No, yes, I don't know."

"Let Vince take a look at it. He's good at stitching people up, I don't even have a scar," I said, remembering the work he did on my neck after Lolita took a chunk out of me.

"You're not going to throw me in the dungeon or anything are you?"

"Where would you get an idea like that? I don't think this

house even has a basement." I looked to Vince raising my eyebrows.

"Jean, we want to help you, not imprison you. Let me make sure you will be OK. You don't want to get an infection, do you?"

Jean was standing facing us but looking in the mirror at her arm. We walked over, and I raised an eyebrow. "Come on, let me see it."

She huffed out a breath and turned giving us a view of an arm covered in blood. I heard Vince inhale sharply then took a washcloth from the counter and ran water on to it. "I can't see anything with all the blood in the way."

I moved to the other side of Jean and touched her arm as Vince cleaned away the blood. "Damn that stings."

"Just wait until I use the hydrogen peroxide." Vince chuckled.

"Do you want to tell me what you were doing now or wait until Vince finishes doctoring you up?" I asked, unable to keep my mouth shut. I wanted to go with the vampires and they wouldn't let me. I should have snuck out and followed them.

"Wait," Vince said, looking at the wound. "She needs stitches and I don't want her moving around while I sew. Can you go into our bathroom and grab the sewing kit out of my toilet kit please?"

"On it." I ran out of the room and to our suite. I went into the bathroom, found Vince's kit in a drawer, and pulled the sewing kit out. I ran back down the hallway to Jean's room and went straight to the bathroom. Jean was sitting on the counter and Vince was holding a gauze pad to her arm.

"Here you go," I said, handing the kit to Vince.

"Thank you, now Jean, you have to hold still." Vince opened the case and pulled out a needle and thread wrapped in a sterile packet.

"I'll do my best." She reached her hand out to me and I took it. I was mad as hell at her for ruining our chance of catching Alex, but she was my friend and injured, the least I could do was hold her hand while Vince sewed her up.

Ten minutes later, and after some grunting and screaming, Vince taped a gauze pad over Jean's arm. "Do not get this wet for twenty-four hours, or you risk infection." He got up, winked at me, then left us alone in the bathroom.

"I have to go Katie," Jean said, hopping off the counter and throwing her toiletries into her makeup bag.

"You aren't going anywhere." I stood by the open door and watched her.

"Am I a prisoner?" she asked, stopping and meeting my eyes.

"In a way. You know too much, and you work for freaking Interpol. Theron can't be arrested; do you understand what I'm saying?"

"You don't understand." Jean went back to putting her makeup in the bag.

"Tell me what's going on and I'll try." I crossed my arms over my chest as she zipped up her bag and tried to walk around me.

"I got an email from my boss, if I don't arrest someone in the next..." She stopped and looked at her watch. "Thirty-six hours they are going to tag me as a rogue."

"What does that mean?" I asked, I knew what the dictionary definition meant, but I didn't understand what it would mean to Interpol.

"It means I automatically go on the top ten most wanted list. You know how it feels to be hunted Katie, and you hid in Kevò. The problem is they know about Kevò, and I'm nowhere near ready to run from them." Jean's shoulders slumped. "I don't know what I'm going to do, but I can't stay here."

"Let me talk to Vince, we will figure something out."

"They won't help me Katie, look what I did tonight." Tears tracked down Jean's cheeks as she turned to me. "I don't have another choice."

"Just stay here, and let me see what I can do, OK?" I asked, backing toward the door.

"Thanks, Katie." Jean sat down on the bed and looked at the floor.

"I'll be back in a little while."

I looked around the room one last time and saw the window was cracked. Vasilis and Yannis were seated outside her door and stood up as I exited.

"Don't let her leave and make sure you keep an ear out for the window. I wouldn't put it past her to try to sneak out that way."

"Yes, ma'am," they said together as I strode down the hall to talk to Theron.

The last thing I wanted to do was deal with more of Jean's drama, but she was my friend and helped me when no one else would. I had to try to help her. I walked down the hall and used my vampire sense to find Vince and Theron. I walked into the office without knocking and found them huddled around the table.

"What are you doing?" I asked, joining them as they looked at a map of Crete.

"Making sure Alex can't leave the island." Theron all but growled. "Thanks to your friend we have to start over."

"About that, I know why she did it." I took a chair and watched them.

"Why does it matter?" Theron asked, not bothering to look at me while he talked.

"Because she's terrified and if we don't find a way to help her, I think we could end up being in more trouble than we already are." I crossed my arms over my chest and waited for the men to pay attention.

"Please, enlighten me," Theron said looking up from the map and mimicking my posture.

"She tried to steal Alex from you because she got an email from her handler. If she doesn't turn someone over in the next two days, they will mark her rogue."

"Again, why should that matter to us?" Vince asked, sitting in the chair next to me. "She has been nothing but a thorn in our side since she

181

arrived on Crete."

"Do you know what happens when Interpol marks someone as rogue?" I waited for them to shake their heads before continuing. "They are automatically put on the top ten most wanted list. Which means instead of having one person with a bounty, you'll have two. Beyond that, if she manages to give us the slip, she might be forced to turn you in to save her own life."

"Fuck," Theron said, running his hands through his hair in frustration.

"At least we know why she tried to arrest Alex," Vince said, leaning back in his chair.

"How do we help her?" Theron asked with a tight voice. His emotions were contrasting, he was mad at her, but there was guilt too, and I didn't understand why.

"I think the only thing her handler will accept is turning someone in on the most wanted list." I had no idea where we would find someone who did something bad enough to satisfy Interpol.

Theron's phone vibrated on the desk and he moved the map to answer it. "Serafeim, sorry we left so abruptly, is everything all right?"

I watched Theron's face as he listened, he wore a mask of indifference, but his feelings were a rollercoaster. It started with anger, then spun around to pity, before giddiness took over. "I think we can help each other with this, but it won't be easy." Theron motioned for us to leave and, as much as I wanted to stay, I knew he had work to do.

I left the office with Vince on my tail. I was still mad I missed out on all the fun and I needed a shower. I was in the middle of my workout when I saw the headlights coming down the drive. The sweat had since dried to my skin, and I felt sticky.

"Katie, wait where are you going?" Vince called from behind me.

I stopped and looked at him. "I'm going to take a shower. I'm covered in sweat, why?"

"Can we talk when you are done?" His voice was soft, and his eyes were hooded.

"Sure." I turned and continued down the hall. So many things had been happening, it felt like we never had any time together.

After I showered, I looked over my new wardrobe. I was done for the night, so I put on one of Vince's button-down shirts that I stole from his closet the day before. It was almost like wearing a dress since it hung just above my knees. Once I was dressed, I found Vince in our sitting room reading a book. "How's the book?"

"Good, I started it years ago and never found the time to finish it. I thought it would help ease my mind tonight." He put his bookmark in, closed the book, then set it on the end table. He crossed his legs and laced his fingers together around his knee. "I worry about you Katie. I have taught you to fight and fight well, but I will never stop worrying when you talk about going after Lolita or Alex."

"I know, you don't think I worry about the same with you?" I sat on the couch and pulled my legs under me. "Vince, if you don't believe in me, I have a hard time believing in myself."

"Oh, Katie, I believe in you. Your ability to beat Lolita is not where my concern lies, you are ready to face her. I worry because no one can anticipate all the variables and if she gets the upper hand, I do not know what I will do without you. I love you as I have never loved anyone in my life." He looked down at his hands then straightened. "I will not keep you from going after Lolita, but do you understand why we did not want you to come with us tonight?"

"Yes, you didn't want to have to worry about me while trying to take Alex down. I understand, but I am just as much a part of this team as Helen and Theron. I want to be included. You need to treat me as you would treat them. I don't need to be protected from everything." I was tired of being treated like some fragile antique that needed to be handled with care. "I'm a

183

big girl and you taught me to look out for myself. Do you think I would've been able to escape Alex in Athens or on the boat without the training you gave me?"

"No, but you have to admit you were lucky to find Ramstein."

"Yes, believe me, I know how lucky I was, but I had plans, I would have been homeless, but I would've been safe."

"The thought of you living on the streets terrifies me almost as much as Alex getting his hands on you." Vince let go of his knee, uncrossed his legs, and leaned forward to rest his elbows on his knees.

"Like you said, I was lucky. I have enough aliases now, if I want to disappear I can, and I won't be living on the streets." I uncrossed my legs and mimicked Vince's pose. "Are you going to let me take on Lolita?"

He sat up and ran his hands through his hair. "Goddess, I don't want to, but I know there is no way of stopping you."

"Good, I love you Vince." I got up and went to him. I leaned forward and kissed him. He grabbed me around the waist and pulled me into his lap.

"I love you too, my queen."

## Chapter 26
### *Jean*

Jean was sitting on her bed, well not her bed, but the bed she was using while she stayed with Katie. Her computer was in her lap and she stared at an email from her handler. She felt like crying, how was she going to tell her she came up empty-handed? She was the reason Alex escaped, and now nothing could stop her from being declared a rogue agent. She huffed out a breath and hit the reply button, with a blank message screen in front of her, Jean debated on whether she should tell her handler she failed. Maybe she should ditch the computer and live her life in the shadows.

She looked up when there was a soft knock on the door. "Go away, there is nothing you can do to help me now," she said, thinking it was Katie.

"I'm sorry Miss, but Theron would like to see you in his office," Yannis said, poking his head around the door.

Jean sighed and closed the lid on her computer. She rose to her feet stiffly, her arm throbbed, and she felt like she had been running with Katie. She never wanted to see the inside of a trunk again. She followed Yannis down the hall to Theron's office, feeling like she was walking to her death. She almost laughed, she was worried about how she would live if she was tagged a rogue, when she should've been thinking about how she would escape the mansion. Yannis stopped outside the door to Theron's office and knocked.

"Come in," Theron's voice said from the other side of the door. He was all business as Jean expected. She wondered if begging would work, or if a stiff upper lip would allow her to keep her life. The head of the Cretan Syndicate would not take being made a fool of lightly.

Yannis opened the door, held it for her and used his head to wave her inside. Jean stood there for a second frozen in place. She was terrified of what Theron might do to her.

"Jean, stop being stubborn and come in," Theron called from his desk.

Jean took a breath and let it out slowly, this was her mess and she was never one to leave things untidy, if it meant her life on this earth was over then so be it. She could take whatever Theron dished out. She took a step, then another, trying not to think of the ways Theron could torture her, until she was in his office and standing in front of his desk. She hardened her features and stood with her legs a little apart and her hands at her sides. "You wanted to see me?" she asked, trying to make her voice strong and confident, and she almost made it, it only trembled a little.

"Yes, please have a seat." Theron gestured to the seat behind her while keeping his face the picture of neutrality.

Jean looked around, hoping Katie would be there for emotional support, but she was alone with the head of the Cretan mafia and there was nothing that could save her from his punishment. "Thanks, but I'll stand," Jean said, turning back to face Theron and lacing her hands behind her back to keep herself from fidgeting.

"Very well." Theron leaned back in his chair and looked at the ceiling. "It has come to my attention that what you did tonight was not to further your career as I originally thought, but to keep yourself from being branded a rogue agent. Is this correct?"

Jean nodded her head, she couldn't believe Katie ratted her out. "Yes, when I learned about the ultimatum it was too late to call you back, and I knew you wouldn't give me Alex, so I had to go with my own plan."

"A plan that failed miserably and caused us both pain." Theron looked at her shoulder and she registered the blood on his shirt for the first time.

"Hindsight's twenty-twenty," Jean said, relaxing her arms. If he was going to blame her she was going to defend herself, not roll over like a beaten dog.

"As you say, nonetheless, I'm faced with a problem." Theron locked his eyes with hers, it almost felt like he was trying to work his way into her mind. "It's hard enough keeping Katie safe with the price on her head, I don't think I could keep you safe even if I had the men I had before the attack on my compound, and Katie wasn't here."

Jean narrowed her eyes at him. "I'll be fine on my own, you don't have to worry about me. I'll be gone before the sun comes up."

"What if there was a solution to your problem?" Theron asked, leaning forward and resting his elbows on the desk.

"Unless you want to let me turn you in, there is no solution. My handler wants someone on the most wanted list." Jean crossed her arms over her chest, confused. Why did he want to help her? He made it plain from the beginning that he didn't want her there. This was his chance to get rid of her for good.

"I will never be arrested, but that is beside the point. I know of someone who, while not on the most wanted list, is still wanted by Interpol and his father wants to teach him a lesson." Theron folded his hands together.

"You're saying this guy's dad wants him thrown in jail?" Jean took a step back, it was a new definition of tough love.

"Yes, and all you have to do is find him and arrest him. You'll have all the help you desire from myself and Serafeim."

"Why are you doing this?"

He let out an audible breath, ran a hand through his hair, and stared at his desk while putting his thoughts together. "You are in this situation because of me. You wanted to leave when Katie arrived, and I wouldn't let you. If you had, you wouldn't be where you are now. I want to make sure you have every opportunity to live your life. If Interpol makes you rogue, I don't think you will last long."

"Thanks for the vote of confidence," Jean huffed and stared at the ground. He was trying to help her, but only because he thought it was his fault she was in this mess. "What do you have on this guy? Is there a chance he's still on the island?"

Theron's mask cracked, and he smiled as he turned his laptop around for her to see. "Everything you need is in this file. The island is on lockdown for the rest of the night, there's a storm coming in that will stop all commercial traffic from leaving and his father has taken care of everything else. What do you need from me?"

"I need this file," Jean said, pulling a chair closer to the desk and sitting. She paged through the information about Grigoris: where he lived, who he fucked, where he liked to hang out. "I need a recent picture too." Jean chewed on her bottom lip as she continued to read.

"Very well, if you give me back my computer, I'll email everything to you, then you can track him from the comfort of your own room," Theron's voice grew tight and Jean snapped her head up.

"Sorry," she said, pushing the computer back to him. "And thank you for helping me. I'm sorry about what happened tonight. I want to catch Alex just as much as you do."

"I know, but, next time, let's work together. If you would have told me what was going on at Interpol, we could have figured something out to help you." Theron's voice softened, and he looked at Jean with his eyes half-lidded, until he blinked, and put his mask back in place. "You can go now, I will send this to you in a moment."

Jean stood robotically and left the room. She thought they

were working on being friends, he sounded like he cared for a second but then it was gone. She shook her head as she walked back down the hall to her room with Yannis trailing behind her. Why did she care if they were friends or not?

## Chapter 27
### *Katie*

I rolled my head from side to side and closed my eyes; I had been staring at the computer for hours. Jean and Theron had a plan to get Interpol off her back, but for the plan to work we had to find Grigoris and, so far, we found nothing. I looked over at Jean; she was out like a light. It didn't surprise me; she hadn't slept since she was at The Sanctuary and who knows how long ago that was. I looked at my watch; it was four in the morning and I needed sleep which was probably the reason why we couldn't find the bastard; he was sleeping too.

I set my cameras to record, then went over to Jean and slid her computer off her lap. I covered her in a blanket then set her cameras to record. I tiptoed to the door, opened it, flipped the light off and closed it behind me.

"Katie?" Theron asked, coming from his office. "What are you doing up? It's late."

"I was helping Jean, but now I need sleep." I yawned and stretched my arms over my head.

"No sign of Grigoris?"

"No, he's probably sleeping." I leaned against the wall to keep from falling over.

"True, did Jean hear back from her handler?" Theron asked, moving to lean on the wall opposite of me.

"Yes, she said, *we will see*, which stressed Jean out even more. If she can't get an affirmative that catching this guy will get her out of trouble she is wondering what the point is."

"What's she doing now?"

"Sleeping. All the cameras are recording, and we loaded his picture into the facial recognition software, maybe we should get a hit in a few hours."

"Very well, goodnight Katie."

"Night." When I reached our suite, I stripped, then went into the bedroom. I was too tired to wash my face and brush my teeth I needed sleep. I approached the bed silently and was about to climb in when I noticed Vinny was in my spot. Vince had one arm around him and was snoring softly. Who would've thought vampires could snore?

Vinny picked his head up and thumped his tail on the mattress when he saw me. I held my hand up in a stop gesture telling him to stay. I quietly made my way to the bed and pointed to the end of it. Vinny wiggled out from under Vince's arm and belly crawled to the end of the bed. I slid into where he had been, and Vince pulled my back against his chest.

"I didn't think you would ever come to bed," he whispered in my hair.

"You're awake?" I asked, leaning into him, my mind already half asleep.

"Vinny's tail," he said as an explanation.

"So, you were cuddling with him on purpose?" I asked, really wanting to go to sleep, but I couldn't pass up the opportunity to poke fun at the love of my life.

"He was getting your spot warm, and what can I say? He isn't as bad as I thought he was. Go to sleep, love."

"I'm already halfway there. I love you," I said before my mind relaxed and sleep took me.

There were vampires everywhere, they were barely clothed and looked starved. They were beating at the walls of a courtyard, trying to escape their prison, but they were too weak to jump over the wall or dig under it. I could feel their hunger and was surprised they weren't feasting on each other. As if one could read my mind he took the vampire next to him in his arms and bit down on its neck. The vampire screamed in pain and tried to push the one drinking away, but he only succeeded in drawing the attention of the other vampires. Seconds later, there was a crowd of vampires biting and drinking wherever they could find a spot of bare skin.

The one who had begun the frenzy pulled away and let out a bellow. He looked at the wall and jumped. He sailed to the top and looked around at the sea surrounding him. His nose went to the night sky, and he inhaled loudly before jumping off the wall and going to the water's edge. He looked over his shoulder, pausing for a second, before he waded into the water and swam to the nearest land. I looked back over the wall, more of the starved vampires jumped the wall and took off after him. They were free, and they were hungry. They were going to feast in Venice.

I sat up in my bed and looked around. Vince was lying next to me, and I was safe. But the dream. A war was coming whether Lolita started it or not. "Vince." I shook his shoulder as I spoke. His eyes popped open.

"What is it? What is wrong?" Vince sat up and pulled me into his arms.

"Lolita's army is hungry, if they find a way to escape the island there will be no stopping them." My voice sounded faraway and goose bumps covered my skin.

"You had a dream?" Vince asked, pulling me back so my head rested on his chest and he pulled the covers over us.

"Yes, the vampires were too weak to get over the wall, but one of them drank from another and he jumped the wall then swam toward Venice, others followed him." I was shaking in fear, fear I would only let Vince see. Vinny whined from the floor then jumped on the bed and stuck his nose in my face. I ran my fingers through his soft fur, absorbing his heat. "Vinny, I love you but get down." I snapped my fingers and pointed to the ground. He jumped down but stayed close by.

"Do you know when this will happen or if it already has?" Vince asked, rubbing his cheek across the top of my head.

"No, but you might want to check on Miguel, he might have a better idea of what's going on in Venice."

"I will contact him today. We have not received an update from him in quite some time." Vince put the arm that wasn't around me over his head and rested it against the headboard. "Are you going back to sleep or getting up?"

"Getting up. I need to pee, then I need to get my workout in before I help Jean look for Grigoris." I pulled out of Vince's arms and went into the bathroom. The dream was still freaking me out, and my hand shook so badly while I was brushing my teeth I almost didn't have to move the brush up and down. I closed my eyes and breathed, there was nothing I could do about Lolita's army right now. I needed to let it go, we would deal with her soon enough. When I came out of the bathroom Vince was still in bed and Vinny had weaseled his way next to him.

"Enjoy sleeping in boys," I said, slinging my katana behind my back and taking off for the ballroom.

I ran laps to warm up and my thoughts drifted to the conversation I had with Vince the night before. I wondered what it would take for Vince to let me be the person I was destined to become. I had to fight Lolita, not to prove to him or anyone else that I was Asteria's daughter, but to get my life back. I thought of the picture of my dad going to work. He looked so sad and withered. What would he do when I could finally call him? Would he go back to his old self? I still couldn't find a photo of my mom and I worried about her. With the way my dad looked, there was no way my mom was looking any better. It was time to stop hiding from Lolita and end this, if only so I could talk to my parents and tell them I was all right. Done with my warm-up, I cleared my head of all my worries, and worked through my forms.

After I finished, I went upstairs to the kitchen and found Jean sitting at the bar eating cereal. I went to the fridge and pulled out a bottle of water. I chugged the bottle before turning and looking at her. "How's the arm?" I asked, leaning on the bar across from her.

"It hurts, but not bad. Vince is really good at sewing people up."

"Yeah, he has a talent for it." I didn't know what else to say. "Any luck finding Grigoris?"

"We didn't get any hits on the facial recognition software, but I haven't started going through all the video, hopefully I'll find something there." She looked down at the counter. "How's Theron? He was shot. Did Vince sew him up too?"

I blinked, almost forgetting I watched Helen pull the bullet out of his shoulder the night before. "He'll be fine, Helen pulled the bullet out and Vince doctored him." I wished I could tell her what was really going on.

Her head dropped, and she sniffled. "I'm sorry, I guess there's a reason I'm not in the field." She looked up with bloodshot eyes, her face glistening from the tears falling from her eyes.

"You don't have to save the world on your own. We have to work as a team if we are going to prevent the war." I went back to the fridge as I felt Helen approach and took out the carton of orange juice.

"Good morning," Helen said, taking a seat next to Jean as I pulled out a glass and filled it.

"Morning," I tried to sound happy, but my voice came out flat.

"Aren't you just a ray of sunshine," Helen said, folding her hands together.

"Sorry, long night, bad dreams." I gave her a look telling her it was more than just a bad dream.

"Is there anything to be done?" she asked and glanced at Jean from the corner of her eye.

"No, not right now. We just need to continue with the plan."

"I had a weird dream too," Jean said in a faraway voice. "Zombies were trying to get over a wall then they swam to Venice. Wait, Katie, they were on the island where we found Lolita." Her eyes went wide and Helen looked from Jean to me.

*Is that what you dreamt?* Helen asked, surprising me, she'd never thought to me on purpose before. I nodded my head. "Sorry you had a bad dream, dear. I had better go check on Theron." She slid off the stool and, without waiting for a reply, was down the hall knocking on the door to Theron's office.

"Do you have dreams like that a lot?" I asked, fishing for information.

"Not like this. It was so real. It was terrifying."

"Do your dreams ever come true?" It was scary enough that we had both had the same dream, but the thought of the vampires escaping Lolita's island had me shaking with fear.

"Yeah, but not very often."

"Katie, can you come in here please?" Helen asked from the doorway of Theron's office.

"Yeah, I'll be right there." I put my glass in the sink then turned back to Jean. "Don't worry, it was just a dream. Zombies aren't real." I turned without waiting for her reply and almost ran to Theron's office.

"You had the same dream," Helen said from her seat in front of Theron's desk once I was inside with the door closed.

"Yes, only they were vampires not zombies, but I understand her reference, they looked like zombies."

"Who is this girl? How is she able to share your dream?" Theron asked, slamming his hand down on the table.

"When I first met her, she said she dreamed of her father. He told her someone new would come to Kevó and she should be friends with her. That person was me." I paced around the room unable to settle myself.

"Did she have any other dreams while she was in Kevó?" Helen asked, watching me pace.

"No, that's the thing about Kevó, it's a dead zone. The Gods don't know what's going on there, they can't reach us. I didn't dream of my mother once. When I was unconscious on the boat with Alex, Asteria freaked out, she thought I was dead because she couldn't feel me."

"Are you saying that Jean has a connection to the Gods?" Theron asked, leaning back in his chair.

"I don't know, but she had the same dream I did last night. If those vampires get loose, there will be a war whether or not Lolita lives. No matter what we do we need to contain her army."

"We will rally support at the party. When the vampires see what you can do, they will help us, either out of loyalty or fear of war."

"I hope you're right." I stood to leave. "I need to go help Jean find Grigoris."

"Do you think she'll find him?" Theron asked, concern flooding his system. He made a promise to Serafeim and needed to make sure he could follow through on it.

"Yes, she's the one who found Lolita," I said, turning toward the door. "I bet we have him before lunchtime."

"I found him," Jean said a few hours later as she stretched her arms above her head. We were in the sitting room of the master suite combing video feeds.

"Where is he?" I asked, jumping from my seat and running over to her computer.

"He's in downtown, he's trying to hide from the cameras but that's him, the program pinged him." Jean typed like she had ten minutes to turn in her term paper and a thousand words to go.

"What do we do now?" I asked, standing behind her and watching her type. I had no idea how to arrest someone.

"Now we watch him, see where he goes, and what he's doing."

"I'll go get Theron," I said, walking toward the door.

"Can't we do this without him?" Jean asked, looking up from the screen with fear in her eyes.

"He knows this island better than anyone. He'll know the best way for you to arrest Grigoris." I opened the door.

"Fine, I'll keep an eye on him," Jean said, bending back to the screen.

I ran down the hall to Theron's office and went in without knocking. "Jean found him," I said, looking around and finding Theron standing in front of a mirror with only a suit jacket on and a man on his knees facing him. "Oh, sorry, I didn't know you were busy." My face turned crimson, and I turned around ready to run from the room.

Theron laughed at my discomfort. "Katie, this is my tailor. Nothing more." Theron turned to the side allowing me to see an old man with pins in his mouth and bushy eyebrows behind a set of wire-rim glasses.

"Oh, OK. Well, when you're done here we need to talk."

"I'll be there in a half hour. Tell Jean good job for me, will you?" Theron gave me a fake smile.

"Yeah, sure." I turned and walked down the hall back to my suite while finding Vince with my mind. *We found him.*

*Great, I will meet you in our suite. Did you tell Theron?* Vince replied from the ballroom. He was supervising the party planner Agapios sent over.

*Yes, he'll join us when his tailor is done.* I opened the door to my suite and looked at Jean who was clicking back and forth between pages. "Did you lose him?" I asked going over to her.

"No, kind of. He got into a car and drove away. I'm trying to follow him with traffic cameras but there aren't enough of them to keep up." Jean sounded frustrated.

"Did you get the license plate?" I asked, picking my computer up and moving to sit next to her on the couch.

"Yes, but what good will that do us? If we call it in stolen, the police will get credit for catching him, not me."

She had a point. "It's too bad the facial recognition software couldn't do the same thing with license plates," I said, thinking out loud.

Jean looked up at me with a slacked jaw. "It can, or it could easily enough." Jean got up from the couch and moved to the only desk in the room.

"What are you doing?" I moved to stand behind her.

"I'm creating another program, piggybacking off the facial recognition, only this one will read license plates. There's probably already one on the market, but this will be easier. Jean opened a window filled with code and began typing.

"Where is the bastard?" Theron asked, not bothering to knock before coming in and looking over Jean's shoulder. "Did you lose him?"

"Kind of," I said, pulling Theron away from Jean. No one liked it when someone watched them type. "He got into a car and drove off. There aren't enough traffic cameras to keep tabs on him. Jean is rewriting the facial recognition software to look for plates."

"We could just call the car into the police." Theron crossed his arms over his chest.

"And let them arrest him? Then Jean wouldn't get credit. Kind of defeats the purpose, doesn't it?" I asked, cocking an eyebrow at Theron.

"You're right, I'm not used to dealing with all these rules. If there is something I want, I take it."

"This will work, Jean is amazing at this stuff," I said as the door opened, and Vince walked in.

"Where is he?" Vince asked, and I rolled my eyes.

Once I finished telling him everything, Jean finished the program and was running a search. "There he is," Jean yelled to get our attention.

"Where?" We all asked at once.

"He is leaving Heraklion on the coastal road." Jean turned around in her chair and looked surprised to see Theron and Vince standing next to me. "What do we do now?"

"This is your party, what do you think we should do?" Theron asked, relaxing and taking a seat on the couch facing Jean.

Jean looked excited and nervous, I hope she didn't throw up on the rug, it would be a pain to clean. "Well, we could cut him off and force him out of the car, but we want him alive, right? His dad doesn't want him dead, just to be taught a lesson."

"Right." Theron leaned back and rested his right ankle on his left knee.

"We wait until he settles in for the night, then we take him."

"Good plan," Vince said, sitting in the chair next to Vinny and reaching down to scratch between his ears.

"Let me know where he ends up and we'll go from there." Theron stood and walked to the door. "In the meantime, I have work to do."

Jean watched Theron leave while the smile she had a moment ago faded. She looked at me then Vince. "Well I'm going to go back to my room and keep an eye out. I'll let you know when I find him." Jean stood, grabbed the charger for her computer, and stalked out of the room.

"At least we are getting somewhere," I said, sitting on the couch next to Vince and resting my head on his shoulder.

"Yes, I would hate for you to lose your friend." Vince put his hand on my thigh. "You look tired, do you want to take a nap?"

"Yeah, it was a long night." I slowly got to my feet and looked down at him. "Do you want to join me?"

"I would, but I have to meet with the tailor now that Theron is done with him."

"A new suit?"

"Yes, we all need to look our best for the party." He stood next to me and took me into his arms. "You don't even have to try though. You could wear your workout clothes, and no one would be able to take their eyes off you." He bent his head and brought his lips to mine for too brief a moment.

"Kissing a little ass, are we?" I asked when he pulled away.

"Is it working?" He gave me half a smile.

"Maybe, we will see what happens later." I walked to the door of our bedroom. "I love you, Vince."

"And I you, have a good nap."

"Have fun with the tailor between your legs," I said, trying not to laugh as I left him to crawl into bed.

*Vangel is here.* I had been sleeping so hard I was surprised a thought from Vince could wake me. Once I comprehended what he thought I sat up.

*On my way,* I thought back, getting up and dressing in one of the new suits Helen had ordered for me. It was blood-red, and slim-fitting. I wore a black silk shell and my heels with it. I checked myself in the mirror before I left and couldn't believe I was the same person. The woman staring back at me in the mirror reminded me of a CEO of a huge company, not a college graduate trying to stop an army of vampires taking over Europe.

I shook myself and hurried into the sitting room, realizing I forgot to tell Jean that Vangel was coming with everything else going on. I had no idea how she would react, but it was too late now. *Where are you?* I asked, pulling a water bottle out of the mini fridge and leaving our suite.

*The great room, what is taking so long?* Vince asked, stressed about something.

*I had to get dressed, chill out.*

When I reached the great room Vince and Vangel were standing a few feet apart with their hands on their hips saying nothing. "Vangel, hi," I said, a little louder than necessary. His head jerked and when he saw me he smiled.

"KK, we thought you were dead." He moved to me and wrapped me in a hug before I could stop him. I lightly patted his back not taking my eyes off Vince.

*Just friends?* Vince thought, crossing his arms over his chest. He was pissed, I didn't think I'd ever felt him this upset.

*Yes, just friends. I hug Theron and you don't get mad,* I thought back to him before pulling away from Vangel. "I'm sorry, I should've contacted you sooner, life has been a little crazy." I took a step back.

"Where's Uni? Hound told me she emailed him saying she was staying with you." Vangel asked, his eyes looking skeptical.

"She is in her room working on a project." I went to Vince's side and took his hand in mine, even though he didn't hold mine back. *Jealous much?* I thought to him. "I take it you've met Vince."

"Yes, he's the lover you thought was dead, correct?" he asked, folding his arms across his chest.

"Yes, please let's sit down. You guys look like you are about to tear each other's throats out." I tugged on Vince's hand and dragged him to the couch. I sat and pulled on him until he sat next to me while Vangel sat down across from us.

"Vince, Vangel's the one who helped with the asshole who tried to take me to Lolita," I said, trying to ease Vince's anger and jealousy. *Would you calm down?*

*He hugged you like you were more than friends*, his eyes shot to me before looking back at Vangel. "Thank you for helping Katie get away from the man," Vince said in a tight voice.

"Yeah, no problem." Vangel leaned back on the couch and took in Vince. "So, KK, you need a bodyguard. Is Vince too busy to keep you safe?"

*He is, and was, nothing but a friend. I think he's trying to get your hackles up. You have nothing to worry about. I'm still going to bed with you at the end of the night,* I thought to Vince. "Yes, Vince's work keeps him indoors most of the day. Uni and I have already had to deal with one sniper, and I'm tired of being stuck in the house."

"I see, well I think I can take care of you while Vince is busy working." Vangel put one leg over the other.

"Katie, I think I found him," Jean said, coming into the room and stopping in her tracks as she saw the back of Vangel's head.

Vangel jumped to his feet and turned when he heard Jean's voice. "Unicorn, there you are. Thanks for letting me know where you were. I had to find out from Hound."

"Well, I wanted to make sure Katie made it here safe, I didn't do a very good job though." She shrugged and gave Vangel a hug.

Jean's eyes shot daggers at me as she looked at me from over Vangel's shoulder. He pulled back and looked her up and down. "I'm glad you're all right."

"Yeah, I needed a break from everything back in Kevó." Jean bounced from foot to foot.

"Jean, just tell him. He isn't going to hate you and you've done nothing wrong," I said, putting my hand on Vince's leg trying to calm him. Between Jean and Vince, the tension in the room was so thick, I would need a chain saw to cut it.

"Tell me what?" Vangel asked, pulling Jean to the couch and forcing her to sit next to him. "I take it Jean is your real name."

"Yeah," she looked at Vangel then turned to me. "Thanks for throwing me under the bus Katie," Jean muttered, staring at her hands before looking up at Vangel. "What I am about to tell you is classified information. Tad knows and allowed me to stay so please keep that in mind." Jean took a deep breath and let it out. "I work for Interpol, I was assigned to Kevó to report back any and all nefarious acts that go on there."

Vangel jumped to his feet and ran his hands through his hair. He looked ready to kill someone, probably Jean after what he had been through with his wife. "Wait, you said Tad knows?"

"Yes, and he allowed me to send back reports that would not

jeopardize the town. I was a double agent Vangel. I love Kevò and everyone there, except for maybe Mordor. I would never do anything to hurt Kevò."

"And I can confirm this with Tad?"

"Yes."

"Why didn't you come back?" Vangel paced around the room shooting glances at Jean every few seconds.

"Because I was tired of Kevò, I wanted to be a field agent and catch bad guys not report back on the good things the people in Kevò do."

"What are you doing now? Reporting to your bosses on what *good* things The Syndicate does?"

"No." Jean scrambled to her feet. I had to smile, she didn't want anyone to think she would turn them in. "I'm trying to get out of Interpol."

"Why?" Vangel crossed his arms over his chest.

"Because they are too black-and-white for me. There are no shades of gray with them, and I learned through Kevò and Katie that there needs to be. Plus, I'm tired of sitting behind a computer all day."

"How do you get out of Interpol? I'm guessing you can't just tell them you quit."

"No, that's what we're working on right now. There's an arms dealer on the island that needs to be taken care of. We almost had him last night, but I messed everything up."

"Tell me what happened."

Vince and Jean told Vangel what happened while I sat listening to the story again. I balled my hands into fists when I thought about how close they'd been to capturing Alex. There was nothing we could do about it except try again, but it was frustrating. When they finished telling the story Vangel shook his head.

"Well Jean, I hope you learned your lesson. How are we

going to find this Grigoris guy?" Vangel sat back down next to Jean.

"We are tracking him, waiting for him to settle down, then we will arrest him," Jean said.

"Katie?" Helen called from not far away.

"We're in the great room," I called, remembering to raise my voice even though she could hear me if I whispered.

"I thought you were in your room," Helen said, coming into the room, and halting when she saw Vangel. "I didn't realize we had company." She smoothed down the front of her suit jacket.

"Helen, this is Vangel, Katie's bodyguard," Vince said with his lips pressed so tightly together that I was amazed we could understand him.

Vangel got to his feet and offered her his hand. "Nice to meet you Helen." She gave him her hand, and they shook.

"Nice to meet you too." Helen couldn't take her eyes off him. I'd never seen her anything but calm and collected. Sometimes I thought she must have seen everything in the world and there was nothing left that would surprise her. "You helped Katie when she was in Kevó, correct?"

"Yes, I taught her how to use guns and helped her with a guy who wanted to take her to Lolita." He let go of her hand and put his hands on his hips.

"Thank you, she is a very special person to us." Helen folded her hands together and let them hang.

"Yeah, she is pretty special to us back in Kevó too. Hey, where's Vinny?" he asked, looking around. "I thought the dog never left your side."

"He's outside," I said, getting up and going to the back door. "Vinny, come, someone is here to see you," I called after opening the door. Vinny ran up the steps to the veranda and bounded inside. He went straight to Vangel, sat down, then offered him his paw.

"Hi Vinny, it's good to see you." Vangel shook Vinny's paw then scratched him behind the ears. "Are you taking good care of Katie?"

"He is. You should have seen him when the sniper tried to get us, he pulled me down, so I hit the ground before the bullet could hit me, then I let him go and he barked all the way back to the mansion making all the dogs in the neighborhood bark to let people know something was wrong, but then the poor guy got his paws cut up by glass."

"Trouble just follows you around doesn't it?" he asked still giving Vinny love.

"Only for the past year or so. Helen, do you want to show Vangel to his room? I'm sure he's ready to unpack and get settled."

"What?" She looked at me startled like she couldn't believe I would leave Vangel alone with her. "Of course, if you'll follow me." Helen waved toward the hallway leading to his room. "I'll be right back."

"I need to keep an eye on Grigios, I don't want him to get away," Jean said, backing toward the hall.

"Let me know when you have a plan," I said, wishing I would get to help her, but I doubted anyone would let me go with them when it was time to make the arrest.

Vince and I sat in silence while we waited for Helen to get back. Vince was humming with anger and jealousy and I didn't see the point in talking to him about it until he relaxed.

"Right, I was coming to see if you want to visit my dress designer tomorrow night," Helen said, coming back into the room.

"Oh, I thought I was just going to buy a dress," I said, feeling awkward. Why did I need someone to design a dress for me?

"You are going to make yourself known to the vampires of Europe. You will be making a statement and an off-the-rack dress isn't the kind of statement you want to make." Helen tsked as she glanced back down the hall where Vangel had gone.

"Vince, is it OK with you if I leave the mansion with Helen tomorrow night?" I looked over at him daring him to say no.

"If you are out with Helen, and take your bodyguard, I do not see why there would be a problem."

"So now you're OK with Vangel?" I asked, shaking my head.

Helen looked between us then back towards the hall. "Good, now that it's settled I need to find Natalia, she's helping me with the party plans." She turned and streaked out of the room.

Once Helen was gone, I turned and stared at Vince, waiting for an answer. "That is why we brought him here, right?" Vince asked, pulling his arms over his chest, locking his emotions down and putting his sensei mask on.

"Jealous much?" He hadn't hidden his feelings from me since I finished my training and I wasn't sure what to do.

"You are right he looks like me. It looks like the two of you are close," Vince said, turning his head to make eye contact with me.

"Not really, although dealing with Mordor probably brought us closer."

"I get a weird feeling from him. Are you sure you can trust him?"

"Yes, he didn't turn me over to her once, why would he now? Plus, his wife changed sides and tried to kill him. He is very loyal after what she did to him."

"And you say you're not close. If he told you about his traitor wife, you must have spent some time together."

"We were both lonely and missing our dead loved ones. We talked, he taught me how to use guns, and I showed him a few things with the katana. That was it. Why would I lie to you?" I asked, running my hand through his hair.

"You let him use your katana?" Vince's nostrils flared, and he pulled away from me.

"I would never let anyone else use my sword." I slapped my hand down on my leg so hard it stung. "You need to figure your shit out Vince. You're the only one for me. I don't know how many times I have to say it. Vangel is a friend, he will never be more." I got up and went out to the yard to play with Vinny. I needed some time to myself.

## Chapter 28
### *Jean*

Jean checked the images again. There was nothing, she knew he was somewhere on the coastal road between Heraklion and the next small town, but there weren't any cameras between the two places. She checked the map, there weren't any side roads he could have taken, there weren't any houses on the road and the terrain was too steep to go off-road. *Where did he go?* she asked herself when someone knocked on the door.

"Come in," she said, clicking back to the tracking software to see if it had come up with anything new.

"Have you found him?" Theron asked, looking around the room.

Jean cringed at the state of her room. Clothes and shoes were scattered everywhere. She was going to clean it up, but she wanted to find Grigoris first. "No, he is somewhere between Palaiokastro and Theseus." Jean tensed, she didn't like being alone with Theron. She wasn't afraid of him, but she felt guilty for messing everything up for him and didn't know how to fix it.

Theron's eyes narrowed. "How long has it been since you lost him?"

"A couple of hours, why, do you know where he is?"

"I have a good idea, get ready, we'll leave as soon as the sun goes down." Theron spun and left the room without another word. Jean watched the closed door half expecting him to come back. When he didn't, she looked at her watch. She had an hour to get ready, she closed her computer and looked around for her black jeans.

"Uni, can I come in?" Vangel asked as he knocked on her door.

"Yeah, come on in and call me Jean," she said, crouching on the floor and looking under the bed. *There they are*, she thought pulling the jeans out and getting to her feet. She went to her half-filled suitcase and pulled out a black turtle neck and put it on the bed with the jeans.

"Did you find him?" Vangel asked, looking around the room with a half-smile on his face.

"No, but Theron thinks he knows where he is." She picked up one of her black combat boots then spun in a circle trying to locate the other one. "Do you want to come?"

"I was just going to ask you." He smiled then picked up the boot she was looking for. "What should I bring?"

"I don't know. I'm bringing my side arm, but only because it's the only gun I have." She went to the bed, sat and looked at her hands. What was she going to do if she failed?

"Jean, what's going on? I've never seen you this freaked out." Vangel sat on the bed across from her.

"If I fail, if I can't bring this guy in, they are going to label me rogue. Do you know what that means?" Her voice cracked, and she kept her eyes open to keep herself from crying.

"Yes, but you can't act like you have already failed. You have to believe you can do it. It's not like you are going in alone. You have me, Theron, Helen, Vince, and Katie. If the six of us can't bring him down, then we will find another way."

"I don't think Katie and Vince are coming. Vince hasn't let Katie out of the house since the sniper."

"Well that doesn't mean we will fail, hell, you have the head of the Cretan mob helping you, that has to count for something." Vangel put a hand on her shoulder and shook her. "You've got this."

"Thanks for believing in me," Jean said, looking up and

210

giving him a smile. "I have no idea what we might need. I guess you can bring whatever you want."

"OK, I'll go get ready. When do we leave?"

"At sundown." Saying it out loud gave Jean an ominous feeling. Like it might be her last chance to watch the sun set on this earth.

"I'll be ready when you are."


An hour later, Jean left her room feeling more like herself than she had in days. She would make everything right. She was dressed all in black, her hair was in a high ponytail, her arm holster held her Walther PP, her handcuffs were in her back pocket, and she had her ass-kicking combat boots laced tight. Vangel joined her in the hall and they walked together, saying nothing, to the living room where Helen and Theron were waiting for them.

Helen gave Jean a smile when she saw her and when Theron looked up he took a step back, his eyes bulged for a second before he put his stony mask back in place.

"You must be Vangel," Theron said, offering him a hand.

"And you must be Theron, nice to meet you." Vangel took his hand and gave it a shake before letting go. "Jean said you know where this guy is hiding?"

"I have a good idea, and it makes me mad as hell." Theron walked toward the garage and they all followed. "The only place to hide along the road where Jean last saw him is a cave his father ran out of before we came to an accord."

"Wait," Vangel said, missing a step. "Are you telling me we are going after Serafeim's son? Are we crazy?"

"You know Serafeim?" Theron asked, looking over his shoulder.

"Yeah, I have made a few purchases from him." Vangel shrugged his shoulders.

"Good, and yes we are going after his son, with Serafeim's blessing. The boy is trying to start his own business while stealing from and undercutting his father. Serafeim wants to make an example of him to teach him a lesson." Theron held the door open as everyone walked through and into the garage.

"I guess that is one way to show him tough love," Vangel said as he went to the back door of the BMW.

"Yes, I would've killed him, but he loves his son, and I can't deny him that." Theron got into the driver seat while Jean got in the back with Vangel, and Helen sat up front.

"What are we going to do?" Jean asked as Theron started the car and opened the garage door.

"Split up, if he's in the cave there are only two ways out, a treacherous path leading from the road or the water. I doubt he has a boat though, so Helen and I will come in from the water and you and Vangel will go down the path. We will cut him off and take him there."

"What if he has a bunch of weapons down there? Is there any cover?" Jean asked as panic made her stomach clench.

"Helen and I will handle that, your job is to arrest him," Theron said as he tore down the road shifting gears. Jean gripped the door handle to keep from sliding into Vangel and trying not to throw up from anxiety.

"Are you sure you can swim in?" Jean asked, Theron's plan sounded crazy to her.

"Yes, we've done it many times," Helen said, flicking her gaze back to meet Vangel's then looking forward again.

"Jean, we can do this, have a little confidence," Vangel said, taking her hand and squeezing it before letting it go.

They rode the rest of the way in silence. Jean couldn't stop thinking about what would happen if they failed. Not only would she be a rogue, but her friends might get hurt, again. She didn't think she could take it if anyone died trying to help her get out of Interpol. She was about to call the whole thing off when they came around a corner and saw a car parked along the side of the road.

"Is that his car Jean?" Theron asked, slowing down but not stopping.

"Yes, that's it. Is it where you thought it would be?" Jean asked, getting excited. This was her chance, she couldn't second-guess herself any longer.

"Yes." Theron stopped the car around the next corner. "We'll get out here and make our way down to the water. You two, turn the car around and park behind his. There are night-vision goggles in the trunk. If you use flashlights, he'll see you coming." He opened the door and popped the trunk.

"What about you guys?" Jean asked, getting out of the car and moving to the seat Helen vacated.

"We have some too," Helen said, going to the trunk and pulling her shirt off revealing a wetsuit underneath.

"We'll meet you there in twenty minutes." Theron closed the trunk and put a pair of goggles on his head.

"See you then," Vangel said, getting into the driver's seat.

Jean sat in the car and watched as Theron and Helen disappeared into the brush along the road. Vangel turned the car around and drove back to where Grigoris's car was. "Are you ready?" he asked.

"No, but I don't really have a choice. I just hope this works."

"It will, just wait and see." Vangel pulled up behind Grigoris's car and turned it off. They carefully got out of the car and pushed the doors closed as quietly as they could. They didn't know how far away the cave was and didn't want to alert Grigoris that he had company. Vangel popped the trunk, and they found the goggles Theron mentioned. They closed the trunk then pulled the goggles down.

Vangel led her to the trail then motioned for her to go first. It was her operation after all. Jean took the lead, and they followed the narrow path down the side of the hill leading to the sea. Jean was relieved Theron gave them the night-vision goggles, there was no way she would've been able to navigate the path, if you could call it that, as quietly as they were without them. Jagged rocks and loose soil made the descent to the cave almost impossible.

When they reached the sandy shore, they wove around the side of a rocky face and pulled off their goggles. The glow of a fire told them they were in the right place. Jean looked out over the water trying to locate Theron and Helen, but it was too dark, and the water seem to swallow any light that might try to reflect back at her.

She could hear a man mumbling to himself and Vangel put his hand on her shoulder making her freeze. She turned to look at him and he held his finger to his lips. She didn't think she had said anything, but who knew? He motioned with his hands for her to look around the corner. She nodded, and peeked around the rock. Grigoris was sitting next to a fire outside the cave's entrance with a bottle of something in his hand. He stared into the flames like he was enjoying a solitary camping trip.

Jean turned and looked at Vangel, she gave him a thumbs-up and pulled her gun from her holster. Aiming up at the sky with one hand she did a count down with the other. Three, two, one and she rounded the rock and pointed her gun at Grigoris.

"Interpol, put your hands where I can see them," she said, leveling her gun on him, her voice more authoritative than she thought was possible.

Grigoris stumbled to his feet, dropping the bottle near the fire, and looked around for an escape. "How did you find me?"

"That's not important. Put your hands up. You are under arrest." Jean kept her gun on him and wondered where Theron and Helen were.

"You're not going to shoot me; my dad will kill you if you do." He laughed and moved a hand behind his back.

Jean aimed at his right foot and pulled the trigger. The blast of the gunpowder echoed off the walls of the cave and Grigoris froze looking at the sand next to his foot. "Are you sure about that? He's the one who told me to arrest you."

"You crazy bitch! You almost shot me."

Little did he know she meant to shoot him in the foot but missed. "Put your hands on your head and turn around. Or I'll aim a little more to the right."

Grigoris slowly turned around and put his hands on his head. Jean moved toward him wondering where all her help was. Vangel was behind her somewhere, but Grigoris hadn't acknowledged him, and Theron and Helen had probably drowned in the water. When she reached him, she pulled the gun out of his waistband and threw it to the other side of the fire. "If you move, I will shoot you. I may not kill you, but it will hurt like a bitch and you'll never walk right again." Jean pulled the handcuffs out of her back pocket with the hand not holding the gun. She put her gun back in her holster and grabbed one hand from the top of his head. She pulled it down and locked the handcuff around it before an explosion from the fire pushed her forward and she face-planted into the rocky ground.

Grigoris stumbled but got to his feet and ran around the fire looking for his gun. Jean popped her ears wondering what happened, then moved to pull her gun from her holster. "Don't move, Interpol bitch," Grigoris said as Jean looked up and found a gun trained on her.

She turned her head back to the ground and closed her eyes. *Can't I do anything right?*

"Where's the key to the cuffs?" he asked, kicking her hard enough to make her roll onto her back.

"In my pocket," Jean wheezed, grabbing her ribs, and remembering she still had her gun.

"Get them out now, if you move in any other direction I'll shoot you."

Jean slowly moved her hand to the front pocket of her pants trying to think of a way she could get to her gun without being shot. *Where the fuck was her backup?*

As if her thought had summoned him, Vangel stood behind Grigoris while he loomed over Jean. She put her hand in her pocket and came up with the key. She held it out to him, but as he moved to take it Vangel pointed his gun at the back of Grigoris's head.

"Drop the gun," Vangel said with a smile in his voice.

Grigoris straighten and dropped the gun while Jean put the key back in her pocket and scrambled to her feet stumbling to keep her balance. The blast, whatever it had been, messed with her equilibrium.

"Nice of you to finally show up," Jean said, grabbing Grigoris's loose hand and snapping the other handcuff on behind his back.

"Theron told me to hold back, let you do it on your own." Jean pushed Grigoris toward the trail leading to the main road. She wanted to turn him in, go home, take a long hot bath, and forget that she couldn't bring anyone in on her own.

"You would've had him if the bottle of ouzo hadn't exploded in the fire. Wait, you're bleeding, let me look at your wound while we still have light." Vangel put a hand on her shoulder to stop her.

*It was the damn bottle that exploded, what were the odds?* Jean thought, pushing Grigoris to the wall of the cave and forcing him to sit down. "Where am I bleeding?" she asked, looking over her shoulder.

"The back of the calf. Come over to the fire so I can see better." Vangel led her to the light of the fire then got on his knees.

Grigoris was watching them with shifty eyes. Jean could almost see the gears turning in his mind. She pulled her gun out and aimed it at him. "Don't move, you bastard." He stopped and stared at her, probably imagining all the ways he wanted to kill her.

"You have a piece of glass imbedded, hold still while I pull it out," Vangel said from behind her.

"I'm doing my best, I don't want him to escape." Jean held still while keeping her gun trained on her prisoner and gasped in pain when Vangel pulled the glass out of her calf.

"OK, I got it. I want to put a bandage on it, then you can call it in." She heard Vangel pull off his shirt then tear a piece of it and wrap it around her leg.

"My father owns the police, I'll be out before you go to bed." Grigoris laughed hysterically.

"No, you won't," Theron said, stepping out from the shadows.

"How long have you been here?" Jean asked, getting pissed. If would've her, maybe she wouldn't be bleeding.

"Long enough," Theron turned to Grigoris. "Why did you go behind your father's back? He was grooming you to take over."

"Because he was taking too long. I was ready to take over years ago, but he wouldn't give it up," Grigoris spat at Theron. "I'll be better than he ever was."

"Not without my backing," Theron said, standing in front of him with his hands behind his back.

"You won't be in charge forever."

Theron laughed. "I will be for as long as you're alive. Now what did you sell to Alex?"

"Alex? Oh, you mean the guy last night? Nothing, but it looks like he found my stash." He tossed his head toward the cave. "When I got here someone had gone through my stores."

Jean shone her flashlight toward the cave entrance. She looked over at Vangel and he nodded his head to her. "Let's check it out."

They went into the cave, leaving Theron and Helen to keep an eye on Grigoris. The walls of the cave were almost smooth, etched by water when the sea was higher. It had a high ceiling, at least fifteen feet and about twenty feet across. The floor was covered with wood crates. Some were square while others were long and skinny. There was packing material all over the floor and most of the lids sat askew on the boxes. Jean  looked at Vangel and nodded her head, then they turned around and went back to Theron and Helen.

"It looks like most of the crates are open," she said, standing at Theron's side.

"What did he take?" Theron asked, growing angrier with each word

Grigoris said.

"I don't know. I didn't keep an inventory list." Grigoris was shaking as he felt the anger pour off Theron. "Look, I know all the C-4 is gone, along with the detonators. Probably some guns too, but I'm not sure."

Theron turned and walked into the cave. Jean stayed where she was with her gun trained on Grigoris. *Shit, if Alex had his way, they would have a fucking war*. Theron returned a moment later and stopped next to Jean.

"Helen and I have to go. Call this in to the police and we'll see you later. We can't be seen here, same goes for Vangel I assume."

"Yeah, I want nothing to do with the police," Vangel said, stepping up to Theron. "We'll see you back at the house."

"Jean," Theron said, and she looked up. "You did well, don't give up on yourself."

"Thanks," she murmured, staring at the ground. She couldn't believe she had messed up again. It was nice of Theron to say she did a good job, but she would be dead if it wasn't for Vangel's help. "See you guys later," Jean said as they left her alone with Grigoris.

Three hours later, the police let Jean go back to the mansion for the night. They took her statement, verified her identity, then allowed her to leave. Her handler called to tell her she would be in town the next morning for a debriefing. Jean wasn't sure how it would go, but at least she arrested Grigoris.

She got out of the cab when it pulled up to the mansion and swayed on her feet, she needed a shower and sleep. The house was quiet as she made her way inside and walked to her room. She was halfway down the hallway when a door opened, and Theron peeked his head out.

"You're back. How did it go?" he asked, moving into the hall.

He was wearing silk pajama bottoms and a matching robe. It was untied showing her his pale, rigid set of muscles and she jerked her head up.

"Fine, they took him into custody and were cataloging what was left of his stash when I left. My handler is arriving in a few hours. I need to get some sleep before she gets here," Jean said in a low voice, not wanting to wake up everyone in the house.

"She's coming here?" Theron froze where he stood and snorted out a frustrated breath.

"Here, as in Crete, not here as in the mansion." Jean shook her head. "Sorry, I'm exhausted. I haven't slept more than a few hours in two days. I'm meeting her at the police station later this morning."

"Good, sorry, I didn't mean to sound angry, it's just that I have no idea what to expect from you. You constantly surprise me."

"Me too," Jean said, thinking about everything that had happened the night before. "I need sleep, we can talk more later."

"Goodnight Jean, thank you for your help." Theron turned and went back into his room closing the door behind him.

Jean finally made it to her room and stripped off her clothes. She ran a hot bath then slid into the water and closed her eyes. She was almost free of Interpol, thanks to Vangel, Helen, and Theron. Now she needed to convince her handler she wouldn't do anything to jeopardize Interpol if they let her leave.

After her bath, she crawled into bed and set her alarm clock for an hour before her meeting. She wanted sleep more than she wanted to look nice for her handler. She closed her eyes and willed sleep to come, but her mind kept rolling over everything she had done wrong since leaving Kevò. She didn't know why Katie and Theron let her stay after everything she did to hurt them. She owed it to them to do whatever she could to help them get rid of Alex and Lolita.

She wondered if her handler would let her go. What would she do if they told her she couldn't quit? She was terrified of being labeled a rogue and, if she was, how would she survive? She could always make money hacking on the dark web, but how long could she go without being found? She needed to protect herself, make sure she had a way out if she needed one. Unable to sleep, she pulled her computer out and set up her backup plan.

## Chapter 29

*Vince*

Vince paced back and forth across the living room running his hands through his hair. He did not know why he was acting so jealous of Vangel. Katie was right, he needed to figure his shit out, but there was so much going on, and it seemed every day there was more to add to the list. Vangel would be an asset if Vince would let him. He needed to trust what Katie said, that nothing had happened between them except friendship. Although, what man could ever just be friends with Katie?

He stopped his pacing when his phone vibrated in his pocket. He dug it out and looked at the screen. "Miguel, is everything all right?" Vince asked, leaving his room to find Theron.

"Yes, and no, that's why I'm calling. Is Katie safe?"

"Yes, she is safe and sound. I am just getting to Theron's office, I know he will want to hear what you have to say."

"Very well, take care of her Vince. She is more than all of us combined." Miguel sounded sullen and wistful, and Vince wondered what was going on.

Vince opened the door to the office and motioned to Theron whom was talking to Natalia in quiet tones. Natalia looked at Vince when Theron stopped talking and rose to leave. Once she was gone, and the room was empty, save Vince and Theron, Vince said. "OK, we are both here."

"Good, nothing has changed, except Lolita forced me to change Katie's ex-boyfriend," Miguel said in one breath.

"That tool from San Sebastian?" Vince asked playing dumb, Miguel saved them, but Vince didn't want him to know that they had Lolita under surveillance.

"Yes, and he's going to make a terrible vampire, but I had no choice. Do you think Katie will hold it against me?"

"I have no idea, but now isn't the time to worry about it. Tell me about Lolita's army," Theron said, taking control of the conversation.

"They are well trained, she's been working on this for much longer than I realized. They fight as a group and can kill anything in their path. They may be young, but they're just as ruthless as Lolita, which makes them dangerous."

"How are you feeding them?" Vince asked, setting the phone down in the middle of the desk.

"Bagged blood, Lolita keeps them on a strict diet. Why?"

"Katie dreamed they were starving. After feasting on each other they went over the wall and swam toward Venice. We wanted to know how accurate her dream was." Theron leaned back in his chair.

"She gives them just enough to keep their bloodlust at bay, but they aren't starving. As long as the blood shows up on time I don't see it becoming an issue."

Vince looked over at Theron and their eyes met. It wasn't an issue yet, but it sounded like it would not take much for it to become one. "Very well, is there anything else we need to know about?" Vince still did not know if he could trust Miguel and he was not about to tell him what had been going on in Crete.

"No, except..." Miguel dragged the word out as if he was trying to find the words to explain. "One of Lolita's elite guards was sent on a mission. He has been gone for a week."

"You don't know where she sent him?" Theron asked.

"No, Lolita keeps much of her plans to herself. I don't know if it is because I haven't regained all her trust, or if she forgets I'm on her side."

"If he comes here, it will cost him his life," Theron said.

"Yes, well I must go, someone is coming. Stay safe."

The call ended, and Vince looked over to Theron. "Do you think we have another vampire coming to take a shot at Katie?"

"I don't know, but we need to be prepared. Maybe we should keep her on the grounds just to be safe."

"I don't think she will go along with that," Vince said, thinking back to their talk about Lolita.

"I know, we spent all this time training her to take care of herself and we are keeping her grounded. It's driving her up the wall."

"Between us we should be able to keep her safe," Vince said, getting to his feet.

"I hope so," Theron said, turning back to his computer.

## Chapter 30
### *Jean*

Jean found a parking place a block away from the police station, and got out of her car. She slung the strap of her satchel over her head, so it rested across her body and looked around her car one last time. She probably would never see it again if things didn't go the way she planned, and hell when had anything gone to plan for her lately?

She would miss it if her handler didn't come through for her. It was an Interpol issued vehicle, and it was loaded with trackers and low jacks. There was no way she could keep it if they forced her to go rogue. She smoothed down the basic black trouser suit she was wearing, hoping it would make her look older and more mature.

She walked the block to the station, taking her time. She wasn't early, but she wasn't late either. Being right on time was prized in the spy business and since she was one, she would play the part. She went in through the front doors and stopped at the receptionist desk.

"Jeanette Vang, here to see Special Agent Vang, Interpol." Jean pulled her badge out of her back pocket and put it on the counter. The waiting room was empty this early in the morning and even the sounds from the offices behind the receptionist were quiet.

"Through that door," the woman pointed to a door to Jean's left. "Then take the third door on the right."

"Thank you." Jean put her badge back in her pocket and went to the door. She waited while the receptionist buzzed her in, then walked with a confident stride down the hall, trying not to limp from the cut on her calf, until she reached the third door. She stopped outside it, looked at the camera on her left, and smiled before opening the door and walking into the interrogation room. Her mother was seated at the table dominating the room staring at her computer.

"Right on time I see," she said, not bothering to get up or even make eye contact with Jean, she was pissed all right.

"As I said I would be." Jean sat down, putting her satchel on the floor beside her.

"You look tired Jean, when was the last time you slept?" Her mother, and handler, cocked her head to one side and gave her a pitying look.

"It's been a while, I've had a lot on my plate the past few days." She hated when her mom tried to be motherly toward her. It always came across as fake.

"That's too bad, but if you hadn't left your post in Kevó none of this would be happening."

"Well, it's too late for that now. Look, can we get to business? I brought in the arms dealer as per our deal, can I get off the shit list now?" Jean folded her hands together and rested them on the table. She wanted to get this meeting over with and find out if she would be running for her life.

"Yes, and you found his stash too, how convenient. Why don't you walk me through how you got him?" Mom took her phone out of her pocket and hit a few buttons. "You know I have to record this for the report."

Jean rolled her eyes and went over everything from the night before, less the help she received from Theron and Vangel. Theron swore the night before that Grigoris would remember nothing about him or Vangel being there. She wasn't sure how he did it, but she would stick with what happened without bringing the guys into it. When she was done her mom stopped recording and put her phone back in her pocket.

"What happens now?" Jean asked, wishing she brought a bottle of water with her. Her throat felt like it was coated in sandpaper.

"Now, you come in and we send you to advance covert operations training. You proved yourself Jean, the higher-ups want to see what you can do with the proper training."

It was what Jean had been dreaming about since she was ten, watching James Bond movie marathons. Now they were actually going to train her to be a real spy? It was almost too good to be true. "What's the catch?"

"You tell us what you know about Theron, you've been a guest of his since you arrived on the island, correct?" Mom asked, opening her computer and beginning to type.

"Yes, I have, but he knows who I work for. Do you think he's dumb enough to let me see or hear anything about his criminal activities?" Jean asked, crossing her arms, leaning back in her chair, and crossing her ankles.

"You had to see something. The smallest detail might be what we need to land the biggest crime boss on this side of Europe."

"And if I tell you nothing?" Jean asked, not liking the hungry look in her mother's eyes.

"Then you will be marked rogue and placed on the most wanted list."

"That wasn't the deal Mom. Let me walk away and I will never cause another problem for you."

"Deal? What deal? My email said, 'we will see.' This is what I am offering you. It's what you have always wanted, why don't you want to take it?"

Jean didn't reply right away. She closed her eyes and thought about it. If she took this opportunity, she would get what she always wanted, but she would create an enemy she had no hope of beating.

Chapter 31

*Theron*

Theron looked at the clock. It was past noon, Jean should've been back an hour ago. It wasn't like they would arrest her. She was the one who caught the bad guy. He hoped her handler would honor the deal and let her leave Interpol without being marked a rogue. The woman was insufferable and a pain in his ass most of the time, but he didn't want her running for her life like Katie.

There was a knock at his door and he smelled a human, he cursed himself realizing he was hoping it was Jean. "Come," he said a little louder than usual since it was a human. The door opened and Vangel came in, closing the door behind him. Theron didn't have much of an opinion of the man yet. Vangel had done well the night before helping Jean catch Grigoris but that wasn't saying much, the man was drunk. The only reason Jean hadn't had him all by herself was because of the liquor bottle that fell in the fire. Vince didn't like him because he was friends with Katie, but jealousy could be evil like that.

"Vangel, what can I do for you?" Theron asked, leaning forward in his chair and resting his hands on the desk.

"I came to talk to you about Alex, I'm sorry he got away from the trap you laid for him before I arrived." Vangel took the seat on the other side of Theron.

"Yes, well some people don't know how to stay out of things that don't concern them," Theron said tightly, trying not to think about how Jean

229

screwed up.

"I might be able to help you catch him." Vangel's eyes glanced around the room as if someone would strike him down for saying anything.

"How?" Theron leaned back in his chair, not believing this human could capture Alex.

"I did a few jobs with him many years ago."

Theron thought Vangel was tense, as if he didn't know how well this news would go over. "Why are you telling me this?" Was there no one he could trust?

"Because I didn't like how he did the job and I left, but I talked to him at Sanctuary when I arrived on Crete. I think I can lure him into a trap." He spoke quickly trying to get it all out in one breath.

"I don't know, after what happened with Jean he will probably be more paranoid than ever." Theron cocked his head to the side and looked at the man. Katie was right, he resembled Vince. "Why are you so willing to help us?"

"Because Katie didn't ask for any of this, and she deserves to live her life in peace."

He was telling the truth, the man cared for Katie, Theron didn't think it was romantic, as Vince thought, more like a brotherly love. It wasn't a bad idea and Alex wasn't leaving the island. He had made sure of that.

"What are you thinking?" Theron finally asked.

"I set the stage of a jilted lover, I'm here to fill the hit on Katie to get back at her for *screwing* me over when she found out Vince was alive. Being her bodyguard is my *cover*. He needs help and I'm the only one who will help him."

"Very well, but if you double-cross us, I will hunt you to the ends of the earth. When I do catch you, I will give you to Helen to skin alive. Then we will slowly bleed you to death. Do you

230

understand?"

Vangel gulped and nodded. "Yes, I'm on your side. I want Alex out of the way too."

"Good, and he knows you're here as Katie's bodyguard. How are you going to play it when he asks why you haven't filled the contract yet?"

"I have a few things up my sleeve. You guys are overprotective and never leave her alone. I don't know why you hired me when you won't let her leave the house," Vangel said calmly.

"Good, but are you sure you want to do this? You know how Alex can be."

Vangel was about to answer when there was a knock at the door and they both turned to look at it.

Theron took a breath, another human, Jean. *She came back.* He smiled. "Come." He sat up a little straighter in his chair.

Jean walked in, looking dead on her feet. "I'm back, and I need your help. Where's Katie? Everyone will want to hear this."

Theron picked up his phone and sent a text to the rest of the house. *Katie, Jean is back, and she wants to talk to us all. Can you come to my office?* Theron thought to her. If only there was a way he could relay messages to everyone with his thoughts. "They should all be on their way."

"Good," Jean said, pacing back and forth in front of Theron's desk twisting her hands back and forth.

Theron wanted to make her stop, but the girl had endless energy, even the night before, when she said she was going to bed, he heard her tapping away at her keyboard until the sun was up and she had to leave.

"Jean, take a deep breath and stop moving for two seconds," Vangel said, stepping in front of her. "I don't think I have ever seen you so tired."

Jean stopped, wiped at her eyes, and gave him a tight smile. "Thanks, just what a girl wants to hear."

The door opened as Vince came in, followed by Katie, Helen, Natalia, and Argyris. "Jean what happened? Is everything all right?" Katie asked, running to her and pulling Jean into her arms.

"No, everything is not all right." Jean hugged her back, then moved away from her. "Just let me get this out."

Theron moved out from behind his desk and went to lean against the wall. He wanted to see her as she told them what happened. It didn't sound good.

"My handler, who is also my fucking mother, didn't honor her word." Jean looked down at her clasped hands and let out a sob. "She said if I told her about Theron she would send me to advance covert training, but if I didn't, I would be marked rogue. I told her I wanted out, and that Theron wasn't stupid, he hadn't told me or let me see anything illegal. Of course, she didn't believe me, but there was nothing more I could do. I turned in my badge, my gun, my phone, and my computer, and left. I am now rogue. I took so long to get back because I had to leave my car. It's Interpol issued and had tracking devices installed."

"Your own mother did this to you?" Katie asked, holding her hand in front of her face in disbelief. "I thought Interpol hired you because you hacked their system?"

"Yes, if you could call her a mother. All she has ever done is train me to be the best agent Interpol has ever had. When she saw I had a talent for hacking, she dared me to hack into their mainframe. After I did it, she showed me off to all her friends. She got a promotion, and they recruited me. Now she's tagging me rogue. What am I going to do?" Jean stopped moving and went absolutely still. Theron didn't think he had ever seen her so motionless before.

"You will stay with us. I have work for you, we will protect you. I'll get you a new computer, and phone. We'll work on a car later." Theron couldn't believe the words coming out of his mouth, this woman had been nothing but a pain in his ass since she arrived, and he was going to keep her safe now? There was something wrong with him.

"I don't want to stay where everyone hates me." Jean sprang

into action and resumed her pacing.

"Do you want to go back to Kevȯ?" Vangel asked, watching her pace. "Tad would take you back, you're a valuable asset to the team."

"That's the first place they will look for me. I won't put everyone there at risk. Barkley is working on new aliases for me as we speak, and Copperhead already moved my money into untraceable accounts, but who knows how long I'll last on my own. Theron, thank you for the offer to stay here, but I know it isn't what you really want. As soon as I get my paperwork I'll be out of your life." Jean turned and ran for the door.

"Jean, wait," Katie called, but it was too late Jean was down the hall and locking the door to her room before Katie made it to the hallway. "What are we going to do about that?"

"We will help her anyway we can," Helen said, sitting in one of the visitor chairs. "She needs rest, after she has some sleep Theron will talk to her and convince her to stay."

"I will? She already said no. Why would I try and convince her?" Theron turned his head to look at Helen, where did she get off?

"You will, because this is more your fault than it is hers. You forced her to stay here until Katie returned, you knew who she was from almost the moment she arrived. Even though you didn't want to look too closely at it. If you wanted to save her, you should have sent her away after she dropped Katie's things off, but you kept her here. Allowed her into your inner circle, you gave nothing away, but there is no way her handler will ever believe that. You owe it to her."

Theron didn't appreciate being called out in front of everyone, especially one he barely knew, but Helen was right. This was partly his fault. "I'll make good on what I said. She'll always have a place here."

"Good, now moving on. Katie, we will be leaving for the seamstress at seven this evening. Please be ready to go. Are you bringing Vangel and Jean with you?" Helen asked, moving toward the door.

"I'll be there, I'm the bodyguard, right?" Vangel nodded his head.

"And I'll talk Jean into coming, there is no way someone will come

233

after her so quickly," Katie said.

"Good, I will see you tonight then."

Helen turned to leave, and the rest of the group took their cue from her and left Theron alone. He sat at his desk and got back to work, trying to keep the hurt look Jean gave him out of his mind.

## Chapter 32

*Katie*

I took Vinny outside after the meeting in Theron's office and we played for over an hour while I kept track of all the vampires in the house. If we were going to be inundated with them, I needed to go back to the training I had at the compound. Before the bombing, I could locate almost every vampire on the grounds. Since I had been in Kevò, I let my sense atrophy and I was going to need it. Once Vinny was tired out, we went back to our suite.

Vince was close by feeling guilty, Theron was in his office concentrating on something, and Helen was in her office talking to Natalia, frustrated about something. Argyris and another vampire I couldn't place were in the barn.

"Who's the vampire Argyris is with?" I asked Vince as I entered the living area of our suite. He was sitting at the desk looking at his computer.

"Takis, the one Ilhami enslaved. Theron turned him to save him from dying. He is fighting bloodlust right now." Vince got to his feet and came to stand in front of me. "I am sorry. I am not used to you having friends who are male who I do not know."

"If it was you and a woman, I would feel the same way." I grinned at him. "Vince, you are the only one for me. I'll never let you go, it took me too long to find you and when I thought you were dead..." I trailed off, blinking the tears back. "I thought I would never know what it was like to feel love from someone or love someone in return again."

He took me into his arms and held me. "I will never be worthy of you, but I will be here for as long as you want me."

"I will never not want you Vince." I stood on my toes and brought my lips to his. No matter how often we argued, I would always want him. I pulled away before the kiss would derail my thinking on the new vampire. "Take me to see him."

"I don't know if that's a good idea," Vince said, looking at the ground.

"Why?" I watched him, feeling the tension behind his eyes. "Is it because you fear for my safety?" I waited, and when his feelings didn't change, I moved on to the next question. "Are you afraid he'll scare me?" Vince winced. "You don't want me to see the monster you really are." Vince's head jerked up and his eyes met mine, he was feeling ashamed. "You think that when I see him, I won't want to be with you anymore."

"I don't know what I would do if I lost you Katie," Vince finally said. He took another step toward me but stopped himself from coming closer.

"Vince, don't you think I've seen the monsters you can become? Look at what Lolita did to me. Look at what Miguel did, they weren't fighting for control of their bloodlust, they truly are monsters. Whatever Takis is going through, I know it's temporary. If I'm to be the queen of the vampires, I have to know what you all go through when you're changed." I went to him and rested my hand on his cheek. "Nothing you show me will make me change the way I feel about you." I pressed my lips to his in a chaste kiss.

"I can deny you nothing it seems. I will take you to see Takis after you've return from the seamstress." He leaned down and pressed his forehead against mine. "All I want to do is protect you."

"I know, but you can't protect me from everything. I love you Vince."

"And I you, but you had better go shower and change. Helen

236

will be upset if you're late."

I rolled my eyes but kissed him on the cheek then went to get ready.

After I showered, I dressed in a slim pair of chocolate-brown slacks with a copper-colored camisole, and a tan, loose-fitting cardigan. My katana fit nicely under it even if the red handle looked out of place. I looked down at Vinny who was sitting on the tile floor next to the vanity. "Vinny, you have to stay here and be a good boy, I'll be back in a little while." I bent over and scratched him behind the ears before going in search of Helen, Jean, and Vangel.

I felt Helen in her office, but I had no idea where Jean and Vangel were. I went toward their rooms. Jean's door was closed, but I heard voices behind it, so I knocked softly.

"Come in," I heard her say and went inside. Jean was sitting on her bed looking at the phone Theron had arranged for her, Vangel was doing the same, only sitting in a chair.

"What are you guys doing?" I asked, putting my hands on my hips.

"I took Theron up on his offer to help me. I'm setting up this phone and trying not to think about how long I will last as a rogue," Jean said, looking at the computer box sitting on her desk. "I'll start with the computer next. Hey, can I borrow yours? I want to clone the programs Hound put on it."

"Yeah, sure. It's in the sitting room, feel free to grab it whenever you need it." It set my mind at ease knowing Jean wasn't going to run off.

"Do you guys still want to go with me to the seamstress?" I still wasn't sure how I felt about having a dress made for this party. It was just a party after all, why couldn't I wear something off the rack?

"I don't know if it's safe for me to be seen in public," Jean said barely looking up from her phone, but when she did, I saw her bloodshot eyes. The poor girl had no idea what to do with the rest of her life.

"It'll be fine, all we're going to do is drive to her shop, go in, get measured, look at some fabric, then leave. It will be good for you to get out of here for a while."

237

Jean looked up at me and gave me a half smile. "OK, I'll go, but don't blame me if I get us killed."

"Dress shopping? Is that the only reason you invited me here?" Vangel asked, rolling his eyes.

"I invited you here to help protect me, so I'm not stuck in this stupid house all the time."

"I'm kidding, a bodyguard goes wherever his body is." Vangel rose and checked his pockets. He took out a Glock, pulled the slide back, made sure it was loaded, then put it back in his shoulder holster. "When are we leaving?"

I looked down at my watch, "in a few minutes. Let's go find Helen." I turned to leave when Theron thought to me. *Katie, can I see you for a moment?* I looked over my shoulder at Vangel and Jean. "Crap, I need to stop by Theron's office real quick, I'll meet you in the garage."

"OK," Jean said and Vangel cocked his head at me.

I knocked on the door to Theron's office. *Come in,* he thought, as I left Jean and Vangel in the hallway.

"What's up?" I asked, approaching his desk and taking a seat next to Vince.

"Vince told me you wanted a gun." Theron pushed a polished wood box toward me.

"I do, but what is this?" I asked, gingerly opening the lid and peering inside. There was a matt-black, 9mm Smith & Wesson nestled in foam inside the box. Beside it sat two, loaded, ten-round clips. "Wow, this is beautiful," I said, pulling the firearm out, and checking to see if it was loaded. There was a clip loaded, I pulled the slide back and found a bullet in the chamber. I let the slide fall back in place then engaged the safety. "This is exactly what I wanted. Thanks guys." I tucked the gun into the back of my slacks but pulled it out, it wouldn't work there. I looked down at my clothes. I had nowhere to put the gun.

"I'm glad you like it." Theron opened a drawer and pulled out a shoulder holster. "Here, this will probably be the best with your current outfit. Theron handed it to Vince, I took my cardigan off, and I let Vince help me put it on and adjust it, so it wouldn't interfere with the shoulder straps of my katana sling.

"You are looking more and more like a bad ass," Vince whispered before kissing the side of my neck. "Promise me you will be careful."

"I will, remember what we are doing when I get back," I said before leaning in and kissing him.

"Katie," Helen yelled from the hallway. "We are going to be late. Let's go."

"Of course." Vince kissed me back.

"Coming," I said, backing toward the door. "Really, thanks you guys. I feel safer already."


"Is that a gun?" Jean asked as we walked to the BMW.

"Yeah, Theron just gave it to me." I smiled and patted it.

"I wish I didn't have to turn mine in."

"Why don't you ask Theron for one? I'm sure he can get one for you too." I went to the back door and opened it. "I'm guessing you guys want me to sit in the back?"

"Yes," Vangel said, moving to the driver's door only to be stopped when Helen beat him there.

"I will be driving, you're lookout," Helen said in a cold voice that made me wonder why she was in such a bad mood.

"I'm the bodyguard though, shouldn't I be driving?" he asked, looking down at her. Vangel dwarfed Helen's five foot two. Little did he know she could beat the crap out of him with one arm tied behind her back.

"You're the daytime bodyguard. When I'm here, I'm in charge." Helen opened the door and got in. I had never seen Helen be such a hard-ass unless we were training, it kind of made me feel better. I wasn't the only one who was on the receiving end of her bitchiness.

I got in behind Helen, while Jean got in the back-passenger side, and Vangel went to the front. Helen peeled out of the garage and we drove into the city. After we left the mansion behind, I realized I had no idea what had been happening in Kevȯ since I left.

"What is the latest gossip back in Kevȯ?" I asked Vangel, leaning forward in my seat.

"Not much, same old thing. I was so excited you invited me here." Vangel turned his head to make eye contact with me for a second before looking out the windows and checking the side-view mirror to make sure we weren't being followed. "Oh, there is some news though. Hound proposed to Copperhead."

"What?" Jean yelled. "What did she say?"

"Yes, of course. Those two have had a thing for each other since Hound joined. They are getting married this summer. I think they are planning on inviting you both."

"Really?" I asked surprised. "I would love to go," I whispered, wondering where I would be when summer came around. Would I be free of my enemies to do normal things, like attend my friends' wedding? Or would I still be hiding, trying to figure out a way to kill Lolita and Alex? Would I be alive? I was just about to say, 'we'll see,' when Vangel tensed and pulled his gun from his holster.

"I think we have a tail." He turned around in his seat, so he could see out the back window.

"I was just thinking the same thing," Helen said, looking into the rearview mirror. "He has been back there for too long."

"What are we going to do?" I asked, pulling my new gun from my holster.

"You are going to get on the floor, now," Vangel said, leveling his stare on me. "Put the gun away. It's my job to keep you safe, right?"

I huffed, put my gun back in my holster, and moved to the

floor.

*Can you tell if it is a human or a vampire?* Helen thought to me and I jerked my head up to stare at the back of her seat. It always surprised me when she spoke mind to mind with me. My gift creeped her out. I wanted to smack myself. I never thought of using my vampire sense first.

I closed my eyes and sent my feelers out. I felt Helen, she wasn't worried, the prospect of a fight excited her, she had a lot of pent-up aggression she needed to work out. Moving past her I searched out behind us, it was a vampire. "I don't think it's Alex," I said instead of 'hey there is an unknown vampire behind us.'

"How can you be sure?" Vangel asked, keeping his eyes on the car.

Well, that backfired, at least Helen knew it was a vampire. "I don't know, just a feeling."

"There's a dead-end alley up ahead," Helen said, picking up speed. "I'm going to pull into it. As soon as we stop, I'll jump out and go to the entrance. If I can get past him, we can surround him and find out what he wants."

"That is the stupidest idea I've ever heard. Can't you lose him?" Vangel asked, turning his head to stare at Helen. "What's Katie supposed to do, sit here like a sitting duck?"

"This car is bulletproof, you are going to stay with her and make sure she stays out of sight until we have whoever it is in our custody." Helen hung a hard right drifting around a corner. "Besides, we're on an island, we might lose him, but it won't be hard for him to find us again. Get ready." She slammed on the brakes and turned hard to the left. The car came to a stop and, in the next instant, I heard Helen's door shut softly.

"What the fuck?" Jean asked. "Where did she go?"

"Shut it Jean," Vangel said, rolling his window down. "Katie, no matter what happens, stay in the car. Like Helen said it's bulletproof." Vangel opened his door as the vampire following us started shooting. Vangel slumped in his seat and cocked his head to look at the door. "Yep, bulletproof." He slid from his seat to crouch behind the door with his gun

241

ready.

"What are you doing?" I asked in a low voice as he looked around.

"Trying to distract him from Helen." Vangel pointed his gun toward the headlights blinding us from our attacker's car. He pulled the trigger and one of the headlights went out followed by the sound of glass breaking.

"Be careful. Don't hit Helen," Jean said.

Vangel shot again and the other headlight went out. There was a barrage of return gunfire and it finally dawned on me. This wasn't a human. I found the vampire's mind and looked for a doorway. Maybe if I could get inside his head, I could control him.

I started poking around in his head, but it was sealed tight, so I kicked at his shield with my mind. Forgetting about everything else going on around me, I battered it until I felt it crack. A few more roundhouse kicks with my mind and his shield fell. I was in.

*She has nowhere to run now,* he thought. *Lolita will be impressed when I come back with Katie.*

*Great, one of Lolita's vampires was here to get me. Well not today. STOP, drop the gun, and lay down on the ground,* I thought, forcing my will onto him.

"He just dropped his gun," Vangel said, standing up and peering over the door.

Keeping my will in place I opened my door and untangled myself from the floor of the car. "Let's go get him. He can't hurt us now." I stood and walked toward the vampire on the ground behind his open door.

"Katie, what are you doing?" Vangel yelled, running to my side, and trying to stop me.

"Helen, I've got him," I said a little louder than I needed to and ignored Vangel's attempts to stop me from going any further. "It's fine, he can't move. Grab his gun." I pointed to the gun on the ground a few feet away before I pushed his car door closed and stood over the vampire.

*Who are you? What did you do to me?* The vampire was trying to talk, but I had taken away all his motor functions. All he could do was think. He was full of panic and, where he was full of excitement a few seconds ago, he was now terrified.

*I am your queen, and you just tried to kill me. That's high treason.* I pulled my foot back and kicked him in the gut as hard as I could. "That is for ruining my night out."

"You have him?" Helen asked before I could kick him again.

"Yes." I brought my foot back but then paused. I wanted to take out all my frustration and pain on this vampire, but it wasn't his fault. It wouldn't be right to make him pay for the sins of another. "Anyone have any zip ties or handcuffs?" I asked, we wouldn't need them, but I had humans with me, and I needed to keep up appearances.

"I've got it," Vangel said, pulling a pair of handcuffs from his back pocket, and rolling the vampire on to his stomach so we could cuff his hands behind his back.

"Katie, are you all right?" Jean asked, putting a hand on my shoulder.

I jumped at the touch, but then relaxed. "Yes, why wouldn't I be?" I turned to Jean.

"You got this weird look in your eye while we were in the car. It was almost like your eyes were glowing, then you got out of the car saying this guy was done. How did you know?" Jean crossed her arms over her chest.

I looked at Helen and she stared at me with wide eyes. Vangel was staring at me as well, waiting for an explanation. "I counted his bullets," I finally said. It was the best excuse I could come up with without telling them the truth.

"Whatever, all that matters is you're safe, and we have him." Helen walked over to the vampire, grabbed his cuffed hands, and tried to pull him into a seated position, but his body was stiff as a board. *Little help Katie, we need to get out of here before the police show up,* Helen thought.

I shook my head to clear it. *Get up and go with Helen and keep your mouth shut.* The vampire grunted and got to his feet.

*You will pay for this bitch,* he thought as Helen helped him to his feet. *Lolita will dissect you while you are still alive, bleed you till you are almost dead, then she will let you recover only to drain you again.*

"Vangel, would you pop the trunk? Jean, do you want to move the asshole's car onto the street and leave the keys in the ignition?" Helen asked as she walked the vampire to the trunk of the car. Vangel hit the key fob but nothing happened. He moved in front of it and banged on the lid, when that didn't work he hit the fob and pulled up on the lip.

"Why won't it open?" I asked, keeping half my mind on the vampire's and the other half in the real world.

"Asshole over there shot it. It's jammed," Vangel said, giving it one last heave before it opened. "There we go."

*Wait until Theron sees what you did to his car. Then we'll see whose torture is worse,* I thought before blocking his swearing from my mind and holding the lid up while Helen and Vangel maneuvered the vampire inside. The car the vampire had been driving started, and I watched Jean back it out of the alley then turned to move it to a parking spot on the street.

The sound of the trunk closing had me turning around to see Helen and Vangel staring at each other. "Do we still have time to go to the dressmaker?" I asked, looking at Helen.

## Chapter 33
### *Katie*

The tiny Cretan woman forced me to strip down to my underwear as she critiqued my body and took my measurements, all the while I kept my hold on the vampire's mind in the trunk of the car. He was pissed and wanted me to release him, but I kept my hold on him and forced his body to relax in the trunk and not move. Jean was quiet and never took her eyes off me while the dressmaker went on and on about what I would need. When we were done, we piled back in the car and drove home. I relaxed into my seat and closed my eyes trying to rest my body while my mind grew weaker with every minute I kept the vampire's mind in my control.

I had never controlled a vampire before; I didn't even know I could. I could make them stop and yelled in their mind enough to distract them, but keeping control for so long was new and, like anything new, I needed practice to build up my stamina. Once we were home, I could let go of him, I hoped. I opened my eyes when we stopped at the gate to the mansion and let out a relieved breath.

"Katie, are you OK?" Jean asked, putting her hand on my shoulder.

I jumped and almost lost my hold on the vampire. "What? Yeah, just tired. I think I spent all the adrenalin I had when we caught the bastard."

"It was pretty intense there for a minute." I could tell by the tone of her voice that she didn't believe me. I didn't really care at the moment. I just wanted to get the vampire locked in chains, so I could release him, and rest.

"Why do you think he stopped attacking so suddenly?" Vangel asked

245

as he kept an eye out for threats.

Helen's eyes met mine in the rearview mirror. "I don't know, maybe he ran out of ammo."

"No, I checked his clip," Vangel turned in his seat to look at me. "It was half full."

"I don't know, Vangel, maybe he realized he was outnumbered and there was no escape." I leaned my head on the window and closed my eyes, wishing he would stop asking questions.

"Maybe that was it," Vangel said, not sounding convinced. He didn't believe for a second that was what happened. I didn't have the energy to come up with a plausible lie. I wanted to be home before I became too exhausted to keep my hold on the vampire.

Helen pulled into the garage where Theron and Vince were waiting for us. I jumped out of the car and ran to Vince's arms. *Katie, are you all right?* Vince thought, pulling me away from his chest and looking at my face.

*Keeping a hold on this guy is taking a toll, I need a break, but I don't want to let go with Vangel and Jean here.* I gave him a sad smile and leaned back into his chest. I heard the trunk pop and forced myself to turn.

"Hello there, I will be your host while you spend time on the island," Theron said, leaning into the trunk, grabbing the vampire's arm, and pulling him out. *Katie, let go a little, so he can talk, otherwise the humans will wonder what's going on,* Theron thought. Helen must have told him what I'd done when she called him to update him while I was being measured.

Relieved, I let go of my control over his voice, but not his body. *Go with Theron, and do not struggle, there is nowhere to run.*

"You stupid bitch, you will pay for what you've done. When Lolita finds out she is going to make you pay."

"She already wants to make me pay," I said in a monotone

246

voice. "What are we going to do with him?"

"Shouldn't we call the police?" Jean asked, earning her an eye roll from everyone, including the prisoner.

"Jean, he already admitted that he works for Lolita, if we turn him over he'll escape then come back after me." It was becoming more and more difficult to keep the truth from Jean and my mind was tired enough as it was.

"Let's take him to the barn," Theron said, walking the prisoner toward the side door of the garage. *Katie, can you grab ahold of Takis's mind before we get there?* Theron thought. *Once he smells humans he will make a lot of noise, and I don't want to try to explain it to them.*

"I'll try," I said out loud. I could barely control one vampire, and now they wanted me to control another one?

"What?" Vangel asked, turning his head to look at me.

"Nothing, sorry I'm just tired." I leaned into Vince and let my vampire senses find the newly made vampire. Once I found him, I tapped on his mental shield and it shattered. At least I wouldn't have to fight my way in, when I opened my mind to his, I staggered, and Vince kept me from falling.

*Are you all right?* he thought, looking down at me.

*Just grabbing Takis's mind, I need to keep him quiet until we can get rid of Jean and Vangel.* Keeping my mind on two vampires and talking to Vince was draining me.

*So hungry, if I could only have one more bag of blood, I know I can control myself,* Takis was thinking as we came near the barn. *Just one more bag then maybe I can think straight. Wait, what is that? Someone is coming, and they smell good, too good. Is Theron bringing me a human to drink from? They smell amazing.*

*Takis, I need you to stay quiet and be good,* I thought, feeling like I was treating him like Vinny. *If you're good, I will bring you another bag of blood.* I didn't know if I would have the strength to silence him and control him like I was Lolita's vampire, but I would try if he couldn't control himself.

*Promise?* he thought, sounding hopeful.

247

I hated promises, but if it was what he needed to keep quiet, then I would do it. *Yes, but only if you are so quiet we forget you're here.*

*Deal,* he thought as we approached the door of the barn. Theron looked over his shoulder at me while pulling his keys out of his pocket. I gave him a nod, and he unlocked the door. Vangel pushed the vampire inside and we followed. Helen hit the lights, and Argyris came out of a door at the other end with a worried look on his face.

*We have a prisoner,* I thought to him. He relaxed and nodded his head.

It was a nice barn. The floor was gray concrete without a trace of hay, but I could still smell it. There were six stalls on each side with doors that led outside, they were all barred and locked, and I wondered if they would be strong enough to hold a vampire hostage. Theron led us to a stall in the middle and opened the door. Vangel pushed the vampire inside and Vince let go of me to pull iron manacles from his back pocket. Jean, Helen, and I watched as the men shackled the vampire's arms and legs to chains as thick as my calf. When they finished, they left the stall and closed the door made of wood and heavy iron.

*Release him if you wish,* Vince said, coming back to my side and pulling me into his arms. I let go of my control of his body but kept my control on his voice. As soon as I released him he thrashed and pulled at his bindings. We all took a step back.

"Why wasn't he trying to fight before?" Vangel asked, looking around at us.

"I don't know, maybe he knew he couldn't get away before. Now he's testing the strength of his chains," Helen said, taking a step closer to the stall. "What is your name?"

I let my control slip enough for him to answer the question. "Thomas," he said as drool fell from his mouth.

"How old are you?" Helen asked, cocking her head to the side.

"Sixty-two."

"There is no way this guy is sixty-two," Jean said, taking a step toward the cell. "Why would you lie about your age?"

Thomas cracked a smile, and I caught him before he said what he was thinking. *Human, you do not know who you are involved with.*

"What are you doing on my island?" Theron asked, changing the subject quickly.

"Lolita sent me as a spy. She wants to know what you are up to."

"What have you told her?" Vince asked.

Instead of answering Thomas laughed long and hard. *That you only have two vampires, but I was wrong about that. Katie is alive, and well protected,* he thought.

Theron looked over at me when he didn't answer out loud and I gave him a nod. "Not going to talk?"

The vampire just continued to laugh. *Lolita will save me when she comes for you and your island,* he thought.

"Let's let him stew for a while," Vince said, walking over to a switch in the wall. "I'll open the skylight for some fresh air."

Thomas's laugh was cut short as we all turned to leave. "You can't leave me here with a hole in the roof. Are you crazy?" he asked with a quiver in his voice.

"I'll check on you later, see if you're ready to talk," Theron said, holding the door open for us to walk through. I staggered, and Vince held me close.

"Please don't leave me here," he called as Theron closed and locked the door. *We need to get rid of the humans, so we can talk,* he thought.

*Agreed, but they will want to talk about what happened,* I thought back. When we made it to the garage door, I let go of Thomas's mind and lost control of my legs. Vince swung me into his arms and walked through the door Vangel was holding.

"Katie, are you all right?" Vangel asked, his eyebrows pulling down

249

to form a V.

"Just exhausted. Can we talk about what happened tomorrow?" I made my voice sound weak and rested my head against Vince's shoulder.

"Yeah, get some rest." Vangel took Jean's hand and started toward their rooms.

*That was easy,* Vince thought, giving me a wink and walking toward our suite with Helen and Theron at his heels.

"I'm exhausted, controlling him for such a long time kicked my ass," I said in a voice only the vampires could hear.

When we reached our suite Theron closed the door while Vince laid me on the couch. He left me for a few seconds then was back with a sports drink and an energy bar. "I'm sorry, but we are not done yet and we need you strong."

"I know, thank you." I sat up and opened the wrapper to the bar and waited for them to start with the questions.

"How did you do it?" Helen asked, crossing her arms over her chest.

"I'm guessing you mean control him?" I asked before biting off a mouthful. After chewing and swallowing, I tried to find the best words to explain what I'd done. "So, when I was in the labyrinth fighting Ben, I found my way into his mind and I told him to stop, and he did." I took another bite and talked around the food. "Tonight, I was trying to figure out how I could help catch Thomas without being in the line of fire. I told him to lie down on the ground and drop his gun and he did. I forced my will on him. I didn't want the humans to know what was going on, so I kept control of him until we left the barn."

"Are you telling me you controlled him the whole time we were in the dressmaker's shop? I thought you were acting weird because of shock." Helen uncrossed her arms and sat in one of the wingback chairs. "The thought of you controlling a vampire is

250

terrifying, but I'm glad you could tonight."

"How is this possible?" Theron asked, pacing back and forth in front of the roaring fireplace and running his hands through his hair.

"Mom." I opened the lid on the sports drink and drank half of it before coming up for air. "What are we going to do with Thomas now?" I asked, keeping the conversation on track.

"We need to find out everything he knows about Lolita and her army. See if he knows the layout of the island and where security is, then we need to find out if Lolita knows he's here and when he is expected to check in." Theron stopped pacing and looked me in the eye. "We'll need you, are you up to it?"

"Yeah, but I need to rest for a while first." I closed my eyes and tried to relax my mind. It had been a stressful night. It was one thing to control a vampire so completely for the first time, it was another to have to control him and keep his true nature from Vangel and Jean. I opened my eyes as a thought hit me and looked at Theron. "What are we going to do with Vangel and Jean while Theron introduces me?"

"I'm sure Theron has a plan," Vince said, lifting up my legs, sitting and letting my legs rest on his.

"Did you know Vangel used to work with Alex?" Theron asked, putting his hands on his hips and changing the subject.

"What?" Vince asked.

"Yes, he told me it was a long time ago. He stopped because he didn't like how Alex did things." I uncrossed my arms. "Why does it matter?"

"I talked to him earlier today, and he agreed to spy for us."

"What?" Vangel was a man and he could take care of himself, but if Alex found out I didn't think Vangel would survive.

"At least he is good for something," Vince muttered.

"It might be our best chance of catching Alex," Helen said, trying to calm me down.

I took a breath, why was I worried? Alex was human and Vangel knew him, he had firsthand experience of how devious Alex could be. If there

251

was anyone who could get close enough to Alex for us to get him, Vangel would be the one. "How is this going to work?"

"We're not sure yet, he is going to hook up with Alex tomorrow, then we'll know more," Theron said, and I shook my head. I didn't like the sound of this. "Don't you see? If Vangel wins him over, we will know exactly how Alex plans to abduct you and we can finally capture him."

"What if Alex finds out and kills Vangel?" I asked.

"This isn't the first time Vangel pretended to be someone he isn't. He can do this, Katie." Helen was being softer than usual, and I didn't know what to think of it.

I shook my head and thought about it. Alex would be wary of everyone on the island. If he already knows Vangel, and he set the stage, it could work, and I would have one less person trying to kill me. "OK, but if something happens to him because of this, there will be hell to pay." I looked at my watch, "I'm going to take a nap if it's all right with you guys."

"Please," Theron said, getting to his feet. "And Katie, you did great tonight."

"Thanks." Theron and Helen left, and Vince picked me up, then carried me to the bedroom and laid me on the bed. I was too exhausted to complain. He got onto the bed next to me and pulled me into his arms. "Rest, Katie."


After my nap, I woke up feeling refreshed and ready to get to work. I wanted to know what Thomas knew just as much as my vampires did. I dressed in a pair of black slacks, a green shell with a plunging neckline, and a black blazer. I forced my feet into the black heels with red soles and wished I was in jeans and a T-shirt, but Helen was right; I needed to start dressing the part if I wanted vampires to take me seriously. I put my katana on my back and my gun was in its holster to finish the look.

We met in the great room and silently went out the back door to keep the humans from knowing what we were doing. Theron unlocked the door to the stable, opened the door, and led us inside. As soon as Vince flipped on the lights both vampires started yelling.

Takis wanted to know where the blood I promised him was, and Thomas was yelling profanities. "Argyris, can you give Takis a bag of blood? I promised him one if he stayed quiet while Vangel and Jean were here."

He bent from the waist. "Of course, he deserves it, he behaved very well." Argyris went into what I thought must have been a tack room or an office, then came back with a bag of blood.

"Do you still want to meet him?" Vince asked.

"Yes, but first." *Thomas be quiet please,* I thought to him, laying on some compulsion. His yelling stopped, and the ensuing silence made my ears ring.

"Thank you," Helen said, pulling a chair over to sit in front of his stall.

Vince took my hand and led me to the last stall in the room. Inside, a forty-something vampire was pacing back and forth, dragging a chain attached to his ankle behind him. "Blood, where is the blood you promised me?" His gaze met mine, and I kept myself from taking a step back in horror. It looked like he had been wearing a suit, but it was now torn and filthy, with dark stains covering his once white shirt. The knees had been ripped out and the sleeves of the jacket were frayed and torn. The smell coming off him made me want to retch.

"You could at least let him shower," I said, holding my hand in front of my nose, trying to smell anything but the rancid, dried blood.

Vince took the bag of blood from Argyris and held it out to Takis. "We will let him shower when he learns not to waste his food." Vince took a step back after Takis snatched the bag from his hand.

Takis ripped the bag open with his teeth and sucked the blood from the bag with slurps and sucking noises that, combined with the smell, made my stomach want to revolt again. I couldn't let Vince know how much the sight of this newly turned vampire affected me. I wouldn't lie to him, but if I was going to be the leader of the species, I had to handle every aspect of them. *Fake it till you make it,* I thought to myself as I watched him empty the bag.

"That is so much better," Takis said calmly, walking over to a trashcan and putting the bag in it. "Vince, are you going to introduce me to your friend?"

I blinked and felt out Takis's mind. The vampire who could think of nothing but blood I first felt was gone, the man who stood before me now was sane and almost regal in the way he held himself. I probed his mind and found it quiet and satisfied, at least for the moment. But there was a small part still thinking about blood and how good mine would taste on his tongue.

"Takis, this is Katie, daughter of Asteria, the mother of our kind." Vince took my hand and pulled me to his chest. "She is my lover."

"Pleasure to meet you Katie. Thank you for the blood." *Although I think your blood would taste much better than the bagged shit they keep giving me.*

*You will never find out,* I thought back to him, raising an eyebrow. *Has the vampire down the way said anything to you?*

Takis blinked up at me and took a step back. "You can read my mind?" he asked in a low voice.

*Yes, I can. Can you answer my question?* I felt his sanity leaving as the smell of my blood became too much for him.

*No, he has said nothing. Will you please go? I don't know how much more of your smell I will be able to take before I turn into a monster again.*

"Thank you," I said, turning to Vince. "Shall we see if we can make Thomas talk?"

"Of course, are you going to tell me what you talked about?" he asked as we walked back to the stall Thomas was in.

"I asked him if Thomas had said anything while we were gone. He hasn't." We stopped outside the stall and glanced at Theron who was standing with his fist clinched staring at the vampire. "What's wrong?" I asked, putting a hand on his shoulder. Theron shrugged it off and turned to me.

"This is the second time since the attack that a vampire has come on to my island without permission. This will not stand."

"I'm sorry, we'll find a way to keep them off but, in the meantime, let's find out what he knows." I turned to Thomas. "Are you going to tell us what we want to know or are am I going to have to force the information from you?"

"You can't force me to tell you anything," he scoffed. "Lolita trained me to withstand all types of torture. You're no match for her."

I rolled my eyes and jumped into his mind. "Ask him whatever you want." Thomas might have acted like he wasn't scared, but he was thinking about how he had lost control of his body when we captured him and how he had not regained it until we left. He was nervous and terrified that he wouldn't live to see another night.

"Why did Lolita send you here?" Theron started.

He said nothing, but his mind told me everything I needed. "She sent him here to spy on us, she wants to know what we are doing. He wasn't supposed to engage until she gave him permission." Thomas jerked and met my eyes.

*How in the hell are you doing that? Does Lolita know you can read minds?* he thought, while trying to use his thrall on me. I rolled my eyes.

"Yes, she knows I can read minds, and your attempt to capture my mind is a waste of time. Thrall doesn't work on me. Just answer the questions," I said, sitting in the chair. "What will she do to you when she finds out we captured you?"

"She will kill me when she comes for you." He hung his head. He wasn't lying, he fucked up.

"Tell us what you know about the island where she is staying," Vince

255

said, putting his hand on my shoulder from behind the chair.

"No," he said, but then thought. *This woman can read my mind, if I don't think about it, I won't give away what Lolita has built.*

"Except I can make you talk," I said before thinking to him. *Show me Lolita's island.* He fought my command but only for a second. "From first glance it looks like nothing has changed since she bought it. Everything is overgrown with ivy and trees. There are two main buildings. She houses the army in the old sanitarium, there's a twenty-foot wall surrounding it. It has been outfitted with UV windows. The inside has been completely redone, it looks brand new. They train the soldiers in shifts, there are five older vampires who oversee the army and two, including Thomas here, who oversee the five. Only Thomas and Stephan report the progress directly to Lolita and Miguel. Lolita's house is grand, with many rooms. She has on-site donors that only service the vampires Lolita deems worthy, everyone else drinks bagged blood which is delivered weekly. There's a dungeon where she keeps anyone who breaks the rules and new vampires who have not overcome their bloodlust yet."

"When is Lolita going to attack?" Vince asked, moving around me, to stand closer to the bars.

Thomas laughed. *Don't tell them, you can't tell them. When they have no more use for you, they will kill you.*

*Answer the question,* I thought and closed my eyes to try to sooth the pounding headache starting at the base of my skull.

Thomas jerked then stared into my eyes when I opened them. *Lolita does not tell anyone her plans, we won't know until she tells us. Leave me alone.*

"He isn't high enough in the chain of command," I said as he relaxed his muscles and hung loosely by the manacles. "How are you keeping in touch with her?"

*I must call her at four in the morning, with an update.*

256

*Where's your phone?* I asked, looking at Theron and Vince. "We may have a problem."

*It's in my pocket, bitch, why don't you come and get it?*

I stood and motioned for my friends to follow me out of the stables. When we were out of earshot, I stopped and faced them.

"What's the problem?" Vince asked, rubbing his hands up and down my arms.

"He checks in with Lolita every night, he calls her at four. What will happen when he doesn't call in tonight?"

"Lolita will think we killed him," Theron said, crossing his arms and staring at his feet.

"Will she send another vampire to take his place?" I asked.

"Hard to say," Helen said, putting her hands on her hips.

"Maybe she won't send anyone else. It's not like he has all that much information for us anyway," Vince said, looking down at me.

"But do we want to risk it?" Theron asked, looking up from his shoes.

"What other choice do we have?" Helen asked, cocking her eyebrow at him.

I knew where she was going, and I didn't know if I could do it or not. "I think I can speak through him, but I don't want him to know what is happening until it's too late."

"Why would you want to put yourself at risk doing this?" Vince asked, bending to look into my eyes.

"What risk is there? I have a headache from what I have already done tonight, but if it means Lolita doesn't know we have him, it could be a huge win for us."

"What will you tell her?" Theron asked.

"A version of the truth, that he followed us to town where we went shopping then we came home."

"What good will that do us?" Helen asked, looking confused.

"It gets us through tonight, tomorrow night we can think of a way to feed her false information, but we have five minutes before he is due to call.

What other choice do we have?" I asked, crossing my arms over my chest.

"Katie makes a good point, if she can speak through him, we can feed Lolita information to keep her off our trail and what we plan to do." Theron's frown turned into a smirk. "Let's do it."

## Chapter 34
*Lolita*

"It's almost time," Lolita said, leaning back in her chair and staring at the ceiling. It had been a good night. The club was running smoothly, and the virgin she had for dinner made her feel young again. "If we could only find a way to get rid of Katie, we could start our war."

"Why don't you have Thomas kidnap her and bring her to us?" Miguel asked, sitting in the club chair on the other side of the desk with an ankle resting on his thigh.

"You honestly think Thomas is strong enough to bring her in?" Lolita let out a shrill laugh and brought her chair down to look at Miguel.

"She is only human." Miguel shrugged his shoulders.

"The best assassin in the world has missed her three times, and we know compulsion doesn't work on her. Thomas is good, but he isn't that good, especially since we know there are at least two vampires with her. I wouldn't be surprised if there were more."

"You're right, as usual, but how are we going to get her?" Miguel pulled his ankle from his leg and set it on the ground before leaning toward the desk and clasping his hands together with hunger in his eyes.

"I won't know until I have a clear picture of what we are up against." Lolita looked at the clock, Thomas should call any second. If he doesn't call by five, then something must have gone wrong. "How is Mark coming along?" She needed to take her mind off what was happening in Crete for a while.

"Slower than I would like. He still has no control over his bloodlust." Miguel shook his head.

"You made him too weak, he should be over the worst by now." Lolita pulled her eyebrows together and frowned at her brother.

"I did not." Miguel surged to his feet and leaned over the desk. "I made him as strong as I could without compromising myself. He was a poor candidate, he always went after what his body desired, thinking nothing of the consequences. Until he can master his cravings, he will be of little use to us."

Lolita stood and leaned toward Miguel, ready to put him in his place, even if it meant he left, she would not be treated as less than his equal, but her phone buzzed on the desk stopping her. She looked at the screen then to the clock. Right on time. She snatched the phone, hit the answer button then relaxed into her chair. "Thomas, I was starting to wonder if you were still alive."

He cleared his throat then began. "I'm fine, but it was a busy night."

"Do tell," Lolita purred into the phone, mildly annoyed she had to ask for more information.

"Katie left the compound at dusk with one vampire and two humans. I followed them at a safe distance. They went to a seamstress then went home."

"And this makes it a busy night how?" Lolita rolled her eyes, they went shopping, what was the big deal?

"It was the first time Katie left since I've been here." Thomas didn't sound like himself, but Lolita was sure it was her vampire.

"Have you been able to figure out how many vampires Theron has?"

"No, but there at least three, Vince, Theron, and a woman. I suspect there are more. It is hard to keep an eye on everything since they moved to the new house. There aren't very many places to watch from without being spotted, and there's a dog that knows what we smell like."

"Do you think she will leave at night again?" Lolita asked, she wasn't sure she wanted to risk Thomas attempting to grab Katie, but she was tiring of waiting.

"I don't know, but I will follow if she does."

"Do you think you could take her and bring her to me?" She relied on Thomas's honesty. If he didn't think he could take Katie, he would tell her.

"I'm sorry, but I think she is too heavily guarded for me to take her on my own."

"Very well, continue as planned. We will speak again tomorrow at the same time." Lolita hit the end button on her phone and looked at Miguel to gage his reaction of the news. He seemed to be far away as he was most of the time when they talked about Katie. Would he never give her up? "Miguel, let's go see how Mark is doing."

## Chapter 35
### *Katie*

The next day I was making lunch when Vangel came in. "You're back," I said surprised. "Are you hungry? I can make you a sandwich too if you want."

"No, I'm fine. Did Theron tell you what I'm doing?" he asked, taking a seat at the bar and resting his forearms on it.

"Yes, how did it go?" I asked, cutting the sandwich in half, and putting it on a plate. Jean would be coming for it soon.

"Alex hates you like you killed his puppy." Vangel tried to laugh, but it didn't reach his eyes.

"The feeling is mutual," I said, cutting the other sandwich in half, and dumping some chips on my plate.

"The difference is you are not a sociopath with no feelings. I'm scared for you."

"That's why you're on our side, right?" I asked, moving over to the bar and sitting down to eat.

"Yes, but I don't know how much help I'll be. I've never seen anyone so hell-bent on getting what he wants, which is you." Vangel ran his hand through his hair.

"The man is delusional, I never acted like I wanted to be more than friends. I don't know what made him think he had a chance." I took a bite of my sandwich, pretending what Vangel told me wasn't as big of a deal as it was. I saw Alex on the boat, I saw the hate in his eyes.

263

"I believe you. When we were on a job, before I decided I didn't like him, he opened up to me about his past. You need to understand he has never had a real relationship with a woman, his mother was killed when he was five. His father raised him to be heartless and unforgiving. The only time he deals with women is to satisfy his needs. You treated him as a friend, and he has very few of those. Can you understand why he thought you wanted more? He thought he was in love with you."

I said nothing while I ate my sandwich and thought about my summer in Crete with Alex. He always seemed in awe when I did normal things, like he had never seen a woman eat more than a salad. It was adding up. Just like his reaction when I rejected him. "You know, he was a really nice guy for a while. What you told me explains a lot, but it doesn't make up for what he did."

"I'm not trying to make excuses for him. I'm trying to tell you how dangerous he is because you made him feel for a woman for probably the first time in his life. That you rejected him, made him go insane. He won't stop until you're dead. I don't think the money matters to him anymore. You hurt him. Now, he'll hurt you the only way he knows how."

"Katie? I thought you were going to bring me a sandwich," Jean said, coming into the room and stopping when she saw Vangel.

"Sorry, Vangel and I were just catching up. It's on the counter." I pointed to the plate on the other side of the bar.

"Thanks, where've you been, Vangel?" Jean asked, picking up the plate and sitting next to me at the bar.

"Well..." he trailed off as if he wasn't sure he should tell her.

"You can tell her," Vince said, coming into the kitchen and standing behind the island facing us. "She's part of this too."

"Part of what?" she asked, around a mouthful.

"Alex, of course. We sent Vangel to meet with him. He is spying on him for us and will lure him into a trap."

"Can I help? What's the plan?" Jean bounced in her chair, her sandwich forgotten.

"Yes, and we don't have one yet."

Jean looked at me grinning. "Why are they going to let me help?"

"We'll have a better chance of getting Alex if you are working with us than on your own." I narrowed my eyes at her.

"Oh, yeah, I guess that's a good idea." She lowered her head and picked up her sandwich.

"Do you know what he's planning yet?" I took a bite of my sandwich.

"No, but I let it slip that Theron was having a party and a bunch of bigwigs from all over Europe will be attending."

"Good idea," I said, staring past him as I thought about how it would work. "Have you told Theron yet?"

"No, I was going to after I grabbed a bottle of water."

"Sorry to keep you. Let me know what you guys come up with."

"See you later," Vangel said, leaving us to find Theron.

"Where are you at with setting up your new computer?" I asked, wishing I could've gone with Vangel to talk to Theron.

"I finished loading all the programs last night. Now I need to set everything up the way I want, and I'll be back in business."

"I'm glad you're embracing your new life. Have you chosen a new code name yet?" I asked, she hated to give up Uni, but Interpol would look for it.

"No, but I'll figure one out. Theron has me working security for him and he is going to see if anyone else in The Syndicate needs help too. I think I am going to make it."

"I'm glad to hear it." I gave her a smile and peeled a banana I found on the counter.

"Yeah, I was thinking I could introduce myself around at the party and see if anyone else could use my help. Word of mouth is the best advertising."

I wondered if Theron knew what he was going to do with Jean and

Vangel during the party yet. "Yeah," I forced myself to say. "It will be a great place for you to network." I shoved the banana in my mouth and reached out with my mind to find Theron. He was in his office as always and, based on his feelings, Vangel had just left. "Hey, I need to go talk to Theron about something. I'll see you later, OK?"

"Sure, I will be done with your computer in a few hours if you need it back."

"I'm not in any hurry." I went to Theron's door, knocked, waited a beat, then went inside. Theron was sitting behind his desk staring at his computer. "Have you figured out what we are going to do with Vangel and Jean during the party yet?"

"There will be other humans at the party who don't know about vampires. Why would there be an issue?" Theron asked, raising his eyebrows.

"How are you going to introduce me if there will be humans there?"

"I plan on having all the humans arrive after we talk about you and Lolita." Theron straightened in his chair and leveled a look at me.

"How are you going to do that?" I asked, "Vangel and Jean will already be there."

"I haven't worked it out yet, but they'll join us with the other humans who we can't make forget. That reminds me. You are going to have to make a speech."

"What do you mean?" I shook my head.

"You are to be our queen. You have to convince them that you are who you claim to be. You might need to do something to prove it to them."

I looked at my feet, of course Theron was right. I wondered why I expected the vampires to believe Theron with me standing there smiling. "I guess you're right. What am I going to say?"

"I don't know. You'll think of something."

"I guess I know what I'll be working on for a while." I stood and went to the door.

"You'll be fine Katie, just be yourself," Theron said as I left to go back to my room.

## Chapter 36
### *Katie*

Over the next three days I fell into a routine, Vince would wake me up at three-thirty in the morning, we would go to the barn, make the nightly call to Lolita, tell her about the *fifty vampires* on the property then I would go back to sleep for a few hours before getting up, working out, and helping Theron with whatever I could for the rest of the day. To say life was boring was an exaggeration. Vangel was gone most of the time. He was spending as much time with Alex as he could, trying to cement a bond with him, which meant I was stuck in the house. Which left me time to work on my speech and worry about how I was to prove myself to a bunch of vampires.

I was getting ready for my nightly call to Lolita, hoping taking control of Thomas's mind would become easier with time and practice; the night before had almost been too much for me. Vince was with me, I could have done it alone, but he didn't trust me to go on my own. "What are we going to tell Lolita tonight?" I asked as we exited the door of the main house closest to the barn.

"Same thing we have told her for the past three nights, that he saw another vampire, but not you." Vince took my hand as we walked, and I relished the feel of his hand in mine. I didn't think I would ever get used to having him in my life.

"Don't you think Lolita will get suspicious?" He was here to spy on us, nothing more, but still, how could she think I would just sit around and do nothing. I thought about that for a moment, it was all I had been doing

269

since the sniper came after me. I rolled my neck from side to side. I was tired of being a prisoner. Would there ever be a time when I wouldn't have to look over my shoulder constantly?

"No, he was sent here to observe, he is following her orders, which is what she expects. I think we were lucky he tried to snatch you and failed, otherwise, who knows what information he could have taken back to Lolita." We reached the door to the barn, and I grabbed Takis's mind. He was getting better, the bloodlust he was feeling was half of what it had been the night I met him, but it didn't matter, I still bribed him to keep quiet while Thomas talked to Lolita.

Vince opened the door and allowed me to enter first. Argyris was sitting on the floor with his legs folded and his hands resting on his knees. He was meditating and looked so calm he could've been asleep. His eyes popped open when I took a few steps into the room.

"Katie, is it time already?" he asked smoothly, unfolding himself and getting to his feet.

"Yes, how are you this evening?" I asked, giving him a warm smile. He was the calmest, chillest vampire I had met so far. If we were in the states, I would have thought he had been a hippy before he changed, smoking weed and tripping on shrooms hoping to achieve enlightenment.

"I'm well, and the vampires are calm for a change." He looked at Takis's stall then to Thomas's. I didn't have Thomas's mind yet, and it was strange that he was sitting in the corner and not yelling at the top of his lungs

"That is strange. How long has Thomas been like this?" Vince asked, walking up to the bars and staring at the prisoner.

"Since midday," Argyris said, joining Vince. "I think he finally accepted his fate and is pondering what the punishment for his crimes will be in his next life."

"Could be, or he is coming up with a plan," Vince said,

looking over his shoulder to me. "Are you ready?"

"Yes, let's get this over with, I would like to get some sleep before the sun comes up." I took a few steps closer and took Thomas's mind. He stood and walked over to the bars at my command. "I have him."

Vince pulled Thomas's phone out of his pocket and gave it to him. He took it with the barest whisper of a command from me. It was odd, normally he fought me the entire time. Something was going on with him and I needed to keep my guard up. We couldn't afford for me to slip up and allow him to tell Lolita what was really going on.

He dialed the number, hit send, then put the phone on speaker phone. It was easier for me to hear Lolita when I didn't have to do it through Thomas's mind. The phone on the other end rang and rang which was strange. Lolita almost always picked up between the first and second ring. The phone went to voice mail, and I looked at Vince. What was I supposed to say? I didn't have time for him to help me, I had to say something as the phone prompted me to leave a message.

"This is Thomas, checking in. There has been no change." I forced Thomas to hit the end button and pass the phone back through the bars. Vince took it and stepped away.

"Has Lolita ever not answered your call to check in?" Vince asked, putting the phone in his pocket and rubbing his chin with one hand.

"No, she always answers," Thomas said after I gave him a nudge. He was excited about something.

"What do you think it means?" I asked, putting my hands on my hips.

"She's coming for me." His smile grew into an evil grimace. "You will all pay for what you have done," he said as I released my hold on his mind.

"What is her plan?" Vince asked, grabbing the bars.

"I don't know but I know she will come for me."

"She doesn't know you've been captured, why do you think she's coming for you?" I asked with a half laugh, Thomas was becoming delusional. I didn't know how much longer he would be of use to us, and I wondered what we would do with him when that time came.

"Because you're here, her goal is to gain control over you." He laughed and turned, going back to his corner of the stall where he sat down with his back to us.

"Do not be overly concerned about his words," Argyris said, putting a hand on my shoulder. "He is not in his right mind."

"I'm not worried, I almost hope he's right," I said in a low voice. "I'm tired of living this way."

"Your time will come, and you will be victorious."

"Katie, you are tired. Let's go to bed," Vince said, holding his hand out to me.

"Yeah, thank you, Argyris, for your help and your kind words." I smiled at him before taking Vince's hand and letting him lead me back to the house and our bed.


We slept late the next morning. I'd been sleeping late almost every morning since I had to stay up so late to make the call to Lolita and laying in Vince's arms made me not want to get up. Vinny was whining from somewhere nearby, and I cracked my lids. When he saw my eyes open, he gave me a short quiet bark. He needed to go outside. I pushed the blankets back and got out of bed. I let him out, then stretched and thought about what I wanted to do with my day.

I wanted to work out, but the ballroom was now off limits since the party planners had taken it over to prepare for the party. The thought of the party had my gut tightening. I wasn't sure Theron's plan would work. What if I couldn't convince them to help us? I would be in a room full of vampires, and only five of them were on my side. I pushed the thought away, I wasn't getting anywhere by thinking about it.

I went into the bathroom and got ready for the day. Since the ballroom was off limits, I was going outside to work out on the lawn. It made Vince nervous, but Jean was monitoring all the security cameras on the property. There was no way anyone could sneak onto the property while she was in charge.

I left Vince sleeping in bed and stepped outside into the late morning light. I did my normal workout, then showered and stared at the suits hanging in my closet, there were a few dresses too, but it was too cold out for a dress. I opted for another black suit with a white shell, at least the jacket would hide my gun and I could wear my katana under it. I went in search of food when I was done and found Jean in the kitchen staring at her laptop.

"Hey, how's it going?" I asked, going to the fridge and pulling out eggs and cheese.

"Pretty good, just keeping an eye on things. I set up alarms on the proximity cameras. If someone tries to enter the property, I'll know about it." Jean looked up for a moment before going back to her computer.

"Did they put you on the most wanted list yet?" I asked, going to the stove and pulling a skillet down from the rack above it.

"No, which is strange. I've seen it done before, usually it happens right after they tag someone rogue."

"Do you think your mom was just messing with you?" I cracked an egg into the skillet. "I'm making scrambled eggs; do you want some?" I looked over my shoulder.

"No thanks, I already ate. I'm not sure what my mom is playing at. Maybe she is giving me a chance to change my mind. It isn't like her to not follow the rules."

I whipped the eggs while they cooked then sprinkled some cheese on top. I pulled two pieces of bread out of the bread box and stuck them in the toaster. "Do you think it might be because you're her daughter?"

"That's a good one Katie." Jean laughed. "She couldn't care less I'm related to her. She wants to move up in Interpol, she hasn't cared about me since I could wipe my own butt."

I turned around to face her, there was no way that could be true, but when I looked at her face, there was no joking going on. "Jean, I'm sorry."

"Don't be, I've learned to deal with it, but now do you see why I think it's so strange?" she asked as I turned back to the stove and turned the burner off. I went to the cabinet and pulled out a plate.

"Yeah, if she didn't care, why hasn't she followed through on her threat?" A thought burned through my mind, but it would have to wait until after I finished eating before I found out.

"Afternoon, ladies," Vangel said, wandering into the kitchen and getting a bottle of water out of the fridge. "Katie, you should have told me you were working out, I would've joined you."

"Sorry, I forgot," I said as the toaster finished my bread. I put them on the plate then covered my eggs with it. I hadn't forgotten, I was tired of Vince turning into a jealous monster. "I'll grab you next time." I got a fork out and sat down next to Jean at the bar. "What happen with you and Alex last night?"

Vangel stared at the counter for a second, then looked up at me. "We came up with a plan to kidnap you and kill everyone at the party."

I was bringing a fork full of eggs to my mouth before he started to talk, but it never made it to my mouth, instead, I dropped it back on my plate. *Theron, Vince, Helen will you please join us in the kitchen?* "What's the plan?" I asked, forcing myself to eat while I waited for the vampires to join us.

"First," Vangel started as Theron, Vince, and Helen appeared in the room. "I'm going to plant C-4 in and around the ballroom, then an hour or two before the party, I am going to kidnap you and meet Alex in the gardening shack behind the house. Once the party is in full swing, we're going to blow up the ballroom, killing everyone inside."

"Sounds simple and doable," Theron said as he began to pace.

"Easy to foil," Vangel said, looking around the room.

"Yes, it is a plan we can turn around on him easily," Vince said, not taking his eyes off me.

"Let's think about it then meet later to finalize it," Helen said, looking around the room.

"Yes, and thank you, Vangel," Theron said, stopping his pacing. "I don't know what we would have done without you." Vince rolled his eyes. "Can I see you two in the office?" he asked, looking at Helen and Vince.

"Of course," Helen said as Theron was already making his way down the hall.

"What are we doing today?" Vangel asked, changing the subject.

"I'm stuck here," Jean said, typing on her keyboard. "I still have a bunch of cameras to set up, plus I don't want to tempt fate."

"I don't have any major plans. Did you have something in mind?" I asked, taking a bite of my food.

"Alex thinks I'm your bodyguard and that you're a cocktease, it would look good if we went out. It would help the story."

I blinked and felt around for my vampires. I didn't want Vince to find out about this the hard way. "It's not a bad idea, but shouldn't we stay here and help them come up with a plan?"

"We both need a break, let's go shopping, we will only be gone for a few hours." Vangel finished his water and threw the bottle in the recycling bin. The head of The Syndicate recycled, who would have thought?

"OK, but I need to tell Theron and Vince what we're doing." I ate the rest of my eggs. "Do you want to meet in twenty minutes?"

"Sure thing," Vangel said, moving to the other side of the bar as I got up and took my plate to the sink.

"You guys have fun," Jean mumbled, barely noticing what we were talking about.

I went down the hall to Theron's office and knocked lightly on the door. "Come," he called.

I went inside, closing the door behind me. "Katie, what can I do for you?" I didn't know where Helen and Vince went, but I was glad they weren't there.

"Did you do something to Jean's mom?" I asked, sitting down in the

275

chair across from his desk.

"Me? What would I do?" He was feeling very proud of himself, almost gloating.

"Theron, you know you can't lie around me. What did you do?" I asked.

"I wasn't lying. I answered with another question."

"Point made, what did you do?" I crossed my arms over my chest.

"I might have forced her to let Jean go." He leaned back in his chair still smiling.

"Why?" I asked, he seemed to hate the girl and only put up with her because she was my friend.

"Because it was her mother. Jean has the best intentions, even if they don't turn out how she wants them to." He tried to shut down his emotions like Vince did, but it didn't work. I wasn't going to call him out on them, because he was torn, he didn't know why he was feeling like he was, and it wouldn't be fair. At least I knew he wouldn't kill her.

"Are you going to tell Jean?"

"No, I think I'll let her think her mother loves her enough not to make her a rogue."

"I didn't know you had it in you," I said, letting my arms fall to rest on my legs.

The door behind me opened, and Vince came in. "What are you two doing?" he asked, taking the seat beside me.

"Just chatting about what a nice guy Theron is," I said, unable to hold back. Theron's smile turned into a frown.

"Don't let the word out or my street credit will be ruined."

"Hey, Vangel and I are going shopping today. He thought it would be a good idea to play up the whole cocktease thing." Vince froze, and he locked his emotions down, but not before I felt his jealousy.

"Do you think that is a wise idea? I still do not know how much we can trust him." Vince looked at me from the corner of his eye.

"Yes, plus I'm tired of being stuck in the house. He needs to build trust with Alex, this is the best way. We will be gone for a few hours, no more."

"Fine." Vince crossed his arms over his chest. "Maria and her entourage will be here a few hours after sundown."

"Good, I'm glad she will be here before the party. We need more vampires on our side before the other guests arrive. Marios also arrives this evening," Theron nodded his head.

"Guys, how are we going to keep the vampire thing a secret from the humans?" I asked, it had been weighing on me and I didn't think Jean or Vangel would take it very well if they found out.

"We'll do our best. As soon as our guests arrive we will tell them that none of the humans here can be touched and they must hide their true nature from them. It isn't anything new. We have been hiding what we are since the beginning."

"Good, so no one will try to make the humans a snack?" I asked, looking between the two.

"If they tried, it would be a grand *faux pas*. We do not drink from another vampire's human without permission," Theron said, shaking his head at me.

"Good to know. I want to make sure everyone is safe, or as safe as we can make them." I looked at the vampires, and they looked back at me like I should already know vampire customs. "Well, Vangel and I are going to take off then." I stood, and Vince followed me.

"Katie, a word?" he asked, following me to the door.

"Sure." I stopped and turned to him. He still had his emotions on lockdown and it was making me mad. Yes, he had every right not to share his every thought or feeling with me, but when he locked me out completely I felt like I was out in the cold on my own.

"I need to go talk to Helen," Theron said, walking around us to the door. "You can have the office to yourselves."

"Thank you," Vince said as the door quietly clicked closed.

"What's going on?" I asked, crossing my arms over my chest. I wasn't going to like whatever he had to say.

"I know you have cabin fever and you need to get out of here, but is going out in the middle of the day with Vangel a smart idea?"

"Would you prefer I go by myself? What if I went in the middle of the night?" I asked, knowing it would just make him angry.

"I am trying to keep you safe."

"And by doing so you are driving me insane. It's a big house and there are lots of places to explore, but I need to see the sun, see people, act normal for a change. I have got to get out of here for a while Vince."

"What if I take you out tonight?" he asked, running his hands through his hair.

"Maria is coming tonight. Don't you want to be here when she arrives?"

"Fuck, I should have done this weeks ago." One moment he was standing a few feet in front of me and the next he held me in his arms and his lips were coming down on mine. He unlocked his emotions then, and I felt the fierce love he had for me. He was driving himself mad with thoughts of something happening to me when he couldn't reach me. I kissed him back and tried to pour all the love I felt for him into the kiss, but also my independence, and the strength he had given me. He needed to trust me.

When our kiss finally broke he took a step back. "Go, I trust you." He took my hand and kissed it.

"Thank you, I love you, Vince."

"And I you, my sweet, strong Katie."

We drove to the shopping district in Heraklion with the windows down and the stereo blasting since it was a warm sunny

278

day for a change. I hadn't felt so normal since before I came to Europe. Vangel laughed as I sang along with my favorite songs and danced in my seat. When we arrived, he parked the car, and we walked around.

"What are we shopping for?" he asked, as we passed designer stores advertising end-of-season sales.

"I don't really need anything, but maybe shoes. I need something to wear with my dress at the party." I paused outside a store with shoes on display.

"Then, let's do it." He grabbed my hand and pulled me into the store.

I tensed when he touched me, but we were trying to play a part, a part Alex would believe as me being a cocktease. I needed to play along so it would be easier for Vangel to *kidnap* me before the party. Once inside, I wandered around the store and picked up a few pairs of black heels. My dress would be red, but I wasn't good enough to know the exact shade, so black would have to do.

While the salesperson was in the back getting my size, I sat on a chair and realized how surreal it was to be doing something so normal. Vangel was standing by the door with his phone out. "Is everything all right?" I asked as he bent his head to text something.

"What? Yeah, Alex is texting me. He wants me to take you now."

My body tensed, what were we going to do? "What are you telling him?"

"That it would be stupid, you have a sword and a gun. There's no way I could take you without causing a scene," he said, rapidly typing onto his phone. "And I wouldn't be able to place the explosives."

"Do you think he'll believe it?"

"Let's hope so, otherwise we're screwed. He either figures out I'm lying about being on his side or you have to kick my ass. I'm not looking forward to either."

"What if we did what you did when Mordor was chasing me? Pretend to take me, then we can take him?" The idea sprung to my mind unbidden, but it did work before.

"I don't know if he would fall for it, but let's see what he says and then decide."

The salesperson came back out at that moment with a pile of boxes so high he could barely see over the top. I went back to my seat and tried to enjoy trying shoes on, but I couldn't help worrying about where Alex was, and if he would try something. Going out was turning into a disaster.

"He agreed with me, we're good to go," Vangel said, sliding into the seat next to me.

I let out a deep breath and gave him a smile. "Thank God, do you know how pissed Vince would be if we had gone with the other plan?"

"Again, I don't want to get my ass kicked. Which shoes are you going with?" he asked, looking at the strappy heels on my feet.

"I don't want any of them, but I need something I can move in. These won't come off if I have to move quickly and they look good." I got up and took a stroll around the store. My feet would hate me by the end of the night, but I would sacrifice them for fashion.

"What do you think?" I asked, stopping in front of him.

"I think they are semi-functional and look great. Can we get out of here now?" Vangel looked toward the door. The idea that Alex wasn't far away was getting to him. It should've been getting to me too but, between the two of us, if Alex came after me directly I knew we could take him.

"Yeah, these will work." I sat and took them off, telling the salesperson I would take them. He put them back in the box and went over to the cash register. I paid him, and we left, hurrying, but not too quickly. We didn't want Alex to think I knew what was going on.

Once we were in the car and strapped in a thought hit me. "You don't think he would have put a bomb in the car, do you? He did steal a bunch of C-4," I said as Vangel's finger hovered over the ignition switch. "Let's check." Vangel pulled his phone out and dialed a number.

"What's up? You guys coming back already?" Jean's voice asked, coming from the phone, Vangel must have turned the speaker phone on.

"Yeah, Alex tagged us. I want to get Katie out of the way," Vangel said, looking through the mirrors then out the windshield for threats. "You've been monitoring the car, right?"

"Yeah, no one has come within five feet of it. Why?"

"Alex stole a bunch of C-4, I wanted to make sure the car hasn't been tampered with."

"Good idea, you're good," Jean said. Vangel pushed the starter button right before Jean continued, "Except for the panel van that was blocking my view for five minutes, otherwise, I never took my eyes off the car.

I screamed, but it was too late for Vangel to turn the car off, we both tensed and stared at each other for a moment. When nothing happened, we both looked at the phone. "Jean, what the hell? Vangel started the car right before you told us about the panel van."

"I was just messing with you guys. Nothing blocked the camera." She laughed in the background. "I wish I could have seen the look on your faces when I said that."

"I'll show you a look when we get back," Vangel said, ending the call and driving back toward the mansion.

We drove in silence, thinking of ways to get Jean back, at least I was, while Vince constantly checked the mirrors. After watching him for a few minutes, I couldn't take it anymore. "Do we have a tail?" I looked out the side-view mirror, thanks to movies I knew not to look behind me.

"Yes, and I would put money on it being Alex," Vangel said, his voice was harder than I had ever heard it.

"What are we going to do?" I asked, pulling my gun from the holster.

"Not shoot out the window at him. I'm supposed to be helping him, aren't I?" he asked, bringing his phone up and typing out a quick message.

"Are you trying to get us killed? Keep your eyes on the road." I shook my head and eyed the car. "Wait, are you talking about the red Mini Cooper? That's Jean's car, she left it at the police station after she walked out on her mom."

"Are you sure it's hers?" Vangel asked, eyeing the car behind us.

"No, but I know how to find out." I pulled my phone out of my pocket and sent a text to Jean asking for the license plate number.

**Why?**

"Jean always asks too many questions," I muttered.

**I'll tell you later, I need to know, NOW.**

**SFI-042**

I recited the plate number to Vangel.

"That's who's following us," he said, shaking his head.

I dialed Jean. "What's wrong?" she asked as soon as the line connected.

"Your car is following us. What did you do with the keys?"

"I left them in the ignition. I wouldn't be surprised if they put a tracker in the key fob. Where are you?" After I told her, she sighed. "There aren't any cameras near there. What are you going to do?"

"I don't know, but don't tell anyone what is going on."

"OK, I won't. Just keep the line open."

I put my phone on the dash. "What do you want to do?" I asked Vangel, he had more experience with being followed than I did.

"We could try to lose them, but that is easier said than done. I don't know the island very well."

"I could tell you where to go, Katie has the GPS on her phone turned on," Jean said.

"I don't trust computer maps unless I'm in a big city, they aren't always current or correct," Vangel said and looked at the gun in my lap.

"We could find a place to confront them. Find out what they want." I offered, it had been way too long since I kicked some ass.

"What if it's Alex?" Vangel whispered, not wanting to let Jean know who he thought it was.

"Alex? You think it's Alex?" Jean screamed into the phone.

"Jean, remember when you said you wouldn't tell anyone? Vince and Theron have excellent hearing," I said, trying to keep my voice calm when I wanted to yell at her.

"Sorry," she whispered. "You think it's Alex?"

"There is a chance," I said, looking at Vangel. "Then we go with plan C."

"Plan C? Crap, Theron is at my door. I have to go. Sorry Katie." The call ended, and I put my phone in my pocket.

"Can she do nothing right?" Vangel asked, turning off the highway and onto a dirt road that wound its way up the side of a hill.

"Sometimes I wonder," I said, picking up my gun and looking through the mirror. The Cooper had just turned off behind us. "So, plan C?"

"Plan C: we park the car, I point my gun at you, and force you out of the car. If it's Alex, you pull your gun and shoot him in the knee." He down shifted as the grade became steeper.

"What if it's not Alex? We pull our guns on whoever it is and find out what they want." At the top of the hill, Vangel parked at a pull out on the side of the road, and killed the engine.

"OK, get out, and follow my lead."

My phone vibrated in my pocket and I cursed myself for not leaving it in my purse. I hit the button on the side to make it stop and put my gun back in its back holster. I got out the car and held my hands out to the side of my body, leaving the door open.

Vangel had his gun out and was standing behind me with the muzzle pointed at my back. The Cooper came to a stop, and a woman got out with her gun pointed at the ground.

"Interpol, put your hands where I can see them," the woman said as I looked at my hands already in plain sight.

Vangel quickly tucked his gun in the waistband of my pants, so the woman wouldn't know he was packing and brought his hands up. "What can we do for you?"

"Where's my daughter?" she asked, holding the gun out in front of her, but not pointing it at us.

"Who's your daughter?" I asked, I was pretty sure I knew, but I wanted to make sure.

"Jeanette Vang, where is she?" The woman was clearly distraught, and with a gun in her hands that made her dangerous.

"Why would I know where she is?" I asked. I didn't want this woman to know I knew she was the one who was making Jean a rogue agent.

"Listen, I know who you are, and I know Jean has been staying with you since she left Kevó. I need to find her." There was concern in her voice but, if she was an Interpol Agent, chances were she knew how to act.

"Wait, how do you know who I am?" I asked as a shiver of fear ran down my spine.

"You're Katie Hunter, you disappeared from San Sebastian, Spain last May. Your parents are worried sick about you. I don't know or care who you are running from or how you got mixed up with the Cretan Syndicate."

"I'm trying to keep my parents out of harm's way." I pulled my shoulders back and stared at her. If I blinked I would start to cry, and this woman didn't deserve to see me cry.

284

"Should I tell them I've seen you?" she asked, tapping a finger on her lips.

"No, they think I'm in the witness protection program. It's better this way." I crossed my arms over my middle, like I was trying to hold in the hurt she was causing me.

"Fine, just tell me where I can find my daughter."

"I thought she was with you. She never came back after her meeting with you." I was lying, that might make me a bad person, but Jean didn't want to see her mom.

"What do you mean she never came back? She left all her things in her car and left it on the side of the road."

"She called me as she was leaving the station." We needed to wrap this up, I wanted to be away from her. "She said you wouldn't honor your part of the deal and she was going to disappear."

"I was upset," she said as the rage melted away and became despair. "I would never tag her as rogue."

I didn't know what Theron had done to her, but whatever it was, it worked. "I'm sorry. If I hear from her, I'll tell her what you said." I had no idea how to handle this and I hoped I was doing the right thing.

"Please, she's all I have left." A tear escaped and trickled down her cheek. She pulled a phone out of her pocket and walked over to us. "If you see her, give her this. It isn't traceable, please ask her to call me."

I took the phone, not believing her for a second when she said it couldn't be tracked. "If I see her I'll tell her. Can we go now?"

"Yes, sorry if I scared you." She turned around and went back to Jean's car.

I looked at Vangel and he shrugged his shoulders at me. "Let's jet?"

"Let's let her go first."

The vibrating in my pocket started again, and I pulled out my phone while the Mini Cooper turned and went down the road we had just come up. I'd missed ten calls and had fifteen text messages waiting for me. I shook my head, vampire fingers moved fast when they wanted to.

"Before you reply, let me see the phone she gave you." I handed the phone to him and waited. He took it over to the car, pulled out a multi-tool and cracked the back off it. He inspected it for a few minutes then put the back on. He turned it around and looked at the screen. "Go ahead and call them, I don't see any bugs."

I dialed Vince even though I had missed calls from everyone at the house.

"Katie, are you safe, was it Alex?" he asked as soon as he answered.

"I'm safe, and it was Jean's mom, not Alex. Everything is fine."

"Why was Jean's mother following you?"

"She misses Jean and wants to talk to her." I would tell Vince what Theron did when there weren't any humans around.

"What did you tell her?"

"I told her," Vangel cut me off and pointed at the phone, maybe it was bugged after all. "I told her the truth, that Jean never came back after being tagged rogue. That I had no idea where she was and didn't know if I would ever see her again. She gave me a phone to give to her in case I saw her."

"Write down the phone numbers stored in it then ditch it."

"I was thinking about the same thing. We will be home soon."

"Good, please be careful." Vince's voice softened, he'd been worried.

"OK, see you soon." I ended the call and held my hand out for the phone. "This is a great view," I said, taking the phone and opening the notepad in my phone.

"Yeah, I wonder why no one has built up here. You can practically see the mainland," Vangel said, watching as I copied the three numbers into the phone.

"It's getting late. Should we go?" I asked, giving the phone

286

to him.

"Yeah, let's get home."

We got in the car and Vangel drove down the dirt road. When there was no sign of Jean's car nearby, Vangel rolled down the window and dropped the phone to the ground. "That was messed up," I said as we drove back to the mansion with no tail this time.

"No kidding, I wonder what changed her mind about labeling Jean rogue," Vangel asked.

"I don't know, but I hope it was out of love and she doesn't change her mind."

"Me too."

Chapter 37

*Katie*

The sun was about to set when we got back to the mansion. Vangel parked the car in the garage and took a breath before he opened the door.

"Are you all right?" I asked, seeing the tension in his shoulders.

"I don't know. Do you think Vince will kill me for allowing us to be followed?"

"I won't let him, it wasn't your fault, and we took care of the problem without anyone getting hurt." I squeezed his arm then went to open the door, but it was already open, and Vince was pulling me out and wrapping his arms around me. "Hey, I'm fine, it was no big deal," I said, hugging him back. He was still panicking, and I couldn't imagine what it would have felt like to be close to him when he thought Alex found me.

*I thought Vangel had double-crossed us and was taking you to Alex,* he thought, squeezing me even tighter. *I'm so glad you are safe.*

"Calm down, everything is fine. Let's go inside and we'll tell you everything." I pulled away from Vince and grabbed my bag from the back seat.

Vangel was already halfway to the door leading to the rest of the house. "I'll meet you in the office, I need to go to the bathroom," he said before disappearing through the door.

"What is wrong with him?" Vince asked, taking my bag from me with one hand and holding my hand with the other as he led us to the door.

"He thinks you'll blame him for what happened. It wasn't his fault, he was doing everything he should've. We had no idea who was behind us, but we had a plan if it was someone after me."

"You did?" Vince asked, holding the door as we entered the house. He was still worried, and he was trying to hide it from me, but he was too amped up.

"Yeah, we were going to do what we did when Mordor tried to get me. Pretend Vangel was on their side then I was going to shoot whoever it was. I'm glad we didn't have to, it would've been a mess."

"I'm glad everything went to plan then." Vince's voice sounded calm, but he was still pissed. We went into Theron's office without knocking and found Theron and Jean having a stare down.

"What's going on?" I asked, getting tired of playing peacekeeper for them.

Theron snapped his head in my direction. "We were just discussing what to do about her mother."

"Well, let's wait for Vangel, then we'll tell you what happened," I said, taking a seat on the couch and yawning. I needed a nap if I was going to stay awake for Thomas to call Lolita.

After Vangel joined us, we told everyone what happened; how Alex had wanted Vangel to take me while we were shopping but Vangel talked him out of it. Then about the tail and our plan when we found out who it was. Jean was shocked when she heard what her mother had to say.

"So Jean, here are the numbers your mom had in the phone. We ditched it because Vangel thought it was bugged." I threw my phone to her, so she could look at the numbers. She pulled her phone out and entered them in.

"Thanks, I don't plan on calling her anytime soon." She threw the phone back to me when she was done. "She'll never understand me, and I can't deal with her right now."

"So, crisis averted. What are everyone's plans for the night?" Theron asked, looking at his watch.

"I'm off duty, so I need to make contact with Alex," Vangel said, getting to his feet.

"I'm going to research these numbers and take the first shift of security detail," Jean said, getting up and going to the door.

"Jean, we are expecting a few guests tonight. Don't worry about any cars that come through the gate," Theron said, looking at his computer.

"OK, thanks for the heads-up." She left the room followed by Vangel.

With the humans gone I looked around at Vince, Helen, and Theron. "Is there anything we need to do before Maria and Marios arrive?"

Helen looked at me like I smelled.

"What? Did I step in dog poop or something?" I asked, wanting to check my armpits for BO but stopped myself.

"No, you smell as lovely as ever, but you might want to change into something with less wrinkles," Vince said, taking over for Helen. "A queen would never receive company in a wrinkled suit."

I looked at my suit, the day's activities had not been nice to it. My top was wrinkled and somehow, I had gotten dirt on the knee of one of my pant legs.

"I'll help you with your hair and makeup," Helen said, getting up and waiting for me to join her.

"Fine." I got up and followed Helen out of the room, it had been less than a week and I was already tired of dressing up.


Thirty minutes later I looked at myself in the mirror. Helen knew how to make me look like a professional badass, that was for sure. I was wearing a black pantsuit with a cream, silk shell with a neckline that almost came to my belly button and a black blazer that framed my twenty-two-inches of cleavage. The sleek lines made it more femme fatale than slutty, barely.

Vince was waiting for me when I came out of the bedroom and lust thundered through him. "I guess I look OK?" I asked, smoothing down my jacket. It felt like if I leaned too far to either side I would show the world my breasts.

"You look more than OK, you are a knockout." He made his way toward me and bent to touch his lips to mine for the briefest moment. "Let's go to the great room to wait." He took my hand when I agreed and led me through the house.

When we arrived in the great room Helen and Theron were staring at their phones. Sometimes I found it hard to believe they were ancient vampires and not millennials. Helen looked up first and smiled. "You look fantastic," she said.

"Thanks for your help. If I had to fight in this, I don't know if flashing my enemy would work for me or against me."

The mention of nudity had Theron looking up from his phone. He gave me a once-over and nodded, his face blank, but I felt what he was feeling: lust and guilt, I would never tell Vince about it. He was jealous enough of Vangel. Besides, didn't all men feel lust when they looked at something they thought was beautiful? I sat on a lone, high-backed, upholstered chair, positioned to let me see the whole room and crossed my arms over my chest. I wasn't used to so much exposed skin when I wasn't at the beach.

"The seamstress will be here tomorrow for the final fitting of your dress," Helen said, seeming to want to end the silence that had descended on the room.

"Perfect," I said, wondering what she was going to come up with. I had given her a few specifications, it had to look good with my katana on my back, I wanted everyone to see my tattoo, and I needed to be able to dance in it. When I told her dance, I meant fight, but there wasn't much difference between the two, and she didn't need to know I might have to fight for my life while wearing it. The ring of the doorbell brought me out of my thoughts and into the present.

"Our guests have arrived," Vince said, getting to his feet. I moved to follow him, but he stopped me. "Wait here, I will bring her to you."

"OK." I was confused, she was supposed to be on our side, why didn't he want me to greet her at the door?

A few minutes later, I felt six new vampires enter the house, and I straightened in my chair and rested my arms on the armrests as they walked down the hall to join us. Vince entered first and came to stand behind me. Three women and three men came to a stop in the doorway.

"Katie, this is my very old friend, Maria," Vince said, putting his hands on my shoulders. Maria was about five-foot four with bright red, curly hair, she was dressed in a long, black dress with a sweetheart neckline giving her the illusion of more cleavage than she had, it had long sleeves that accentuated her long, blood-red fingernails. Her stark white skin made her look more like a vampire than most of the ones I had met. Her lips were painted red and held a look of contempt.

"Nice to meet you." I offered her my hand. "Vince told me you helped him while he was drugged. Thank you."

She came forward and took my hand with a wet noodle grip before quickly releasing it. "Nice to meet you as well. You're welcome." *If it hadn't been for you, he wouldn't have needed my help in the first place*, she thought as jealousy raged through her.

"If it wasn't for Lolita, none of it would have happened," I said, returning to my seat. If I was to be queen, this woman needed to know what I was about. *This chair will be my throne*, I thought, sitting with my back straight and my hands gently resting on the arms.

*What did she say?* Vince asked.

*That it was my fault you were drugged in the first place.*

"What?" Maria asked, confused.

"You blame me for what happened to Vince. I could blame you for letting a spy into your home, but I blame Lolita for the entire situation."

"Please sit down, Maria, so we can talk," Theron said, motioning to the empty seat next to him and giving me a critical eye. He was confused as well, no one had ever heard me speak so sternly. They would have to get used to it. I decided while I was getting dressed; I couldn't let any of the new vampires I met see me as anything but a queen. If I showed them how terrified I was about what was happening, they would walk all over me.

"Very well, Juan, please join me. The rest of you get our things out of the car and take them to our quarters," Maria said, sitting next to Theron. Juan took the seat next to her and the others filed out the room, upset because they didn't get to stay.

"Maria, this is Theron and Helen. I do not think you have met them before. Theron is my son, and he turned Helen," Vince said.

"It is nice to meet you," she said, but she did not really care, she was still fuming about what I said to her.

"Likewise," Theron said, flashing her a smile that didn't reach his eyes.

"You as well," Helen said.

"Vince, you asked me to come, and I'm here. Tell me what you're planning, and how I'm involved?" Maria asked with introductions done.

"First, we plan to introduce Katie to the vampires of Europe, in hopes of gaining more allies in our fight against Lolita. Then we are going to Venice to destroy her army, sending her to hell." Vince opened the wine bottle sitting on the coffee table and filled glasses for everyone. He pulled a flask out and put a few drops of blood in all but one and passed them around.

"You still believe she's 'The One?'" Maria asked, before taking a sip of her wine. *When did Vince become so gullible?*

"It's fine with me if you don't believe it. Helen doesn't either. All I care about is stopping Lolita and her army. Vince believes it because he has seen what I can do."

"How are you doing it?" she asked.

"Doing what?"

"Answering questions I haven't asked out loud." She sat up straighter and Juan tensed next to her.

"You're projecting your thoughts."

"Are you telling me you can read my mind?"

"If I want to but, right now, you're thinking loud enough I don't have to."

Maria opened her mouth but closed it before saying anything. *How am I going to have any privacy when she can read my mind? How does Vince deal with it?*

"You need to stop thinking so loudly to start. Vince deals with it because he trusts me and thinks quietly. He knows I won't read his mind unless it is an emergency."

"As we all do," Helen said, taking a sip of wine and leaning back in her chair.

"You believe in the prophecy then?" Maria looked at Theron.

"I do," Theron said, looking around. "She proved herself to me the first night we met."

"I believe she has powers I have never seen before. I don't believe in the myth, but I believe she is the key to stopping Lolita," Helen said.

"OK then," Maria said, turning and looking at me. "Please stay out of my head."

"I will, as long as I can trust you."

"What do you need us to do?" Maria leveled her gaze on Vince.

"I need you to help me protect Katie and support our cause during the party. Even if you do not believe it. It would do us little good if you are not on our side."

"What are you going to be saying at this party?"

"We will tell everyone who Katie is and ask for help to stop Lolita's war with the humans."

"Someone will tell Lolita, how will your plan work when she crashes the party?"

"I will kill her here, then we will travel to Venice and dispose of her

295

army," I said, believing the words as I said them. I was going to kill her if it was the last thing I did in this life.

"Vince, I'm on your side in this, but don't get me and mine killed."

"I will try not to," Vince said, moving around my chair.

"Then I will help protect Katie from any harm that may come her way. I'm not swearing my life for hers, but I'll help." She relaxed back in her seat and sipped her wine. "How many vampires did you lose in the attack Theron?"

"All but myself, Helen, and Vince. I have already started rebuilding my forces, but as you well know, it will take decades." Theron blew out a breath and ran his fingers through his hair. "I had my children, who were not at the compound during the attack, join us which adds three to our numbers.

"What of the other humans I'm sensing here?" she asked, closing her eyes and taking a deep breath. "Are they donors?"

"No," I almost yelled. I didn't want any of my friends becoming blood-addicts or slaves. Vince put his hand on my shoulder and squeezed. "Sorry, they are my friends and I will not allow them to be hurt."

"I was just asking Katie; don't be so quick to judge those you do not know." Maria rolled her eyes at me, and I felt myself tense further.

"I will always protect what is mine. We have bagged blood here, if you want something else, Theron can tell you where to go." I sat up straighter, I wouldn't apologize for protecting my friends.

"As Katie said, we have a bagged blood service and, if you would like, I can show you the vampire bar we set up for a limited time. With so many coming to the party, we needed to have somewhere for us to eat without making ourselves known to the people on the island."

"We ate before we left, but I may need something tomorrow.

For now, I think I'll retire to my rooms and make sure we are all settled in." She gulped the rest of her wine then stood. "Vince, will you show me where to go?"

"Of course." *I will be back in a few minutes,* Vince thought before holding his arm toward the same wing our suite was located in.

I waited until they were far enough away to be out of earshot. "Why are they staying in our wing?" I asked Theron. I didn't know why it mattered, but I was getting used to having the wing to ourselves.

"They're guests, I wanted to give them the nicer, bigger rooms." Theron's eyebrows climbed up at my words. *Is she jealous?*

"I'm not jealous, I'm just used to having that side of the house to ourselves." I huffed.

"Giving her more than a bedroom will also keep her out of our hair more." Theron looked back down at his phone and frowned.

"What's wrong?" I asked, trying to get a read on him but getting nothing. "There seems to be an issue with the caterer in the ballroom I need to look into." He rose to his feet.

"Do you want me to come?" I asked.

"No, Helen and I can handle it, but thank you." Theron left with Helen trailing after him.

I was alone in the great room with nothing to do. My mind was bouncing around everything happening. Maria was here, and she didn't like me. Vince was trying to keep both Maria and me happy. The party was in less than two days and we had no idea where Lolita was. Things were coming to a boil, and I wondered how we would get through it.

I needed to take my mind off everything, so I went back to our suite. I was thinking about changing out of my suit when the door opened and Vince walked in. "What are you doing?" he asked, seeing my black heels on the ground in front of the couch.

"I was thinking about watching a movie. Do you want to join me?" I asked, pulling the remote control for the TV out.

He stared at me with his hands on his hips thinking. "Yes. We have not had a lot of downtime, have we?”

"No, and I need to take my mind off my problems for a while." I gave him a smile and made room for him on the couch.

## Chapter 38
### *Jean*

Jean watched the first car come through the gate. Part of her wanted to get up and see who it was, but she had a job, and leaving her post was not in her job description. She didn't mind watching the security footage, but it was getting old fast, mostly because nothing was happening. There had been no sign of anyone on the property since she started. That didn't mean someone wouldn't show up at any second though.

She looked around her room, looking for something to keep her busy but still allowed her to keep an eye on the computer, but there was nothing. She wished Vangel was there, then she could at least have someone to talk to. Katie was hanging out with Vince and they needed their alone time, it didn't seem like they got very much of it.

She didn't understand a lot of what was going on with these people. She understood why they were doing what they were doing, but it felt like she was missing part of the big picture, like they were hiding something from her. Her computer chimed, and she looked up as a man with a rolling suitcase in his hand walked through the gate and headed toward the front door.

Jean pulled her phone out and called Theron. She kept an eye on the man as the call went to voice mail. "Theron, someone is coming to the front door. He is on foot with a suitcase. Are you expecting someone?" She ended the call and dialed Helen. Her phone went to voice mail too.

She looked at the contact information for Katie and Vince, she didn't want to bother them. They needed this time. Instead, she opened the security app on her phone and went to the front door, keeping one eye on where she was walking and one on the cameras in case anyone else wanted to sneak onto the grounds.

When she reached the door, she clicked on the camera for the front door. The man on the other side had short, black, straight hair, a large sharply angled nose, and thin lips. He looked to be in his mid-twenties and was dressed in a light suit too cool for the chilly night. He was about to ring the doorbell when Jean opened the door.

"What do you want?" she asked, leaving the door open only a crack with her foot on the other side of it to keep it from opening any further.

The man looked at her and laughed. "Theron knows me too well," he said in a low voice, shaking his head and looking at the ground. "Let me in girl, I am a guest of Theron's." His eyes locked with hers.

"Who are you? Theron didn't tell me about anyone arriving on foot." Jean blinked, his eyes were such an intense shade of brown it felt like he was trying to hypnotize her.

The man shook his head and lost his smile. "I am Marios. Theron invited me for the party. Let me in."

Marios? Theron mentioned he would be arriving, but Jean was getting a weird feeling from him. "Fine." She opened the door and moved out of the way, allowing the man to enter.

"My suitcase?" he asked, leaving it outside.

"What about it? I'm not a bellboy." Jean turned and went into the great room, sending a text to Theron that Marios had arrived.

"What does Theron keep you around for then?" he asked, and it felt like he was staring at her neck. The house was warm, she only had a tank top on and her hair was up in a ponytail.

"Security," Jean said, leading him into the great room and

rubbing her neck.

"I doubt that's all," Marios said, then he moved faster than anyone she had seen before, except Katie. One moment he was standing on the other side of the room, then in the blink of an eye, he had his arms around her in a tight embrace.

Jean screamed and tried to push him away, but he was too strong. She didn't know what he wanted, he wasn't kissing her or groping her. It felt like he was trying to get to her neck. She took a step back then kicked forward and connected with his balls. He released her, and she ran for her room. There was no way she could beat him in a one-on-one fight.

She was halfway there when he was on her again. "You will do what I say," he said, yanking her by the arm, back down the hall and throwing her on the couch. "There's only one reason Theron would have a human working for him." He loosened a button on his shirt.

Jean kicked out, hoping to distract him long enough for her to escape, but she missed. He sank to his knees and lowered his head to hers. "Now, be a good girl and hold still." She felt the niggling in her head again, and she shook it. She was about to headbutt him when he was gone.

"Marios. What are you doing?" Theron bellowed at him and Jean sank deeper into the couch cushions.

"She is not to be touched. Do you understand me?" he bellowed, picking Marios up like he weighed less than a piece of paper and drug him into his office. "Wait here and don't touch anything." He shut the door behind him and went back to Jean.

"Are you all right?" Theron asked, offering her a hand up.

She took it, getting to her feet. "What was he talking about? Do you usually have your house full of hookers or something?" Jean asked, letting go of his hand as soon as she could trust her legs.

"Something like that." Theron blew out a breath and held his arm toward her room. "I'm not like that anymore. Marios has been gone for a long time. Are you hurt?"

"No, I'm fine, just surprised. He wanted me to get his bag like I was a servant or something." Jean rubbed her arms and shook her head.

"Get some rest. I'll have Natalia take over security for the rest of the night." Theron walked with her to her door. "And don't worry, Marios won't bother you again."

"Thanks." Jean went into her room, closed and locked the door behind her. What was going on here? Theron didn't seem to notice or care that Marios could move faster than a speeding bullet. Jean hit her palm to her forehead, Marios wasn't Superman, but he was something different, maybe they all were, and why did he refer to her as human? Wasn't he one too?

# Chapter 39
## *Katie*

"I wonder what's going on." I asked Vince as we left the stable and walked back to the house. "Lolita doesn't seem to be the type to blow off her vampires."

"I don't know. I'll call Miguel when we get inside and see if he knows what is going on." Vince put his hand on the small of my back and led me toward the door.

"Are you sure we can trust him?"

"Yes, I wish I could take away all the horrible things he did to you, and you have no right to forgive him, but he is trying to help." Vince led me down the hall to our suite.

"What if he is telling Lolita everything we tell him?" I stopped in the middle of the hall. "Does he know we have Thomas?"

Vince stopped and turned to face me with a pained look on his face. "No, Theron and I thought it was best if we did not tell him everything that is going on around here. Lolita can be very manipulative, and we do not know if Miguel is strong enough to withstand her."

"Thank the Goddess." I blew out a breath.

When we got to our suite, I opened the door and heard Vinny growling. I pulled the katana from my back and tiptoed into the room following the sound of the growls. It was coming from the bedroom. I looked at Vince from the corner of my eye and noticed a knife in his hand.

*Is it a vampire?* he thought.

I let my feelers out, there were so many vampires around that I muted my sense, so I didn't have them bouncing around in my head all the time. *Yes, but I have no idea who.*

*Stay here, I will go see.* Vince pushed me back and flashed into the bedroom.

"Get this beast away from me, Vince," a heavily accented voice boomed through the door.

*Katie, will you call Vinny please?* Vince asked. He wasn't afraid or angry, he was paranoid.

"Vinny, come," I called, taking a few steps toward the bedroom. Vinny growled one more time then came bounding to me. I gave him a rub down. "Good boy, keep the bad guys out of my bedroom."

"Katie, we are coming out, please keep control of your dog," Vince said, and I heard him and the other man's feet clop across the floor. I led Vinny over to the couch and sat down with him between my legs. I kept my sword in my right hand and held onto Vinny's collar with my left.

Vince came into the room followed by a man who looked like he had been in his early forties when he was changed. His olive complexion had not seen the sun in millennia and the frown lines on his face proved he had never been a happy man.

"Katie, this is Livius, my maker, Livius, this is Katie, 'The One' who was prophesied by Asteria's oracle."

I stood, keeping my eyes on the vampire who looked me up and down before laughing. "She has really schooled you boy. When did you become so naïve?" he asked out loud. *This girl must be a good fuck if she has Vince wrapped around her finger.*

"I am a good fuck, but that isn't why Vince is with me," I replied, running my hand down Vince's chest.

His eyes went wide. *Did she just hear my thoughts?*

"Yes, I can hear your thoughts, now if you wouldn't mind,

304

please stop thinking about what I look like naked. You will never find out."

"That is impossible," he almost shouted and rubbed his hands over his eyes. "You are human, correct?"

"Half human, half god. Asteria is my mother, I dream of her almost every night. Why else would I be able to hear the thoughts of vampires?" I was bored repeating myself.

Livius believed me, and it made him want me more. I could almost see his desire, it was so powerful. "Vince, why don't you show Livius to his rooms? I'm sure he had a long journey and needs to rest." I wanted him out of my suite before he got any ideas and I had to kill him.

"Yes, come. Theron has given you a wonderful suite." Vince held his hand out toward the door leading to the rest of the house.

"This is the master suite?" Livius asked, turning on his heel and taking in the room.

"Yes, it is mine and Katie's," Vince answered, and tension filled his body.

"I am the master, so I will take this suite. You can move with, or without Katie. I wouldn't mind letting her warm my bed."

*Is he serious?* I thought to Vince.

*Yes.* Vince was fighting for control of his body. I wasn't sure if it was a vampire thing, or the fact that this man had once owned him.

"Livius, you are not the master here," I said, resting my katana on my shoulder as a show of strength. "This is Theron's island. He gave us the master suite. Now, your room is the second door on the right. I suggest you go now or risk earning Theron's displeasure." I moved to hold my katana in both hands in front of me.

"How would I earn his displeasure?" he asked, trying not to laugh at my sword.

"This mansion is a rental. If I get your blood everywhere he won't be pleased," I said out loud. *Do not tempt me old man, I am more powerful than you know.*

He jumped and looked at the door. "You said it was the second door on the right?" He moved to the door. "Very well, I will find it myself. See you later, Vince," he said, shutting the door on his way out. I relaxed, sheathed my katana and locked the door.

Vince stood frozen and blinked at me. "I'm sorry if I made you look weak in front of him, but there was no way I was changing rooms."

"How did you do it?" Vince asked, ignoring my words.

"Do what?" I asked, looking at him.

"Get him to leave without bloodshed. If you were anyone else, one of you would have been bleeding by now."

"I broke into his mind and threatened him. I think he believes me." I went back to the couch and sat. "Can he really make you do what he wants?" I asked, wondering if it was part of the magic associated with vampires or if it was something else.

Vince sat on the couch next to me and ran his fingers through his hair. "If you are wondering if it's vampire magic, it's not. We have free will just like humans. He cannot force me to do anything, but I was his slave for hundreds of years and old habits die hard."

"So, you feel like you have to do what he says from your time as his slave?" I asked to clarify. I couldn't imagine the conditioning it would take for a man, or vampire, to feel like they had to obey their master thousands of years after he was set free.

"There is a reason why I haven't seen him in a long time. As soon as he is near I feel like I must do what he says. I know I do not have to, but part of me wants to earn his goodwill." Vince leaned back and stared at the ceiling.

"I'm sorry, Vince, I can't even imagine what that would be like. Is there anything I can do?" I asked, taking his hand in mine.

"You have already done it." He looked at me from the corner of his eye then moved faster than I thought possible, and I was in his arms and he was carrying me to bed. "Goddess, I love you."

306

Chapter 40

*Katie*

The next day, after I did a light workout and practiced my speech for the party, Theron gathered everyone in the great room. It was time to plan. I was sitting in the armchair I had used as a throne when Maria arrived. Vince was standing next to me and Theron was behind me. Helen sat on the loveseat next to Maria while her vampires stood at ease behind her. Vangel and Jean shared the couch with Livius, where they put as much room as they could between Livius and themselves. Marios, Argyris, and Natalia stood near the doors, as if they were expecting an attack at any moment.

"We need to talk about the game plan for tomorrow night," I said, looking around the room at the group who had agreed to help us. "Theron, why don't you brief us on the schedule for tomorrow night?"

Theron moved around my chair and stood next to me. "The party is scheduled to begin an hour after sunset. Guests will enter through the doors nearest the ballroom where we will contain them. I don't want them wandering around the house." Theron walked around inside the circle of furniture we were sitting on. "We know, thanks to Vangel, that Alex is planning on attacking the party and he doesn't care how many he kills in his effort to get his hands on Katie. What we don't know is where Lolita is. It's safe to bet that she will make an appearance tomorrow night. Miguel said she left days ago with dozens of her most elite soldiers. We need to be prepared for an attack."

"How are we going to capture Alex and how are we going to deal with

Lolita?" I asked, feeling Vince's worry as he no doubt thought about Lolita and I fighting.

"I will place the C-4 under and around the ballroom when we are done here," Vangel said, pointing to the backpack by the door. "Alex put trackers on them, so I have to set them up, but he doesn't have the blueprints, so I will place them where they will do the least amount of damage if they are detonated."

"How are we going to keep them from being detonated?" I asked, looking from Theron to Vangel.

"All Alex really wants is you, he wants to kill all your friends too, but you are the top of his list." Vangel stood and walked around the room. "As far as he knows, I will kidnap you before the party begins, then we will meet in the garden shed. There is no power in the shed, so if one of you ladies would agree to pretend to be Katie we will have a decoy. Once we have Alex in the shed, we can overtake him and capture him. After we have him, we will chain him up in the stables and join the party."

"I'll pretend to be Katie," Natalia said, taking a step forward. "I don't want to miss the party but capturing the man who destroyed the compound is more important than rubbing elbows with the heads of Europe."

"Good. Jean, you'll be on the lookout for Alex?" Theron asked.

"Yeah, I'll be waiting for him," she said, sounding excited.

"Once they are in the shed, I want you to backup Vangel and Natalia. Alex was stronger than ever when we fought him in the bar." Theron paced around the room. "Once we have Alex out of the way, we will be ready for Lolita."

"How are we going to deal with her?" Vince asked, almost growling with anger.

"We will all be armed, and we will be ready for her. If Miguel's right, and she shows up with a bunch of soldiers, we need to break into teams and bring them down as quickly as possible." I touched his arm to calm him, and he shied away.

"Katie's right. If she shows up, she will make a grand entrance." Theron stopped pacing and stood at my side. "I want everyone who is not going after Alex spread out through the ballroom. If Lolita attacks, go after the soldier nearest you. The goal is for Katie not to have to fight anyone but Lolita."

"Are you sure you are ready to face her?" Vince asked, placing his hand on my shoulder. His worry turned to icy fear as we talked about the details.

"Yes, only because of the training you and yours have given me." I put my hand on top of his and gave it a squeeze. *I need you to believe in me.*

Vince pulled his hand away. *I do believe in you.* He meant his words, but he was holding something back.

*Thank you, I can't do it without knowing you believe in me*, I thought back to him.

"While Katie is fighting Lolita, it will be all our jobs to make sure no one else interferes," Vince said after I felt him accept my fate. "I will be at Katie's side throughout the night." I felt a calm wash over him as if he finally understood what Theron, Helen, and I were trying to tell him since we came back to Crete: I could, and would, defeat Lolita.

"Good, now I have a drawing of the ballroom, let's break it up so everyone knows where they need to be." Theron pointed to the dining room where a large piece of paper was draped over the table.

Chapter 41

*Katie*

When we finished with our pre-party meeting, Helen took me to her room where the seamstress was waiting to do a final fitting on my dress, then I went to our suite feeling that Vince was waiting for me there. I felt lighter since he was finally all right with me fighting Lolita. It had been an argument weighing on my mind for too long. If he hadn't agreed with everyone else during the meeting, I might have lost the confidence I needed to beat her.

I opened the door and saw him standing by the fireplace. "Vince," I wanted to thank him for being at my side and ask him what had changed, but he put a hand up to stop me.

"Wait, please come and take a bath. You need to relax, then we will talk." He swept his hand toward the bedroom.

I didn't realize how tense I was until he mentioned it. I walked past him and into my closet to undress, I hung the suit up then took my robe and wrapped it around my body before going into the bathroom. Vince was nowhere in sight, but he was close by. He already drew the bath, wisps of steam were rising from the water, and a glass of wine sat on the ledge. I hung my robe up on the hook and slid into the bath. The hot water smelled of lilies and lavender. I leaned back and rested my head against the edge, closed my eyes and let my mind wander. This might be the last time I got to relax and enjoy the luxury I was surrounded in and I wanted to take advantage of it.

I would beat Lolita, and as I let the hot water relax my muscles, I visualized fighting her. It would be a fight where I used everything I learned in the past year. She was old, older than Theron, I thought, but no one seemed to know how good of a fighter she was. Yet, they all thought she would know how to fight. I would have my work cut out for me.

The feel of something touching my arm made me jump. I opened my eyes and Vince grinned down at me. "You need to use your senses more."

"How long have you been here?" I asked, realizing the temperature in the water had gone down a few degrees.

"Long enough, and never long enough. I could watch you for the rest of my life and never tire of it." He picked up a luffa and squeezed soap on it.

"Vince, about earlier," I started as he picked up my arm and washed me. "Thank you for supporting me."

"I've been an ass about it, I know. I wanted it to happen under conditions we set, not her crashing our party." He moved down my arm, then back up to my shoulder and over to my collar bone.

"The chances of getting her exactly where we want her are almost zero," I said, leaning back and letting him wash me.

"I know, and I fully support your decision, but it feels like we just found each other and, with everything else going on, it feels like we have barely had any time together."

"No kidding." It seemed like all we had been doing is dealing with other people's drama or trying to catch Alex. "Maybe after the party, and we take care of Lolita's army, we can disappear for a while. Just the two of us."

"We can go to my house in Sorrento, it is private, and no one knows about it." He ran the luffa over my chest and leaned over to take my other hand. "It's right on the beach, we can play in the ocean and teach Vinny to swim."

"That sounds like the vacation I need." I closed my eyes and envisioned us walking along the beach hand in hand as Vinny ran and played in the waves. I didn't know what I would do with no one after me. It had been so long since I truly felt free.

"Yes, we can take as long as we want and just be together." Done with my arm, he circled my breasts without touching my nipples and I shivered wanting more. Being washed by Vince was almost as good as one of his massages. He moved down to my belly, circling, and coming close to my center but never touching it.

"It is a beautiful town surrounded by slabs of lava rock. There are beaches made of nothing but rocks smoothed down by the water. You will love it."

"Can we visit Pompeii?"

"Of course." He moved to my foot, pulling it out of the water and washing it before moving up my leg.

"I can't wait," I said, and we lapsed into silence. Thinking about being alone with Vince and Vinny on a beach far away from the enemies who had been ruling my life was a touchstone I wanted to keep with me as I fought Lolita. I had something to fight for and I wasn't going to let it go.

"Lean forward, I want to get your back."

I pulled my knees up and wrapped my arms around them allowing him access. When he finished, I laid back.

"Stay here and enjoy your wine, when you are ready I will be in the sitting room waiting for you." He rose and was gone, leaving me horny and ready for him to take me to bed, but it was obvious he had other ideas on how we would spend the evening. I picked up my wine glass and took a sip. I couldn't pass up on enjoying some relaxing alone time. I wondered what everyone else was doing with their night, but not enough to find out, as long as they left me and Vince alone.

After I finished my wine, I climbed out the tub, the water was cooling, and I was getting cold. I dried off, then pulled my robe on. I went into the bedroom ready to go straight to my closet when something on the bed caught my eye. A long ruby-colored nightgown was spread out on top of the comforter. I ran my fingers over the fabric. The silk was so smooth it felt like I was touching air. I pulled my robe off and let the nightgown flow over my body. It was floor-length with a slit on each side. The thin straps holding it led down to a perfectly fitted bodice that cupped my breasts before flowing to the floor.

I hung my robe in the closet then went to the sitting room. The lights were off, and the room was only lit by candles and the fireplace. Vince was standing in front of the fire, staring into the flames, lost in his own thoughts. A bottle of wine with two glasses and a covered plate were sitting on the coffee table.

I went to him and took his hand, startling him. "Are you all right?" I asked, forcing him to look at me.

"Eat, then we will talk." He led me to the couch and took the cover off the plate while I sat.

"Tell me what you're thinking, Vince," I said, putting the napkin on my lap and cutting a piece of fish.

"Can't you tell?" he asked, going back to the hearth and staring into the flames.

"If I tried, but tonight I would like to hear it from you." I ate a carrot and watched him.

"I'm terrified. I don't think I have ever been more scared in my life." His voice cracked on the last word.

"And you think I'm not?" I asked, forcing myself to eat. I wanted to go to him and tell him everything would be OK, but I couldn't tell him something I didn't believe. I put on a good show, but I didn't know if I would win this battle. It was nice to talk about the future but, the reality was, I had a feeling that nothing would go as we planned.

"You're scared too?" He turned to face me, and I put my fork down and got to my feet.

"Vince, I act confident because, if I don't, no one will think I have a chance of beating Lolita, not even me."

He came to my side in a flash and took me in his arms. "I don't want to lose you."

"I don't want to lose you either, but you know I have to do this if I want to be free."

"Yes, that is why we are still here and not on a deserted island somewhere. You will be queen of the vampires, and your first step to taking the throne must be defeating Lolita."

"So why are you freaking out about her crashing the party? We have more help than we did before, and I don't think I will ever be more ready to fight her."

"Because I don't know what I will do if you die." Vince pulled away from me and went back to staring at the fire.

"You will take revenge. You will find a way to make that bitch's life hell. Then you will move on, we've only known each other for one percent of your life. You will mourn me and move on, just as I would want you to."

He turned to look at me. "You are it for me, don't you see? If I lose you, I see no point in living." He ran his hands through his hair and stepped to me, putting his hands on my upper arms. "Of course, I would avenge your death, but then I would seek my own. My work on the earth would be done."

"Vince, don't say that." The last thing I wanted to think about was Vince killing himself because I was dead.

"You have to win Katie, I need you, Theron needs you, all the vampires need you. Without you to rein us in, there will be another like Lolita who will seek to take over the world, and we cannot allow it to happen. The humans will destroy the world to kill us."

"Then I have to win," I said, leaning into him and wrapping my arms around him. "Can we put all this save the world stuff on the back burner for the rest of the night? I want to just be with you."

"That is what I was hoping for, but I needed to tell you what I was thinking."

"And I'm glad you told me, but enough for now."

"Yes, finish your dinner. You will need your strength."

"Why? What do you have in mind?" I asked as he led me back over to the couch.

"Wait and see." He sat next to me and poured the wine.


When I finished eating, Vince led me into the bedroom and helped me onto the bed. I lay back with my head on the pillow wondering what he was planning. He took off his robe, revealing the body I would never tire of looking at. I dreamed of him this way every night I was in Kevò. His broad shoulders packed with muscle tapering down to his eight-pack abs, and the deep V of his hips, leading to one of the things I loved the most about him. "Just relax," he said, taking my foot in his hand and digging his thumbs into my instep and rubbing.

I moaned as he massaged first one foot then the other. He slowly worked his way up my legs stopping when he reached the top of my thighs. He pushed my nightgown up with his nose then buried his face in my center, inhaling deeply like it would be the last time he would smell what he loved most in the world. Then he licked and sucked me, causing my back to arch. I buried my fingers in his hair and moaned. He added a finger to the mix, bringing me to the edge of the abyss before pulling away and leaving me wanting. "More," I moaned, trying to force his head back down, I was ready for him to take me even higher.

He moved up my body and settled between my legs. *Now, I will make love to you,* he thought, capturing my lips with his as he slowly penetrated me, causing me to moan around his tongue.

*Then what?* I asked, clenching down around him, I was already so close.

*Then, I will fuck you,* he thought, slowly moving in and out of my sex. I could feel him trying to control himself.

*What then?* I moaned as he moved faster.

*Then we will do it all again until you pass out from*

316

*exhaustion*. He increased his pace moving the tiniest bit, so he could hit the spot that would send me soaring.

"Perfect," I said as the first of many orgasms pulled my ability to think away from me.

I was standing on the stage in the ballroom. The two chandeliers overhead cascaded light across the room bouncing off the mural of the Trojan war covering the walls and ceiling. Vampires of all shapes and sizes were facing me, waiting for me to speak. They were dressed like movie stars at an award show. The men wore tuxedos, and the women wore dresses in every color of the rainbow. Some wore ball gowns while others wore short dresses with plunging necklines. Most of them had a drink of some sort in their hands. I was so nervous I didn't know if I could speak. I cleared my throat. "I am your creator's daughter," was all I could say, my speech forgotten.

There were laughs and murmurs from everyone. They didn't believe me, I could feel it. I looked to Theron. *What should I do?*

He shrugged his shoulders. *You must do something, prove to them you are who you say you are.*

*But how? What can I show them?* I looked from Theron to Vince.

*I don't know, but you must do something,* Vince thought.

"Katie, what are you talking about?" Jean asked, suddenly appearing at my side.

"Why would we believe you? You are just a slave," one vampire said, taking a step toward the stage. "Let's show her what she really is." There was a cheer from the crowd as the vampires closest to the stage started making their way to the stairs.

"Jean, what are you doing here?" I asked as the vampire closed in on me. "Run, they are going to kill us."

Jean must have seen the fear in my eyes because she turned and ran. I looked around at my friends, the ones who were supposed to be helping me. They were frozen in place with stunned looks on their faces. My chest was tight, and it was becoming hard to breathe. *How did I think this was going to go?* I wondered. *Why did I let Theron talk me into this when I wasn't ready?*

The first vampires were just out of reach when everyone in the room froze. "What are you going to do daughter?" my mother asked from behind me.

I turned and ran into her arms. "I don't know. How am I going to prove to them I'm here to save them?"

"You have power, you need to learn to use it," she said, pulling away from me. "Show them what will happen if they defy you." She took a step back and dissolved into nothing.

"Wait," I called, but it was too late, she was gone, and the vampires were moving again. I closed my eyes waiting for them to pull me to pieces when I felt it. I felt them all, every vampire in the room was a part of me, part of my mother's magic, which made them part of my magic. I looked out across the room and found my way into their minds.

*Kneel before your queen*, I demanded as they dropped to their knees and bowed their heads. I backed up a step, it worked, they obeyed me. If they didn't believe me now, I didn't know what would convince them.

"Do you still not believe me? I tried to be civil and explain who I was, but you called me a fake. I do not wish to be a tyrannical leader, but I will if I'm forced to." I released them from the command and they rose to their feet.

"What say you now?" I asked aloud and in their heads. Over half the vampires genuflected of their own free will, while others went to the door, some stood looking at me dumbfounded, like they didn't understand what I had just done.

I sat up straight and looked around the bedroom. It was a dream. I wasn't surprised, but it answered a question I had been

318

pondering since Theron said he wanted to introduce me to the vampires of Europe. I finally knew how to convince them I was Asteria's daughter. I grimaced at the thought of what holding onto all those minds would do to me. I could only hold on to Thomas for a few minutes before I felt like I would pass out. How was I going to stay on my feet while I forced over a hundred vampires to their knees?

"What is it?" Vince asked, sitting up next to me and touching my shoulder. I looked back at him and laid down to rest my cheek against his chest.

"I know how I'll prove to the vampires that I'm Asteria's daughter." I closed my eyes wanting to go back to sleep.

"How?" he asked, running his hand up and down my arm.

"I'll make them kneel before me." I thought of the power I used in my dream, and how easy it was to break in to their minds and control them. It had never been that easy before, but it gave me a place to start.

"I cannot wait to watch you stun the most powerful vampires in Europe. They will be speechless." He bent his head and kissed the top of my head. "It's early, go back to sleep, tomorrow will be a long day."

Chapter 42

*Katie*

When we finally got out of bed, it was near noon and Helen had a crew of people waiting for me. I spent the afternoon being fluffed and buffed. When it was time to put on my dress, I was panicking. This was happening, by the end of the night we would have Alex, and, with some luck, Lolita would be dead, which only left us with disposing of her army before I would be free to live my life.

After Helen helped me put the dress on, I turned and looked in the mirror. The dress looked amazing. It was red with gold highlights spiraling throughout the fabric. The spaghetti straps allowed me full motion with my arms while keeping the bodice from falling. The side with my tattoo was open from my armpit to my hip bone and with the help of some special glue, it stuck to my skin without pain. The dressed flared to the floor with an A-line skirt giving me the mobility I needed. The red handle of my katana stuck up behind my head like it was part of the dress. Helen put my hair up, so it looked like curls exploded from the top of my head.

"Vince will pass out when he sees you," Helen said from behind me.

"This is so not me." I turned to look at her while smoothing down the fabric.

"It's a far cry from the girl who showed up on our doorstep last summer scared and confused. This is who you have become, a strong, confident woman who will become the leader of the vampires."

As Helen spoke, I felt the truth behind her words. She believed it

321

and so did I. It was time to take my place as queen. "Thank you, Helen."

*Are you ready?* Vince asked before knocking on the door.

"Come in, we're ready." I stood in front of the door as it opened. My mouth dropped at the sight of Vince in a tuxedo. It was mat-black with narrow lapels that rested on his chest and the bright white shirt created an inverted triangle pointing the way to his narrow hips. His hair was loose and just touched his shoulders. He was the sexiest man I had ever seen. "Wow."

Vince stood just outside, his mouth open, and fumbled with a box in his hand. "Katie?"

"Close your mouth." I turned in a slow circle for him to get the full affect.

"You almost look like a queen." He walked in with a barely concealed smile on his face.

"Almost?" I asked, turning back to the mirror. What could be missing?

"I'll see you in the living room, I need to find Theron," Helen said, before leaving.

"You are missing one very important accessory." Vince opened the box and smiled.

"What?" I asked, looking into the box. Inside was a crown dripping with rubies. My hands trembled as I reached in to take it out. I turned it in my hand, it was five inches high at its peak then sloped down to nothing on each side. The crown must have been designed around the ruby in the middle. It was large, with only the smallest pieces of gold holding it in place. The jewels shrank proportionally as the crown tapered down to the gap in the back. "They aren't real, right?"

"Only real gems for the real queen, otherwise who would believe her?" Vince asked, taking it from my hands and placing it on my head. He pulled my ringlets out, so they fell over the crown then he took bobby pins from his pocket and secured it in place.

"Where did you learn how to use bobby pins?" I asked, still shaking. I was wearing more money on my head than I would likely ever make.

"I picked up a few odd talents over the years. There, now you look like a queen." He took my shoulders and turned me around to face the mirror.

My mouth dropped open again, the crown was the topper on the cake, now, even I believed I was a queen. The smoky eyeshadow and thick, black eyeliner made my green eyes almost glow, the red of my lipstick made my lips look covered in blood, and since I hadn't been spending much time outside my skin was almost porcelain-looking. "Wow."

"Come, we are meeting everyone in the great room for one final briefing." He offered me his arm, and I took it, still in awe at my transformation.

Vince led me down the hall as I practiced moving in the dress. I could move my legs freely, but my upper body felt trapped by the bodice. I had full movement in my arms, but I didn't know how well I could twist around without ripping it. It wouldn't be easy to fight in it, but it could have been much worse. The heels were a little high, but with the straps I wouldn't have to worry about them falling off. When we entered the great room, everyone turned and stared at us.

"Katie?" Jean asked, running to me but stopping a few feet away, thank Goddess. She was dressed in a ghillie suit and had black grease all over her arms and face. "You look amazing, and don't worry I dreamed about the party last night, you won them over then, and you will tonight too."

"Thanks," I said, shocked she brought it up. "Are you ready for this?"

"Yeah, we work as a team and bring the bastard down," she said, giving me a salute before moving toward the door.

"I always thought you were hot, but wow, you look like royalty," Vangel said, taking my hand in his and kissing it.

"Thanks, are you ready?"

"Yeah, look at Natalia, she looks almost just like you." He waved his hand toward the vampire standing next to Theron. She was wearing a red dress similar to mine but not as nice. There was no point in spending the money on a dress that would probably be ruined while they captured Alex.

"Thank you for helping us," I said as she went toward Vangel.

"It is a pleasure to help 'The One.' May you reign forevermore." She curtsied then she moved to join Jean by the door.

"Katie, what's she talking about?" Jean asked, and I froze, my eyes locked with Vince's.

"Natalia has some strange ideas about the world is all," Theron said, stepping up to Jean and resting a hand on her shoulder.

Jean jumped at the contact and I watched as her eyes went huge. "What?" She shook her head and took a step away from Theron. "Yeah, never mind."

*Thank you*, I thought to Theron. I wasn't sure how much longer we could keep from telling Jean what was really going on, but I wanted to do it after the party. I looked around at the vampires. They were all impeccably dressed and staring at me. "You all look great," I said, trying to sound excited, but the butterflies in my stomach were threatening to break out and cause me to throw up all over my dress.

"Are we ready?" Vince asked, walking around me.

"As ready as we will ever be. Natalia, Vangel, and Jean, take your positions. Helen and I have radios in our ears tuned in to your frequency. If you need help, call, and we'll be there." Theron nodded at them and they left to get ready for Alex's arrival.

"Vasilis and Yannis, you will stand guard outside the entrance of the ballroom. Once Helen and I enter, no one comes in or out until I give the OK. Marios, Argyris, Maria, and Livius, you are to spread out and take the positions we talked about yesterday. If you think there's a problem, I expect you to neutralize it before it becomes an issue. We don't want this to turn into a bloodbath. Vince, you will stay with Katie, as much as I would prefer you at my side; I need to appear strong without my maker. Helen, as always you're with me. Are there any questions?" Theron looked around the room and I wondered if I would ever command a group of people the way he did. They all shook their heads, indicating they were ready. "Let's have a party then, shall we?"

"Theron, Helen?" I asked before they could leave. "Could I have a word?" They stopped and turned. Vince moved to leave, but I grabbed his hand. "No, stay."

"What's wrong?" Theron asked.

"Nothing, it's just..." I trailed off as I looked at the vampires who had sacrificed so much for me. "I have a feeling everything will change after tonight and I wanted to tell you how much you mean to me. There is no way I would've survived this long without everything you've done for me, the safe haven, the training, believing in me when I didn't believe in myself." I turned to Helen, "Thank you."

"It has been an honor to serve you," Helen said and curtsied, bending low but never taking her eyes from mine. I was so shocked, I didn't know how to respond for a moment. Finally, I nodded my head to her.

"Katie, you are one of the most incredible women I have ever known. Thank you for allowing us to help you become the warrior who stands before us." Theron bowed from the waist. "No matter what happens, it has been an honor to know you." He offered Helen his arm, and she took it without another word, leaving Vince and I alone.

"Why did that feel like a goodbye?" Vince asked, taking me in his arms.

"I don't know but I agree. I just wanted everyone to know how important they are to me in case tonight doesn't go as planned," I said, being careful not to touch my face to Vince's jacket.

"Are you going to tell me goodbye?" he asked, pulling away from me and looking into my eyes.

"I will never tell you goodbye, Vince," I said as he frowned and looked at the floor. I cupped his cheek in my hand and pulled his face up to meet my eyes. "I won't tell you goodbye because we will never truly be apart again. If I die, I will wait for you in the afterlife. No matter where you go, you will take a piece of me with you and I will take a piece of you with me."

Vince's frown turned to a smile, and I swore I saw moisture in his eyes before his lips met mine in a kiss that said everything he needed. He loved me more than he loved anything in this world and, no matter where I went, he would follow me. To the end of the world and beyond.

## Chapter 43
### *Katie*

"I thought we would watch the guests arrive from the balcony," Vince said, offering me his arm.

"Good idea, then I can see what I'm up against." I took his arm and let him lead me to the other end of the house and up a flight of stairs to the balcony. It had been closed for the beginning of the party, so I could make my grand entrance on the staircase, but once the party got going, it would be open for people to explore.

I looked over the railing and watched as the servers and escorts, who had all been personally screened by Theron for their capability to be open to his thrall, move around the gleaming hardwood floor below. The servers were moving quickly from table to table, making last-minute preparations in their white tux jackets. While the escorts, or donors as I thought of them, stood around in small groups with champagne flutes in their hands, talking about the fun they would have tonight. I hoped they all would go home at the end of the night and not end up in body bags.

"I hadn't thought of it that way, but you're right. Knowing what you are walking into will help you stay calm." Vince squeezed my hand. "Would you like to sit?"

"I would love to, but I don't want to wrinkle the dress." I smoothed it down for the hundredth time then checked the katana on my back.

"Why don't you at least take your shoes off until it's time to go," Vince said, looking down at my feet.

"Good idea," I slipped the shoes off and let my bare feet dig into the thick carpet beneath them.

We silently watched the humans below us until the doors to the ballroom opened and vampires came in. The men, as in my dream, were dressed in tuxedos while the women were dressed better than anything I had seen on the red carpet. I understood why Helen said I needed a custom dress. I would've looked like I was going to a prom while being surrounded by vampires going to the Met Gala, if I would've wore something off the rack.

Vince pointed out the head of the Roman vampires, followed by the head of the Parisians, it went on and on. The heads of almost every capital city in Western and Eastern Europe were there, and my butterflies ramped up again. Remembering my dream, I closed my eyes and started to work my way into their minds. It wasn't taking as long as it normally did.

*Breathe with me*, Vince thought, taking my hand and placing it on his chest. *There is nothing to be afraid of, you will win them over.*

I forced myself to breathe with him, his slow, methodical breathing helped me find my center and diminish the butterflies in my stomach. I looked at him and smiled. I could do this, I was going to be a teacher before the vampires found me. I was planning on spending my days talking to groups of people. This would be no different. Who was I kidding? It was like going from pitching in a little league game one day to pitching in a major league game the next.

Finally, the doors to the ballroom slammed shut and everyone turned to watch Theron walk toward the stage with Helen on his arm. When they took the stage, applause began, along with a few shouts of encouragement. Theron bowed, then held his arms out at his side and motioned for the room to go quiet.

"Thank you everyone, for joining me in celebrating my

recuperation and retaining control of my island, but it is not the only reason I invited you here." He walked across the stage making eye contact with a few people and waving before turning and walking back the way he came. "It hurts me to tell you that dark times are upon us. Beyond what I have already been through, we are facing a war. I invited you onto my island, not only to celebrate my recovery, but to urge you to join my side in a coming battle." He paused as whispering erupted.

"You are all familiar with Lolita. What most of you are not aware of is that she is intending to take over Europe, I do not mean just the vampires living here but the humans as well. She wishes to conquer the world."

"She can't, she doesn't have the numbers," someone from the back said, and I squeezed Vince's arm.

"That's where you are wrong, my friend. She started creating an army almost a century ago and trained them to fight."

"Why don't we let her? Let the humans take care of the problem?" a woman near the front asked.

"Because she will make her true nature known. Do you know what that means for us? With the technology the humans have, it will take no time for them to find a way to track and kill us. Many of you weren't around when the last cleansing occurred. We were on the run, there was no way to beat them when they burned our houses down, and we were forced to hide in caves, sewers, and mausoleums. Believe me when I say we do not want another cleansing."

There were murmurs of agreement and whispers of people confirming what Theron said. Realizing it was almost my turn, I slipped my shoes on, making sure the straps fit snugly over my feet. When I was done, Vince pulled me around the balcony to the stairs as Theron let the vampires talk.

"What should we do?" a woman with a heavy Greek accent asked from the middle of the room.

"We need to band together and kill Lolita and her army," Theron answered.

"How? No one knows where she is," another guest asked.

"I learned a few weeks ago she's in Venice. She purchased an island there. It is where she will start her campaign," Theron answered.

The murmurs began again, it sounded like some wanted to help, while others wanted to leave the continent and watch from afar, then there were the silent ones. They stood stoic with neutral expressions. I dove into their minds. *Vince, some of these vampires, the silent ones, are already on Lolita's side. We need to watch them.*

*I wondered about the quiet ones, thank you, lover. I will keep an eye on them this evening.* Vince squeezed my hand. *It is almost time, are you ready?*

I pulled my hand out of his, smoothed my dress again, and checked my sword. *As ready as I'll ever be.*

"If you are interested in aiding me in preventing this war, so we may continue to live as we do, please let me, or my people, know. In the meantime, I want to share some news with you." Theron waited until the crowd quieted down. "As many of us older ones know, and whether you believe it or not, our mother, our creator, Asteria, sent us a prophecy centuries ago. She promised to send a savior, a messiah, a daughter to us. She is with us here tonight, and it is my greatest pleasure to introduce her to you." Theron turned to the side and held his hand out to me. "Your Highness, will you join us?"

My breathing calm, I let a small smile form on my lips as Vince took my left hand and led me down the staircase into the ballroom. I kept my face forward and let my eyes roll back and forth across the crowd, making sure I had a lock on every vampire's mind. I didn't want to force their acceptance, but it was better to be prepared. Their feelings were across the board, from astonishment to hatred, from glee and excitement, to disbelief and boredom. When I reached the stage, Theron offered me his hand. I let go of

Vince and took Theron's, letting out a breath before I turned and looked over the crowd. Vince took his position behind me and to the left while Theron and Helen went down the steps to keep vampires away from the stage.

"Good evening, I am Katie Hunter, daughter of Asteria, creator of vampires. I come here tonight to beg your help. If Lolita starts this war, there will be no turning back for our kind. We will be, once again, forced to the shadows to survive. I am here because I want nothing more than to help us thrive." I had practiced the speech so many times it came out calm yet demanding.

"You are human, why would we believe you?" someone from the middle of the crowd called.

I pulled my back up straight, ready to force them to kneel, when the double doors of the ballroom slammed open, and the bodies of Yannis and Vasilis were thrown down the aisle without their heads.

## Chapter 44

### *Jean*

Jean crouched under the olive tree and breathed quietly. Her legs were cramping, and it was so quiet she felt like she had cotton in her ears. She hadn't moved from her position in at least a half hour. She kept her eyes and ears tuned into any sound or movement. She watched Vangel and Natalia go into the shed a few minutes ago which meant Alex should be along shortly.

She thought about what she and Vangel talked about before they came outside earlier. Once Alex was inside, Vangel would pacify Alex with a passed-out *Katie,* then while he was making sure Vangel had the right girl, Vangel would hit Alex on the back of the head with a shovel already staged in the shed. Then Jean would come in, they would cuff Alex, and take him to the barn to hang out with Thomas. She wanted to be the one to catch Alex, but this was a team effort and she had to be a good sport. It made sense for Vangel to capture Alex, he would be the closest and Alex wouldn't see it coming.

She heard a branch break to her left, and it took all her concentration not to jerk her head around to see what was coming. She sat as still as one of Medusa's statues and waited while the footfalls she could now make out, came closer to her. She held her breath, not wanting whoever it was to hear her, and wished her heart would stop pounding so loudly. The footsteps stopped two feet from her and turned in a circle. It was like he knew someone was watching him, but he didn't know where they were. Jean let her breath out slowly and silently before inhaling as quietly as she could. She wanted to look up and confirm it was Alex but giving away her location would mean not only her death, but probably Vangel's and Natalia's too.

The feet finally turned toward the shack then moved toward it. She moved her head a little, so she could watch the dark silhouette reach the door and go inside. She waited until the door closed and for them to start talking before she got to her feet and stretched her legs out. When she could feel them again, she snuck to the door and pressed her ear against it to listen.

"Where's Katie?" Alex asked.

"I had to knock her out," she heard Vangel say. "She's in the corner."

"Where does everyone think she is?" Alex sounded paranoid.

"They think she is still primping, the prima donna."

Jean shook her head, Vangel could be such an ass when he wanted to be.

"How long do you think she'll be out?"

"I don't know, she's been out for at least ten minutes already."

"Let's tie her up and get out of here then."

"What about the C-4? It was a pain in the ass to hide."

"Fuck, I forgot about it. Here, take the detonator and we'll do it on our way out."

Jean shook her head. Vangel better get his shit together and take care of Alex already, they were running out of time.

"What the fuck?" She heard Alex say and pulled out her gun. If Vangel didn't get him knocked out soon she would have to go in. Now that the moment was here she wasn't sure she was ready to take him down. What if she missed and hit Vangel or Natalia? What if Alex turned on Vangel and shot him before she could get through the door? There was a scuffle going on inside the shack and she closed her eyes, trying to center herself. She was a trained agent, she could do this.

The shot of a gun had her moving before she opened her eyes all the way. She kicked the door in and quickly moved to the side.

"Vangel, you lousy piece of shit," Alex yelled. "How could you do this to me?"

Jean heard the unmistakable sound of a foot connecting with a body. She turned and leveled her gun on Alex. "Interpol. Put your weapon down." Jean blinked at the light from the lantern Vangel must have staged earlier in the day. The room wasn't too bright, but she could make out the moldy walls with shelves holding gardening tools, the hard-packed dirt floor, and nothing else except for the three people and a shovel.

"Not you again," Alex said, turning and leveling his gun at Jean.

Not wasting a second Jean pulled the trigger just as Natalia streaked through the air and tackled Alex. Jean cursed as the two tangled on the floor and prayed she didn't hit Natalia. She looked at Vangel who was lying face down on the ground and wondered if Alex had hit him with the first gunshot or if Vangel had been the one who shot first. She couldn't check on him yet. She needed to make sure they captured or, who was she kidding? Killed Alex first.

She kept her gun aimed at the two people grappling on the floor, trying to get a clear shot of Alex, but Natalia was a better wrestler than Jean thought. As they rolled back and forth across the floor, Jean wondered what happened to the gun Alex had been holding. She moved around the shed sweeping her feet across the ground feeling for it while keeping her eyes on Alex. She didn't trust him, if she took her eyes off him for more than a second, he would find a way to escape.

Jean found something hard on the ground and looked down for an instant to verify it was the gun. She bent down to pick it up when Alex saw her, he threw Natalia off him and lurched forward, hitting Jean in the knees. She lost her balance and ended up on her butt. She still had her gun and had it trained on Alex, but he had grabbed the gun on the floor and was swinging it around between Natalia and Jean.

"Nice try ladies, but you'll never be as good as me." He laughed while wiping blood from the corner of his mouth and taking a step toward the door.

"You won't get away," Jean said as her arm shook from holding the gun out with one hand for too long. She brought her other hand up to disburse the weight. "There are people all over the orchard looking for you. Give up now and I'll make sure it's quick."

"You're a horrible liar." Alex took a step toward her while keeping Natalia in his peripheral vision. "Everyone else is at the party."

"Did you hear that?" Jean cocked her head to the side like she was listening to something outside. "We're in here, and we have Alex." She knew no one was out there, but with the gun going off in the shed a few minutes before, Alex wouldn't trust his hearing.

"Fuck," Alex said, looking over Jean's shoulder. While Alex was distracted, Natalia leapt at him, but he heard her coming. Before Jean had time to shoot, Alex had Natalia in his arms and the muffled sound of gun fire between Alex's and Natalia's bodies told Jean everything she needed to know. When his gun clicked empty, he looked at Jean with wild, bloodshot eyes that made him look like he hadn't slept in a week.

She couldn't let Alex leave, after everything he did to the people she cared about: Ted, Theron, Katie, and now Vangel and Natalia. He wasn't leaving this shed alive unless it was in chains. She sighted down the barrel of the gun, but she still didn't have a shot unless she wanted to shoot through Natalia. She was probably already dead from the lead Alex filled her with, but Jean couldn't bring herself to take the shot.

"Put her down and drop your gun," Jean said, her voice cracked, and tears leaked from her eyes. The last thing she wanted to have happen was someone die while they captured Alex.

336

"Why would I do that?" Alex asked, running straight for Jean with Natalia still in his arms. Jean tried to spin out of the way and get a shot at his back, but she was too slow. As soon as Natalia made contact with Jean he let go and gave them a push. Jean lost her footing and fell backward, hitting her head on something as she fell.

"I'll let you live this time," Alex said from the opening of the door. Jean's head was spinning and pounding from whatever she hit her head on. "Someone has to be alive to tell the others what happens when you try to catch me."

Jean tried to raise her gun and take a shot at him, but she was stuck under Natalia, who outweighed her by at least fifty pounds. Her head hurt, and her vision was fuzzy, but she didn't miss Alex turning and walking away before consciousness left her.

## Chapter 45
### *Katie*

Three vampires, dressed in black fatigues, combat boots, and baseball hats entered the room with assault rifles pointed at the ceiling. I went for their minds just before they fired and commanded them to stop. They froze in place, their guns still aimed at the ceiling and their fingers on the triggers. I forced them to drop their guns as Lolita glided into the room like she owned the place. She wore a black skin-tight bodysuit, and I wondered if she was trying to channel her inner cat woman. *She is mine,* I thought before pulling my katana from my back.

"Theron, my invitation to your little soirée must have gotten lost in the mail. It's a good thing Geovanni told me about it or I would have missed it completely," Lolita said as the crowd parted for her.

*Find your breath, stay calm,* Vince thought as I shifted my grip on my katana. I banged against her mental shields. It would be the easiest way to defeat her. Making her do my will would solve all my problems, but she was old, and her shield was almost as hard to get through as Vince's.

"After you sent your man to take over my island, and he failed, I didn't think you would want an invitation." Theron stepped in front of Lolita stopping her progress.

"Silly Theron, I had just released him from my service. He came here on his own and never asked for help. If he had, you wouldn't be standing here blocking my way to the stage. Are you afraid for the little human who wishes to rule us?" She ran one long, glossy, red fingernail down his cheek, and I felt him want to flinch away from her touch, but he held his position.

"Afraid for her? Never, you have no idea what she is capable of. If you were wise, you would destroy your army and do as the Goddess demands." He grabbed her hand and placed it at her side before moving out of her way.

"The Goddess? How do you know she's real? And if she is, how do you know it's what she wants?" Lolita climbed the stairs, gave me a twisted smile, then turned to face the crowd of vampires. Some were smiling and taking their jackets off, preparing to fight. Some were backing to the edge of the room wanting to watch, and others were heading for the exit.

"I am here to give you all the opportunity to join me in overthrowing Europe. Together, we can rule and turn the humans into our slaves. We have lived in the shadows for too long. It is time for them to bow to us. We are superior to them in every way, so tell me why aren't we ruling the world? I have an army of five hundred vampires ready to do my bidding, if you join me there will be no stopping us." She brought her hands up to the sky and stared at the ceiling ending her rant.

"You are wrong, Lolita, you will create a war that will end vampires. Even if you can take Europe, the other countries of the world will stop you, causing a war that will leave our homes in ruin, and vampires living in caves," I said, moving in front of her and holding my sword in front of me with two hands. There was no doubt in my mind that she came here to kill me, recruiting allies was only a side benefit.

"Boys, please dispatch the human," Lolita said, turning away from me and inspecting her nails. I glanced at her soldiers, still frozen in the middle of the aisle.

"No, Lolita, you brought this fight on yourself," Vince said, moving to the first guard. He pulled a short sword from under his coat and took off the guard's head in one smooth motion. Blood sprayed, and a few vampires gasped and backed away from the torso as it shrank to the ground.

Lolita made a grab for me, but I was ready for her, and spun out of her grasp. My concentration broke though, and I lost my hold on her guards. I wanted to see what they were doing, but I couldn't risk taking my eyes off Lolita. "How do you do it?" she asked, pulling a knife from her sleeve.

"Do what?" I asked as we began circling each other.

"Make everyone help you, I have never seen anyone who was more annoying, yet gains so many allies."

"I tell the truth and people believe me, it's kind of amazing how it works." I was desperately trying to move in on her, but the petite vampire was fast. Remembering I could move just as fast as her, I faked right and came in on her left side, swinging my katana in an arc aimed to take her head off. She ducked at the last moment and instead of connecting with her neck my sword sliced into her shoulder.

"Bitch, you are ruining everything," Lolita said as I spun around, ready for her counterattack, but she stopped and ran her finger through the cut before putting it in her mouth and sucking the blood off it. "Looks like you learned how to fight since our last meeting."

"You would be surprised how much I've changed since Spain, no thanks to you," I said, believing that she would be dead before the night was over.

She looked at me with fire in her eyes as we circled each other once more. "But it is all because of me. Vince would not have taught you to fight, and Miguel would have never hurt you if it wasn't for me." She lunged at me, I moved to the right bringing my sword down aiming for her right arm. I missed and spun around to face her again.

"You're right. You will be the cause of your downfall." I was looking for a weakness, the blood on her shoulder had already stopped dripping to the floor, she was well fed, and healing faster than I thought possible. "What do you mean Miguel would have never hurt me if it wasn't for you?"

341

"He didn't want to rape you at first," Lolita said, lunging toward me, I brought my sword up to block her attack, but she wasn't there. She laughed. "I had to convince him that raping you would put you in your place. I guess I was wrong."

I didn't have time to process what she said before she rushed me with the knife held high above her head; I exhaled and waited, lowering my center of gravity ready to strike at her extended arm, when a blow came from my side. I flew through the air and lost my grip on the katana as I hit the ground hard. There was nothing I could do about the sword, it was halfway across the stage. I rolled to my feet, ready to take on another adversary. Her soldier must have fallen to the floor as he hit me because he was just regaining his feet when I reached him. I brought my arm around in front of him grasping his shoulder; I took his head under the chin with my free hand and yanked so his body went one way and his head went the other. A loud snapping sound echoed through my mind as I let his limp form fall to the floor. He wasn't dead yet, but he would be out of my way for a while.

I turned in time to see Lolita running at me with her knife held low. There was nowhere I could go and no way I could reach my katana in time. I hit the floor and rolled away from her and toward my sword, but she was on me before I made one revolution. I caught the wrist holding the knife with one hand, keeping it away from my body, and scratched at her face with my other as her fangs slid out and she moved toward my neck for what was the bite of death. My mind wanted to panic, but my free hand found an eye and I dug my thumb into it until she screeched in pain and pulled away. I bucked her off me and jumped to my feet. I needed to disable her, with no weapon I was going to have to do it with my body.

I took my fighting stance and waited for her to come. She wasn't as good as I was; I needed to find an opening and break her neck, like I did her guard. With her disabled I would have time to find my sword and cut her fucking head off. There was a chance, a small chance I could do it with a kick, but I would have to hit her in just the right spot. She came at me with the knife slashing and jabbing the air, trying to distract me. My arm seemed to move of its own accord as it lashed out, grabbed her wrist, and snapped it back, forcing her to drop the knife. I pulled my leg around in a roundhouse kick as fast as I could, hoping to make contact with her neck when something hit me in the back of the head. I felt myself falling to the floor. *I beat her. She should be dead not me*, I thought before everything went black.

## Chapter 46

*Vince*

The party was not going to plan. After the fight between Katie and Lolita started, Vince had been busy fighting Lolita's guards and a bunch of her zombie-vampire-soldiers flooded the room. Now, everyone was locked in combat. Vince sliced through the head of the soldier he was fighting and looked toward the stage just in time to see one of Lolita's bodyguards hit Katie on the back of the head. "Katie," Vince yelled as she hit the ground.

He had to get to her now. Lolita didn't play fair, it was what he had been afraid of from the start. He pushed his way through the crowd of vampires all locked in battle with either Lolita's soldiers or her allies who attended the party. He was almost to the stage when he heard someone behind him. He turned just in time to block the knife coming down on him with his short sword. One of Lolita's bodyguards had found him.

Vince pushed the knife away, faked a thrust on the right side, as the guard moved to block it Vince sliced the sword through his neck. His head fell to the left while his body fell to the right. It had been many years since Vince was in a good fight and adrenaline pumped through his veins making him feel alive. It reminded him of his days in the ring, fighting for his life against others who had just as little to lose as he did. He lived to fight another day then, and he would do it now, as long as he got to Katie in time.

He ran to the stage where he watched Katie fall a moment before, but she was gone. *Fuck, Katie, where are you?* he thought, waiting for a reply, but none came. He vaulted the stage and scanned the crowd, Theron was finishing off one of the guards, and Helen was in the middle of battle with one of the zombie-vampires. Maria was standing in the center of a circle surrounded by her entourage. Livius was fighting off two of the zombie-vampires, and Marios was leaning against the wall watching the fight. There was no sign of Katie.

Vince jumped off the stage and ran for the door, Lolita was trying to kidnap her. He pushed vampires out of the way as he ran, not caring if they were friend or foe. He had to get to Katie. As he exited the ballroom, he heard a low thrum, almost like someone beating on a drum. The thrumming went faster and faster as he ran for the door leading outside. He pushed through it as the helicopter left the ground. Without stopping, he took a running leap trying to grab the landing feet, but it was already too high. When his feet hit the ground, he wasn't sure his legs would hold him. His only reason to live was being taken from him. He sank to his knees and stared into the sky. "Why would you let this happen?" he yelled into the clear night. He didn't know if he was asking it of himself or Asteria.

Vince did not know how long he knelt on the ground feeling as though his life was over. He thought about all the good times he and Katie had together, and what an overprotective ass he had been since he gotten her back. After what happened tonight he should have never left her side. From the few glimpses of the fight he saw while fighting his own battle, Katie was winning. If he would have stayed on the stage, he would have been able to attack the guard who bludgeoned Katie, and she would have killed Lolita. Shaking off his guilt, he got to his feet and stormed back into the ballroom, ready to kill any of his enemies left alive.

He walked through the door, expecting everyone to still be locked in combat, but instead Theron was on the stage, his tuxedo torn and covered in blood. He had just begun to speak. "This is why I called you here tonight," he paused and looked around the room. "Lolita will unleash her army on Europe and reveal our true nature.

346

Do you want to live in another war-torn Europe, where instead of country against country it's us against the humans? We know where Lolita is, and we know what she has: young vampires trained to do nothing but kill. Help us end this threat, so we can continue to live in the safety of anonymity."

As Theron talked Vince looked around the room. It was impossible to tell how many on their side were lost. Piles of ash was all that was left of those who did not survive, and ash littered the room. *Some of it ours, most of it hers*, he thought. Most of the guests who began the evening impeccably dressed now were in torn, bloody rags, their perfectly arranged hair, matted and ruined. The ones who gathered around Theron looked mad, not at Theron but at Lolita, revenge was in their eyes. It was exactly what Vince was feeling, and he smiled. At least he wasn't alone in his anger.

"We must now come together as a community and take down the plague that is Lolita, once and for all," Theron bellowed through the room. He touched his finger to his ear and looked at the floor before shooting a glance to Helen who was standing at the edge of the stage. Something must have come through on the radio. Vince had forgotten about the trap Jean and Vangel laid for Alex. Hopefully the nod meant Alex was in custody.

Vince watched as most of the vampires nodded their heads while others murmured their agreement. Theron was rallying his troops. They might not be of his blood, but he was a true leader. If anyone could get the vampire leaders to fight, Theron would be the one.

"Now, we will talk and plan more later, please make use of the mansion as you would like, I have a situation that needs to be dealt with." Theron looked to Helen, jumped off the stage, and hurried to Vince. "Katie?"

"Taken by Lolita, they left in a helicopter. Alex?"

Theron shook his head and started for the door, pulling Vince with him as Helen trailed behind. "Got away, Jean's calling for help; Natalia and Vangel were shot."

"Natalia?" Vince asked, giving Theron a concerned look, he couldn't afford to lose another child.

"She will be fine, but Vangel..."

"Are you going to give him the choice?" The man drove Vince up the wall with the friendship he had with Katie, but he would be a good vampire to have on their side.

"Yes." Theron looked to Helen. "You will have to do it, are you ready?"

"Of course, he is too good to lose." Helen moved to the door leading to the orchard.

"Good, I'll help you." Theron followed behind her.

"What about Jean?" Vince asked.

"I will send her in here to help you find Katie," Theron said before running into the night following Helen.

Vince paced back and forth waiting for Jean. Vampires moved around him, asking him where bathrooms were and if more donors were coming, they needed blood after the battle. Vince tried to answer them with respect, these vampires had helped them fight Lolita's soldiers, but when Katie was out there with Lolita and there was nothing he could do, it was hard not to tell them to fuck off.

"Vince," Jean asked, running through the doorway and looking around. "Where's Katie?"

"That is what we are going to find out." Vince took her by the shoulder and started to walk her to her room. "Can you hack into Greek Airspace Patrol?"

Dear Reader,

Thank you for reading, Taken by Vampires. I hope you enjoyed another installment of Katie's journey.

If you liked this story, please tell a friend, and leave a review on **Amazon** or **Goodreads**.

Look for the next book in 2019.

Happy reading!

Joy


Visit Joy's website at: www.joymosby.com or follow her on social media:
https://www.facebook.com/joymosby81625
Twitter: **@joy_mosby**

**Books by Joy Mosby**

Found by Vampires (Asteria's Daughter Book 1)

Trained by Vampires (Asteria's Daughter Book 2)

Hunted by Vampires (Asteria's Daughter Book 3)

Taken by Vampires (Asteria's Daughter Book 4)

**Books by Ann McCune**
**(same author different pen name)**

Knight Flyers (Knight Flyers Book 1)

# Acknowledgements

This book would not have been possible without the help of so many people.

The biggest THANK YOU goes out to my readers. Without you this would be a pretty boring job.

A huge thank you goes out to my husband, who reads everything I write and gives me the feedback I need to hear, whether it's good or bad. I could not do what I am doing without your love and support. Love you.

Leah and Amy, my own personal cheerleaders and beta readers. Your enthusiasm and support make me want to continue.

Mom and Dad, I would not be where I am today if you had not gotten me tested for dyslexia.

Anelia, your covers are amazing! They are the first thing my readers see, and I wouldn't sell a book without them. Thank you!

# About the Author

I love to write about the Heroines Journey in the paranormal universe because writing about everyday life is boring for me (hence I am horrible at blogging). I love taking a character who thinks she is weak and showing her how strong she really is.

I live on forty acres in Northwest Colorado with two dogs (Ajax and Achilles), and my amazing husband. I love not having any neighbors, being outside in the summer, and inside in the winter. I have traveled to many places in the world, but I have many more places to visit before I am done.

When I am not staring at the monitor writing, I am staring at my Kindle reading, or spending time with my husband and animals.

Check out my website: Joymosby.com to find out about new releases and join my mailing list. I am not very good at updating it but bear with me I am working on it.